ON NOWHERE ST.
Jennnie's Journey

a novel by
RON HANDBERG

HAWK HILL
LITERARY
AN IMPRINT OF INGRAM

ON NOWWHERE ST., Jennie's Journey

A Novel

Layout & Design: Susan O'Reilly

Author Photograph: Gregory Handberg

Cover Model: McKenzie Louwagie

Inquiries should be addressed to: Hawk Hill Literary, LLC
13274 Huntington Terrace Saint Paul, MN 55124
Voice and Text: (612) 812-6060

ISBN: 978-1-7366108-4-8

ebook ISBN: 978-1-7366108-5-5

Printed in the United States

For our four great-grandchildren,
Nolan, Florence, Brady and Brighton
Who All Have Loving Homes
And
For the Homeless youth of our communities
Who Do Not

ONE

. . .

As Gabby slipped on her coat, she glanced out the newsroom window. And caught her breath. Snow. Swirling, dancing, big flakes, pushed by stiff winds that rattled the window.

Minnesota. Early November.

Walking to the window, she watched people hurry by, hunched over, backs to the wind, coat collars snug around their necks.

The Minnesota Hunch, she would soon learn.

Gabby came to Channel Seven from California in the spring, and this was her first sight of the snow she knew would be coming. And dreading. But already? The very sight of it gave her the shivers inside her lightweight coat.

Damn. Time to layer-up.

The station meteorologist had predicted the snow would come, but not until later that night, when she'd be warm and cozy in the Uptown apartment she shared with her fiancé, Zach Anthony, one of the station's news photographers.

Who now stood next to her, his arm around her shoulders. "Ready to go?" he asked.

With the last of the afternoon newscasts over, the day staff had begun to scatter, shouting quick goodbyes as they left. Many of them were headed for home, a few for one of the bars or restaurants down the street.

"Look at that," she said as she pressed her nose to the window-pane and pulled her coat more tightly around her body.

He laughed. "It's snow, Gabby. Better get used to it."

"Never," she replied.

"Then you're in for a miserable few months."

Gabby, short for Gabriel Gooding, had grown up in Portland, where it did snow occasionally, but she'd spent the bulk of her adult life in California, both in college and working as a reporter and weekend anchor at a television station in San Jose.

Where it never snowed.

Before they could turn to leave, a shout came from Harry Wilson on the assignment desk, pointing to his phone. "Hey, Gabby, you've got a visitor waiting in the lobby."

"*What?* Who?"

He could only shrug before turning away.

She glanced at Zach. "Who could that be? I wasn't expecting anybody."

He checked his watch. "Don't know, but could you make it quick? I'd like to get the hell out of here. It's been a long day."

"Tell me," she said as she started across the newsroom toward the lobby.

Both had been up since shortly after dawn, she to cover a double-murder in Pine City, some seventy miles to the north, and he to capture video of a multi-car train derailment about the same distance to the south, near Rochester. By the time both were back at the station and had finished working on their stories for the five and six o'clock newscasts, they were exhausted.

Entering the lobby, she at first saw no one, then—following the head-nod of the receptionist—spotted a small figure, a young girl, huddled in one corner, wrapped in a thick coat that looked two sizes too large, a backpack by her side, her head encased in a scarf that left only her eyes and nose visible. A half-frozen waif.

She walked across the lobby and sat down next to her. "I'm Gabby," she said. "You're looking for me?"

For a moment, the girl refused to look up, and when she did, her eyes were filled with tears. "Yes," she said, wiping at the tears with a mittened hand. "I need help."

"Okay," Gabby said. "But, first, why don't you tell me your name?"

"Jennifer," she replied, "but most people call me Jennie."

"Jennie what?"

"Nystrom."

"And how old are you?

"Fifteen, almost sixteen."

"Do you want to take off your coat, Jennie? And the scarf? You'd be more comfortable while we talk."

She removed the scarf but kept the coat tightly around her. "I can't stay long."

"That's all right," Gabby said, now seeing her face clearly for the first time. Cheeks still flushed from the cold, blue eyes, full lips, a perfect nose, and blond hair cut short, but ragged. A normal teenage girl from what she could see, pretty but not quite beautiful.

Hearing a noise behind her, Gabby glanced over her shoulder to see Zach standing impatiently at the lobby door. "I'll be back in a minute," she said as she hurried across the lobby. "I don't know what's going on, Zach, but take the car and head home. I'll Uber it and get there as soon as I can."

"Who is she?" he asked.

"A girl who says she needs help. That's all I know."

Puzzled, he said, "All right. I'll get dinner going."

By the time she got back to her, the girl was halfway out of the chair and putting her scarf back on. "Don't go yet," Gabby said. "Let's talk."

Slowly, cautiously, she settled back into the chair.

"You said you needed help. Tell me more. What's going on? What's the problem?"

"My friend's disappeared. I can't find her. Not for three days. I've looked everywhere."

"Hold on and back up. You told me your name, but not where you live. Or anything else so far. Do your parents know you're here?"

"I haven't seen my parents for a couple of weeks. They don't know where I am and I don't want them to know."

"So you're a runaway? From where? And why?"

"You don't need to know that."

"If you want my help, I do."

She was clearly uncomfortable, again appearing almost ready to flee. Finally, "I come from Elsa. It's a little town up north. I'm sure you've never heard of it."

She was right.

"And I ran because I couldn't stand it at home."

"What do you mean? Were you abused?"

She looked the other way, ignoring the question.

"So," Gabby said, "you're a runaway from Elsa whose girlfriend has gone missing. She's a runaway, too?"

"Yeah. I met her at the bus depot a couple of weeks ago. We kind of hit it off right away."

"And what's her name?"

"Hannah. I don't know her last name."

"Have you gone to the police?"

She laughed. *"Are you shitting me?* That's the last place I'd go. They'd have me on a bus back to Elsa before I could spit on the sidewalk."

"So why are you here?" Gabby asked. "Why'd you come looking for me?"

She hesitated. "I saw you on television a couple of months ago. I hardly ever watch the news, but that night I did. You'd been stalked by some guy who was out to kill you or something. And he ended up getting killed himself. You seemed like a really brave lady, you know, and smart. And I remember thinking that I'd like to be like you some day."

She was talking about Craig Jessup, a demented and abusive former boyfriend who had followed Gabby from San Jose in a frantic effort to get her back. In a final showdown, as he tried to abduct her, he was shot and killed by a bodyguard the station had hired to protect her. It was a story that had received wide coverage in Minnesota, both on television and in the newspapers.

"Are you being stalked?" Gabby asked.

"Not exactly," she replied. "But there are a couple of guys who'd probably like to know where I am."

"What kind of guys?"

"I don't want to talk about them."

"Because you're afraid?"

She stiffened up. "I told you I don't want to talk about them."

"Could they have had anything to do with your friend's disappearance?"

"I don't know. Maybe." Standing up. "I'd better go."

Gabby stood with her. "Where are you staying?"

She shrugged. "Who knows? On the street. Some shelter, if they have room. Wherever."

"And when was the last time you ate anything?"

"Ha! I can't even remember."

Gabby thought for a moment, deciding, perhaps foolishly, that she couldn't just let the girl go back into the cold and snow for another night in nowhere. But what did she know about her? Nothing beyond what she'd just been told. Was she as helpless and innocent as she seemed? She'd been living on the streets for two weeks and surviving. But how? Who were the guys who'd like to know where she is? All of that flashed through her mind before she finally made the decision. That she hoped she wouldn't regret.

Without knowing if Zach would approve, but fearing he wouldn't, she took Jennie's hand. "Let's do this. You come to my place. Just for the night. We'll get you some food, a shower, and a clean bed to sleep in."

"No way," she protested. "I don't need that kind of help. I'll make it on my own."

"Up to you," Gabby said with a shrug of her shoulders, "if that's the way you want it, fine. I thought you came for my help. But I can't sit *here* and talk forever. Not with the snow coming down like it is. I've gotta get home." With that, she got up and began to walk away, but stopped midway across the lobby to look back.

"Wait, please," the girl said, following her. "You're sure, just for tonight?"

"That'll be up to you."

"You won't call the cops?"

"No, but I will ask you to call your folks. You don't have to tell them where you are if you don't want to, just that you're safe. They need to know that."

"But just for tonight. I can't stop looking for Hannah."

"I understand," Gabby replied, "but, hey, maybe I can help with that."

As they walked from the lobby back through the newsroom, Gabby couldn't escape a feeling that this could be more than a ride home, but the beginning of a journey...which could lead anywhere.

TWO

• • •

Alerted by her phone call on their way from the station, Zach was waiting at the apartment door, working on a smile. "Hi, there," he said, holding out his hand. "I'm Zach. And welcome. I'm the cook around here."

The apartment was filled with the aroma of spaghetti sauce simmering on the kitchen stove.

Jennie held back, eyes wide, moving from Zach to the little dog standing at his feet, staring up at her. Zach said, "And that's Barclay. He's my dog, but Gabby thinks he's hers. And spoils him."

Gabby laughed as she picked up the dog. "And, Zach, this is Jennie, Jennie Nystrom. She's going to spend the night with us. After dinner and a shower and time to talk."

His smile slipped away.

Jennie stood quietly, still clutching her coat and backpack, but then moved next to Gabby and tentatively scratched Barclay's head. "He's cute," she said. "What kind of dog is he? He's so tiny."

"A teacup poodle," Zach said. "He's a rescue dog we got from the pound."

"Does he get any bigger?"

"Nope. He's about as big as he's going to get."

"C'mon, Jennie," Gabby said as she put the dog down. "Let's get that coat and scarf off. And I'll show you where you'll be sleeping tonight."

Reluctantly, Jennie followed her across the living room and down the hall to the second bedroom, pausing at the door as Gabby said, "The bed's newly-made up and there are fresh washcloths and towels on the dresser. And while you're smaller than I am, I bet some of my clothes will fit you in a pinch. So, after dinner, I'll get you some of them out and put the ones you're wearing in the wash. Okay?"

Jennie hadn't moved. "Why are you doing this?" she asked. "You don't even know me. I don't understand."

"Gosh," Gabby replied, kneeling down to be at eye level with her. "I guess because I didn't want you out on the street in the snow by yourself. At least not for tonight. And because I truly would like to help, if I can. I have two kid sisters back home and you remind me of them when they were younger."

"I don't have any sisters. Just a brother. And he's a lot older."

"What's his name?"

"Jesse."

"Does he live with you and your folks?"

"No. He's in the Army. In Texas, right now, I think."

With that, she slipped off her coat and scarf and walked to the bed, sitting gingerly on the edge, booted-feet dangling. She was wearing a tattered white sweatshirt with a faded Elsa Eagles legend on the front and an even more faded image of an eagle behind it.

Shyly, she asked, "Are you and Zach married?"

Gabby grinned. "Not yet, but I hope we will be some day."

"You're very pretty, you know. Prettier than when I saw you on TV."

"Really?" Gabby replied, glancing at the bedroom mirror. "That's nice of you to say."

"My mom's pretty, too."

"I bet she is. To have a lovely young lady like you."

"But she's not as pretty as she used to be. She's sad, so much. Like she's ready to cry all the time. Makes her not as pretty as I saw in some of her old pictures."

"I'm sorry to hear that. But maybe knowing you're okay will make her feel a little happier."

"Maybe." Then, "So will you help me look for my friend tomorrow?"

Gabby sat down next to her. "I'll try, but I'll have to check with my boss at the station first. He might have something else for me to do. But let's not think about that until tomorrow, okay?"

Before she could reply, Zach was at the bedroom door. "Spaghetti's done and waiting for you two. I hope you're hungry."

If there was any doubt about her hunger, it disappeared as soon as they sat down. She politely waited for permission, but then filled her plate to the rim with the noodles and sauce and salad, glancing sheepishly across the table before digging in with a famished abandon. Zach and Gabby had taken no more than a couple of bites before Jennie's plate was empty and she clearly was ready for more.

Gabby had to smile. "I'll ask you again, Jennie. When was the last time you ate?"

She wiped the sauce from her lips. "About this time yesterday, I think. But it was only what I could scrounge out of a garbage can."

"No kidding?" Zach said. "Where?"

"Behind an apartment house over Northeast. They leave a lot of stuff out, pretty good stuff, all wrapped up, like they know people like me may be picking through it. I think they spotted me and Hannah one day a while back, but didn't say anything. Didn't shout at us or give us any crap."

"How about the last *real* meal?" Gabby asked.

"At a Perkins. A guy we got to know works there and got his boss to give us a couple of free meals."

"That was before your friend disappeared?"

"Just before. We split up after eating. She said she had to meet some guy and that we'd meet up later at the shelter."

"What guy? Do you know?"

"No. I asked, but she wouldn't tell me."

"That was three days ago. And you haven't seen her since?"

"No, and that's why I came to you."

"And you haven't had a real meal since?" Zach said.

She managed a shrug. "I can stop by the food shelves or the drop-in centers, but I don't need that much."

Despite those words, she continued to eat, and as she did, they were able to elicit a few more pieces of information from her. That she'd saved enough money for a bus to the Cities; that she knew from friends back home that her parents and the sheriff had issued a missing persons alert, but that she had no plans to return home.

"But why?" Gabby asked again.

"Because I got tired of getting the shit kicked out of me, that's why," she blurted, her eyes welling. "I told him, one more time and I was out of there! He just laughed and slapped me across the face."

"Your dad?"

"Duh. Who else?"

"How long has that been going on?" Gabby pressed, leaning in.

"Like forever. Started with like a slap on the rear, then he'd twist my ear, like almost off, then, later, he started using his belt on me. Pants down, then whop! The older I got and the more he drank, the worse it got." She hesitated for a moment. "I probably deserved some it. I was kind of a wild kid, but so were a lot of my friends and they didn't get hit on like I did."

"Did you tell anybody?" Zach demanded. "Your teachers? The cops? Anybody?"

"Are you kidding? In that town? Nobody would believe me. My dad's the goddamned mayor. Everybody's buddy."

"But what about your mother?"

"She's helpless. Like, hopeless. I love her, but she's as afraid of him as I am. He slapped her around even more than me. Broke her arm once when she tried to get between us. She'd never say it, but I bet she's glad I got away."

Gabby and Zach could only stare at one another. Could they believe this horror story? From this teenager who was, in ways, still a child? But how could they not? Seeing the pain etched in her face, a few tiny tears sliding down her cheeks. If this was a tall tale, an act, then she should be on the stage at the Guthrie.

But they also knew her story was not unique. The news they covered was filled with stories like hers, of abused children, of abusive parents or relatives who often had been abused themselves. If not an epidemic, it was a growing phenomenon that swept into the headlines virtually every week. And, like Jennie, stories of children who escaped the brutality by seeking refuge with hundreds of others like them on the darkened, anonymous streets of cities like Minneapolis or St. Paul.

"How about your brother? In the Army?" Zach asked. "Does he know what's been happening to you?"

"Not from me, he doesn't. He left a couple of years ago and hasn't been back since. But he knows about my dad. He took some of the same crap from him. That's why he joined up as soon as he could. I think if he knew what was happening to me, he'd come back and kill my dad. And I don't want that to happen. Not because of me."

"Have you heard from him?" Zach said. "Has he tried to call you? He must know you're missing."

"He doesn't know my number and I don't know his."

Gabby asked, "Do your folks know you're here? In the Cities?"

"Maybe. But I don't think they've come looking for me. I would have picked that up on the street. They probably think I'll be back sooner or later. Like I have before." Then, "But not this time."

"You have to call them, though," Gabby said. "That's our deal. They need to know you're safe. You owe that to your mother, if not your dad."

She thought for a moment. "Okay. But only that. That I'm safe. Not where I am."

"Where's your phone?" Zach asked.

"In my backpack, in the bedroom."

"Then bring it out here, will you? So we know you actually made the call."

She gave him a look, but got up and slowly headed for the bedroom.

Once out of earshot, Zach looked at Gabby. "Do you really know what we're getting into here? Harboring a kid, a minor, who the cops may be looking for?"

"*Harboring her?* We're protecting her, for God's sake."

He was unconvinced. "I don't know. We've gotta think this through, Gabs. What about tomorrow? And the next day?"

"Let's get through tonight before we worry about tomorrow."

By then, Jennie had returned, cell phone in hand. Without a word, she touched the keypad. And waited. Finally, "Mom, it's Jennie." A pause. "I'm okay. That's why I called." Another pause. "I can't tell you. I just wanted you to know I'm safe." One more pause. "I don't know when I'll come back. Or if I will. Not with *him* still there." She shook her head. "Are you kidding? No, I won't talk to him. No way." Then, "Are *you* okay?" Pause. "You're sure? Okay. I have to go. I'll call again when I can. Don't worry. I can take care of myself."

She put the phone aside with a glance at both of them. "There. I did it."

"Your mother's okay?" Gabby said.

"Says she is, but she wouldn't tell me if she wasn't. Not if he's standing there."

"So, let's get you in the shower and into an old pair of my PJ's. Then we can talk more, if you feel like it."

An hour later, the three of them were in the living room, Jennie—in a pair of striped pajamas and a rose robe, her hair still damp from the shower—sat next to Gabby on the couch, Barclay the poodle snuggly in her lap.

"So tell me about your friend, Hannah," Gabby said. "The only thing we know is you met her at the bus depot and that you haven't seen her for several days. And that you're worried about her."

"I really don't know that much about her," she admitted.

"Except that she's a little older than me and really nice. To me, anyway. We connected, like right away. It was like I'd found the big sister I never had. I can't really explain it, but she kind of, like, wrapped her arms around me. Said we should stick together, watch each others' backs."

"What else?" Zach asked.

"She never told me a lot more. Not her last name, not where she's from. Only that, like me, she's on the run from her dad, her stepdad actually, who sounded even worse than my dad. He kept trying to get into her pants. One night she found him on top of her and said she'd finally had enough and cut him."

"Cut him?"

"Stabbed him with a kitchen knife she kept under her pillow. That's what she told me. Didn't kill him, but hurt him bad enough that the cops got called. That's when she took off."

"Holy shit," he muttered.

"And you haven't seen her since that night at Perkins?" Gabby said.

"No. And I've looked everywhere. All of our old haunts. The drop-ins. The Mall. The depot. The homeless camps. Under the bridges. On the trains. Everywhere we used to hang. I've tried to call her a hundred times, but it keeps going to her mailbox. I leave messages, but she's never called back."

"Maybe the cops found her," Zach offered. "If she stabbed her stepdad there must be a warrant out for her. This is no simple runaway we're talking about."

"I don't think so. I would have heard. It's like our own little world out there. Word gets around, especially if the cops are making the rounds."

Gabby said, "And when you last saw her, she was off to meet some guy?"

"Right."

"But you don't know who?"

"She wouldn't say. But we know lots of guys. Some of them are bad dudes. Which is why I came looking for you. I'm scared for her."

Zach said, "Was one of these guys a pimp?"

She recoiled. "*What?*"

"C'mon, you know what I'm talking about. Was Hannah out hustling?"

She turned to face him, sputtering. "Not that I know of. Not when I was with her!"

"But you weren't together all the time, right? So she could have been."

She looked to Gabby. "Why is he asking me all of these questions?"

Zach answered. "If you want our help finding her, we need to know as much as we can about her. Understand?"

She gave Gabby another plaintive look.

Zach pressed on. "Was she on drugs?"

"Maybe. I don't know. Not with me. But a lot of kids on the streets are."

"Were *you?*"

"Jesus, no! All I've ever had was a shot of whiskey…and I puked."

Gabby finally broke in. "Okay, okay. Enough for now. We can talk more about all of that later. But, first, tell us what Hannah looks like. We'll need to know that."

Jennie picked up her phone. "I have a picture. She doesn't know I took it. Probably would have killed me, if she knew."

She flicked through the phone photos until she found the right one and held it up. A young, dark-haired woman, slim, and at first glance a few inches taller than Jennie. With a more mature build, breasts that pushed at her sweater and a face that had lost any girlish features sometime in the past. She may have been a teenager, but could easily pass for a woman in her early twenties.

Which didn't escape Zach's notice. "You said she was only a couple of years older than you. Are you sure?"

"She told me she was seventeen. But I have no proof."

Gabby said, "While the photo's not that clear, she seems quite attractive."

"Hot, that's what all the guys say. They couldn't keep their eyes off her."

Gabby got up off the coach. "Okay. That's enough for the night. It's time to get you to bed and a real night's sleep."

Jennie held Barclay up. "Can he sleep with me? Would he?"

"You might have no choice," she laughed. "He loves to cuddle, but Zach and I don't let him up in our bed. So if you invite him, I'm sure he would oblige."

"Good," she said, getting up.

"But listen up," Gabby went on, aware she could be taking a chance, but trusting her instincts. "Zach and I have to go to the station first thing in the morning. We'd like you to stay here during the day, while we're gone. We need to talk to our boss, whose name," she smiled, "is also Barclay. To talk to him about what's going on. There's plenty of food in the kitchen and Netflix on the TV. So you can just make yourself at home until we get back. Then we can talk about what's next…and what we might be able to do to help find Hannah."

Jennie looked doubtful.

"I'll get your clothes out of the dryer, and try to pick up some warmer stuff for you while we're gone. It's still snowing out there and no time for you to be back wandering the streets. I'll give you my cell number in case you need anything."

"Okay," she finally said. "But only for tomorrow. After that, I'm gone."

"Let's just wait and see about that," Gabby said.

Through this whole exchange, Zach had said nothing. But, Gabby knew, his silence spoke a thousand words. Words she was not eager to hear.

As it turned out, she only had to wait until Jennie and the pooch were in the bedroom and the door shut.

"So," Zach said, "do I get a say in all of this? I mean, do I live here, too?"

"Of course," she replied, girding herself. "I thought you'd agree with me."

"Without discussing it?" There was a touch of anger in his voice, anger she rarely heard. "Without talking about the implications? Without knowing my concerns?"

"I thought you'd already expressed them," she replied, reflecting a little heat herself.

"You said one night. Now it's tomorrow, too. And then what? Another day, another night? We're on dangerous footing here, Gabby. Face it. This is not some hooker we've taken in off the street. She's a *child*. A runaway. Who we know virtually nothing about, aside from what she's told us. And who knows if all that is true? We could be in a shit pot full of trouble, Gabby."

"So what do you suggest?"

"I don't have an answer. But we've got to do something. Talk to somebody. Child protection. Some counselor. Whatever. I don't want to put her back on the streets any more than you do. And I don't want to send her home, if what she says about her father is true. But we can't keep her here for days on end. There has to be another way."

"I hear you. Let's talk to Barclay in the morning. Maybe he'll have an idea."

"Don't count on it. He may be a great news guy, but I bet he's no smarter in these kinds of things than we are."

"Maybe not, but you know what, Zach? There could be a story here, a story that he might want to pursue. Homeless kids, abused kids. Kids like Jennie."

Zach leaned back, slowly shaking his head. "My, God, is that what this is all about? A story? Jesus, I don't believe this. Or you."

With that, he headed off to bed himself. Regretting, perhaps, that the spare bedroom was occupied.

THREE

. . .

By morning, while the tension between them had eased, it had not disappeared. They exchanged only a few words in the drive to the station, but even those words were more than they'd spoken at breakfast or before. Give it time, Gabby thought as they walked into the newsroom. This, too, will pass. Hopefully.

After shedding their coats, they immediately headed for the assignment desk and editor Harry Wilson. "Anything you need us for right away?" Gabby asked.

"Not that I know of. But the news huddle hasn't started yet. So hang tight."

"Is Barclay in?"

With a grin, "Like he reports to me? Check his office."

They crossed the newsroom and stood outside Barclay's door, which was almost always open. Zach poked his head inside. "You have a minute, George?"

He looked up from his desk. "Sure, but not a lot more than that. We huddle up in fifteen minutes or so."

George Barclay was the legendary news director of Channel Seven, having served in the same capacity for more than twenty years, ignoring offers of front office advancement or moves to larger markets or the network. He had outlasted three general managers and had developed and nurtured dozens of first-class reporters and photographers—some of whom had moved on to the network or to bigger stations and bigger salaries. He had chosen to stay because of his love for the station, the quality of its journalism, and Minnesota.

Over that time, he had transformed himself from an overweight, socially-inept bachelor into a trim married man who maintained the respect and admiration of virtually everyone who had ever worked for him. And in that time, he and his staff had broken more big stories than any other station in town—or in the country for that matter. But he could also be tough. As one reporter once said, "He might break your balls, but he'll never break your heart."

He was also the man who, when asked by the desk if he wanted to cover the birthday of a one-hundred-year-old lady, had replied, famously, "Only if she's pregnant!"

And the man an admiring competitor once described as having "the journalistic balls of an elephant."

All of that and more is where the label "legend," came from.

"We'll try to make it quick," Gabby said as she and Zach took seats across from him. "But we may have to get back when you have more time."

"So what's up?" he said.

She glanced at Zach and repeated Jennie's story as simply as she could. "She stayed with us last night and is still at our place as we speak. We're not sure what to do. As Zach reminds me, we can't keep her there forever, and neither of us want to put her back on the street or send her back to an abusive home. We thought you might have some sage advice."

He smiled. "Thanks a lot."

"Even more," she went on, with another glance at Zach, "I think there may be a story here. I did some online research last night. There are hundreds of kids like Jennie alone on the streets of the Twin Cities on any given night. *Hundreds.* Throwaway kids, many of them kids of color, gay or trans-gender. Without money or food or a family or a roof over their heads. At the mercy of who knows what or who. Except for a lot of people who may want to do them harm."

He sat back in his chair. "That story's been done before, Gabby. Mainly by the newspapers…"

"But not by us. Or by the other stations. Not the kind of story I have in mind."

"Which is?"

"Up close and personal. I'd want to get close to these kids, to tell their stories in a way nobody else really has. See their faces, hear their voices, sense and show their anger, their despair."

He studied her. "How?"

"By being out there with them. Mixing with them. Earning their trust, if possible. Use hidden cameras, if necessary. Or the small cameras or phones. With those you can be virtually invisible these days."

"We'd have to be careful," he said. "Doing a story about them is one thing, exploiting them for the sake of a story is something else. They're just kids."

"I understand."

"And if they're minors, I don't think we could name them or show their faces on the air without parental consent. And my guess is that would be hard to get. We'd have to talk to our lawyers."

"I'm not saying it would be easy," she replied. "But I'm sure we could find a way. It's a story that needs to be told."

He looked at his watch, then got up and went to the door to summon his assistant news director, Jeff Parkett. "Can you take the huddle, Jeff? I need some more time with Gabby and Zach."

"Sure, but do I get to know what's going on?"

"I'll fill you in later," he said, returning to his desk.

"Thanks," Gabby said.

"What about this missing girl? This Hannah?"

"She just seems to have disappeared. At least Jennie can't find her."

"But is that so unusual?" he asked. "That these kids come and go? Isn't that what you're suggesting for a story? That kids like this Jennie or Hannah have no roots…no real reason to stay in one place?"

"That's true, but…"

"Especially if, as you say, this Hannah did actually stab her stepdad and may have the cops on her tail."

"That's also true. But the last Jennie saw of her, she was off to see some guy and had promised to meet up later. Jennie claims she never would have just run off without some sort of goodbye. They were that close. Like sisters, she says. Even after just a few days of being together. And that's why she's so worried."

Barclay could only shake his head, clearly torn. Over the past several months he had developed an enormous respect for Gabby as a reporter, admiring her instincts and impressive perseverance. Not that long ago, she and Zach almost singlehandedly had exposed a federal fugitive who had been living undercover in the Twin Cities for years. Who was now behind bars, along with a couple of his cohorts.

"So what do you want to do?" he said finally.

"I want to go find her. I want to take Jennie and Zach and go search for her. Walk and drive the streets, visit some of the places they used to hang out. And in the process, find out if there's actually a story for us out there."

He turned to Zach. "You haven't said anything. What do you think?"

He hesitated, carefully choosing his words. "I think she may be right about the story, but whether we could actually capture it on video is another thing. And who knows how long it would take? With winter setting in? It may be worth a try, but that doesn't solve the more pressing issue. As I keep asking, what do we do about Jennie? We can't keep her at our place indefinitely, we can't put her back on the streets and we can't send her home. Or call child protection. She'd be gone like a flash."

"I have no answer for that," Barclay admitted. "But I do have one suggestion."

"What's that?"

"Talk to that cop friend of yours, Philips. See what he has to say."

He was talking about John Philips, a Minneapolis homicide

detective who had been at their side in the investigation and capture of the federal fugitive. They had not seen or talked to him in weeks, but Gabby knew he'd be willing to help—if he could.

"Good idea," she said. "A place to start anyway."

"I'll talk to the desk and see if they can spare you for the day, or at least for part of it. But let's not get ahead of ourselves on all of this. One step at a time, okay?"

"Fine with me," she said.

"And with me, too, I guess," Zach added, not bothering to disguise his doubts.

As it turned out, their dilemma was quickly resolved. For no sooner had they left Barclay's office than Gabby got a call.

From Jennie.

"I'm sorry, Gabby, but I can't stay here. Just sitting here. I have to find Hannah…"

"No, no, wait a minute!" Gabby said, frantically.

"Thanks for everything. I mean that. You and Zach were really nice and I know you want to help, but I'll go crazy if I don't get back on the streets looking for her."

"But we're ready to help," Gabby protested. "Our boss gave us some time. You have to wait for us!" She looked out the window. Still snowing. Still blowing. "You'll freeze to death. Just look outside."

"I'll be okay," she said. "I know places I can get warm. And I've got your number in case I need it. Don't worry about me."

"But you wanted our help…we can be…"

By then she was gone.

"Damn," Gabby muttered, repeating Jennie's words for Zach.

He shrugged. "We tried. You tried. She's on a mission. Not much we can do now."

"Yes, there is," she said, again glancing out at the snow. "Only now we have to look for both her *and* Hannah."

"Okay," Zach replied with a deep sigh. "But you'd better bundle up."

FOUR

...

O nce in the car, as they pulled out of the garage and on to the snow and ice-covered street, she put a tentative hand on Zach's thigh. "So are we okay?" she asked.

"What?" Giving her a quick glance. "What do you mean?"

"You know what I mean. Are we friends again? Is our little tiff over?"

They were at a stoplight. "Of course. I just don't quite get you sometimes."

"Like last night?"

"Exactly. To me, sometimes a story comes last, not first. And I'm not sure you always understand that. Or me."

She leaned back in her seat, not sure how to respond. Finally, "That's who I am, I guess. And I'm not sure I can change. The story has always come first for me. And sometimes that gets me in trouble. So you may have to live with it, if you can."

"I think I can manage that, but don't expect me to roll over and play dead."

She had to smile. That's the last thing she would expect of him. And one of the many reasons she loved him.

It seemed a long time ago now, but she had first met him on her first day on the job, when she was told to ride along with him as he responded to an apparent suicide that seemed a little strange. Sure enough, the body of the guy found in a basement had gone undiscovered for more than a year and was not a suicide, but a murder. And the victim, it turned out, would become a key character in their later investigation of the federal fugitive, who had been involved in an elaborate Ponzi scheme years before.

Of course she knew none of that then. Only that Zach seemed like a nice enough guy, handsome in a disheveled sort of way, not unlike most of the photographers she had known. But she quickly learned that he did not consider himself as just a photographer but as a photo-journalist who cared as much about the words in a reporter's mouth as the images in his camera.

He had treated her kindly on that first day and—in fact—had offered to let her stay with him until she found her own place. She had, and as the weeks passed, that first day friendship grew and became what it is today.

Now, as the light turned green, they found themselves trying to navigate in the face of the wind-whipped snow. The flakes were like tiny pellets pounding the windshield, challenging the wipers. And the streets themselves had turned slick as the snow melted on the still-warm pavement, then quickly froze again.

"Jesus," she said as she tried to wipe away the fog from the side windows. "Does it always snow this early? Halloween's hardly over."

"That's why we brag about this being the 'theater of seasons.'"

"Who brags?"

"We Minnesotans. You're one of us now, you know."

"Temporarily, maybe. But I'm still a Californian at heart."

"And how did that work out for you?"

"Smartass."

Even this early in the day, traffic was heavy and—thanks to the snow—barely moving. They were heading toward the neighborhood around their apartment, in hopes of catching a glimpse of Jennie before she was able to get too far away. "Once we get close," Zach said, "I think we should get out and walk. We're never going to spot her this way, and she has to be on foot herself."

"I still don't get it," she said. "Why would she come to us and then walk away?"

"Because she's a kid. And we're not inside her head. She may have decided she doesn't want to be seen on the streets with a couple of adults, or thinks we may slow her down. Who knows what she's thinking?"

"Still…"

"And how are we ever going to spot this Hannah? We've only seen one crummy picture of her and don't even know her last name, or anything else about her. It'll be like looking for a white needle in the snow."

Gabby took out her cell and punched in a number and waited. "We know that she may have stabbed her stepdad and the cops may have a warrant out for her."

"So who are you calling?"

"The desk."

A moment passed, then, "Harry, Gabby here. I need a favor. Can you have an intern check our files or the *StarTrib* or *Pioneer Press* archives, or Google Search, LexisNexis, wherever, for anything about a girl named Hannah. Yeah, Hannah. No last name. She may be wanted for stabbing her stepdad somewhere in Minnesota." She paused, listening. "Probably outstate. Happened fairly recently, I think, and she may be here in the Cities now, on the run. I'd do the search myself on my phone, but we're trying to find our way through the snow, looking for her and another runaway that Barclay may have told you about. Got all that? Good. Thanks." With a sigh, she slipped her phone in her pocket and watched the enormous flakes still coming down.

By the time they got close to their apartment the snowfall and wind had worsened, cutting the visibility even further. "This is silly," Zach said, eyes straining. "We're never going to spot her in this weather. I can barely see the sidewalk."

"Let's at least check as many of the bus stops as we can. She's probably trying to get back downtown."

"Okay," he agreed, after a long pause.

They inched their way up and down stretches Hennepin and

Lyndale avenues, hugging the curbs, gliding by each and every bus stop, finding few people willing to brave the weather at any of them. And no sign of Jennie.

"Where did she go?" Gabby wondered aloud.

"Who knows?" Zach said, clearly frustrated. "She may have called one of those guys she knows for a ride."

"Let's hope not. I wouldn't trust any guy who hangs around kids like Jennie."

As they headed back downtown to cruise some of those streets, Gabby got a call from a young intern named Andy, a University of Minnesota student who was new to the newsroom and whom Gabby had not yet met. She didn't even know his last name.

"Harry Wilson said I should give you a call. Is this a bad time?"

"No, no," she said, "it's great, Andy. You've got something for me?"

"I think so," he replied.

"That was quick. Good work."

"The *StarTribune* did a short story three weeks ago about a girl named Hannah Hendricks...from a small town in western Minnesota, someplace called Delroy."

"And?"

"And if this is the girl you're looking for, you were right. She *is* accused of stabbing her stepdad and the cops *do* have a warrant out for her. Stepdad's name is Arnold Klinger. He survived the attack, but that's about all I can tell you so far. There was nothing in the *Pioneer Press* that I could find and nothing more in the *Strib* after that first story. And I haven't had a chance yet to really check the social media stuff."

"Good work," she said, impressed. "Did the paper include a picture of this Hannah?"

"No, but that's what I hope to find on Facebook or some other place out there."

"Great. You're saving me some time. If you find a picture,

please text me or shoot me an email."

"Sure."

"One other thing. While you're scanning the web, see if you can find anything on a Jennifer, or Jennie, Nystrom. She's a young runaway from Elsa, up north. I'll tell you more about her when we get back to the station, if you're still there."

"I'll be here until early this afternoon," he said.

"I'll come find you. Thanks again for the help."

She put the phone aside and quickly repeated the conversation for Zach.

He took a moment. "If it's small enough, this town of Delroy may not have its own police department, but the county sheriff should be able to give us the information we need, and maybe some pictures of the girl."

"And maybe something about her family," Gabby replied, "although I'm not sure I'd want to talk to the stepdad. If he's the creep Hannah told Jennie he was, he may have deserved what he got."

Neither spoke for the next few minutes. Until Zach finally said, "So where are we going with this, Gabs?"

"What do you mean?"

He paused. "I mean, is it the story of a kid who stabbed her stepdad after an attempted rape and took off? Or the story of Jennie's abusive dad? Or is it the story of both girls and others like them, the young, lost kids, who are walking the streets and sleeping in culverts, or tents, or in the jam-packed shelters? Or maybe the story of the guys preying on them?"

"Maybe all of the above," she replied, after a moment.

"That's a big order."

"The truth is, I don't know. It's too soon to really know. We've spent less than a day on it so far. But I think there is a story…a good story…that neither we nor any of the other TV guys in town have done. At least that I know of. These kids, Jennie, Hannah, and scores of others like them, they *are* the story. We just have to find a way to tell it. Or at least part of it."

FIVE

. . .

When they returned to the newsroom, having failed in their search, they found Andy the intern sitting comfortably at Gabby's desk. Wearing a shy smile, he got up and introduced himself, last name Simmons. "Mr. Wilson told me you were on your way back and that I should just wait here. I hope that's okay."

"Of course it is," she said, as she and Zach returned his smile and handshake.

Tall and slender of body and face, with reddish hair hanging down to his shoulders and spectacles the size of small saucers clinging to his nose, he could have been fifteen or twenty-three, a young student or a young professor. Hard to tell.

"So you have something for us?" she asked.

"I do," he replied as he checked a small notebook. "Wasn't hard finding Jennie Nystrom's Facebook page, although she hasn't posted anything for like three weeks. But her parents have posted several appeals on her wall, reporting her disappearance and seeking her friends' help in locating her. The sheriff in her home county of Wadena has also posted a missing person appeal."

"You'll show us that?" she said.

"Sure. I'll cue it up on my laptop in a minute."

"And you've got more?"

"Yeah. Wadena County has a weekly newspaper, *The Wadena Villager*, with its own website. And it carried a short article two weeks ago, reporting that Jennie had gone missing and that her parents and the sheriff were asking the public's help in locating her."

"Did it say she's a runaway?"

"No, not exactly. Only that she's disappeared and that they're very concerned."

"Nothing since?" Gabby asked.

"Not that I could find."

Zach said, "You've done a lot since we talked on the phone."

"It didn't take that long," he said, handing them a sheet of paper. "This is a copy of the website story. I was able to use your printer."

"You're amazing," she said.

"One more thing. I hope I didn't overstep myself here, but I also put a call into the Lyon County sheriff's office...and they agreed, with some hesitation, to email you a picture of this Hannah Hendricks...and a copy of the criminal charges in the stabbing of her stepdad...along with copies of the local newspaper stories."

"No shit!" Gabby blurted. "Zach, go away. I think I'm going to marry *this* guy!"

Andy laughed. "The deputy I talked to said he'd have to talk to his boss about the privacy issues involved before they could say anything more, but he was very curious as to why we're so interested. Of course, I didn't tell him anything."

"Good for you," she said. "Now let's see Jennie's Facebook page."

He sat down again in her chair and quickly found the page. The image was definitely that of Jennie, posing, unsmiling, in her Elsa sweatshirt. And while it contained the parental appeals he had mentioned, there were few of Jennie's own postings. Yes, there were the predictable pictures of herself and her friends, more girls than boys, and a few somber selfies in a number of different locations, mostly in and around her school, Gabby guessed. There was one picture of her brother, Jesse, in an Army uniform, but none of her parents. And few details that Jennie had revealed about herself, like her favorite music or movie or TV shows, or her other likes or dislikes.

As Gabby studied the page, she decided there was far less there than she'd expect from an active, happy teenage girl. "I think it's kind of sad," she said. "I didn't see one smile in any of her pictures. It shows what we saw in person yesterday…a lost, unhappy child."

"Hard to disagree with that," Zach said.

"If she has or had a Twitter account, I couldn't find it," Andy said. "Same thing for Instagram and Snapchat."

"How about the other girl, Hannah?" Gabby asked. "Did you have time to look for her in all those places?"

"I made a quick check, but couldn't find anything. She may have dumped everything."

As they pondered the next move, Barclay strode across the newsroom. "You're back. What's happening?"

"We've been getting briefed by Andy the Great," she said with a grin. "I don't know where you found him, but you should hire him, fulltime, immediately."

He laughed as Andy stood shyly to one side, clearly embarrassed. "Didn't he tell you? He's in the U's Law School. Like near the top of his class. He thinks he can somehow combine law and journalism."

"I don't know about that," she said, "but he's done a hell of a lot for us in the last hour or so."

"Like what?"

She quickly repeated everything Andy had learned, and of their fruitless search on the streets for Jennie.

"Where does that leave us?"

"About where we were," she admitted. "We know a little more about the two girls, but are no closer to finding either of them."

"So…"

"So, we keep looking, I guess. Get back on the streets when we can. And talk to some of the people you suggested. Like our cop friend and some of the people who work with homeless kids. I still think there's a story there, but it's going to take more time, that's for sure."

"I'm not sure I've got that much time to give you," he said. "As you well know, we're already down a couple of people."

"I know."

Channel Seven, like most other local stations in the country, had faced cutbacks ordered by its corporate owners. With no assurance that more cuts wouldn't be coming.

Barclay turned his attention to Zach, who again had said nothing. "What do you think?"

"I think I should go back on the regular photo schedule. To help out there. Because so far there's nothing to shoot and I'm not doing much to help Gabby, except driving her around. When she needs me, I'll be there."

"Gabby?"

"I think he's right. I'm wasting his time. If you let Andy work with me for as much time as he has, I should be fine. And if the desk needs me for some other assignment, I'll be available."

"Is that all right with you, Andy?" Barclay asked.

"For sure. I'll give you as much time as I can."

"Then let's leave it there for now."

As Barclay and Zach walked away, Gabby turned to Andy. "Since we'll be working together for a while, why don't you tell me something about yourself?"

He sat down next to her desk. "Not much to tell, really. My full name is Andrew, but everybody calls me Andy. I grew up in St. Paul, graduated from Central High, got a B.A. degree from the University, and am now in my second year of Law School."

"Family?"

"My dad's a lawyer, surprise, and my mom's an accountant. I have an older brother and sister, both married with a couple of kids each, and both living out-of-state. We don't see much of them except at Christmas and a week or so in the summer."

"So you're in Law School, but sitting here in a television news-room. How come?"

"Growing up, most of my buddies were into sports, but I spent a lot of time watching television news, especially some of the stuff your I-Team did over the years. Going after the bad guys and apparently having a good time doing it. Not good in the sense of ha-ha, but enjoying the effort, getting satisfaction out of it. I thought maybe I could combine some of the rigors and tedium of the law with the excitement of journalism. Probably a pipe dream, but that's why I'm here."

"It's not all excitement," she said.

"Maybe not, but I saw what you and Zach did to that Ponzi scheme guy and his buddies. That had to be exciting."

"More satisfying than exciting, maybe, but, yeah, it feels good when you get your man. Your story."

"Also," he grinned, "as you've probably noticed, I don't really have the looks for television. Certainly not in front of the camera. Looks aren't that big a deal in a courtroom, or sitting in some conference room taking depositions."

"Believe it or not," she said, "even in television, brains are more important than looks."

"Then why don't I see any ugly people on TV?"

She had no ready answer for that.

"Let's get back to business," she finally said. "Let's figure out where we go from here. If we stand a chance of finding these girls, we'll have to know more about where kids like them hang out. The shelters, the libraries, the trains, shopping centers. Any place that's warm, I suppose, and more or less welcoming. Places they won't get booted out of right away."

"From what I've read," he said, "a lot of them are couch-surfing, hopping from place-to-place or squatting in some of the encampments that pop up around town."

"Or with their pimps or the sex-traffickers," she offered, looking away.

"That, too, of course."

She got up and moved to the window. The snow seemed to have diminished a bit, but was still thick on the streets and sidewalks. Somewhere, she thought, Jennie and Hannah probably were in the middle of it all. Each looking for the other.

SIX

• • •

Had she been able to look over or around the high-rise office and apartment buildings, she may have spotted Jennie as she trudged through the snow in the heart of downtown, almost unrecognizable in her long coat, and the scarf wrapped around her head like a turban. Eyes watering and nose running from the cold wind in her face. When she'd left the apartment, she'd used the last of the little money she had left to grab the first bus that came along, eluding Gabby and Zach's search by a half hour or so.

As she'd stood crammed and jostled in the bus, recoiling from the sour breath of the man leaning against her, she couldn't help but wonder if she'd made a serious mistake in leaving the apartment, foregoing the help Gabby had promised to provide.

Isn't that what she'd wanted? What she'd asked for? Yes, but as she'd sat in the kitchen early that morning, looking out at the snow, she knew she couldn't wait longer. Not an hour, not a minute. She had to be back on the street. An hour or a minute could make a difference. She would never know if she simply sat and waited.

Once off the city bus, she had stopped at two of the near-downtown drop-in centers that she and Hannah had once frequented. But with no sign of her at either place, she was now heading for the bus depot, where the two had met weeks before. The depot had once been a temporary refuge for kids like her, but in recent years had tightened security, trying to limit entry to those who actually held a ticket to somewhere. Knowing this, Jennie waited until the ticket agent's eyes were elsewhere before she scooted through the gate unnoticed.

Suddenly, she could feel her breath quicken, her mind slipping into rewind. To those two weeks before, when she had—literally—first run into Hannah.

Moments after getting off the bus, tired and still frightened from her run from home and the long ride to Cities, having spent the last hour in darkness, huddled in her seat, confused and disoriented by the lights and buzz of the highway traffic flashing by outside her window.

Not knowing if her father might have guessed she would be on this bus. And if he had, would he have the police waiting? Or would he be there himself, smoldering with the anger she was trying to escape?

She was the last to leave the bus, looking furtively in every direction, clutching the strap of her backpack with one hand, her cell phone with the other. A small figure alone in the big city. With no idea of what to do or where to go. For her, at this moment, Minneapolis could have been the moon.

As she walked through the door of the depot, blinking at the bright overhead lights, caught in the middle of the moving crowd, she was pushed roughly to one side by a man rushing past her, flinging her into the arms of a girl caught totally unaware, idly leaning against a wall. Whatever drink she was holding went flying with the impact, splattering her and a guy next to her. "What the hell?" she shouted, recovering her balance just in time to grab a falling Jennie before she could hit the floor. "Hey, girl, hold on!" she yelled, grasping her by one arm. "I gotcha."

Momentarily stunned, Jennie tried to pull way, but then leaned over, frantically searching for her phone that had skittered away as she fell. "Lemme go," she shouted. "I lost my phone!"

"Hey, hey, relax," the girl said, reaching down. "It's here by my foot."

"Thank you, thank you," Jennie said, taking the phone, and in the confusion, actually seeing the girl for the first time. Several inches taller

than her, dark-haired with fair skin and eyes that seemed to have a smile of their own. Maybe, Jennie thought, the most beautiful girl, or woman, she had ever seen outside of the movies or TV.

Before she said anything more, and before she could walk away, the girl said, "Hey, young lady. You look a little lost. Need some help?"

Jennie turned back. "No, I'm fine. I'm meeting some friends."

"Really?" the girl said, looking around. "Funny, I don't see anybody waiting for you. Probably just late, huh? Maybe you can give them a call."

Jennie turned again without replying.

"My name's Hannah," she said. "What's yours?"

"Why do you care?" Jennie replied.

"Because I'm betting you're not even sixteen and I'm seeing you arrive on a bus by yourself. From somewhere you don't want to be, I'm guessing. And I'm also guessing you don't really have any friends waiting, that you're on your own. Am I right?"

Jennie looked down, staring at her boots.

"And I know what this town can do to young girls like you, lost and living on the streets or in the shelters, if you're lucky enough to find a bed. I've been there, done that, girl. Still doing that, actually."

Jennie studied her. While young, Jennie knew that big city predators didn't have to be male. They come in all sizes and colors and genders. Be careful, be afraid, she'd been warned by others who had made trips like this before her.

Still, there was something about this girl, the warmth of her smile and her easy manner that allayed some of those fears. But not enough. "I've got to go," she finally said.

"To where?" Hannah asked.

Jennie shrugged. "I'll find a place."

"Okay. Good luck."

Jennie hesitated. "Why should I trust you? Why are you being so nice?"

"For one thing, you kind of remind me of one of my kid brothers. He's about your age and probably just as clueless. I'd hate to see him

standing where you are, ready to walk out that door to who knows where. And to what. If you'd like, there's a drop-in center two blocks away that would probably take you in on an emergency basis, just for the night. And you can figure out what to do after that, in the daylight."

"Okay, I guess," Jennie said.

"You still haven't told me your name," Hannah said.

She hesitated. "Jennie. Jennie Nystrom."

"Nice to meet you, Jennie. And welcome to the big city."

With that, the friendship began.

Today, there were no crowds in the depot and, again, no sign of Hannah. But she did spot one of the street guys she knew only as Jake, who, like herself, must have snuck in. He was slouched in a chair, apparently asleep. His ragged-fleece jacket was pulled up around his neck and the flaps of an old blaze-orange hunting cap fell over his ears. A silver circle pierced his nose.

Pulling the scarf from her face, she sat down next to him and gently nudged his shoulder. "Hey, Jake, it's Jennie." His eyes came half open, "Get lost," he muttered. "Can't you see I'm trying to get some sleep."

"Please, Jake. I need some help. Please."

His eyes opened to slits. *"What?*

"I'm looking for my friend, Hannah. You know her. You've seen us together. I haven't seen her for days and I'm really freaked out, Jake. Have you seen her anywhere? Please."

He sat up in the chair, smirking. "No, I haven't seen her, but, yeah, I remember her. Beautiful bitch. Big tits." Then he laughed. "If you do find her, send her my way, okay? I'd love to have a piece of that."

She gave him a shove and stuck her middle finger in front of his nose. "Jerk!"

He pushed her hand away, laughed again, and sank back into the chair, his eyes closed again before she could walk away.

Back on the street, she found herself all but alone. The wind and snow were keeping most people inside, in the skyways, or hurriedly hustling from building to building. Busses passed by, the passengers ghost-like behind the fogged windows. But she kept going, down Hennepin Avenue, sometimes turning her back to protect herself from the penetrating, numbing chill of the wind. She stopped at two or three bars and restaurants along the way, and took a quick look inside each, knowing there was almost no chance of spotting her friend in one of those places.

But where?

She finally reached the Central Library, another temporary haven for the homeless, and began a search from floor to floor, wandering the stacks, checking every nook and corner, but again without success.

Back on the main floor, she sat slumped on one of the benches. Cold. Discouraged. Defeated. And, for the first time since boarding the bus from home, began to really cry. Silently, head bowed, allowing the tears to fall, unheeded, until one of the library security guards, a tall Black man, approached and knelt beside her, sympathy written across his face. "Hey, kid. What's going on?"

She turned away, slipped off one of her mittens and tried to wipe away the tears with the back of her hand. "Nothing, nothing, I'll be okay."

"Doesn't look that way to me," he said. "Can I call somebody? Your folks? A friend?"

She waited, finally saying, "No, thank you." Then, "But could you look at a picture, please?" Taking out her camera, she found the photo of Hannah and held it up to him, "Have you seen her? Her name is Hannah. My friend. And I can't find her. I've been looking forever."

The guard took the camera and studied the picture. "Can't say as I have. But we get a lot of young girls passing through here, you know. Girls like you. Come and go, come and go."

"I know," she said.

"Want me to ask some of the other guys?"

"Would you? It's really important."

He walked away with the camera, showing the picture to two other guards down the hall, then entering the library itself. After about ten minutes, he returned. "Sorry," he said, "Nobody seems to remember seeing her."

"Thanks for trying," she said, reclaiming the camera.

"Are you sure I can't call somebody? Maybe somebody from one of the shelters? An outreach worker? They'll be happy to come, I know."

"No, I'll be fine," she replied.

"If you say so," he said, giving her another close look before walking away.

Only then did she notice another man, not a guard, standing across and down the hall, staring at her. Showing a small smile.

The face staring at Gabby and Andy from the computer screen was that of Hannah Hendricks, emailed to them, as promised, by the Lyon County sheriff's deputy. This picture provided a much closer and clearer image of the girl than Jennie's photo. A portrait that looked as if it may have been taken for the high school yearbook. Dark hair, falling to just above her shoulders, a straight but not pointed nose, full lips, slightly dimpled cheeks, and eyes that seemed to be trying to penetrate yours. A beautiful young woman, no doubt about that.

The deputy had included a copy of the criminal complaint, listing in legalese the assault charges against her, along with an article from *The Lyon County Record* that described the event: namely, that Hannah was accused of stabbing her stepfather, Arnold Klinger, with an eight-inch kitchen knife in the early morning hours of October 12th in their rural Delroy home. She then fled before law enforcement arrived. The knife was recovered at the scene, and Klinger was hospitalized in nearby Marshall. A later newspaper clipping revealed that the stepfather had since returned home and that Hannah remained at large.

Gabby looked over at Andy. "So what do you think?"

"That she's gorgeous."

She grinned. "Other than that?"

"Not much, really. It's about what we knew before. Except that the stepdad is back home, apparently recovering."

"But we know nothing about *her*," she offered. "If she did dump her Facebook and other web accounts, as you suggested, then we're left with a picture but a blank page. And if we have a chance of helping Jennie find her, or hope to find her ourselves, we'd better learn more about her. Habits. Personality. Does she drink or do drugs? Sell herself? What other friends does she have that Jennie might not know about?"

"I hear you, but tell me why you care so much about this girl? I don't get it."

"I'm not sure I can explain or even know. But if we really hope to do a story about kids like Hannah and Jennie...they could be a key. A place to start." She thought for a moment. "But one more thing. In the back of my mind, I'm starting to share some of Jennie's concern about where this Hannah might be, or what might have happened to her. Silly maybe, but still. Like who is or was the guy or guys she was supposed to meet? And why hasn't Jennie been able to find her after all this time?"

"Maybe because she doesn't want to be found," Andy said. "Or maybe she's moved on...to Chicago...New York...the West Coast, wherever."

"You're probably right, but I'd still like to know more about her."

"So what can I do? I've still got a couple of hours here."

"Good. Get on the phone to our deputy friend and try to find out as much as you can about Hannah...and the names of any of her friends, male or female, that we might contact. Especially friends she was close to."

"What if he says 'bug off'?"

"Then we'll figure something else out. Like maybe a trip to Delroy."

"What about you now?" he replied, moving away.

"I'm off to see a cop."

As Jennie sat in the library and tried to figure out what to do next, the man who'd been staring at her walked down the hall and stood by her. "Saw you talking to the guard," he said, his voice gentle, non-threatening. "Looked like you're having a tough time. Anything I can do to help?"

She studied him. Six feet or so, blond, tan, maybe in his thirties, wearing a long overcoat, expensive. His expression gentle, like his voice. Smooth.

"No, I'm fine," she replied, turning away. Knowing immediately why he was there.

"You're sure?" he said, settling down next to her, closer. "You look pretty lost."

She turned back, irritated. "I told you. I'm fine. And why would you care?"

"Hey, hey," he said, holding up his hands. "I'm just trying to help. Maybe buy you a cup of coffee or some hot chocolate."

She laughed. "Want to help me, right? And why's that? Like I remind you of your little sister, maybe? Or is it your niece? That's why you hang around the library, hoping to help girls like me, right?"

"Hey, hold on…"

"No, *you* hold on! I may be a kid, but I've been on the street long enough to know about dudes like you. So leave me the hell alone, okay? Find some other little chick."

"You got me all wrong, girl. I know what you're thinking, but I'm a married man, got two kids of my own, five and seven if you want to know. But you're right, I do have a niece about your age. I *was* thinking of her when I saw you here."

"Then go get her a book and one for your kids. Just leave me the hell alone."

At that moment the same Black security guard approached. "Everything okay?"

"Sure," the man said as he got up. "I was just offering to help this young woman."

The guard shot him a look. "Well, from what I can see, it doesn't appear that she wants your help, so you may want to move on."

The last thing Jennie heard as the man walked away was a muttered, "Bitch!"

SEVEN

...

Gabby waited patiently outside an office in City Hall for her appointment with John Philips, the former homicide detective who had helped in the Ponzi investigation, and who, because of his role, had then been promoted to the white collar crime unit. He was not only a good cop, but a good friend who—before Zach—had secretly hoped he and Gabby could become more than just friends. But that was now a thing of the past.

After about ten more minutes, the door opened and he stepped out, his hand extended and a broad smile flashing across his face. "Hey, stranger...great to see you. Sorry to keep you waiting." She took his hand and gave him a quick kiss on the cheek. "Thanks for seeing me on short notice," she said, following him into his office.

It had been a few weeks since she'd seen him, but in that time he'd allowed a little tire to form around his slim waist, and now sported a closely-cut beard. But in all other respects, he was still the same lanky, good-looking guy. And still with no ring on his finger.

"How's Zach? How's Barclay?" he asked, settling in behind his desk. "And how about you? You're looking great."

"Thanks. Except for your dreaded Minnesota snow, I'm fine. And Zach and George are good, too. But busy. Everybody is. Trying to keep up. Smaller staff, more pressure, more competition."

"The same over here. More bad guys with guns on the street, and more crazies. And never enough cops. The uniforms are always looking over their shoulders and keeping their body cameras rolling. They make a mistake and they've got a hundred people with signs shouting at them. Or suing the department."

Gabby knew there was another side to that story, but simply said, "Maybe we should retire."

"And run away," he replied. Then, "Oh, yeah, you're engaged."

"Happily," she added, with another smile.

After spending a few more minutes updating their lives, Phillips asked, "So what can I help you with?"

"I'm not sure you can, but I hope you can put me together with someone who *can* help." She told the story of Jennie and Hannah as quickly and concisely as she could, pausing once to show him the picture of Hannah and a copy of the criminal complaint from Lyon County. "This could be just another story of a couple of runaways and nothing more. But I'm afraid for both of them and am looking for some kind of help in finding them."

"That's a big order," he said. "I'm no expert, but I know there are scores, if not hundreds, of homeless kids on the streets and in the shelters on any given night in the metro area."

"That's right, and I know they move around a lot. But I think it's a story that needs to be told and one I hope to do. But I'd like to find these two girls first. And maybe get their help in telling the story."

He thought for a moment. "There's a woman in the Second Precinct, Sergeant Sarah Chan, who I've heard is spending a lot of her time chasing after these kids. She works with the shelters and the street outreach workers. Trying to intervene, to keep the kids safe and out of trouble, off booze and drugs, out of the hands of the pimps and traffickers, and into some kind of safe temporary housing. And counseling, if that's possible. That's not her full-time job, but the brass down the hall has given her some time and resources."

Gabby was taking notes. "That's great. Can I use your name when I call her?"

"Sure, but I don't know her that well. I wish you good luck."

"Thanks. Anything else?"

"If you give me the picture of this Hannah, I'll try to get it spread around the precincts. They may already know about her because of the warrant, but maybe this will goose them a little bit."

Blocks away, as Jennie was about to leave the library and return to the streets, she heard the ringtone of her phone, which she had stuffed into a deep pocket of her parka. As she took it out, she saw an unfamiliar number. Hesitantly, she put the phone to her ear.

"Hello?"

"Are you Jennie?"

The voice, deep, almost guttural, was like the number. Unknown. "Who is this?"

"Never mind. You don't know me."

"How'd you get my number?"

He ignored the question. "Word on the street is you're looking for Hannah. That right?"

Stunned, she waited a moment. "Yes...so do you know..."

"Don't."

"What?"

"Forget her. Stop hunting. Got it?"

She could feel her breath quicken. "Who *are* you? What do you mean, *stop?*"

"Just what I said. And I won't say it again. Give it up. For your own sake."

She slumped onto the bench. Shaking, feeling the same fear she'd often felt facing her enraged father. Finally, barely able to speak, "Where *is* she? What have you done to her?"

"You aren't listening, kid. Don't screw with this. Don't screw with me. You got a life. Keep it."

Then the phone went dead.

She stared at it, rehearing what she'd just heard. Disbelieving. Her young mind raced. Who knew her number? Only a few of her street friends, but they were all girls. No guys that she could remember. Certainly no one with a voice like that.

Then it dawned. Hannah. Could she possibly have given her number to someone like that? Willingly?

And why the call now, after all this time?

Suddenly. Jake. At the bus depot. She hadn't given him her number. But he might know someone who did know. Everybody has phones.

Think!

The fear she felt was real, now as much for herself as for Hannah. What to do? Where to go?

She held up her phone and punched in a number.

Gabby was walking through one of the downtown skyways, from City Hall to the station, when she got the call. She stopped short. "Jennie? Is that you?"

"Yes, it's me."

Gabby took a breath. "Where are you?"

"At the library, downtown."

"Are you okay?"

"Not really. I need to talk to you."

She could hear the quiver in her voice. "Okay. Can you come to the station? Or should I come to you?"

"I can come to the station."

"And you won't run off again?"

"No, I promise."

"All right. I'll see you there."

Strange, Gabby thought, as she put the phone away. Strange call, strange child. Something had happened to cause that quiver. But what?

When she got back to the station, she found Andy still there, at her desk.

"I thought you had to leave," she said.

"I do, but I wanted to talk to you first."

"Go ahead."

"I talked to the deputy again, but he's clammed up. Wouldn't

45

tell me anything more about Hannah and wouldn't give me the names of any of her friends. Says he's already in trouble with the sheriff for doing what he's already done for us. Cited privacy issues. That's bullshit, of course, because what he gave me were public records. But for now, it's a dead end, I guess."

"There may be other ways."

"Like?"

"Like the local newspaper. Where the clippings were from. They may be willing to exchange some information with us."

"Want me to make that call?"

"No, I want you to go hit the books, or whatever you do. You've done enough for today, and I appreciate it."

He got up, but hesitated.

"Scat!" she said. "I'll see you tomorrow."

No more than fifteen minutes had passed before Zach walked into the newsroom with Jennie in tow. "I found her outside the front door," he said when they reached Gabby. "Standing there, freezing, like she was afraid to come in."

Gabby got up and gave her a hug. "I'm glad you're here, Jennie. Let's get that coat and scarf off and go somewhere we can talk."

Jennie returned the hug, and mumbled, "I'm really sorry."

Zach stood looking puzzled. He'd been on assignment and knew nothing about Jennie's call to Gabby. "So will someone tell me what's happening?"

"In a minute," Gabby said.

Once they'd put Jennie's coat and all aside, they found an empty conference room. "First of all," Gabby asked, "where have you been all day?"

Looking away, in a voice almost too faint to hear, she described her fruitless search of the shelters, the bus depot, the restaurants, and, finally, the library. Ignoring her encounter with the well-dressed predator. "It was just like every other day. She was nowhere I looked."

Gabby said, "On the phone, you sounded afraid. I could hear it."

Jennie turned to face her, the fear returning. "Someone called me. A guy. I don't know who he was or how he got my number."

"And?"

Hesitantly, voice choking, she repeated the telephone threats, as best she could remember. "In the end, he said something like, 'You have a life. Don't give it up.'"

"Jesus," Gabby breathed.

"You have no idea how he got your number?" Zach said.

"No, no," she replied, almost in tears. "No guys know it. I did run into this kid, Jake, at the bus depot, but didn't give him my number."

"But Hannah knew it," Gabby said as she exchanged glances with Zach.

Jennie didn't miss the looks. "You think she gave him the number, don't you?"

"We may never know," Gabby replied. "But I do know this. You can't wander the streets any more. Not after that phone call threats. You could be in real danger, and we can't let that happen."

Plaintively, "So what do you want me to do?"

"I want you to give me that guy's number from your phone, then wait at my desk until either Zach or I get a break. Then we'll get you back to the apartment. Where you'll be safe."

Jennie quickly checked her phone and retrieved the number. "I told you, I don't know the number," she said.

"I understand, but I'll try to check it out."

"Wait a second," Zach said. "Hold on. We need to talk about this."

"I know, I know," Gabby replied. "But right now, I don't think we have a choice. We need to get Jennie to a safe place."

If Zach was swayed, he didn't show it. Instead, there was another sign of his lingering frustration and muted anger. "We'd better talk to Barclay."

He was at his desk, but on the phone…so they waited until he waved them in. "Why do I have a feeling I'm not going to enjoy this conversation," he said as they sat down across from him.

"You may not," Gabby replied, "but we need your advice again."

He looked across the newsroom and saw Jennie sitting at Gabby's desk. "That's the girl you told me about? Is it Jennie?"

"Yes, Jennie Nystrom. And a lot has changed since we last talked to you."

He sighed. "Tell me about it."

She filled him in on everything that had happened since they last spoke—including Jennie's telephone threats. "So, in a way, we're back where we began," she said. "Only now Jennie may be in real danger, and there's still no sign of Hannah."

"And you think something may have happened to her? Prompting the threats?"

"It's possible. If not likely. Which is why I want to get Jennie back to the apartment."

"You, Zach?" Barclay asked.

"I don't know, boss. I agree the kid could be in danger, but we come back to the same question. Is it our job to protect her? To house her? Gabby and I obviously disagree, which is why we're talking to you. I just don't want to find our asses in a sling."

Before Barclay could reply, Gabby said. "I don't disagree, but I would like one more day to pursue this. My cop friend gave me the name of another cop, a woman in the Second Precinct, who knows a lot about these homeless kids. Who may be able to help us sort this out and maybe help find a place for Jennie."

He thought for a moment. "Okay. I want to give you some room, but you've gotta remember that if you get in trouble by keeping this girl, the station is in trouble, too. And it's my job to prevent that."

"I understand," she said. "I'll try to set up a meeting with this woman first thing in the morning. And get back to you."

"Good. And if Andy has the time, take him with you. His law studies could help."

"I'll see if he's available."

That night, at the apartment, after dinner and after tucking Jennie into bed with the teacup poodle, Gabby put in a call to one Howard Hooper, the editor and publisher of the *Lyon County Record*—whose name and home phone number she had found through a Google search.

He answered on the third ring.

"Mr. Hooper?"

"Yes, who's calling?"

"My name is Gabby Gooding. I'm a reporter for Channel Seven in the Twin Cities."

"Really."

"Yes. And I'm sorry to bother you at home and in the evening, but I didn't have a chance to call earlier today."

"That's okay. But what can I do for you?"

"We've become interested in the case of Hannah Hendricks, whom I'm sure you know about. We've received a couple of clippings from your newspaper."

"Of course I know about her. That's all they're talking about in Delroy." He paused. "But I don't understand why you'd be interested in the Cities."

"It's hard to explain, especially on the phone, but she could be part of a larger story we're trying to do on missing and homeless kids."

"She's not *homeless*," he objected. "She's a *fugitive*, for God's sake. Damned near killed her father."

"You mean her stepfather."

"Okay. Her stepfather."

"Who she says tried to molest her."

"*What?* Did she tell you that?"

"No, she told a friend of hers. Who told me."

"That's hard to believe. Better double-check your sources."

From his voice, Gabby tried to picture the man. Older, probably in his late fifties, early sixties. A bit grizzled. Grouchy. Impatient. Probably like her own dad, her journalistic idol, who had dropped dead of a heart attack several years before—at the peak of his storied reporting career at the *Portland Oregonian*.

"I realize there's a warrant out for her arrest," Gabby said, "but I thought we might work together on this. It could be a story for both of us."

"What kind of story?" Dripping skepticism.

"About what may have led her to do what she did. Why she took off? And where she is now? We've talked to your sheriff's people, but they've stopped being very helpful."

"What would you expect of me?"

"To tell me as much as you and your staff know about her. And her family. And the names of some of her friends we might speak to."

"I don't know," he said, clearly reluctant. "I can't afford to irritate the sheriff and his people. We depend on them and work with them."

"They wouldn't necessarily need to know that you're working with me. At least not right away. And *I* certainly wouldn't tell them. What I really need are the names of some of her close friends, those who know her best. They might help us find her, if she's in the Cities."

"And if you did find her, would you tell the cops?"

"That's an open question. We work *with* the cops up here, not *for* them."

"I don't know. I'll have to think about this," he finally said. "What I might get out of the kind of cooperation you're looking for. Give me your phone number and email and I'll let you know."

"That's all I can ask," she replied, giving him both. "I'll just wait and hope to hear."

But, truth was, she didn't hold out that much hope.

EIGHT

• • •

B y morning, the snow had stopped and the sun was out, the temperature supposedly heading toward the low sixties—as Zach had predicted it might. It would take a while, Gabby decided, to figure out this Minnesota weather. With yesterday's snow melting at her feet, she could only wonder what tomorrow might bring.

Meanwhile, she was content to savor the warmth of the sun on her face.

Andy was standing next to her outside the police Second Precinct on Central Avenue in northeast Minneapolis, an attractive brick and stone structure that occupied almost half a city block. And standing next to them was a more-than life-sized bronze sculpture, turned green with age, of two policemen—one from perhaps the turn of the century, the second a more modern figure, one protectively holding the hand of a child.

The woman cop whom John Philips had recommended, Sergeant Sarah Chan, had agreed to meet them, but since they were about ten minutes early, they'd decided to bide their time outside in the sun.

Then, as they started to saunter up the sidewalk, Gabby said, "You're sure you're not missing a class or something?"

"No, no classes 'til this afternoon."

"If you say so, but I hope you're not screwing up your life for this."

"Not to worry." Then he stopped, mid-step. "But, tell me again, what we're going to talk to her about?"

"We'll have to wait to see, depending on how much time she'll give us. But I'd like to drain her brain as much as I can about homeless kids like Jennie and Hannah, and to ask her specifically if she's aware of the hunt for Hannah. And whether she has any advice on how we might go about finding her."

"That could be tricky," he said, "if you tell her about Jennie, that you're housing a runaway. I'd be careful about that."

"I understand."

"I'm not sure you do."

By then, they'd made it inside the precinct and found Sergeant Chan waiting for them with a welcoming, if slightly curious, smile. A petite woman with dark, short hair and striking facial features. In plain clothes. As they shook hands, Gabby introduced herself and Andy, and said, "Thanks for agreeing to see us on such short notice."

"No problem. Detective Philips told me about you...the work you did together. But he didn't really need to. I've seen you on television and remember your story on that Ponzi guy. And the close call you had with your stalker."

"That's good. Then I don't need to tell you much about myself."

"But I don't know anything your friend here. Is it Andy?"

"Right. Andy Simmons. I'm just a tagalong. I'm an intern at the station and a second-year law student at the U. Trying to be of whatever help I can."

"Then follow me," she said. "There's a small conference room down the hall."

She led them through a locked door and down a long hallway to a room with a round table in the center. Once settled, she said, "Philips tells me you're thinking of doing a story on youth experiencing homelessness. Is that right?"

"I hadn't heard it put that way, but that's right. Homeless kids. And he tells *me* you know a lot about them, which is why we're here, taking your time."

"So shoot."

"It gets a little complicated," Gabby said, "so maybe we can talk off the record, if that's okay."

Looking puzzled, she replied, "I can't talk off the record until I know what we're going to talk about. So let's just make it a woman-to-woman conversation for now."

"Fine," Gabby said, momentarily regretting she hadn't listened to Andy. But she then launched into the story—from her first meeting with Jennie to the subsequent unsuccessful search for Hannah. It took her about ten minutes and Chan listened without interruption. Finally, she said, "So let me get this straight. You're helping this young runaway try to find another young runaway, who apparently stabbed her stepfather and is on the run from the likes of me."

After a warning glance from Andy, Gabby said, "That's right."

"And you also think this Jennie may be in danger because she's out looking for this Hannah?"

"That's also right. Because of that frightening call she got."

"So what would you want from me?"

"Advice on where to look. And maybe some official police help in finding Hannah before something bad happens to her. And, in the longer run, to help me tell the story of kids like these two. Where they hang? How they get by? The dangers they all face? What's being done to find and help them? All the stuff I'm told you know about."

"Where is this Jennie now?"

Gabby glanced at Andy. "Staying with us. Temporarily. To keep her safe."

"And how old is she?"

"Fifteen going on sixteen, she says."

Chan shook her head. "You know it's against the law. Harboring a minor."

"Protecting, not harboring," Gabby replied, repeating what she'd once told Zach.

"That may be your way of looking at it, but it's not the way the law does."

Andy broke in. "She's right, Gabby. As I was going to tell you outside, I looked it up last night. Minnesota Statute 609.26 says it's illegal to hide a child from their parent. And while the law seems to be aimed at custody battles, one parent taking a child from the other, it could apply in your case too. If someone wanted to pursue it."

Tiredly, Gabby said, "Then we've come back to the same question: Do we send her back to what she says is an abusive home, or back on the streets to face whoever made that phone call? It's an impossible situation."

Chan leaned in. "You live alone or with somebody, Gabby?"

"With my fiancé. Zach Anthony. A photographer at the station."

"Another possible problem. What if Jennie was to claim you or he touched her inappropriately?"

"*What?* Zach would never do that! I wouldn't do that! And I can't believe Jennie would ever make up a story like that."

"Then that may be naïve on your part. You don't know these youngsters like I do. While they're more often the victims of crime than the perpetrators, they're not always as innocent as they seem. Even a girl like Jennie. They can get street-wise in a hurry, and if they get desperate enough, they may try anything to survive. "

"Like blackmail?"

"It's happened. To well-meaning people like yourself."

Gabby leaned back and clasped her hands behind her neck. Finally, she said, "So what do you suggest?"

"You have to get her to an agency that deals with young people from abusive homes. Like Jennie. There are several of them around town and I can help connect you with one. I'll even talk to this Jennie if you'd like. But you've got to get her out of your apartment. For her well-being and for your own sake. And before I have to come and get her."

"She'll just run again. She won't stay put anywhere until she finds out what's happened to Hannah."

"That's a chance you'll have to take. Trust me."

Resigned, Gabby said, "We'll see. I may take you up on your offer. I'll talk to Jennie. But what about Hannah? Can you help us find her?"

"Tell me more about her."

She took out Hannah's picture and the other material they'd received from Lyon County. "She may no longer be in town, but if she is, she could be in trouble. If you believe Jennie's phone call. She could be linked up with a pimp, out hustling, doing anything to keep clear of the law."

Chan studied the picture and the other material. "I'll be out making the rounds this afternoon. I'll ask around all the usual places...show the picture...and see if I can get any leads. With the warmer weather, more of the kids will be out and about. So I'll see what I can find. But I wouldn't count on it. There are too many kids, too many places to camp."

"I'd appreciate whatever you can do," Gabby said as she reached into her purse to retrieve her card. "All of my cell and work numbers and email addresses are here. If you find anything, please call me, day or night."

"Will do, but what about Jennie? What are you going to do about her?"

"Talk to her. Maybe get her to talk to you. Maybe make the rounds ourselves. We need to find Hannah. That's the priority. For her and for us."

"Okay. But don't push me on your keeping Jennie. I'm a cop, first and foremost."

As they got up to leave, Gabby handed her a slip of paper. "One more thing. I have the number of whoever called Jennie. I tried it several times, but got no answer. Not even an answering machine. Could you possibly trace it?"

"With that kind of call I'd guess it's a throw-away phone."

"I guessed that, too, but I'd appreciate your checking."

Once back in the car, Gabby asked Andy, "So what do you think?"

"Give her a couple of days, but if you haven't dealt with Jennie by then, I suspect she or somebody else will be at your apartment door, ready to take her away."

"I think you're right. I just hope we have a couple of days."

NINE

...

Turns out, it wouldn't be a couple of days. Less than twenty-four hours, actually.

Gabby was in the midst of a deep sleep when the phone's ringtone suddenly brought her awake. At first, in the darkness and fog of sleep, she thought it was her alarm, but quickly realized it was the phone on the bedside stand, next to the clock that read 2:45.

Reaching across Zach's still-sleeping body, she picked up the phone. "Yes?"

"Gabby?"

"Yes."

"This is Sergeant Chan. Sorry to bother you this late, but you told me to call."

Gabby sat up straight, poking Zach as she did. "No, that's fine."

"I think we found your girl, Hannah."

"What? Where?"

"Are you fully awake?"

By now, Zach had raised himself up and turned on the bedside light, his expression a mixture of concern and confusion.

"Yes, I'm awake," she said.

"Then brace yourself," Chan replied. "The news is not good."

"Tell me."

"It's not official, but the body of a young woman we believe is Hannah was found a couple of hours ago..."

Gabby gasped. "No, no. Please no."

"The body was stuffed in the back seat of a stolen SUV found in a parking lot across from the bus depot. The parking lot manager was emptying the pay box when he noticed the single car still in the lot. He checked and found the body. I'm terribly sorry."

"Hold on, please," Gabby said as she repeated the news to Zach, swallowing a sob. Then she put the phone on speaker.

Chan went on, "Homicide called me at home because they knew I'd been asking around about a missing girl, and the description seemed to fit. They also found a driver's license stuffed in one of her pockets. I really am sorry."

"Are you still there? With the body? Is Homicide still there? Is it still a crime scene?"

"Yes, I'm still here, and, yes, it's still a crime scene. Will be until the sun's up and they can more thoroughly search the area."

"Give us a half hour and we'll be there. And thanks for the call."

She scrambled out of bed and started to search for clothes. "Quick, Zach. Get dressed and get the camera gear. We've got to go!"

He was on his feet. "What about Jennie?"

"We'll leave a note. That we were called out on an emergency. Tell her to make some breakfast and we'll be back."

In a flurry, after both were dressed, Zach went to round up his gear and write the note while Gabby made a quick phone call to George Barclay, at home.

When he groggily answered after three rings, she apologized for the call, but then quickly told him what had happened. "We're on our way now, but I wanted you to know so you can alert the dispatch shack that we've got it covered."

"They may already have sent the overnight photog."

"Then we'll meet him there."

"Are they sure it's her?" he asked, sleep still in his voice.

"Not positively. But her picture apparently matched the body and they found a driver's license."

"Jesus. So how do we play this?"

"As a normal homicide, I guess. We'll get the video back to the station and I'll leave a note for the morning crew with everything I know. Or don't know. But I'll have to get back here to somehow break the news to Jennie."

"All right," he said. "I'll head to the station to manage things there."

By the time they arrived at the parking lot, the area around the white CRV was awash with light from the police floodlights and surrounded by yellow crime scene tape. Several squad cars were parked in the lot, with a mixture of uniformed and plainclothes cops milling about. The warmth of the day before had crept into the night and the lot was now all but free of snow.

As Gabby stood in the shadows, outside the field of light, she tried to absorb what she was seeing. It had the feel of a dream. Or a maybe a nightmare from which she had suddenly awakened. Unreal. Surreal. Elusive. In her years as a reporter she had covered more murders and more death scenes than she cared to remember, but never, not once, had any of those been *personal.* Not that she *knew* Hannah Hendricks, but, still, in a way she did. Because of Jennie, who now slept peacefully, sadly unaware her young life was about to be changed. In a most horrible way.

She was quick to notice they were not the first television news crew to be there, including their own overnight photographer, Ted Manning, who spotted them and came over. "The dispatcher told me you guys were on the way, but he didn't tell me why."

"It's kind of complicated," she replied. "But we're thinking of doing a story on homeless kids and this dead young woman," nodding at the CRV, "might have been part of it. And we've been helping to search for her. That's about all I can tell you right now. We don't know much more."

"I've shot about as much as there is to shoot," Manning said.

"The body's still in the car, we're told, although we can't get close. The M.E. is supposedly on the way."

"Good," Zach said, "but I'd still like to get a little video of my own."

"Be my guest," Manning replied.

At that moment, Sergeant Chan approached them, accompanied by a squat, heavyset man clad in a long overcoat, whose gray, thinning hair reflected the shine from one of the photographer's LED lights. After a quick hello to Gabby, she introduced the man as Homicide Detective John Archer. "I've told Detective Archer of our conversation about Hannah and he'd like to hear it himself."

"Sure, but I'd also like to get some kind of comment on camera before we leave."

Archer shook his head. "We won't have anything to say beyond the obvious until later this morning, at the earliest. We need to make a positive ID and get a cause of death, that kind of thing."

"Can you at least tell me if she died…ahhh…violently…?"

"No. Because we just don't know yet."

"Right," she replied, knowing full well that he did know.

"So tell me," he asked. "What do you know about this girl?"

"Not that much, really," she said, repeating what she'd told Chan the day before. "After Jennie got that call, I had the feeling that something bad could happen to Hannah. And here we are."

"And where is this Jennie?" Archer asked.

With a glance at Chan, "At my apartment, for safekeeping."

"I'll need to talk to her."

"I hear you, but I need to talk to her first. To break the news. She'll be crushed."

"I can't wait too long," he said.

"Give me your card and I'll call you as soon as I've talked to her. If I can keep her from running."

Chan broke in. "We can't chance that. So let me meet you at your apartment when you're ready to talk to her. We'll do it together."

When Gabby and Zach got to the newsroom, Barclay was already there and had briefed the morning news producers. Zach had collected Manning's video at the scene and together with his own was now editing about a forty-five second story for the first of the morning newscasts. Gabby had written the script, acknowledging there was precious little to tell:

Minneapolis police were called to a downtown Minneapolis parking lot early today after the body of a young woman was found in an abandoned, stolen vehicle. At this time, there is no official indication of how the woman died and no confirmation of her identity. The Hennepin County Medical Examiner will be conducting an autopsy and attempting to establish her identity. No name will be released until the family of the victim is notified. Nor will they reveal how long the vehicle and the victim may have been in this parking lot. We'll continue to follow this story throughout the day with the latest details.

Once she was done, as she and Zach sat in Barclay's office, he said, "Here's the plan. You guys head home and take care of your business with Jennie, as painful as that will be. But it obviously has to be done. And I'm glad this Sergeant Chan will be with you. For legal and other reasons. Then, when that's over, and if you have the time, Gabby, we'll have you do a live shot from the parking lot for the noon show. We may have more information by then."

"But what about Jennie?" she asked, plaintively.

"You're going to have to give her up. You don't have a choice. Let Sergeant Chan get her to one of the safe places she knows about. Let them deal with her situation...with the abusive dad. They have experience dealing with kids like her."

"They'll have to lock her up...or she'll run like a damned rabbit."

"That's their problem, not yours. And I have to say this, Gabby. Be careful how close you get to this child. You're a reporter, not a foster mom."

She turned to Zach. "Help me here, please."

He shrugged his shoulders. "I think I care as much about her as you do, Gabs, but I don't think there's an alternative. For her sake and ours."

There was a long pause. Then, after a deep breath, she said. "Okay. I'll call Chan and have her meet at our place in half an hour. But I'm telling you, I'd rather take a stick in the eye than do what we're going to have to do."

TEN

• • •

A rriving at the apartment, they found Jennie still asleep, almost unseen under the covers—with the poodle snuggled practically nose-to-nose with her. Gabby stood at the bedroom door for a moment, Zach behind her with his arm around her. "I'm not sure I can do this," she whispered. "Not you," Zach said into her ear. "*We* will do it."

She walked to the bed and sat gently on the edge, which drew a low growl from the irritated poodle. "Shush," she said, then nudged Jennie's shoulder. "Hey, Jennie, it's me. Wake up, okay. Time for breakfast."

Her eyes slowly opened. "What time is it?"

"Almost nine. Time to get up and go."

She pushed back the covers, yawned, and stretched. "Are you kidding me? I haven't slept this long in a long time. We gotta get back on the streets."

"Not so fast," Gabby said. "Brush your teeth, grab your robe and meet us in the kitchen. We need to talk."

"About what?"

"You'll see."

By the time she got to the kitchen, with the dog trailing behind her, Sarah Chan was already there, seated at the kitchen table, sipping on a cup of coffee.

"Jennie, this is Sarah Chan. She's a friend."

The girl took one look and bolted. Screaming. "She's no friend! She's a freakin' cop! I've seen her on the street. I can spot one a mile away."

Gabby got up to block her way. "Hold on! Okay. You're right. But she is also a friend. And she's here to help…so please sit down and listen to us."

Jennie's anger exploded as she tried to rush Gabby. "Bullshit. You promised. You bitch!"

Chan caught her mid-rush and wrestled her into a chair. "Sit down and settle down, young lady. And be quiet or I'll put the cuffs on you. I mean it."

Jennie pushed her away and defiantly crossed her arms across her chest. "You'll need more than cuffs to keep me."

Gabby looked at Zach, who stood on the other side of the kitchen, as aghast and amazed as she was. Never had she witnessed such a sudden, explosive reaction like this from a child. Not in school, not in her years of covering the news. She knew then that she'd led a sheltered life. And was now seeing a frightening side of Jennie they had not seen before. Or knew existed.

They waited and watched until some of her anger abated, and then Gabby moved closer to her. "You have to calm down and listen, Jennie. We've got some very bad news and you'll have to be brave. Okay?"

Jennie turned to face her, calmer now, but with her anger still simmering. "What news? About Hannah?"

"Yes. I'm afraid so."

"Did you find her? Is she hurt? *Tell me!*"

Gabby glanced at Chan, but before either could say anything, Zach knelt down in front of her, his eyes welling. "We're so sorry to tell you this Jennie, but Hannah is dead…She…"

It took a split second to register, but then she leaped out of her chair, shrieking, her face contorted. "You're lying! That can't be. No, no!"

Gabby reached out to grab her and hold her tightly in her arms.

"Please, Jennie, please. Hold on. We're here for you...we want to help you get through this..."

She fought to free herself. "You *never* helped. You kept me here...kept me from looking for her. I could have found her...I could have saved her."

Gabby continued to hold her, firmly. Then, in a calming voice, "No, Jennie you could not have saved her. If she had wanted you to find her she would have found you. Called you. She must have known you were looking for her, but she didn't want to be found. We don't know why. We may never know why. Maybe she was trying to keep you safe. But you can't blame yourself. You cannot blame us. You tried. We tried."

The tremors in her body stilled. But the quiet sobs continued. "Where was she? Where did they find her?"

Chan leaned forward. "In a stolen car. Parked behind the bus depot. We don't know how she died yet. Whether someone killed her or if she died in some other way. A drug overdose or something else. But we'll find out, one way or another. I promise you."

Jennie reached down and picked up the dog, holding him tightly. "So that man who called me...who tried to put a scare into me. Is he the one?"

"Maybe. That's why we're going to need your help. To find whoever did this."

"Help how?"

Chan continued. "Once you get dressed, pack up your things, and have some breakfast, I'm going to take you downtown, where one of the detectives will ask you everything you know about Hannah. Who her friends were...where you hung out. He'll probably show you some pictures and ask you to try to remember anything that might help us find the people who did this."

"Can I see her?"

"I don't know. Maybe sometime. Her parents don't even know about this yet. So we'll have to wait and see."

"Then what happens? Do I come back here?"

With a quick look at Gabby and Zach, she said, "I'm afraid not. They'll get in trouble if they keep you here. I'm going to take you to a good place where they'll look after you and talk to you about what's been happening in your home. You'll be safe."

"I won't stay, you know. I won't go back to my dad. I'll disappear."

"I suppose you could. I hope you won't. But if you try, I hope you'll remember what happened to Hannah when she tried to disappear."

Gabby held the dog as they waited for Jennie to emerge from the bedroom with her pack on her back and tears in her eyes. She tried to brush past them, but Gabby stopped her. "Sarah will tell us where you'll be and we'll be there to see you as soon as we can, as soon as they'll let us."

Jennie touched the poodle's head, rubbing his ears. "Wherever it is, I won't be there long." But then, as she stepped out the door, she stopped and turned. "I'm sorry I screamed at you. You're not a bitch…and I'm sorry I said that. I know you tried to help…but," shaking her head, "we never had a chance, I guess."

With a final kiss to Barclay's nose, she was gone.

As Gabby and Zach stood watching, he said, "She's right, you know. We never had a chance."

"Maybe not, but I don't regret trying. Not for a minute. And I won't stop trying to figure out what happened to Hannah."

"You're not a cop, Gabby. Leave it to them."

"They'll try to find out who killed her, but I want to know who she was and how she got to the point that got her killed. And whether the same thing could happen to Jennie and scores of other kids still on the street. There's a story there and I hope we can tell it."

He checked his watch. "We should get going."

"You go. I want to make a couple of calls. I'll take my own car down."

"Okay, but don't take too long."

She retreated to the kitchen, poured a cup of remaining coffee, and punched in her first number.

"Hennepin County Medical Examiner," the voice said.

"Is Dr. Maxwell in?"

"Who's calling?"

"Gabby Gooding. From Channel Seven."

"Just a moment."

Dr. Cynthia, Cindy, Maxwell, was an assistant medical examiner whom Gabby had worked with in the Ponzi investigation. Who became her friend.

"Hey, Gabby. Long time."

"Hi, Cindy. Sorry it's been so long. I should have been in touch before now."

"No problem. We're all busy. What can I do for you?"

"Are you working on the Jane Doe who came in this morning?"

"Not directly, but I know about her."

"Off the record, can you tell me anything? Like a cause of death?"

"Off the record?"

"Yes. Promise."

"I can't give you many specifics. The autopsy's not done yet. But it's clearly a homicide. Multiple stab wounds among other things. Like head trauma."

"Brutal."

"You got that right."

"Officially identified yet?"

"Not officially, but the BCA is checking the fingerprints to make sure."

"So the family's not been notified?"

"Not yet. Hopefully in a couple of hours, I'm told."

"Thanks. Can I keep in touch on this?"

"Sure, but why the special interest?"

"I was helping a young friend of hers try to find her. But not in time."

"Too bad. I'm sorry. I'll get back to you when we know more and it's official."

As soon as she'd hung up, Gabby checked her contact list and hit the number of Howard Hooper, from the *Lyon County Record*. He answered on the first ring.

"Mr. Hooper, this is Gabby Gooding. We talked a couple of nights ago."

"Yes, I remember."

"I have some news for you, but it's strictly off the record. And I'm telling you this because—as I said before—I hope we can cooperate on a story about Hannah."

"What's the news?" Still skeptical.

"Hannah is dead."

"What?"

"They found her body this morning in a Minneapolis parking lot. An apparent homicide. They're confirming her identity as we speak, and the family has not yet been notified. So you can't say anything to anyone yet."

"For God's sake. That's terrible."

"If things work out, I may be coming down to Delroy for the funeral, whenever that is, and I would like your help in lining up some of her friends and others in the community to talk to. Could you do that?"

"I suppose so, sure. If you keep filling me in on things up there."

"I will. As soon as we know more."

By the time she reached the parking lot, the station's live truck was already there, its antenna up, with Zach standing by with his camera on a tripod. Two other competing live trucks were also there, situated in such a way that each reporter could report on camera without one of the other trucks in the background.

The white CRV was gone…as was the police presence. Why, then, when there was nothing happening, was a live shot necessary?

It was a question that had never been satisfactorily answered for her, but that's the way TV news operated and she did as she was told. There *was* new video, however, showing the daylight search for any piece of evidence that may have been missed in the darkness.

The police had not yet held a promised news briefing, apparently waiting for confirmation of the victim's ID and assurance her family had been notified. So Gabby, like the others, was limited in what she could say—despite the off the record information she'd received.

"Ten minutes 'til you're on," Zach told her. "Are you all set?"

"I guess so," she replied, holding up her phone. "I've got the script on the phone, but I'm going to pretty much wing it. Not that much new to say."

She fidgeted as the minutes passed—until she finally was given her cue from Zach. The report lasted about two minutes, as she repeated the story of the body's discovery and the search for evidence. She wrapped up by saying, *"We have learned that there are no surveillance cameras in the area, and, from what we know, no eyewitnesses who may have come forward with information about the CRV. Police have promised a briefing later in the day, and we'll continue to follow this developing story. I'm Gabby Gooding reporting from downtown Minneapolis for Channel Seven News."*

ELEVEN

. . .

L ater that afternoon, as she and Zach were about to leave for home, their long day over, she received a call from Cindy Maxwell at the ME's office. "The autopsy on your Jane Doe is over and confirms what I told you earlier," she said. "The girl died of homicidal violence...multiple stab wounds to her upper torso and severe trauma to her head. It was the stab wounds that killed her."

"Jesus," Gabby muttered.

Maxwell went on, "I'm told the cops are going to hold a briefing in the next hour or so. But you'll have to check with them."

"Has her family been notified?"

"I'm told they have been, but the cops should confirm that at the briefing."

"Thanks so much, Cindy. I owe you one."

"How about a drink?"

"For sure. Once I get a break."

As she put the phone down, Barclay approached. "Time for you guys to head home," he said.

"I don't think so," she replied, repeating what Cindy Maxwell had just told her. "I'd like to be at the briefing."

Barclay said, "You'll probably fall asleep."

She looked at Zach. "We're all right. I'd like to see this through."

"Up to you."

Before she left the station, Gabby put in another call to Howard Hooper, reporting on the autopsy results. "I'll call you after the briefing," she said, "but you might want to get started on your story now."

"I already have, thanks to you. Our paper comes out the day after tomorrow, so we're ahead of the game."

"Good. And please get back to me when the funeral plans are made. I think we may be coming down."

"I'll give you all the help I can."

With the warmer weather continuing, the police had cleared an area of the parking lot where the body was found, and had set up a stand for the media microphones. Reporters from the local TV stations and print media were there, standing in a semi-circle around the makeshift podium, waiting for Detective John Archer to speak.

Sergeant Chan was there, too, standing off to one side with another woman and a couple of uniformed cops. When Gabby approached her, she shook her head, mouthing "Wait."

"I'll be very brief," Archer began, "and tell you what we can at this point. Which isn't much. This is an open, ongoing investigation and less than twenty-four hours old. So I'd appreciate your patience."

He then went on to identify the victim as Hannah Hendricks from Delroy, Minnesota, in Lyon County, repeating what Cindy Maxwell had told Gabby about the cause of death. He went on, "We believe she was killed either in the early hours of this morning or late last night. We are trying to determine a more precise time of death and where the murder may have taken place. At this moment we have no suspects. We do know that the car in which her body was found was stolen from a private home in northeast Minneapolis earlier last night. That car has now been impounded as part of our investigation."

At this point, one of the *Strib* reporters, Patrick Cochran, interrupted. "We understand you were looking for this woman…that there was a warrant out for her arrest. Is that true?"

Archer hesitated, glancing at the woman who stood next to Sergeant Chan, whom Gabby now guessed was probably from the Hennepin County Attorney's office. She gave a quick nod. "That's correct," Archer finally said. "She was wanted by the Lyon County authorities on an assault charge. She was accused of stabbing and wounding her stepfather before fleeing."

"Had you been actively looking for her?" the reporter asked.

"We were aware of the arrest warrant," he replied, cautiously. "And we had circulated her picture. But I would not say the search was a priority for us. We were not even sure she was in the Twin Cities."

"Has the family been notified?" another reporter asked.

"Of course, or I wouldn't be standing here talking to you. We expressed our deep condolences and promised them a thorough investigation."

There were several more questions, including some about the stepfather stabbing, but he said he had no more information on that. Then, with nothing more to offer, the briefing ended with a promise to keep the media informed as the investigation moved forward.

Before everyone started to pack up, one of uniformed officers passed out pictures of Hannah—the same one the Lyon County deputy had provided for Gabby. And while that was happening, she walked over to Sergeant Chan. "Okay," she said, "tell me. Where's Jennie…and how is she?"

Chan stepped away from the other woman. "She's all right. Angry and confused and still grieving, of course. But she's in a safe place for now."

"Where?"

"A shelter called The Haven, in Brooklyn Park. They'll keep her until someone from her home county's child protection can talk to her and decide what to do."

"And when will that happen?"

"Hard to tell. We're not responsible for her here, so who knows when her home county, up north somewhere, will be able to get someone down here? They're probably short on staff and over-whelmed with cases like Jennie's."

Gabby asked, "So what do you think they'll do?"

"Want to know the truth? They'll bring her back home…"

"To an abusive father? Give me a break."

"Settle down. Remember, there is no proof of abuse. Just her word. And she's not even sixteen years old. The law may not leave them much choice."

"She'll just run again. Unless they chain her up."

"Maybe. And then we'll have to pick her up again. Round-and-round we go."

"Wait a minute," Gabby said, thinking back. "Jennie told us she has an older brother in the Army somewhere. Texas, I think. And she claims he was also abused…and hates their father. Maybe he could back her story up."

"Did he ever see *her* abused?"

"Physically? I don't know. I didn't ask and she didn't say."

Chan shrugged her shoulders. "If he didn't, then he may not be of much help."

At that moment, Detective Archer walked over to join them. To Gabby he said, "Thanks for your help with Jennie. She's a nice young girl and tried her best to help us."

"Maybe you can help *us* keep her out of an abusive home."

He smiled. "Not my job, unfortunately. But she did pick out a few pictures of guys she and Hannah knew. And gave us a few names, mostly first names or street names."

"What kind of guys?" she asked.

"Pimps. Or other punks we've picked up for things like shop-lifting, purse snatching, disorderly conduct. Pissing on the sidewalk. That kind of thing. A lot of young shits."

"Any of them violent?"

"That's what we're checking, of course. I've got two other guys working the case, but understand, it's only one of many unsolved homicide we're dealing with."

"Have you checked out the stepfather?"

"Dah. Give me a break. He's clear. He was back in the hospital at the time of the murder. Getting some follow-up care for the stab wounds."

"Can I keep in touch?"

"Sure," he said, as he started to walk away. "But don't make a pest of yourself."

As Chan also started to leave, Gabby asked, "So when can I see her? Jennie?"

"I don't know," she replied. "But I'll let you know."

By seven that evening, at home, Gabby already was in her pajamas and robe, the poodle in her lap, a can of Surly beer in her hand, Zach's head resting on her shoulder, and an empty pizza box sitting on the coffee table. Neither she nor Zach had the strength or desire to speak.

2:45 A.M. was a long time ago.

Her last official act had been another live shot from the parking lot for the five o'clock news. Then, on Barclay's orders, she had turned the story over to one of the night side reporters, Ben Ferris, who would carry it through the later newscasts.

The story continued to dominate the local news, even as murders were becoming increasingly common. But with little wonder. The ingredients were captivating and irresistible, especially on a slow news day: a young, attractive woman, a runaway, a homeless fugitive from a small Minnesota town, killed in a most violent way. Who, herself, had been accused of stabbing her stepfather.

She couldn't help but wonder if the story would have gotten the same kind of play had the victim been a young Black woman from the troubled north side of town. Deep down, she knew it wouldn't… and that made her even sadder. More disturbed.

But such was the state of television news…and she, alone, could not change it.

While she was at the briefing, another Channel Seven reporter,

Stephanie Accusi, had been sent to Hannah's hometown of Delroy to get local reaction to the murder. Her report was due to air on the ten o'clock news, but Gabby wasn't sure she could stay awake to see it.

Finally, she nudged Zach's head. "You awake?"

"I am now," he groaned.

"Is it too early to go to bed?"

"I never thought you'd ask."

She took another sip of beer. "We can't. We have to see Steph's report at ten."

"Set the alarm."

She laughed, and then her phone sounded. "Yes?"

"It's Sarah Chan, Gabby. Hope I'm not disturbing you."

"No problem. What's up?"

"I pulled some strings and cleared the way for you to have a few minutes with Jennie in the morning."

"Really? That was quick. Thanks."

"I'll pick you up at eight, if that's okay. Assuming Jennie hasn't fled by then."

"I'll be waiting outside."

"No camera. No recorder. Just the two of us."

"I understand."

Gabby did manage to stay awake until ten o'clock and watched as Stephanie Accusi stood on what appeared to be the main street of Delroy, ankle-deep in a new snow that had fallen in western Minnesota but had missed the Twin Cities.

STEPHANIE: *As you would expect, the small town of Delroy is in a state of shock today, reeling from the news that one of their own young people, Hannah Hendricks, was the victim of a brutal murder in Minneapolis.*

As she began her report the cover video showed a string of small buildings along the main street, a couple of them vacant, two bars, an auto repair shop, a small restaurant, an abandoned movie theater, a gas station and, in the distance, two towering grain elevators. From what Gabby could see, a small, rural Minnesota town that looked to be like many others—dying a slow death.

STEPHANIE: *This is a community of only five-hundred–and-thirty people, a close-knit village in the middle of the rich farmland of western Minnesota. Few of those people were on the streets today; many huddled in one of the bars or cafes, or staying at home, ducking the reporters who have descended on the town. While Hannah and her family lived on a farm outside of town, she was well-known here. She attended a consolidated high school in the nearby town of Travis, played volleyball and softball, and graduated in the top ten-percent of her class.*

STEPHANIE ON CAMERA WITH A GIRL: *This is Amy Kitteridge, one of Hannah's high school friends.*

AMY: *Hannah was one of my best buddies. We were on the volley-ball team together and spent a lot of time hanging out. None of us can believe what happened to her. It's like unbelievable, you know. She was, like, kinda wild, a crazy kid, but we loved her...and she loved us.*

STEPHANIE: *Did she have a boyfriend?*

AMY: *Not a regular one, no. She hung out with a lot of guys. She was kind of, what do you call it? A magnet for guys. They fell all over her. But there was nothing serious. I would have known.*

STEPHANIE: *Had you talked to her recently? Did you know she was in the Cities? Had any of your friends seen or talked to her?*

AMY: *No, none of us have. Not since...you know...that thing with her stepdad. We were all worried about her, but never, like, expected something like this. I can't believe she's gone.*

STEPHANIE: *About her stepdad...did you...*

AMY: *I can't talk about that. My folks told me not to talk about that. I've gotta go.*

Stephanie watched as she walked away, head down, hearing her sobs. Then, the new video began, showing a white farmhouse in the near distance, its siding peeling, with two old cars and a rusting tractor standing outside a lopsided, collapsing barn. A sheriff's car was blocking the driveway.

STEPHANIE: *Hannah's family lives here, three miles outside of*

Delroy on a gravel road now hubcap-deep in snow. A farm that has been in Hannah's family for three generations, we're told. Hannah had two younger brothers, Paul and Devin, in ninth and tenth grades. The local sheriff has made it clear to the media that the family is off-limits, unwilling to speak publicly...that they are in mourning for their daughter. As you can see, a sheriff's car is guarding the house, keeping reporters and the curious away. The sheriff himself has been unavailable to the media to discuss either Hannah's murder or the assault charges that had been leveled against her.

The only person who would speak to us about that case was Howard Hooper, the editor and publisher of the Lyon County Record, who spoke to us exclusively.

HOOPER: *I can only tell you that the stabbing of Mr. Klinger was a major story in this county for days after. Our paper has tried to investigate the case...the motive for the stabbing and the circumstances surrounding it. But we have run into a brick wall. The criminal complaint contains few details and none of our sources has been able to tell us more.*

STEPHANIE: *We're told there are rumors that Hannah may have...*

HOOPER: *We don't deal in rumors, young lady. And neither should you! That's not good journalism.*

STEPHANIE: *So the mystery continues...as does the mourning for a young murder victim in small town Minnesota. This is Stephanie Accusi reporting from Delroy, Minnesota for Channel Seven News.*

As the news went to commercial, Gabby could only smile, remembering Hooper's final words: 'That's not good journalism.' She knew in the same situation, they were the same words her late journalist father would have spoken to her.

Made her smile, but also want to cry.

The next thing she knew Zach was poking her arm. "Hey, sleepyhead, time for bed."

TWELVE

...

The Haven was located on the edge of a residential section of Brooklyn Park, a two-story brick structure that could have passed for an office building were it not surrounded by an expanse of lawn, now lightly-covered by a layer of snow that had fallen overnight, and by several picnic tables and a small play area.

Sarah Chan swung her unmarked squad car into a circular driveway, parking across from the main entrance and alongside several other cars and a small white van with *The Haven* stenciled on its side.

Before she got out, Gabby asked, "How long do you think we'll have with her?"

Sarah shrugged. "As long as they'll give us, I guess. And as long as Jennie wants to talk. I got no guarantees."

Gabby already had learned that the place temporarily sheltered homeless youth through twenty-one years of age. Some for a few days, others for up to a few weeks or longer—depending on the circumstances. "Remember," Sarah said, "you're here as a friend, not a reporter. And one of the rules is that we talk to none of the other kids we happen to run into. We're here to see Jennie. Period."

"I understand," she replied.

Standing outside, Sarah held up her badge to a camera by the door and pressed a button. The door clicked open and they found themselves in an open, but rather small lobby, facing a stern-faced older woman sitting at a steel reception desk, her gray hair tied in a ponytail and with too much blush on her cheeks. "Yes?" she said, quizzically, as though unexpected visitors were rare. Sarah gave her a nice smile and said, "I'm Sergeant Chan and this is Gabby Gooding. Mrs. O'Connell has given us permission to spend a few minutes with Jennifer Nystrom."

"Really?" she said, picking up the phone. "She didn't tell me. I'll have to check."

Julie O'Connell was the executive director of The Haven, who—Sarah had explained on their way there—was a former cop herself, who had quit the department several years before to work with kids like Jennie.

"She'll be out in a moment," the receptionist said. "Please have a seat."

Two hallways led in opposite directions from the reception area. The doors to both were closed, muting any sounds that might have come from within. There were no voices of children or any sign of any.

"How many kids do they have here?" Gabby asked.

"I'm not sure, but I think they're licensed for up to twenty at any one time."

Before they could sit, from a door behind the reception desk, came a tall, slim, blond woman, clad in a striped shirt and slacks, with a smile and an outstretched hand. "Hey, Sarah, welcome. Sorry I forgot to tell Ms. Hansen," with a nod to the receptionist, "that you were coming."

Sarah returned the handshake and a quick hug. "No problem. I'm just glad she let us in and that you've let us come."

With that, she quickly introduced Gabby, whom she already had described in an earlier phone conversation. "It's nice to meet you," Julie said. "Sarah has told me how kind and protective you've been to Jennie, and how difficult it's been to see her come to a place like this."

"Not that," Gabby said quickly. "I'm very glad she's here and safe. It's her future I'm worried about. That she may have to go back to what she says is an abusive home."

"I understand. But that's not up to us, of course. Child protection or the courts will have to decide on that eventually. All we can do is care for her in the meantime…to see she's fed and clothed… and loved, in our own way."

"How has she been since you've had her?"

"Quiet. She keeps to herself, mostly. Still in mourning, I think, over her friend's death. We normally house three of our kids to a room, but Jennie has her own room because of her age and her particular situation. We had her visit one of our therapists, but I'm not sure how much that helped. She's a confused, lonely child right now."

"Has she tried to run?"

"Not so far. But we've kept a fairly close eye on her. This is not a locked facility, but we do try to keep a close watch on everyone."

"Have you notified her parents that she's here?"

"Not her parents, but I was mandated to notify the child protection people in Wadena County, where she lives, within 14 hours of her arrival here."

"So what will they do?"

"I suspect they've notified the parents, and will then assign a screener to investigate Jennie's case and her claim of abuse. But I don't know when that will happen. You have to understand, Gabby, the state's first priority is to reunite broken families, and that child protection in whatever county will do their best to make that happen." She paused for a moment. "In Jennie's case, her claims of abuse by her father may delay her return to the family. But, as Sarah told me, there appears to be no witnesses to that abuse beside her mother, and whether she would be willing to corroborate Jennie's charges is another question."

"So she'll go back to more abuse?"

"Not necessarily to the same situation. If they believe Jennie, they may order anger management for the father or a temporary guardian or foster family for Jennie until her family problems can be corrected. They'll have some options, but—trust me—they're not going to let a fifteen-year-old girl stay on the streets. Not if they can help it."

"Could you keep me or Sarah posted on what's happening?"

"That's a touchy area, but, yes, I'll try."

She went on to say that some of the older kids staying at The Haven have jobs during the day, returning in late afternoon, while the younger ones go to classes either here or in nearby schools.

"I still don't understand," Gabby said, "why some kids are still here? Why aren't *they* sent home, like Jennie might be?"

Julie smiled. "Good question. Some parents don't want them back. Won't take them back. Some of the kids, it's clear, come from horrible home situations and can't go back. Some have mental health issues and keep running. Others are waiting for foster homes to become available or for another solution to their situation. It's different with each child…and it's our job to do our best for them as things are sorted out."

Gabby could only shake her head. "That's horrible. Kids deserve better. No wonder our prisons are overflowing. What chance do they have to grow up healthy and have some kind of normal life?"

"We ask ourselves that every day. That's why we're here, I guess. To help give them that chance."

Sarah broke in. "We don't want to take any more of your time, Julie. I know you're busy. We'll let you get back to work if you'll take us to Jennie."

Julie moved toward one of the doors. "Good. I'd appreciate it if you'd limit your time to say, a half hour. And less if Jennie seems upset. I'm not sure how she'll react to this, but I know she sees you as a friend, Gabby, so maybe it will help."

They had no more than opened the door than Jennie was out of her chair, eyes almost wildly wide, her voice a notch below a scream. *"Did they find him?* Tell me yes!"

Momentarily shocked, Sarah and Gabby stood back as Julie quickly crossed the room and put her arm around her shoulders.

"Settle down, Jennie. Please, settle down." She tried to shake the arm away, but then, after a moment or two, slowly sank back into her chair, her body relaxing, her composure returning. "Okay, I'm sorry. I'm okay."

"Good, good," Julie said, stepping back, pausing. "Sergeant Chan and Gabby are here to see how you're doing and to talk a little. Is that all right? If it's not, just tell me."

Jennie's eyes returned to Sarah and Gabby, still standing just inside the door. "No, that's okay." Then a small smile. "Hi, Gabby. Hi, Sergeant."

"Hey, Jennie," Gabby said as she walked slowly across the room, her hand reaching out to find Jennie's, squeezing it tightly. "I've been worried about you. Both of us have. We're so glad you're here and safe."

Sarah stood to one side before also moving to put her hand on Jennie's shoulder. "You're sure it's okay if we sit and talk for a bit."

"Sure, but you have to tell me what's happening. No one here will tell me anything."

Julie retreated to the door. "I'll leave you three alone. When you're done, just come find me."

"Thanks," Gabby said, as she and Sarah took chairs next to Jennie, studying her. She was wearing jeans and a shapeless blue sweater that looked a size or two too large, swallowing her small body. Her hair was nicely combed, her face fresh, looking well-rested.

Gabby opened a bag she had carried with her. "I didn't have time to do any shopping," she said, "but I brought a few of my own things that I think may fit you. A couple of shirts, some pants and underwear. You're welcome to them, if you like."

"Thanks. I only have the clothes they gave me here and they don't fit too well."

"I can see that," Gabby said with a smile.

"We want to know how you're doing," Sarah said, "but before that, I'll answer your first question. No, we have not found the person or persons who killed Hannah. I know Detective Archer and the other detectives are doing their best, and I know he appreciated the help you gave him. But it may take a while, Jennie. So try to be patient."

It was clear Jennie was fighting to hold back her tears. "I just don't understand why someone would want to kill her? She was one of the nicest people I've ever met."

"We may never know that," Gabby said. "Even if they do catch whoever did it."

"They'll get him. I know it. I can *feel* it."

"I hope so," Gabby said. Then, "Did Hannah ever tell you more about her stepdad? What he did to her? And why she felt she had to hurt him?"

She took a moment. "Not much. She really didn't want to talk about it. But I know he tried to—what do you say?—assault her several times before that night. Whenever her mom and the other two kids were gone…when she was alone with him. Most of the time she just ran away…or locked herself in her room. But that night, when the rest of the family was away again, to an aunt's house or someplace, he came into her room after she went to bed."

"And she kept a knife under her pillow?"

"That night she did. She was afraid of what might happen."

"Did her mother know about any of this?"

"I don't know if she ever told her. Or if her mother just didn't believe her."

"And she never told anyone else? A teacher? Her friends?"

"She never said, but I think she was afraid and ashamed. Maybe she thought it was her fault. Or that she'd be blamed."

"Jesus," Gabby breathed. Then, "Was he the real father of the other two kids?"

"I don't think so. I think her mom married him after she divorced their dad. Hannah really didn't want to talk about all of that."

Sarah looked at her watch. "We don't have much more time, Jennie, and we'd like to know how you're doing? That's why we came, actually."

She thought for a moment. "I'm doing okay, I guess. Except they took my phone away. Which pisses me off. Most of the kids here are older than me...so they kind of ignore me. They seem friendly enough, but, like, they've got their own problems. Their own friends. And I don't feel much like talking to them, either. I just kind of, like, keep to myself. I've got a part time tutor, which is a bore, but I do what they tell me to do. And the food's okay."

Gabby said, "Mrs. O'Connell says you talked to a therapist."

"Yeah. He was kind of a wimp, but nice enough. Tried to make me feel better."

"You're not going to try and run, are you?"

"Not unless they try to send me home. Then watch my dust."

Sarah smiled. "Is there anything else we can do for you?"

"You can tell me when Hannah's funeral is...and whether I can go?"

"We don't know when yet," Gabby said. "But I expect it will be soon."

"What about me?"

"That will be up to other people," she replied. "But I will tell you this. I expect we'll be covering the funeral for the news, and if I can, I will try to let you see the video."

Jennie wiped at a single tear that had found its way to her cheek. "That would be nice, but not like being there. Hannah would want me to be there. I know she would."

"I know she would, too, but not everything we wish for can come true."

As they walked back to Sarah's car, Gabby said, "It's hard to believe that girl is not yet sixteen. She's more of an adult than I was at twenty."

Sarah laughed. "I would have liked to have known you then."

"I'm serious."

"And I'm curious," Sarah said. "Why all of the questions about the stepdad?"

They stopped at the back of the car. "Besides the fact that he's an ass?"

"Yeah."

"Because," Gabby said, "of what he did or was doing to Hannah may have led her to the life she was living. The kind of life that got her killed. I want to know more about him. Who knows? She may not have been his first victim…and he's going to go scot free."

"He did get a knife in the belly."

"And survived. Like most predators do."

"Can I help?"

"Absolutely. You can check all of those criminal data bases of yours. You know, locally and nationally. Find out everything you can about him. What kind of record he's got, if any. And while you're doing that, I'll try to use social media to find out more about who and where he was before he hooked up with Hannah's family. I'd like to get a profile of the bastard, for whatever it's worth."

"I'll give it my best shot," Sarah said.

"Also, if you can please keep me informed on the murder investigation. I don't want to bug Archer."

"Speaking of him, I forgot to tell you one thing."

"What's that?"

"When he was talking with Jennie down at City Hall, he asked her to remember, as best she could, what the guy in her threatening phone call actually said to her. Word for word, if she could."

"Really. And she could remember?"

"I guess so. Most of it. She said the words were hard to forget."

"And then what?" Gabby asked.

"They're asking each potential suspect they're interviewing to repeat the words into a recorder—in hopes that Jennie will eventually listen to them and possibly recognize the voice."

"That's pretty impressive. How many guys have they interviewed?"

"I'm not sure. Several, I guess."

"Great. So please keep me in the loop."

THIRTEEN

. . .

When Gabby got back to the newsroom, she was surprised to find Andy the intern sitting at her desk. Surprised because she hadn't seen or heard from him for several days, and surprised by the way he looked. Instead of the buttoned-up college kid she knew, he could have been one of the homeless himself: with a two-or-three day growth of beard, wearing a dirty, stained jacket, sagging jeans torn at the knees, and a mangy stocking cap that hung over his ears and looked as though it had never seen the inside of a washing machine.

She stood back. "Cripes, who the hell are you?"

He laughed. "Hey, Gabby. It's me, your friendly intern. Have you missed me?"

She grabbed a chair next to him, unable to erase her smile. "I was going to call you, but I've been a little busy. Where have you been and what've you been doing?"

"On the street. Wandering around. Talking to anybody who would talk to me. And," as he pulled a small, hand-held video camera out of his jacket pocket, "recording any of them willing to be recorded."

She couldn't take her eyes off him. "Like a homeless geek with a camera?"

"You could say that, I guess, but lay off the geek part."

"I will, but please take off that hat. I can't concentrate looking at you with it on."

Grinning, he pulled off the hat and shoved it into his jacket pocket.

"How long have you been doing this?" she asked.

"For the better part of two days. Whenever I could get away from school. You didn't see me, but I was in the crowd watching the cops briefing you in the parking lot."

She tried to think back, remembering a small crowd on the edge of the lot, but having no memory of anyone who looked like Andy. "So what were you talking to all of these street people about?"

"How they live, where they live, where they're from. Things like that. Trying to get a feel of the kind of stuff you said you were looking for. I tried to concentrate on the younger ones. Some of them not much older than our Jennie."

"And they were willing to talk to you on camera?"

"Some, not all. I told them I was doing a video on the homeless like myself, in hope of getting us some help. They thought it was a pretty cool idea."

"So you lied to them," she said, challenging him.

"Not totally. About myself, yeah, but I might actually do a documentary someday. Besides, I'm not a journalist like you, bound by your ethical codes. And I was on public property. No law broken."

"Did you have the younger ones sign anything? Like a waiver?"

"No chance. None of them would even give me their full names. And even if they did, who knows if they were their real names? I had no way to check."

"You're amazing."

"I also mentioned Hannah's murder to each of them. Kind of innocently asked if they knew anything about it or about her?"

"And?"

"Not much help, I'm afraid. All of them knew about the murder, for sure. No secrets on the street, I discovered. A couple of them knew her, but not well...and none that I talked to had any clue about who might have killed her. At least that they were willing to admit. There's a lot of fear out there, you know, about getting caught snitching."

"May I see the video?"

"Of course. Your computer was unlocked so I transferred it over while waiting for you." A few quick finger movements cued up the images. "It's pretty raw," he said. "I haven't had time to do any editing...so you'll have to be patient as we roll through it. I'll fast-forward to show you who we have before we start listening to them."

She sat transfixed as one after another of Andy's people appeared. Some looked curious, some shy, some belligerent. One gave him the finger and stalked off. Another stuck his nose in front of the camera and spit on the lens. There were three girls or young women, two white, one Black, and eight guys, four white, three Black and one who looked Hispanic. Some were clad in basically cold weather rags while others could have just walked out of The Gap or Old Navy. All different, but all bore what Gabby could only describe as forlorn expressions, their eyes largely vacant, their shoulders hunched against the cold, shivers showing. Young people, she thought, who came from nowhere with nowhere to go.

"Pretty depressing," she said.

"Maybe, but their looks can be a little deceiving. None of them seemed all that unhappy to me. Sure, they'd like to be off the street, out of the cold, with some food in their bellies, but several of them seemed surprisingly content in that little homeless world of theirs. Here's one example. Her name's Jackie. No last name."

JACKIE: *What the hell, this is where my friends are. We're like a little family, or what do you call it? Like a sorority, you know, just like the college broads have. We watch each other's backs...share what we've got. A little weed, a little booze. (Giggling) Well, maybe more than a little. It's a shit pot better than where I came from.*

ANDY: *And where was that?*

JACKIE: *Some place you never heard of, dude, and someplace you'd never want to go. Trust me on that.*

ANDY: *And where do you live now?*

JACKIE: *On Nowhere Street.*

ANDY: *Really? And where's that?"*

JACKIE: *You know, not that far from Nowhere Avenue.*

ANDY: *I get ya.*

Gabby sat back. "How old do you figure she is?"

"Wouldn't tell me, but I'd guess seventeen, maybe eighteen."

"Looks older."

"So would you, probably. You heard her. It's Nowhere Street, not Easy Street they're living on."

With that, he cued the video to a shot of another young woman. "This is April, who I asked how she manages to get along… to subsist on the street."

APRIL: *You do what you have to do, man. A little begging, a little hustling, some boosting, maybe a little hooking, if you know what I mean.*

ANDY: *Like a little sex on the side?*

APRIL: *If you get desperate enough, sure. I'm not ashamed of it. You gotta live. And when you haven't eaten in a couple of days, been sleeping under a bridge in a cardboard box, and haven't had a shower in a week, well, you do what you gotta do.*

ANDY: *You work alone or do you have a…*

APRIL: *A pimp? Once, but never again. He beat the shit out of me and took the money. So I'm on my own now.*

ANDY: *And how old are you, April?*

APRIL: *Old enough, how's that?"*

ANDY: *Did you know Hannah, the girl that got killed?*

APRIL: *Yeah, kinda. We spent a couple of nights together in some vacant room on the northside. Along with three or four others. So I didn't really know her.*

ANDY: *Have you talked to the cops?*

APRIL: *Are you shittin me? You want me to end up like her?*

To Gabby, Andy said, "You can take your time and look at the rest, but you won't find anything that takes your breath away. But they might be helpful if you do decide to do that series you were talking about."

"That's great. I'll look at them all tonight at home."

He rolled back the video. "There is one guy you might want to see. Said his name was Jeremy. Not the friendliest fellow."

JEREMY: *You shouldn't be carrying a camera like that down here. You'll end up in the goddamned gutter with a busted head and no camera. Hear me? This is no place for a wimpy shithead like you.*

ANDY: *That sounds a little scary.*

JEREMY: *There are some bad asses around here. Black guys, spics, Somalias. You have to watch your ass.*

ANDY: *No bad white guys?*

JEREMY: *Screw you, man.*

ANDY: *So who do think killed that girl, Hannah?*

JEREMY: *Shit, who knows? Probably her pimp. Her Daddy, ya know. That's the way it goes. And there are plenty of them around.*

Gabby reached across the desk to switch off the computer. "That's good work, Andy, although I'm not sure…"

"I'm not done yet," he said, breaking in. "I'm going to get back on the street whenever I can. Talk to more of these kids. Maybe we'll get lucky."

"Wait…wait…wait. Didn't this Jeremy just tell you that you could end up in the gutter with a busted head and no camera?"

"That was bullshit. I'm not out there in the dark, and there are always people around. It's not like I'm some cop…or some reporter like you. I'm just another scruffy one of them with a camera."

"Asking about Hannah's murder," she said. "That word will get around."

He shrugged. "I'll take my chances."

"And if you end up in the gutter, you won't just be one of them. You'll be Andy, the Channel Seven intern. And I don't want that to happen."

He sat up straight in his chair. "Listen, I'm not doing this just for you. Okay? The more I learn about these kids, the more I want to know. And who knows? This may be an area I'd want to pursue when I get out of law school."

"That's admirable, but you're on our dime now."

"No offense," he said irritably, "but you can keep your dime. You're the one who got me into all of this. And I've done a lot of research in the past few days, getting to know just how big a problem this is. Despite what the county and the non-profits and other advocates are doing, we're largely turning a blind eye to it," he went on, clearly wound up. "Not you, personally, but society. This community of ours." He stopped to take a deep breath. "You want to help and so do I. But I can't do that by sitting on my butt in a classroom listening to boring lectures. I want to help you, but I also want to help these kids. And that means getting out among them."

"Wow," Gabby said. "That was quite a spiel."

"Call it a spiel or a speech or whatever you want, but I've lived a pretty protected life. No lack of a roof over *my* head, or food on *my* table. Or a chance for an education. But what about the kids you just saw?" nodding to the computer. "And tons of others like them? Scratching for food every day and for a dry, warm place to sleep every night? And an education? Give me a break. You've helped me open my eyes and I'm not ready to look away again."

Before she could respond, her phone sounded. "Gabby Gooding."

"Gabby, this is Howard Hooper."

"Hey, Howard. How are you?"

"Just fine, but I wanted you to know they've set a time for Hannah's funeral."

"Really. When?"

"Day after tomorrow. Ten o'clock in the morning at the Jensen Funeral Home in Travis. Where Hannah went to school. But depending on the crowd, they may move the services to the school gymnasium. As you can guess, there's a lot of interest down here."

"I imagine so. Do you know if they'll allow cameras inside?"

"I haven't heard. That will be up to the family, I guess."

"Thanks, Howard. Any other news?"

"No. The sheriff still isn't talking about the stepdad stabbing, and my guess is, with Hannah dead, the whole thing will simply go away."

"You may be right," she said, "as sad as that would be. But I do hope to be down for the funeral…so maybe I can buy you a cup of coffee."

"I'd like that."

Hanging up, she shared the information with Andy, who offered, "It'll probably be a media circus."

"I'm not so sure. I think some of the interest in the case up here may have faded by now. People have moved on to other things, and I suspect not all of the media big wigs in the Cities will want to invest the money to have their crews travel that distance to cover it. We'll have to see."

"But you're going to go?"

"If Barclay will let me, yes. I wouldn't miss it."

Getting up, he slipped on his ridiculous stocking cap and drew another guffaw from her. "I'll keep in touch," he said, with a smile. "And let me know if you need me. You've got my numbers."

"I will. But be careful. Don't make me responsible for your flunking out of law school. Or landing in the gutter."

"You've got my word."

FOURTEEN

. . .

B efore she could leave for home, Gabby got an urgent call from Sarah Chan. "Glad I caught you," she said. "We need to talk. Like as soon as possible."

"Okay, but where are you?"

"Just down the street. At the Starbucks."

"Do you want to come here? To the station?"

"I'd rather not."

"Give me ten minutes," Gabby said. "And grab me a cappuccino."

She quickly cleared off her desk and found Zach in one of the editing rooms. "If I'm not back in twenty minutes or so, you should head home."

"What's happening?"

She shrugged. "Don't know, but Sarah wants to see me, like right now."

She found her at a corner table, well away from the few people who were lingering over their coffee. Her cappuccino was waiting. "So what's happening?" she asked as she slipped into the chair across the table.

"I have some news," she replied.

"About Hannah? "

"No, not about Hannah. Nothing new there, as far as I know."

"Then what?"

"Our favorite stepdad, Mr. Klinger. You asked me to check our data bases."

"I remember."

"Hold onto your hat. First, some facts. He's forty-seven-years old, a carpenter by trade, born and raised in a small town in Nebraska. Hershall, Nebraska, to be precise. Married at twenty-two to a Louise Gladden, had two children, a boy and a girl, divorced years later after—*get this*—he was charged and convicted of raping a seventeen-year-old neighbor girl, a babysitter for the family."

"*What?*"

"Sentenced to six years in the Nebraska state penitentiary, but released after three. Was still on probation when he married Hannah's mother four years later."

"No shit."

"She was a divorcee with the two boys and Hannah. Living on that farm outside of Delroy."

"Where did you get all this?"

"Some of it from the data bases, but a lot of it from some friendly cops in Nebraska. The rape of the babysitter was a big deal down there, small town and all, and is still fresh in the memory of a few of the sheriff's people I talked to. Klinger's a real piece of work, they say. Besides the rape, he was also suspected of molesting a couple of other girls while on probation, but was never charged."

"God! Could Hannah's mother have known any of this?"

"Can't tell you that, but I'm told by those same Nebraska cops that he's quite a con man. So maybe she didn't know...or didn't want to believe it."

Gabby said, "The sheriff in Lyon County must know. If he's doing his job."

"Not necessarily. But you'll have to ask him, if you go down there for the funeral."

"I sure as hell will. If he'll talk to me."

"If he won't, maybe the county attorney will."

"Good idea. Anything else?"

"Not really. I'll email you the names of the Nebraska people I talked to. You may want to talk to them yourself. Get a transcript of the trial. And maybe check out the local newspaper coverage at the time, if there was any. I didn't have a chance to do that."

"Another good idea. Hate to say it, but you've done my job for me. If you ever get tired of being a cop, you may want to try reporting."

"Thanks, but I think I'll stay where I am."

As soon as she was back at her desk, Gabby put in a call to Howard Hooper. "I know we just talked," she said, "but I have to ask you a question."

"Shoot," he replied.

"Did you know that Hannah's stepdad is a convicted rapist?"

There was a momentary silence. "Repeat that."

She quickly repeated what she had just been told.

Another silence, but longer. "I'll be damned."

"So you didn't know?"

"Of course not, or I would have told you."

"Do you think anybody in the county knows?"

"I have no idea, but I think I would have heard. There would have been rumors over the years. You know, barroom talk. Coffee shop talk. Which would have gotten back to me."

"Would the sheriff have ignored that record, in view of the stabbing?"

"I can't imagine he would. He's a good man, if not the smartest lawman around. He's a bit set in his ways, but I can't see him ignoring something like that."

"It puts a new light on Hannah's story, doesn't it?"

"Sure does."

"What do you think I should do? Or *we* should do?"

"Can you give me the night to think about it? Call you in the morning?"

"That's fine, but I don't think we can sit on it forever. We can't let Hannah go to her grave with no one knowing her story. We can't let the truth die with her."

"You're right, I guess. But think of what it will do to Hannah's family if this gets out. To his wife and two boys. And to the town."

"Maybe the wife already knows. Maybe she knew Hannah was telling the truth."

"Maybe. But I doubt it."

"It's not an easy call, Howard. But you know...we're stuck..."

"I know. Between that old rock and a hard place. But I'm a small town newspaper guy, Gabby. And out here, that's where I live, between a rock and a hard place."

As she put the phone down, she saw Zach striding across the newsroom. "Ready to head home?" he asked when he reached her desk.

"In a minute," she said. Then, "Is the boss still here?"

He looked across the newsroom. "Looks like it."

"Then I need to talk to him."

Puzzled, he asked, "What's up?"

"I'll tell you both," she replied as she led the way toward Barclay's office, where they found him putting on his scarf and coat. "Do you have a minute?" Gabby asked.

"About that. I'm supposed to meet my wife down the street for dinner."

Standing at the office door, Gabby quickly relayed what Sarah had told her and the conversation with Hooper. "I think we have to go to the funeral," she said, "and talk to the sheriff or county attorney. To see if they knew about this guy's past. And if they did, why they apparently didn't investigate the possibility that Hannah may have stabbed the stepdad in self-defense?"

He appeared confused. "I hear what you're saying, but what difference does it make now? Sadly, she's dead and gone...so there's no way to prove if the attempted rape actually happened."

Gabby took a step toward him, anger in her voice. "So we're

going to let her go to her grave accused of trying to kill her stepfather when she may have been trying to defend herself? With us knowing that her charges could have been true? That we allow her reputation to be ruined, never to be recovered?"

He glanced at his watch. "Okay, okay. Cool down. But then what do we do?"

"We tell the story. We tell the truth. We report on the stepdad's past conviction, and whether the local authorities knew about it and ignored it in charging Hannah."

"Jesus. That's a can of worms."

"It's all part of the story that ended up here with Hannah's murder. If she hadn't been charged, she wouldn't have fled and been hiding here…where she winds up brutally murdered and shoved in the back of some stolen car. The story of her murder begins and ends in what may have happened in the little town of Delroy…and I think we have to tell the full story."

Barclay looked at Zach. "What do you think?"

"This is the first I've heard any of this, but I think Gabby's right. You can't let this young woman be buried as a would-be killer without knowing the truth. And I guess it's our job to try and figure out the truth."

Barclay again, to Gabby. "And what does your editor friend, Hooper, think about all of this?"

"He was surprised, to say the least, about the stepdad's past. And he had no clue as to whether anyone else in the county knows. Including the sheriff. We're going to talk again in the morning."

"And the funeral's the day after tomorrow?"

"Right."

"Then go. Both of you. Let's see where all of this leads. But be careful. This could be full of pitfalls. I know you're concerned about the dead girl's reputation, but we also have to think about the stepfather's. He's served his time, and to accuse him now of an attempted rape we can't prove could get us in a heap of trouble. Legal trouble, big time. I don't want anything to go on the air without my personal approval. Got it?"

"Got it," she replied.

"Then get the hell out of here before my wife drags me away by my ear."

At home that night, she and Zach watched the parade of homeless young people pass by and pause in front of Andy's camera. A few volunteered their first names but never their last and almost none was willing to reveal where he or she had come from or where they were living now. Like the ones she had seen earlier, their dress varied from scrappy cold weather wraps to normal coats and jackets you'd see on any high school or college campus. The difference was in their testimony as to how long they'd been on the street or what circumstances had brought them there. The kind of homes they had come from or escaped from.

But as they listened to their stories, she couldn't help but agree with Andy that none of them seemed desperately unhappy. Some were angry, yes, or bitter about the world as they see it. Some were even amused by it. But all struck her as fiercely independent and street-savvy. Resilient and mostly self-assured despite being alone and literally out in the cold. Without a real home or family.

She turned up the volume as a girl who said her name was Angie stared into the camera with a slight smirk. In her late teens, Gabby guessed, a deep brunette clad all in black, with black eyebrows and lashes, black lipstick, wearing gold earrings the size wristbands that jangled every time she moved her head or the wind caught them

ANGIE: *You know, everybody thinks we're some kind of losers. Like trash. Just because, you know, we don't look and act like everybody else, they think we're weirdos. Like freaks in some freakin' freakshow. Like you, out here with a camera, trying to figure out who we are…so you can do what? Put it on Facebook? Twitter? YouTube? Maybe make a buck or two selling our sad stories? Well, screw you and your mother, too, buddy, because a lot of us are out here because we want to be here. Got that?"*

ANDY: *I'm not out to make a buck or two. I'm just trying to tell your stories.*

ANGIE: *Well, forget it.*

ANDY: *But I'm curious. Do you really want to be out here? Seriously? On the street? Constantly looking for a place to sleep and a meal to eat?*

ANGIE: *If you're so concerned about all of us, you should be talking to the people who pushed us out here.*

ANDY: *Like who?*

ANGIE: *Like the shithead parents who are too drunk or stoned to take care of their kids. Who don't feed 'em or clothe 'em, for christsake. Or the ones who throw you out because you happen to be gay or trans. Or the ones who beat the shit out of you because you don't toe their line. Want to know more?*

ANDY: *Yeah, about you.*

ANGIE: *None of your business. Let me know if I make the final cut.*

Gabby reached across and shut the computer down. "So what do you think?"

Zach smiled. "I think if we ever put some of this on the air, we're going to have to do a lot of bleeping."

Before she could respond, her ringtone sounded.

"Gabby, this is Julie O'Connell at The Haven."

"Hey. Hi."

"Hope I'm not interrupting anything."

"Not at all. We've been watching video of a few homeless street kids. Kids who should be in a place like yours. It's fascinating stuff."

"I can imagine."

"So what's up?"

"I really shouldn't be making this call, but Sarah said I could trust you to keep it in confidence."

"Of course. Is Jennie okay?"

"As good as can be expected, I guess. Which is why I'm calling. Knowing how concerned you are, I thought you'd want to know that child protection in Wadena County is so backed up they won't be able to send anyone down here for a few days, at least. And what's more, Detective Archer has requested that she be kept here temporarily...in case they need her in Hannah's murder investigation."

"Good," Gabby said. "That will keep her away from her father."

"Temporarily, maybe, but there's a long road ahead. You should know that."

"I do." Then, "While I have you, may I ask for another favor?"

"Of course."

"Would you ask Jennie for the full name of her older brother? I meant to do it but forgot. He's in the Army someplace, maybe Texas. I'd like to try to find him. To see if he might be willing to intervene on Jennie's behalf."

"I think I can save you the trouble. We have the resources here to locate family members. I'll have one of my people give it a try and get back to you."

"That would be great. Thanks so much."

"We'll talk again soon."

FIFTEEN

. . .

The sun had just begun to creep over the eastern horizon as Gabby and Zach pulled off the highway and into the small town of Travis. But even then they could see they were not the first to arrive; a long line of cars moved slowly ahead of them, even though it was still hours before this part of western Minnesota would gather to witness the final goodbye to Hannah Hendricks.

Gabby had received a call the night before from Howard Hooper, confirming that the funeral had been moved from Delroy to Travis, where Hannah had spent her high school years, and where the school auditorium was judged large enough to hold the expected crowd of mourners. But before that service, they were told the family planned to hold a small, private gathering at a funeral home on the other side of town, where a visitation had been held the night before. Private meaning no media allowed anywhere near. Period.

They had left the apartment in the early morning hours for the three-hour trip, blessed by a continuing warm spell that had kept the highway snow-free. But both had fought to stay awake, keeping the car windows partly open for the fresh air, the radio on to all-night talk, and stopping twice for coffee. And always alert for a wayward deer to suddenly dart out of the darkness, beyond the reach of their headlights.

But, now, the rising sun and clear blue skies had brought both of them out of their sleepy stupor.

The combination middle-and-senior high school was not hard to find, a two-story stucco building only a few blocks off the highway, flanked by a football field and Friday night lights with long wooden stands on both sides of the field. On the other side of the school was a parking lot already dotted with cars and bordered by a string of six yellow school busses, busses that would remain idle for this day…since school had been cancelled in honor of Hannah.

While Gabby and Zach were in one of the station's news cars, they would be followed in a few hours by a station live truck, driven by a technician, Chuck Dressen, who would handle Gabby's expected reports later in the day.

For now, they passed the school and drove another six blocks to the center of town, finding a four-block-long main street—anchored on one end by combination BP gas station and Subway shop, and on the other end by the City Hall and police station. In the middle was Lannie's Café, identified by a lettered-awning stretched over the front door. The place Gabby hoped Howard Hooper would be waiting for them.

And he was. Huddled in the last of six booths lining one wall, across from a twelve-stool counter and five tables set in between. Most of the stools were occupied, as were about half of the tables and booths. Big crowd for this time of day, Gabby thought, many probably awaiting the funeral. Although she had never seen Howard, she recognized him immediately. He was as she had pictured him on the phone: in his mid-to-late sixties, with thin, graying hair, looking a bit disheveled and a tad grumpy. Much, she thought sadly, as her late father would have looked today.

Rising halfway out of the booth, he waved as they walked past the tables, not oblivious to the stares they were getting. Even down here, Gabby was clearly recognized as a TV personality. "Don't get up," she said as Howard tried to free himself of the booth. She held out her hand to grasp his, "I'm glad we could finally meet," she said. "Although I feel like I already know you."

"Same here," he replied, smiling as he sat back down. "But, of course, I *do* know you from TV."

She and Zach slid into the booth across from him. "This is Zach Anthony, Howard, one of our finest photographers, who's also lucky enough to be my fiancé."

Hooper laughed. "Nice to meet you, Zach, and welcome to one of the finest little towns on the prairie."

"Bigger than Delroy, right?"

"A lot bigger. Although big down here can be a little misleading."

Howard passed over a couple copies of his newspaper. "This just came out yesterday, so you can get the latest on what's going to happen today. Pretty much as I told you. Private family gathering at nine, the big service at ten. They're expecting several hundred people, maybe more when you count all of the school kids and families from across the county."

"Will they allow cameras inside?" Zach asked.

"Lot of debate about it, but in the end, yes. But only after a lot of pressure from us and from the papers and TV stations in Rochester, Austin, Marshall and Mankato. That's the reason the family is having the private gathering first, to avoid the circus."

Gabby asked, "Have you talked to the sheriff or county attorney? You said you'd get back to me."

"Sorry, but no. I wanted to talk to you again first. Figured I could wait until today."

"So what are your thoughts now?"

"I think we should try to corner the sheriff after the funeral. He'll have too much to do before then. Controlling the crowd and handling the media."

"But even then do you think he'll be willing to talk to us?"

"I hope so. I know him pretty well."

"And what do you think his reaction will be, assuming he doesn't know about Klinger's record?"

"Shocked. Like I was. Like this whole area will be if and when this all comes out."

She leaned across the table. "And you're still torn, aren't you?"

"Of course. The news could destroy the family, the kids

especially. I don't care about Klinger, if he really did what Hannah claims he did. But his wife and kids are another matter. They've got to continue to live around here."

Zach said, "So what do you think the sheriff will do, once he knows?"

Howard pondered the question. "I have no idea. But if I had to guess, he'll say what's done is done. What's past is past. Klinger served his time. Let Hannah rest in peace and let the family go on living their lives."

"Living with a convicted rapist," Gabby said as she pulled some papers out of her briefcase. "This is a record of Klinger's trial in Nebraska. The clerk of court in Hershall, Nebraska emailed it to me yesterday. It makes for pretty rough reading."

He took out his reading glasses and studied the document, one page after the other. "Jesus," he muttered when he finally looked up.

"As you see, this is one nasty dude," she said. "The girl wasn't even eighteen when she was attacked while walking home from a football game. He not only raped her, but tried to strangle her. And fled only after she managed to let out a scream. And although he was wearing a mask, she knew who it was by the smell of the cologne he was wearing…something she recognized from babysitting for the family. But it took a DNA sample from her underwear to prove what she was saying."

"And why was his DNA on file?" he asked.

"I don't know that, but I assume it's from a previous crime of some kind."

"Then the question is," Howard said, "whether we let a guy like this continue to walk the streets knowing this," pointing to the court record, "and knowing that what Hannah claimed happened is probably true."

"That *is* the question," she replied. "But from where we stand, there's not much choice."

"I hear you, but let's wait to see what the sheriff has to say."

By nine o'clock, the school parking lot was filled with cars and pickups, leaving only enough room for Channel Seven's live truck and vans from the area TV stations. Three Lyon County sheriff's cars stood off to one side, with uniformed deputies on the street in front of the school, handling the crowd and waiting for the family's arrival.

Gabby and Zach found their technician, Chuck Dressen, standing by the live truck. "Hey, guys," he said, "nice to see you. I was wondering when you'd show up."

"We've been catching a nap," she replied with a grin. "Are you all set?"

"Yeah, but I didn't expect to be the only one here. What happened to our competition from the Cities?"

"This is still big news down here," she said, looking around. "But I think the Hannah story has lost some of its interest up there."

"Then why are *we* here?"

"Because it may be part of a bigger story we're working on," she replied, reluctant to say more.

"Okay, I guess. So what's the plan?"

"I've been told a photographer from the Mankato station will serve as the pool photographer for us and the other stations. Shooting from the center of the gym. Everyone will be allowed to record the arrival of the funeral party outside, and then Zach alone will be allowed to quickly move inside to record the ceremony from the left of the makeshift altar. Those will be the only two TV cameras in the gym, responsible for sharing the video with all of the stations once the service is over."

"How'd you manage to get Zach inside?" Dressen asked.

"By using my considerable feminine charm," she replied, with another grin.

"Of course. Why did I even ask? Then what happens?"

"You can feed some of the video back to the station, and I'll call in with enough information for them to pull together a short piece for the noon news. And later, I'm not sure when, I'll be back outside to do a standup for the five and six o'clock shows."

"Any idea when I can get out of here? My kid's got a game tonight."

"By three, I hope. That should get you home in time."

As ten o'clock approached, Gabby left Zach outside to cover the arrival of the family while she stepped past the deputies and into the auditorium. Even knowing that a large crowd was expected, she was stunned by the number of people she found there…all but filling the bleachers and the scores of chairs that had been set up on the gym floor. Despite the size of the crowd, she found an eerie, respectful quiet in the place, broken only by the soft music of a string quartet made up, she was told later, of Hannah's former classmates. Even young children sat mostly still and silent, squeezed between their parents or other adults. For some, she guessed, this might be the first funeral they had experienced, but still somehow sensed the solemnity of the occasion.

The auditorium was little different from others she had visited or covered over the years in small California towns. Basketball hoops at each end, wrestling mats rolled up at one end, and in the middle of the court, an insignia for the Travis Tigers, the painted tiger growling, showing his teeth. To the left of the tiger, a temporary altar had been set up on a riser, covered in white cloth, holding two lighted candles, a simple silver cross and a large Bible set on a small lectern.

Fifteen minutes passed before she saw and heard commotion at the entry of the auditorium, then watched as the funeral party made its way through the door. At the head of the procession was a man Gabby guessed was probably the family's pastor, followed by three men, the lead one, weeping, carried a small bronze urn. Hannah's biological-father? They, in turn, were followed by a woman, head upright, tightly gripping the hands of two boys, one on each side of her. Hannah's mother and her sons. And behind them, a man Gabby presumed to be the stepdad, Arnold Klinger, eyes straight ahead, seemingly oblivious to the crowd in the gym. He was followed by perhaps a dozen somber-faced men and women, Hannah's other relatives, she thought.

Gabby stood by the bottom plank of the bleachers, not more than twenty feet from the family as they approached their chairs in front of the altar. Mrs. Klinger was a short, slightly overweight woman with reddish-tinted hair and—considering the circumstances—with a sweet smile that seemed to broaden as her eyes swept the crowd. Whatever tears had once been there apparently had been left at the gathering across town.

Klinger had to be well over six feet tall, lean and straight-backed with a tight, weathered face and close-cropped graying hair. He had the look of a man who had spent his life in the sun, his skin tanned and leathery, his body taut. As she studied him, she couldn't help but wonder if tears had ever touched *his* cheeks.

At that moment, Zach crept past her and quietly set his camera on a tripod to her left, concentrating on the crowd while the pool camera at the center of the gym focused on the altar.

Once the funeral party was seated and the music had ended, the pastor—whom the program identified as the Reverend Harley Peterson—stood at the altar and asked the audience to bow their heads in prayer.

"Lord, we pray for those who mourn, for parents and children, friends and neighbors. Be gentle with them in their grief. Show them the depths of your love, a glimpse of the kingdom of heaven. Spare them the torment of guilt and despair. Be with them as they weep beside the empty tomb, of our risen Savior, Jesus Christ our Lord. Amen."

There followed a standing full-throated audience rendition of How Great Thou Art, *"O LORD my God! When I in awesome wonder, Consider all the works Thy hand hath made, I see the stars, I hear the mighty thunder, Thy pow'r throughout the universe displayed"*...to the final refrain... *"There sings my soul, my Savior God to Thee, How great Thou art! How great Thou art!*

As the audience took their seats, the pastor adjusted the microphone and looked first at the family, then to the crowd. "We are gathered here to mourn the passing of a young woman, a daughter, a sister, a niece, a cousin, a friend, whose life was taken suddenly and violently, depriving her loving family and all of us in this gymnasium and beyond of seeing her grow into the wonderful woman she could have become. A woman of substance whose life might have held untold adventures and triumphs. Who would have added to the richness of the world around her. Around all of us."

Forgotten or ignored, apparently, were the assault charges that would be buried with her. Like a ghost hiding in the shadows of the gym, Gabby thought.

As she listened, she studied the faces of the family. The eyes of the mother and both boys were fastened on the pastor, somber but without visible emotion. All of it hidden or lost somewhere in the past. In contrast, the man who had carried the urn was sobbing silently, his face in his hands, reaffirming Gabby's belief that he was indeed Hannah's birth father, listed in the program as Gregory Hendricks. As for Klinger the stepfather, he could have been at the funeral of a distant cousin, his eyes staring up at the high ceiling, one hand rubbing the skin beneath his chin. Making no apparent effort to share in the grief.

There were more hymns, a short sermon, and more prayers, with many in the crowd weeping, wiping at their eyes, until the final words from the pastor. "May you rest in peace Hannah, cradled in the arms of God, as you look down upon us from your heavenly post."

As the recessional music began and the crowd started to head to the school cafeteria for a promised reception with coffee and cake, Howard Hooper slipped into a spot next to Gabby. "The sheriff has agreed to meet us," he said, "in the principal's office down the hall. As a favor to me. But no camera, no recording."

"When?" she asked.

"In a half hour. Once the crowd moves on."

"Does he know what we want to talk about?"

"I didn't tell him, but I assume he suspects it's about the step-dad stabbing."

She glanced at her watch. "I'll catch up with Zach, call the station, and meet you back here."

SIXTEEN

. . .

The sheriff was already in the principal's office as they arrived, leaning against a desk, looking both curious and a tad apprehensive. He wore a carefully-pressed tan long-sleeved shirt and dark pants with a stripe on the outside seams. On his chest, a seven-point metal badge and a gold nameplate bearing the name HENDERSON. At first glance, Gabby guessed him to be in his early sixties, with a ruddy complexion, striking green eyes and a wisp of gray hair clinging to a balding pate.

He held out his hand. "I'm Duane Henderson."

"And I'm Gabby Gooding. Thanks for meeting with us."

"You can thank Howard. We go back a long way."

"I know. He's told me."

Hooper stepped forward. "Can we sit? My knees aren't what they used to be."

As they took three chairs in front of the desk, Henderson said, "You should know I'm not that comfortable talking to the press. I leave that to my chief deputy. In fact, I can't remember the last time I talked to a reporter from the Cities, let alone a TV star like you."

Gabby smiled. "I'm hardly a star, but I do appreciate your time."

"So what can I do for you?"

She glanced at Howard. "This could get uncomfortable, but we need some answers."

"About?"

"Arnold Klinger."

"I'm not surprised. That's what I figured…"

Gabby didn't wait, leaning into him. "So let's not waste our time. I need to know if you are now aware, or ever were aware, that he is a convicted rapist?"

Henderson fell back in his chair, clearly startled, jaw dropping, green eyes bulging. "WHAT?"

She gave him a moment to recover, then pushed on, "It's true. In Nebraska. Almost ten years ago. Spent three years in the Nebraska State Penitentiary. Was still on probation when he married Mrs. Hendricks."

Henderson leaned forward, shoulders slumping, breathing heavily.

Gabby had her answer. "So you didn't know."

It took him a moment. "No, no. Of course not. Are you sure?"

From Hooper, "We're sure, Duane. I've seen the trial transcript."

"How could I not have known?" the sheriff asked, more of himself than them.

"It's probably not that surprising," Hooper said. "It was in Nebraska, after all. Years ago. No reason for you to check his background unless he got into some kind of trouble here in Lyon County."

Gabby leaned in even closer, frustration bubbling over, knowing she was about to cross some kind of journalistic line, but forged ahead anyway. " Maybe you had no reason to know, but now that you *do* know, I'll tell you something else. That Hannah has claimed she stabbed him only as he tried to rape *her*—that she was trying to protect herself."

Doubt filled his face. "Who told you *that*? And do you believe it?"

"A young friend of Hannah's, a girl named Jennie, told me what Hannah had told her before she was murdered. And to be honest, I don't know what to believe, but," angrily, "I do know this: you were quick enough to charge her with assault or attempted murder without ever talking to her."

Hooper stood up, grabbing a knee. "Settle down, Gabby. Please."

"How the hell could we talk to her?" the sheriff said. "She was gone. Disappeared. But we had Klinger with a knife wound in the stomach, bleeding badly when the first responders got there. Just in the nick of time, as it turned out."

"And what did he tell you had happened?"

"We couldn't talk to him for a couple of days. Until he was out of intensive care."

"And then?" she pressed.

"He said he and Hannah got into a big argument...over some boyfriend. She wanted to go meet him and one thing led to another. When he tried to stop her at the back door, she got him in the gut."

"And you believed him?"

Defensively, "We had no reason not to. She was long gone by then."

"So that was the end of the investigation?"

He shrugged. But his anger was not lost on her.

"Where did the first responders find him?" she asked.

"In the kitchen, not far from the back door."

"And when you got there, did you look any farther?"

"Like where?"

"Like elsewhere in the house? Like in Hannah's bedroom? You just assumed he was stabbed where he lay?"

He shook his head in annoyance. "We had no reason to look farther. There was no blood trail. And by then his wife and two boys were back home and it was a pretty chaotic scene."

She looked at Hooper. "So if we are to believe what Hannah told Jennie, that she stabbed him while he tried to rape her in her bed, you would think there would have been blood there. That he somehow managed to get from the bedroom to the kitchen."

"Or maybe," Hooper replied, "Jennie misunderstood what she

was told. That Hannah stabbed him in the kitchen as she tried to get out of the house after the attempted rape."

Gabby, back to the sheriff. "Did you ever question the wife? About what she thought might have happened?"

"No, I saw no need. She wasn't there. And as you'd expect, she was very upset. Distraught. As were the boys."

"Do you think she knows about his past?"

He thought for a moment, stroking his chin. "I have no idea. But if I had to guess, I'd guess no. She's a very decent lady from everything I've been told. A strong Christian, devoted to her family. It's hard to imagine she would have knowingly married a convicted rapist."

They sat silently for several minutes. Finally, the sheriff asked, "So what do you plan to do?"

"That depends in part," she replied, "on what *you* intend to do."

He sat back and looked up at the ceiling. Then, "I'll talk to the county attorney. But I think I know what he'll say. 'Forget it. Move on. There is no proof, no way to determine the truth.'"

"So you won't interview Klinger again, now that you know about his past?"

"What is there to gain? He'll deny Hannah's story, of course, and claim that he's a changed man since that business in Nebraska. And he'll probably threaten to sue if we reveal what we now know."

"But what you should also know," she said, "is that he was suspected of two other attempted assaults in Nebraska while on probation. But he was never charged."

"God, you don't make it any easier."

"Let me ask you this: have you had any unsolved rapes in Lyon County in the last couple of years?"

Henderson cocked his head, thinking. Finally, "Not here, but I know there's one unsolved case next door, in Lincoln County."

She smiled. "You think they'd like to know about our friend, Mr. Klinger?"

"Probably, yes."

"I know Nebraska has his DNA on file. I don't know about the national data base."

"I'll check, but in the meantime," looking at both Gabby and Hooper, "let me ask again: What do you plan to do? The county attorney will want to know."

"For me, nothing at the moment," she said. "I have to talk to my boss and to our lawyers. But I'll tell you what I've told everyone. I'm not prepared to let Hannah be remembered as a criminal if she wasn't. Not as a perpetrator, but as a victim."

Henderson looked at Hooper. "And, you?"

"I will follow Gabby's lead. I can't afford to be sued. But you should know that I'll be watching closely to see what develops. And I trust you're not going to let the matter drop, no matter what the county attorney might want to do."

With that the meeting ended, more peacefully than Gabby may have hoped.

Before leaving the school, Gabby found her way to the cafeteria, where a few people remained, sharing in the post-funeral coffee and cake. She went in hopes Mrs. Klinger would still be there. And she was, apparently having returned after the graveside ceremony. She was seated with her husband and boys at a table with several friends, quietly chatting. Gabby approached and tapped her on the shoulder. She turned and looked up, showing a small, polite smile.

"Mrs. Klinger, I'm Gabby Gooding, a reporter from Channel Seven in the Twin Cities. I wonder if I might have a moment of your time, in private if possible."

The woman's smile vanished, replaced by a puzzled but not unfriendly look. "I'm sorry," she said, "but I really can't talk to the media. Not now."

Gabby knelt beside her. "First of all, I'm very sorry for your loss, but I'm not here to ask questions, but to tell you something about Hannah and her time in the Cities."

After a quick glance at her husband, she turned to face Gabby, her face filled with doubt. "You knew Hannah? In the Cities?"

"That's what I'd like to speak to you about."

With some hesitation, she got up and moved a few feet away. "So tell me."

"I thought you would want to know that Hannah had a very good friend while she was on the streets in Minneapolis. A young girl by the name of Jennie, a runaway from an abusive home in northern Minnesota who Hannah befriended and became something of a big sister to. Watching out for her, protecting her. Until she disappeared several days before her death." She took a breath. "Jennie adored her and was frightened for her…and came to me in a desperate hope I could help find Hannah. We tried, together for several days…but, sadly, did not find her in time."

Mrs. Klinger put her hand to her mouth, tears forming. "So where is Jennie now?"

"In a shelter in the Twin Cities. She wanted very much to come to the funeral, but that wasn't possible. I hope to show her some video of the services when I get back. She'll be very touched, I know."

"Do you think I could speak to her? See her? Talk to her about her time with Hannah?"

"I don't know about that. I can certainly ask. But I wanted you to know about her before I left town. To know that Hannah, in her final days, was a good friend to a young girl in need. I thought it would be important to you. To help ease some of your pain."

Without warning, she put her arms about Gabby, whispering, "God bless you. I can't thank you enough. Please be back in touch with me. Please let me know if I can see or talk to Jennie. It would mean so much."

"I will," she said, slipping one of her business cards into her hand and stepping back out of her arms. "But tell me, did you ever speak to Hannah after that night? After she took off?"

"No, never. She wouldn't answer her phone. If she still had it. I didn't know where she was."

"Or what actually happened that night?"

"No. Only what Arnold and the sheriff told me."

Gabby said, "All right. Please call me at any time. I wish we'd been able to find Hannah. She's a young woman I would have loved to have known. Blessings to you and your boys."

At that, she turned and walked to the door—with one look back, at Mrs. Klinger still standing, unmoving, and at Arnold Klinger, staring after her.

She found Zach in the live truck reviewing the video that he and the pool photographer had shot. "How'd you do?" she asked.

"Not bad. Some of the pastor's audio is a little weak, but I think we can make it work. Good shots of the family and lots of emotion out there in the audience, especially from the high school kids. She must have been pretty popular, judging by the tears."

"I thought the same thing," she replied.

"So what's next?"

She glanced at her watch. Almost 11:30. "Feed the video back to the station…"

"I already have."

"Then I'll give them a call with enough information to put together a short piece for the noon show. I'll look at the video and then find some quiet place inside to sit down and write the reports for five and six. That'll take an hour or two…but we should be out of here in time for Chuck to get home for his kid's ballgame."

"What about the sheriff? What'd he say?"

"I'll tell you after I make the call and write my pieces. But the short answer is he didn't know about the rape conviction."

"Wow."

"I know. He was stunned." Then, as she started to walk away, she said, "Why don't you and Chuck get lunch someplace and bring me back a sandwich and a Coke? I'll be inside the school somewhere, on the computer."

It was a little past two when she took a spot in front of the school. The weather had worsened with the passing hours, temperatures falling, the wind picking up and the snow flurries beginning to swirl around her. While trying to hold the microphone out of the wind, she struggled to wrap her scarf more tightly around her neck and pull her stocking cap down over her ears. "Do I look like a dork?" she shouted to Zach behind the camera.

"Yes, a frozen dork," he yelled back. "But beautiful."

"Liar, liar."

"Are you ready?"

"As I'll ever be."

"Go," he said, giving her a hand cue.

GABBY: *"This small part of western Minnesota came together today to share its grief over the brutal murder of a young woman, Hannah Hendricks, who went to this school behind me in the town of Travis, and where hundreds of people gathered to pay their respects in the gymnasium where she had once played volleyball.*

As the video rolled, she went on to describe the crowd, the mourning family, the prayers, the hymns, and the homily by Pastor Peterson, describing Hannah "as a woman of substance...who would have added to the richness of the world around her. Around all of us."

GABBY: *"Unspoken by the pastor or by anyone else at the service were the tragic circumstances of Hannah's death. Or the fact that her murder in Minneapolis remains unsolved. Or, finally, the fact that she was buried still charged with stabbing her stepfather, the motive for which remains a mystery and went to the grave with her. This is Gabby Gooding, reporting from Travis, Minnesota for Channel Seven News."*

She looked at Zach. "Was that okay?"

"Looked fine to me. I'll check with Chuck to make sure the feed went through."

He returned a moment later. "Everything's fine. But I see you couldn't resist."

"What?"

"The stabbing and the motive still a mystery, going to the grave with her."

"Well, it's true."

"Maybe so. But I'm not sure Mr. Klinger will see it that way."

SEVENTEEN

...

By the time they got back to the station it was past five o'clock and the first of her two reports from Travis already had been on the air. Barclay was waiting for them, pacing in the middle of the newsroom, hands in his pockets, shoulders back. "Good job," he said. "The pieces looked great. I'm glad you convinced me to let you go."

"What did our friends across town do?" she asked.

"Not much. Carried about forty-five seconds or so of the video they got from one of the local stations down there. We made 'em look pretty bad in comparison."

"Good."

By now they had arrived at his office. "Tell me about your talk with the sheriff."

"He's going to talk to the county attorney but, as I expected, doesn't think he'll want to do much. Afraid of stirring things up, of maybe getting sued."

"Go on."

"Then I talked briefly to Hannah's mother, who took some comfort in what I told her about Hannah's and Jennie's friendship. She wanted to talk more and possibly try to see and talk to Jennie herself. So I gave her my card. We'll see what happens, but my guess is her husband will probably veto that possibility."

"And if she does talk to Jennie..."

"I know. She may learn about the attempted rape."

"And you don't think she knows that now?"

"That's certainly my impression. She said she was never able to talk to Hannah after that night. Despite trying. All she knows is what her husband has told her."

"And about his past?"

"Who knows? But I doubt it."

He sank back in his chair. "Where do we go from here?"

"I wish I knew," she admitted. "I want to follow up on the unsolved rape in Lincoln County and keep in touch with the sheriff and my newspaper friend, Hooper. But I don't think anything will happen very quickly. They want to let the sleeping, the dead Hannah, lie."

"What about the homeless kids story you want to do?"

She glanced at Zach. "I still want to do it, more than ever, knowing what I know now. But it's going to take more time and research. And I don't want to give up on Hannah's murder. So I guess we should just hang tight."

"And, remember," Barclay said, "I may need you for other things."

"I realize that. And I'll be here."

He got up. "Head home now. Get some sleep and we'll talk more tomorrow."

Sleep proved to be elusive.

With more than eighteen hours since she had last slept, her body was bone-tired and her mind a jumble of wayward thoughts. But her eyes would not close. She lay staring at the darkened ceiling, feeling the warmth of Zach's body next to her, listening to the rhythm of his deep breathing. And next to the bed, with occasional small whimpers, lay Barclay the poodle in his blanket, letting her know in his own quiet way that he'd rather be in the bed with her.

The images of the funeral would not leave her: Hannah's weeping father holding the bronze urn to his chest, unwilling to surrender it until the pastor gently took it from his arms and placed it on a small stool in front of the altar. Hannah's stoic mother, clasping her boys' hands so tightly that Gabby thought she could see them wince. The stepfather, aloof and alone in the midst of a sea of grief.

She could still feel the mother's arms around her and her whispered words, "God bless you."

Intertwined with those memories were thoughts of her own mother, standing next to her father's casket in Portland, putting a solitary rose atop it as she and her sisters watched and wept. A man who had died too young, too suddenly, for Gabby, who was away in California, to have any chance to say a goodbye. Even now, leaving her with the emptiness she saw so profoundly in the faces of a woman and two young boys in the small town of Travis.

Outside the bedroom window she could hear the muted sounds of late night traffic and the occasional laughter of passersby on the sidewalk below. Like her, awake in the dead of night, but unlike her, not yearning for sleep.

The last thing she remembered before sleep finally came was leaning over to pick up the poodle, holding him tight.

She awoke to the smell of fresh coffee under her nose, the dog's soft licking of her face, and standing over her—holding the coffee—was Zach, fully-dressed and smiling. "Hey, welcome to the world," he said as she struggled to sit up. And wake up.

"Jeez," she mumbled, fighting to shake away the fragments of her last dream, finally glancing at the bedside clock. "Nine-thirty!" Flinging off the covers, she pushed the dog out of the bed and struggled to get up. "Why didn't you wake me?"

"Relax," Zach said, settling down next to her and handing her the coffee. "Barclay called while you were passed out and said to forget about coming in until this afternoon. He said they've got things covered and knew we'd had a long day yesterday."

"God bless him," she said, sipping at the coffee while trying to stay upright. "How long have you been up?"

"A couple of hours. But I think I got a better night's sleep than you did."

"Amen to that. The last time I checked, it was about three o'clock and I know I was awake for a while after that."

"A lot on your mind?"

She looked up at the ceiling, trying to remember. "I couldn't erase some of those images from the funeral. They kept coming back, like different shots from different camera angles. The mom, the dad, the kids, the stepdad, all of them mixed in with memories of my dad's funeral. Crazy, I know, but it was like I was living it all again. In the middle of the night."

"Not crazy," he said, "But I'm glad you got to sleep in." Getting up, he took the coffee cup from her. "While you get your beautiful bod out of bed and get going, I'll take the pooch for a quick walk and make us some breakfast. Then we can decide on what we should do with all of this free time we've been given."

"Like what?" she laughed. "Three hours?"

"Take what we can get," he replied with a grin. "And be grateful, Gabby."

By the time she'd showered and dressed and got to the kitchen, she found a stack of pancakes on the table and strips of bacon crisping on the stove. "Gosh," she said, giving Zach a quick kiss, "if you keep this up, I might actually marry you."

"When?"

She laughed. "You tell me."

"Today?"

Glancing at the clock on the stove, "We've only got two hours."

"Plenty of time."

"We probably should invite my mom and sisters."

Grinning. "I suppose."

Before they could sit down her phone sounded. Puzzled, she picked up. "Andy?"

The intern's voice on the other end was faint, almost a whisper. "I should have listened to you. I'm really sorry."

"Andy? What's happened? Where are you?"

There was a long pause. "At the Hennepin County Medical Center."

"What?" She put the phone on speaker.

"I got the shit kicked out of me. Just like you warned me."

Looking plaintively at Zach, she asked, "When? Where?"

"This morning. Early. A couple of blocks off Hennepin."

"Are you going to be okay?"

"I think so. The docs say I have two broken ribs, a possible concussion, and some pretty ugly bruising on my face. As you'll see, I'm even less handsome than before."

Zach broke in. "Who in the hell did it?"

"A big guy. Wearing a black hoodie and scarf that hid his face. Just walked up to me, kind of out of nowhere, and started beating on me. Before I could do anything, I was on the ground, trying to cover myself. But he had these big boots. Like cowboy boots. With pointed toes. I remember that. But not much more."

Gabby asked, "No one tried to help?"

"No. The two kids I was interviewing took off, running. I didn't see anyone else."

Zach pushed on, "Did the guy say anything?"

"Stop asking questions, buddy. That's all I remember."

"So who found you?" she asked.

"A squad car came by and took me here. They want to keep me overnight to check on the concussion."

"We'll be there as soon as we can," she said.

"No hurry. I'm not going anywhere."

"I'm so sorry, Andy…"

"Forget it. I should have listened to you." A pause. "Oh, yeah. He crushed my little camera with those big boots of his."

"Damn," Gabby whispered. "Take care until we get there."

As they prepared to go, leaving the burnt bacon and cold pancakes behind, Gabby's ringtone sounded again. What now? she asked herself.

"Ms. Gooding?"

"Yes, this is Gabby."

"This is Mrs. Klinger. Hannah's mother. You said I could call."

Gabby stopped at the door. "Of course, Mrs. Klinger."

"Have you talked to the young girl, Jennie?"

"No, not yet. I got back too late from the funeral."

"But you plan to?"

"Yes, but I'm not sure when. A couple of important things have come up since."

"I see."

"You'd still like to try and see her?"

"Very much, yes. As soon as I can."

"I'll see if it can be arranged. But I need to know, would you come alone?"

"Yes, my husband would need to stay with the boys and tend to things here on the farm. But why do you ask that?"

Gabby's mind raced, searching for the answer. "Well, as I told you, Jennie comes from an abusive home, an abusive father, and… is not comfortable around older men."

"Really? Well, I guess I can understand that."

"Then why don't you give me another call tomorrow, Mrs. Klinger. I may know something by then."

"Thank you, I will. But please call me Rosemary. I feel like we know one another now."

"That's fine, Rosemary. Perhaps we'll talk tomorrow."

As they drove to the hospital, Gabby put in a call to Barclay, briefly explaining what had happened to Andy. He was not pleased. "Holy shit," he said, "was he working for us when this happened?"

"Not officially, no," she replied. "He was on his own. He made that clear to me when he ignored my warnings. But…"

"But what?" A touch of anger in his voice.

"In a way he was. I mean, I'm the one who got him interested in the homeless kids story…"

"Okay, okay. I hear you. I just hope he's got insurance."

"He's probably still on his folks' policy. He's probably young enough."

His voice mellowed. "I hope he's okay…and give him my best."

"I will."

"But we've got another problem."

"What's that?"

"I'll brief you when you get here. But it ain't good."

They found Andy sitting in one of the private rooms of the medical center, staring off into space. Only when Gabby touched his arm did he turn abruptly, as if suddenly awakened. "Oh, hi," he said. "Sorry, I was daydreaming, I guess."

More likely the concussion, she thought.

He wore a hospital gown pulled tightly around him. Even knowing what he'd told her on the phone, she was jolted by what she saw. One of his eyes was blackened, almost closed, his face puffed up, bruised and scraped. More splotchy purple than white. One side of his head was shaved to make room for a row of stitches, the ear on that side wrapped in a bandage. For an instant, she couldn't take her eyes off of him.

He tried to smile, but a swollen lip distorted it. "You think I'm ready for that on-camera audition?"

Despite herself, she had to laugh. "You may have to wait a few days."

"I told you it was bad," he said. "I never have liked what I see in the mirror, but this is a little too much."

They pulled up two chairs next to him. "Do your folks know?" Zach asked.

"Yeah. I had to tell them to get their insurance information. They should be here before too long."

"And what did they say?"

"What you'd expect. That I should've known better. But they're glad I'm still alive."

"And so are we. Barclay sends his best wishes."

"But he's pissed, right? Afraid I'll sue him."

Gabby, lying, "No way. He's concerned, just like we are."

"So what are the doctors telling you now?" Zach asked.

"I guess I passed the concussion protocol, and they've wrapped my mid-section to protect the broken ribs. But I can tell you they hurt like hell. That's the worst part of this. I can barely breathe."

They spent a few more minutes going over details of the attack, but learned little more. "The guy had broad shoulders and a kick you wouldn't believe," he told them. "The cop took a statement, but he didn't expect much to happen. I've already talked to the folks at the law school and they're going to give me a break. Let me make up any lost classes. And I plan to be back with you guys as soon as I can."

"School comes first and us a distant second," she said. "I don't want to see you again until you're healthy and ready for that audition."

As they got up to leave, he said, "I saw your report on Hannah's funeral. Nice job. Especially the little jab at the stepdad. Cool."

Then, after a quick hug, they were gone. Thankfully before his parents arrived.

EIGHTEEN

. . .

Barclay was again on the phone when they got back to the station, so they waited patiently, and apprehensively, outside his office—aware of the curious stares from others in the newsroom. As they stood there, Jeff Parkett, the assistant news director, walked over to them. "Can you guys tell me what the hell's going on? He's been in a bad mood all morning."

Gabby shrugged. "You've got me. He just said he wanted to see us right away."

"And what about our intern?" he asked. "I hear he got busted up pretty good."

"You heard right," Zach replied. "We just saw him in the hospital. He's in bad shape, in a lot of pain, but he'll survive."

"So what happened to him?"

Gabby quickly repeated the story. "That's about all we know. The cops took a report, but chances of finding the guy are pretty remote, I'd say."

Parkett, who was not a great fan of Gabby, persisted, not hiding his irritation at being in the dark. "So he was working on your homeless kids story?"

"Not directly," she said. "He was kind of on his own."

Before he could ask more questions, Barclay was at the office door. "C'mon in. We need to talk."

He shut the door behind them. "So how's our young intern?"

Zach repeated what they had just told Parkett. "And he does have insurance."

"Good. I'll try to stop by to see him after work."

"He'd appreciate that," Gabby said. Then, "So what's up, George? You sounded upset on the phone."

He settled back in his chair. "I got a call from Ryan this morning. *He's* the one who's upset."

Sam Ryan was the general manager of the station, brought in to run the place after a media conglomerate, San Lucas Communications of San Jose, bought the station the year before. In that time, he and Barclay had had a strained relationship—over budgets and some of the aggressive reporting the station had done, including Gabby and Zach's Ponzi investigation. He was not a man who liked to rock the boat. However, it was Ryan who had brought Gabby from the San Jose station to Channel Seven. Thanks, in part, because of her college friendship with one of his daughters.

"He's upset about *us*?" Gabby said.

"Yes. Seems like he got a call from a county commissioner in Lyon County, a guy named Lester Updahl, who happens to serve with Ryan on the Governor's Task Force on Economic Opportunity. A group which advises the state on how to spend its tourism advertising dollars. Like on TV. See where I'm going?"

"Maybe," she replied.

"This Updahl guy has been talking to the county attorney who has been talking to the county sheriff. And guess what? Turns out Updahl is a close family friend of the Klinger family, Mrs. Klinger in particular. They went to the same high school."

"Shit."

"And he's heard from the county attorney that we may be planning a story that connects Mr. Klinger's past to Hannah Hendricks's death. A story he says could destroy the Klinger family."

"Word travels fast," she said. "So what did you tell our Mr. Ryan?"

"I told him no decision has been made. That we have more work to do before a story will air, if it ever does. And that I'm on top of it."

"And his reaction?"

"That he'd like us to forget it, but that he'll trust my judgment. If you believe that."

"I don't," she said, with heat. "Not if there's advertising dollars involved."

"Easy, Gabby, easy," Zach said.

"No," she said, standing up. "This story, if there is a story, may never air. But if it doesn't, it won't be because some county commissioner is afraid of hurting the Klinger family. That's bullshit, George, and you know it."

Now it was Barclay who stood up. "Settle down, Gabby. Get off your high horse and listen to me. We're not backing off, but we've got to be cautious. Not because of Ryan, but because we want to be right. And fair. Even to a convicted rapist."

She sat back down, clearly upset. "Is any other reporter on vacation right now?"

He looked surprised. "Not at the moment. Nobody takes a vacation in November in Minnesota."

"Then I'd like to take a few days, maybe a week. I've got the time coming."

"To do what?"

"Poke around a bit. Try to see Jennie. Maybe see Mrs. Klinger, if she decides to drive up. All on my own time, not yours."

"You may be on your own time," he said, "but you're still our employee."

"And what about me?" Zach asked.

"You'll be just fine," she replied. "Between here and home we probably spend too much time together anyway."

"Great. Then I hope you're cooking dinner."

Before leaving the station for her new-found vacation, she put in a call to Sara Chan. "Hey, Sarah, I thought you ought to know about a new wrinkle in Hannah's murder."

"Really, like what?'

She described the attack on Andy and the only words spoken to him: "Stop asking questions."

"What questions?" she asked.

"He's been asking each of the kids he interviews whether they know anything about Hannah's murder. I warned him the word could get around and it apparently did. He's in the hospital now, recovering."

"Damn," she replied. "I'll let Detective Archer know."

"Thanks. The cop that picked him up filed a report, so that should be available."

Then, before hanging up, she told Sarah about her conversation with the Lyon County sheriff and how word of the stepdad's past had already spread to at least one county commissioner. "And now he may be trying to kill any chance of us doing a story."

"So what are you going to do?"

"Take a few days of vacation. I'll be in touch."

On her way home, she took a detour to The Haven—on the off-chance Julie O'Connell would be there and willing to see her on the fly. It had been a couple of days since she'd talked to her or had heard anything about Jennie. She wasn't even sure she was still there.

Luck was on her side. Julie was there and available, although she didn't hide her surprise at seeing her. "This must be karma," she said, "I was ready to call you."

"Really?"

"But I wasn't sure you were in town. I saw your report on the funeral and thought you might still be down there."

"Was Jennie able to see the report?"

"No. I wasn't sure how she'd react. I didn't want to take a chance."

"So she's still here?"

"Yes, but for how long I'm not sure. I'll fill you in on her in a minute, but that's not why I was going to call you."

Gabby waited.

"Remember that I offered to help you locate Jennie's brother, the one who's in the Army somewhere."

"Of course."

"Well, one of my people tracked him down. He's at Ft. Hood, Texas, a huge base somewhere between Austin and Waco. Jesse Oliver Nystrom, a sergeant assigned to the First Army Division West. I was able to talk to his unit's commanding officer and briefly explained the reason for the call. But I also urged him to say nothing to Jesse…that someone other than me would be in contact with him."

"Did you get his cell number?"

"Yes, but only after being my persuasive best. He also gave me the number of one of their chaplains."

"You are a wonderful person," Gabby said. "I can't thank you enough."

"No problem. Is there anything else?"

"As a matter of fact, there is," she replied. "I met Hannah's mother at the funeral and told her about Hannah's friendship with Jennie. She was very touched and wonders if she could possibly see Jennie and talk to her?"

"Jeez, I don't know. That could be a problem. I'd have to check with the child protection people up in Wadena County."

"Would you?"

"I will, but I wouldn't count on a meeting like that happening."

When Zach got home from work, he was greeted at the door with a cold bottle of Beck's beer and the sweet aroma of dinner in the oven—along with a warm, lingering kiss. All before he could take his coat off.

Stepping back, he smiled, "Wow. You should take a vacation more often."

She laughed. "Don't you know, I'm just the dutiful little would-be wife waiting for her hubby to come home."

"I could get used to it," he said, slipping off his coat. "What's the smell?"

"Pot roast, with all the trimmings. Just as you like it, sweetie."

Slyly, he asked, "Do we have time for a little pre-dinner appetizer?"

"Afraid not. Maybe later, for dessert, if you're nice."

"I'll be nice if you'll be naughty," he said with a grin, settling into the couch with his beer. "So what's new?"

She sat next to him and repeated what she had learned about Jennie's brother. "I'm going to try to call him after dinner. See what he knows, if anything, about Jennie and what's happened to her."

"That could be a little touchy," he said.

"I know. I'll have to be careful."

"Then what?"

"Depends on what he says. What he's done, if anything."

Once dinner was over and with some hesitation, Gabby punched in the number for Jesse Nystrom. There were three rings before he answered.

"Is this Jesse Nystrom?"

"Yes. Who's this?"

"My name's Gabby Gooding. I'm a reporter from Channel Seven in the Twin Cities."

There was a long pause. "Is this about Jennie?"

"Yes. Did you know that she's okay? Safe and in a shelter?"

"I just found out yesterday, when I talked to my mother. I knew she'd run away, but I'm just back from overseas...so I've been out of touch until now."

"Do you know why she ran? Did your mother tell you?"

"No, she probably was too afraid of what I might do. It's my dad, right?'

"So you haven't spoken to Jennie?"

"No, I don't know how to reach her. I don't have her number."

"She doesn't have a phone now, anyway," she said. "Not in the shelter."

"So how do you know her?" he asked. "Have you seen her? Spoken to her?"

"Yes," she replied, explaining how Jennie had come to her for help in finding Hannah and the rest of the story, including Hannah's death. "I've grown very fond of her and want to help her, but I may need *your* help to do that."

"How?"

"By supporting her claim that she's been abused by your father...as she says you once were."

"Hey, wait a minute..."

"No, please listen. She may be sent back home...to your father...unless she can prove she's been abused. And right now, it's only her word. Do you want that?"

"Of course not, but..."

"Did you ever see her abused?"

"Not physically, no, but in every other way, yes."

"Then if you're contacted by child protection, you'll have to tell them what your father did to you...that you believe she might also have been physically abused, even if you didn't witness it yourself."

"Man, I don't know. I thought I had gotten away from all of that. Why I'm here, bustin' my ass in the Army. I can't go back there. I hate the man. I can't face him again or I may kill him."

"You may not have to go back," she argued. "You may just have to write and sign a statement, an affidavit, reporting what he has done to you. Or perhaps simply talk with the child protection people. That may be enough to save Jennie."

She could almost hear his mind churning. "This is your sister we're talking about."

"I know, I know," he finally said. "But you don't know my father."

Exasperated, she pushed on, "If you're brave enough to be ready to fight for your country, you should be brave enough to face your father."

"Easy for you to say. And it's not about being brave. I'll have to think about this. Talk to my chaplain. Give me your number and I'll get back to you."

That ended the conversation.

NINETEEN

· · ·

Despite the opportunity to sleep in, Gabby was up early, in time to shower, have breakfast with Zach, take the poodle on his mandatory walk, scan the morning papers, check the internet, and catch the first of the television newscasts. All before ten o'clock.

Then it was time to decide what to do with her free day.

She didn't have much time to think. By the time the bed was made and the few breakfast dishes washed and put away, her ringtone sounded with its familiar tune. It was Zach. "You may want to get down here."

"What? Why?"

"Because you have a visitor sitting in the lobby."

"Who?"

"Mrs. Klinger."

"What?" A deep sigh. "Damn. She was supposed to call first."

"I know. I went out and talked to her. Told her you were on vacation. But she seems very determined. And upset, I'd say."

Gabby's mind raced. Remembering the county commissioner's call to Ryan. Could the word have spread so quickly? "Do you think she knows? About her husband?"

"You've got me. And I certainly wasn't going to ask. But I don't think she'll move until she sees you."

"Tell her I'll be there as soon as I can. Get her a cup of coffee or something."

"I already have."

She found Mrs. Klinger sitting erect, still wrapped in a long, green winter coat despite the warmth of the lobby. "Hello, Rosemary," she said as she approached to shake her hand. "I'm happy to see you, but surprised. I thought you'd call first."

Mrs. Klinger rose and took her hand in both of hers. "I know. I'm so sorry. But I was afraid if I called you might put me off. And I do need to talk to you. I don't know who else to turn to."

"Please sit," Gabby said as she took a chair next to her. "Can I have someone get you another cup of coffee?"

"No, no thank you. I had plenty on the drive up."

"You must have left early."

"I did. Before anyone was up. I left a note."

Gabby folded her arms and waited.

"Did you know about it? At the funeral? When we spoke?"

"About what?"

Her voice choked up. "About my husband."

Gabby took a deep gulp. "Yes, I knew."

"How?"

"By research."

"And it's true?"

"Yes, it's true."

"Tell me. Please. What made you do that research?"

Gabby looked away, then back. "I'm not sure we should talk about this."

"Please. I have to know."

Gabby paused. Thinking. Debating. Then, "I checked into your husband's past because of what Hannah had told Jennie before she was killed."

"Told her what?"

The moment Gabby had so dreaded had arrived. "Are you sure you want to know? It will be painful."

"I have to know," she replied, her face only inches away. "I *must* know."

Gabby met her gaze. "First tell me how you found out about his past? I've told no one except the sheriff and," thinking of Howard Hooper, "one friend whom I trust completely. I know he wouldn't say anything to anyone."

She sighed. "It's a small town, Gabby. A small county. No secrets last long, not one like this."

"Does your husband know that you know? Do your kids?"

"I don't think so. I was only told late last night by an old friend. That's why I left early this morning. I had to see you. To learn the truth."

"Was your old friend the county commissioner, Mr. Updahl?"

Hesitation. "Yes, but how did you know?"

"That's not important, but please listen. I'm not sure I know the full truth. I'm not sure anyone does. I only know what Hannah told Jennie."

"Which was *what?*" The voice demanding.

Gabby swallowed hard. "That Hannah stabbed your husband only as he tried to rape her. That night, while you and your boys were away."

It took a split second....then..."*My, God,*" she whispered. "That can't be true! *To my own daughter? To his own stepdaughter?* There must be a mistake. Hannah must have lied."

"Maybe so. I was unsure myself until I did the research. Then her story seemed plausible. Which is why I pursued it, to try to find the truth. To protect her memory, not as a would-be killer, but as a victim who stabbed your husband to save herself from rape."

The woman buried her face in her hands, sobbing. Gabby waited, unsure of what to do, of what to say, of how to comfort her.

Finally, the sobbing ended and she looked up, wiped the tears away and straightened her shoulders. "My life is ruined, you know.

My kids' lives are ruined if this is true, if the story gets out."

"Maybe it won't. Maybe your friend is the only one who knows and tried to do you a favor by telling you."

"I doubt that, but I still have to face my husband. To demand the truth."

Gabby leaned in. "So, clearly, you didn't know about his past."

"Of course not. Or I *never* would have married him. I had no hint. He never told me much about his life before me and I never pressed him. I knew he was divorced and had two children, but he said they lived in California, not Nebraska, and that he was totally alienated from them." She paused to catch her breath."It was an ugly divorce, he told me, and his ex-wife took him for everything he had. Got a restraining order to keep him away from her and the kids. He was so emotional about it that I never really questioned it." She took another breath. "I went through a bad divorce, too, so I was probably more sympathetic than I should have been. Now that I look back."

"So tell me about him." Gabby said. "Was there ever any hint...you know...that he might not be what you thought he was?"

"Not really. He's a hard worker, keeps up the farm, does carpenter work around the area. He's very handy that way. Helps pay the bills. I can't say he was very affectionate or that we had much of a love life. But I wasn't much interested in that, anyway. I work in the school cafeteria in Travis and by the time I get home at night and take care of the boys and Hannah, I'm usually exhausted."

"How did he act around Hannah?"

She leaned back, momentarily staring at the ceiling. "I don't know. Maybe he was harder on her than he was on the boys. Kept after her about the kind of guys she was hanging out with. Worried about her getting in trouble, that sort of thing. But he could also be kind of flirty around her, in what I thought was a funny, fatherly way."

"Flirty?"

"You know, kidded her about her looks and what she was wearing. Her makeup. But all in fun, I thought. I certainly never worried about it."

Gabby said, "So she wasn't nervous around him? Never came to you with complaints about him? That he tried to chase her around when you were away, that she had to run from him or lock herself in the bedroom?"

"No, *never*! Did she tell Jennie that?"

"Yes. That she was afraid of him. That he came into her bedroom that night and got on top of her...that she kept a knife under her pillow to protect herself."

"Sweet Jesus," she whispered as she got up. "I have to go. I can't hear any more. I have to get home."

Gabby rose with her. "What are you going to do?"

She seemed to shudder. "Face him, I guess. As much as I hate the thought. But I have to know the truth. To hear what he says. For my sake and my boys' sake."

"May I offer a suggestion?" Gabby said, haltingly. "If you *do* confront him, you should do it when the boys are not there...and perhaps have the sheriff or one of his deputies with you in case he gets angry or violent. I would hate to see you get hurt."

"I appreciate that. And everything you've told me. But I don't know how else to do it. I may have to start my life all over again."

Hesitantly, she took Gabby into her arms. "Hannah would have liked you, I know. I'm sorry you never met."

"So am I. But because of Jennie, and you, I feel like I do know her. And miss her. Please let me know how this turns out. And, please, please, be careful."

Holding her hand, Gabby walked her to the lobby door and watched as the green coat disappeared into the parking ramp across the way.

Barclay found Gabby at her desk, staring out the window at a new, lightly falling snow, lost in thought, oblivious to the newsroom hubbub that surrounded her. "How's that vacation of yours?" he said, leaning over.

She turned, surprised to find him there. "A work in progress, I guess."

He pulled up a chair. "I can see that." Then, "Zach tells me you had a visitor."

"Yeah. She left a while ago."

"And?"

"She knows the truth about his past from that commissioner friend of Ryan's. And from me, reluctantly, about what Hannah had told Jennie about the attempted rape. She's on her way home now, threatening to confront her husband."

For the first time ever, she saw what looked like real fear in his face. Not quite panic, but genuine alarm. And anger. *"Are you kidding me?"* he demanded. "She's going home to face—out of the blue—a man who thinks she loves him, a rapist who may think his secret is still safe? A man she may then accuse of trying to rape her daughter? My God, Gabby, what have we done? What have we got ourselves into?"

She pulled back, knowing he was talking about *her*, not *we*. "Hey, hold on," she snapped. "What was I supposed to do? She learned the truth about his past from that commissioner, not from me, and she demanded to know—from me—what Hannah had told Jennie. Should I have refused to tell her? Would you have?"

By now, the tense confrontation had drawn curious looks from others nearby. He lowered his voice, drawing closer to her. "Look, we can't free ourselves from this. The commissioner only knew because we told the sheriff, and nobody would have known if we hadn't pursued it in the first place..."

"Sure. And Rosemary Klinger would still be living in the dark with a rapist, a man who may have tried to rape her daughter and—in a roundabout way—may have gotten her killed."

"What do you mean?"

"Just what I've said before. If she hadn't had to flee the law in Delroy, she may not have ended up here, dead in a parking lot."

He leaned back, hands clasped behind his head, clearly frustrated. "So what can we do?"

She repeated the warning she had given Mrs. Klinger. "And

before you came over, I called the sheriff and told him what had happened. He said he or one of his deputies would watch out for her, and try to stop her before she gets back to the farm. To try and control the situation before it explodes."

"And if it explodes?"

She abruptly got up and walked to the window, stood for a moment, and came back. "If that happens, if the worst happens, then I guess it's my fault. Because of my stubborn, perhaps stupid, pursuit of a story. Of the truth. I don't regret it, but I'd have to live with it. But not here, George. I couldn't face you or Ryan or the newsroom knowing that I'd caused something horrible to happen. That I'd brought down a ton of shit on the station and on you."

"Wait a minute," he said, getting up and leading her away from the desk, out of earshot. "I don't want to hear that kind of talk. Not now, not ever. You were doing your job, okay, with my full knowledge and approval. You aren't alone in this. Let's step back, take a deep breath, and hope for the best. There's nothing to be done now but wait."

She slipped on her coat and scarf. "We'll wait and see, George, but for right now, I'm back on vacation."

TWENTY

· · ·

It didn't take that long. She got the news as she was taking the poodle on a long walk through the neighborhood, the walk more for her benefit than his. To clear her head, to help her decide what the next step could or should be. The snow was still falling, but in a snow globe kind of way. Gently, the flakes lightly caressing her cheeks as she walked, settling on the tip of her nose as she stopped every few minutes to let the dog have his sniffs.

The call came as she was several blocks from the apartment. "Yes?"

"Gabby?"

"Yes."

"This is Sheriff Henderson."

Urgently. "Yes."

"He's gone. Klinger's gone."

"What?"

"And Mrs. Klinger is okay. I thought you'd want to know right away."

She stopped short, holding the leash tight, overcome with relief. "Thanks you, so, so much." The dog looked back, curious. "Tell me, what happened? Please."

"After your call I was able to intercept Mrs. Klinger about three miles from the farm and asked what she planned to do. When she told me, I convinced her to let me go to the farm first. To talk to

141

Klinger before she got there. I asked her to go to the café in town and wait."

"And?"

"No one was at the farm. His truck was gone…"

Quickly, "And the boys?"

"They're okay. In school. I checked."

She waited.

"He left a note stuck to the door. I can't tell you exactly what it said, that's not up to me, but he does know that word about his past is out and that he can't stay around any longer. I called Rosemary at the café and told her. I'm on my way to see her now."

Gabby closed her eyes, breathing deeply. "I am so grateful, Sheriff. Really. As I told you, I was scared to death something really bad could happen and that I'd be the one…"

"Forget that. I'm glad you called…I'm glad I got to the farm before she did. Maybe I can cushion the blow a little, maybe get her to stop by the church and talk to Pastor Peterson. We'll have to see what she wants to do. I'll be as much help as I can, but it's not going to be easy."

"If there's anything I can do…"

"I'll let her know. But remember," the sheriff said. "She has tons of friends around here, from church, from the school, her neighbors, so she should have lots of support."

As Gabby made her way back to the apartment, the sheriff found Mrs. Klinger huddled in a back booth of Lilly's Café, the only restaurant in the town of Delroy. Feigning surprise at seeing her there, he walked over and slid into the booth across from her. "Well, hello, Rosemary. What brings you to town?"

She gave him a tentative smile. "Oh, I stopped at the grocery store and had a little time to kill."

Only one other customer was in the café, an old man, bundled up, sitting at the counter, sipping on a cup of coffee, absorbed in a copy of the *Mankato Free Press*.

As he learned across the table, the sheriff said, quietly, "Well, this is quite a coincidence, because I just stopped by the farm to have a word with Arnold. But he wasn't there."

"Really?" Feigning her own surprise. "He must be running some errands."

At that moment, the waitress came by. "Hey there, Sheriff. What brings you to our little town?"

"Just making the rounds," he replied. "Always on the job, you know."

"Sure, you betcha," she said in her Fargo voice, "So what can I get ya?"

"Nothing, thanks. I'll be on my way in a minute."

Once she was gone, he handed Rosemary a folded note. "He left this for you. I'm sorry, but I took the liberty to read it. Felt I had to, considering the circumstances."

She took the note, but left it unopened. "So he's really gone?"

"For now anyway. I don't know how, but the word must have got back to him."

She put her hand to her mouth, stifling a sob.

"It may be for the best, Rosemary. Saves what could have been a serious situation. Considering."

She took her hand away. "But what will I tell my boys?"

He leaned forward and lowered his voice. "I wish I knew. I wish I could help. The truth, I guess. They'll have to know eventually, but better from you than someone else. I hoped you might talk to Pastor Peterson. I could arrange that, once the boys are out of school."

"No, no, but thanks. I'll do it myself. They're old enough to know the truth, as horrible as it will be for them. I'll pick them up from school and go somewhere to talk."

"You're sure?"

"I'm sure."

Turning away, she opened the note.

Dear Rosemary, I know you now know what I've did in the past. Sorry you learnt about it the way you did. Scumbag Updahl and that bitch reporter. I shoulda told you, but knew you woud never understand or forgiv me. I made some bad mistakes before you and I got together and thought all that crap in Nebraska would never come back at me. Ha! Jokes on me, right. I wish I could take back some of the things Ive did but its too late. I can't stay around here now that everybody will know what I did back then. Laughin behind my back. Tell the boys I'm not all bad and that I'll miss em. And I'm sorry I'm leavin you like I am, you're a good woman and a good wife and I hope you'll find another man whose better than me.

She folded the note and turned back, with a slight smile. "He never was very good at spelling."

"I noticed," the sheriff said. "And l also noticed he said nothing about Hannah."

"I saw that, too," she replied. "For whatever it means."

Henderson slid out of the booth. "Any idea where he might have gone?"

"No, no idea. I don't know of any friends he has, except those around here. He has his old family, but from what he's told me, they're in California. I just don't know where he'd be. But wherever it is, I'm sure he's one angry man."

"So you're going to be okay?"

"No, but I'll survive. I just hope he didn't raid our bank account. And I've got a sister in Marshall who will be there for me. And a lot of friends. I will not let this be the end of my life. Of my boys' lives."

"I'll be there, too, if you ever need me," he said. Then, he added, "One more thing. I spoke to our friend, Gabby, while I was at the farm. She's very relieved to know that nothing bad happened and wanted you to know that."

As he spoke those words, Gabby was home from her long walk with the dog, spending time on needed household chores: a quick vacuuming, two loads of wash and a change of the bed linens. Not her favorite ways to spend her time, but they needed to be done and, besides, it gave her some mindless moments to figure out what to do next.

Again, as it turned out, that decision was made for her.

The call came just as she was moving the last load of clothes from the washer to the dryer. "Is this Gabby?"

"Yes. Who's this?"

"Jesse Nystrom. You gave me your number."

It took her a moment. "Well, of course, Jesse."

"I wonder if I can see you?"

He caught her off guard. "Are you here? In the Cities?"

"Yes. At the airport, actually. I just flew in."

"That's great," she said. "But let me think for a minute."

"I'd like to see Jennie, but I don't know where she is. And I'd like to speak to you first, if I could."

"You're catching me by surprise, Jesse, but let's do this. Grab a cab and meet me at the Channel Seven studios. The cabbie will know where it is. I'm at home now and it will take me about a half hour to get there. So if you beat me, just tell the receptionist I'm expecting you."

"Thanks. I'll see you there."

She waited a moment then punched in Julie O'Connell's number at The Haven. She was surprised to get an answer on the first ring, but then quickly explained the reason for her call. "Will there be a problem in him seeing Jennie?" she asked.

There was a pregnant pause. Then, "Gosh, Gabby, I don't know. We're in uncharted territory here. I don't know if I have the authority…"

"What can it hurt?" Gabby argued. "He's her brother, for God's sake. Can anyone dispute his right to see her?"

"I can't answer that question. Not without talking to some people who know the rules better than I do."

"Well, please do. I'm meeting him in a half hour, and I'd like to bring him to you soon after that. Jennie deserves this, Julie, after what she's been through."

"I hear you and I'll do my best. Call me before you come."

Gabby found him waiting in the lobby, sitting in the same chair she had found Jennie in so many days before. A lifetime ago, it seemed now. He quickly got up, his expression a mixture of curiosity and anxiety. "Hey, Jesse," she said with a friendly nod. "I'm Gabby. Welcome back to Minnesota."

He took her hand. "I've been waiting to meet you," he said. "Ever since your phone call. I'm here because of you."

She studied him. Considering Jennie's small stature, he was taller than she'd expected, but with a definite family resemblance. A long face, deeply-tanned, with Jennie's blue eyes and full lips. By any definition, a handsome man, clad in civilian clothes, but with a straight up, military bearing. She almost expected a salute from him.

"Let's sit," she said. "Can I get you a coffee or something?"

He grinned. "A beer and a bump would be great, but that's probably not possible."

She returned the grin. "Not now, but maybe later."

After an awkward moment, she asked, "What made you decide to come?"

"Your phone call. I couldn't get it out of my head. I finally talked to one of our chaplains, a friend of mine who served with me overseas. He convinced me I had no choice…that I had to come. He helped me get an emergency family leave, and I got on the first plane out."

"Well, I admire your willingness to help. Knowing the history with your father."

He leaned forward. "So how is she? Jennie?"

"I haven't seen her for several days, but I think she's doing okay, considering what she's been through. As I told you on the phone, the child protection people from Wadena County are due any day now—to question her about her claims of abuse. Then they'll decide on what to do."

"Can I see her?"

146

"I'm not sure. She's at a place called The Haven, and the woman who runs it is checking on the rules as we speak. I'm hopeful but not certain."

"So I may have come all this way...and not see her?"

"We should know soon. But, remember, your trip won't be wasted if you're willing to talk to child protection. To tell them what you went through with your dad. It could make a difference."

He settled back in his chair. "I should have known this could happen. He never touched Jennie, physically, when I was there. But he was always on her ass, like verbally complaining about her friends, how she dressed, how she talked. Demeaning her, I guess you'd call it. Took away her phone, locked her in her room, shouted at her when she tried to get between him and me."

"What about your mother?"

"Ha! What's she going to do? Divorce him? It's a small town, Gabby, and he's a big man in town. She has nowhere else to go. No other family up there. She had to put up and shut up or he'd slap her around, too. As he sometimes did. I had to get away as soon as I could, and took the cowardly way out, I guess. And I'm not proud of it. Which is why I'm back here now, maybe to make up for it."

At that moment her phone sounded. She recognized the number. "Hey, Julie."

She wasted no words. "Is Jennie's brother there with you?"

"Yes, sitting right here."

"Can you bring him here, like right away?"

"Of course. You must have talked to someone."

"No, I made the decision myself. Like you said, he's Jennie's brother and deserves to see her. And she deserves to see him. If there's any flak, I'll deal with it."

"That's great, Julie. Thanks so much. We're on our way now."

When they left the station and walked to the parking ramp across the street, they failed to see the man standing in the shadows of Orchestra Hall, a man Gabby had last seen staring after her in the gymnasium in Travis.

TWENTY-ONE

. . .

A s they waited in the lobby of The Haven, Gabby could sense Jesse's nervousness. "Are you ready for this?" she asked.

"I guess so, but I haven't seen her in more than a year. I don't know what to expect."

At that moment, Julie O'Connell emerged from her office, wearing a warm smile as she approached them. "Hey, Gabby," she said, "Welcome back." Then, holding out her hand, "And you must be Jesse. I'm glad you could make it. I know Jennie will be delighted to see you."

"Thank you so much," he replied, his uneasiness showing as he took her hand. "I appreciate your letting me see her. Gabby told me you're taking a chance doing it."

She shrugged. "I hope it's not a problem, but if it is, it's my problem, not yours."

"Does she know I'm coming?"

"Yes. I thought I had to tell her. She's in a fragile state right now and I didn't want to surprise her. To give her some time to adjust to the idea."

Jesse said, "So how is she?"

She thought for a moment. "She's all right, I suppose, but she's worried about what may happen next. And is still terribly sad about her friend's death. A tutor is helping with her studies, but she sticks pretty much to herself. Hasn't made any real friends. But there've been no behavior problems and no attempts to run. She's just a lonely, brittle kid like so many others we see. Only younger than most."

"Have my parents been here to see her?"

"Not yet. Not until the child protection people see and talk to her. But they know she's safe."

"And when will those child protection people come?"

"Soon, I think. Maybe tomorrow. We're still waiting to hear."

"And will I be able to see them, talk to them?"

"I would hope so, but that will be up to them. I can't see them refusing."

At that, she led them through the lobby door to Jennie's room and paused, saying, "I think we should go in together," but then, to Gabby, "After that, we should leave them alone for a time."

"I understand," she replied.

Jennie must have heard them approach—for when the door opened she took one look and flung herself into Jesse's arms, tears streaming down her cheeks. No words, just a muffled cry.

"Hey, hey," he said, holding her, "it's okay, I'm here." Still, she would not let loose, burying her face in his chest.

Gabby and Julie stood back, still at the door, overcome by what they saw.

Jesse finally freed himself of her hug and held her out from him, kneeling to look her in the eyes, "Hey, sis, shut off the tears, okay. Everything's going to be all right."

She wiped at the tears and looked over his shoulder, seeing Julie and Gabby. "Thank you so much," she whispered to them. "Thank you, thank you."

"We're going to leave you two alone for awhile," Julie said. "Come find us after you've had a chance to get reacquainted."

Almost an hour passed before the two came through the door to find Gabby sitting alone, reading the online version of the *Star*

Tribune on her cell phone. They came to sit next to her, Jesse's arm protectively around his sister.

She put the phone aside. "So how did it go?"

Jesse said, "She's told me everything. From the crap she's been getting at home to her time on the street. About you and Zach and Hannah. All of it was hard to take and I still can't believe I knew almost nothing about it."

"She's been a brave young woman," Gabby said.

"No kidding. She's faced more in a few weeks than most kids ever do. And she's not even sixteen years old, for God's sake."

Before Gabby could reply, her phone sounded. "Give me a minute," she said, moving away.

"Gabby?"

"Yes."

"This is Hooper."

"Hey, Howard."

"I just talked to Sheriff Henderson. You remember that unsolved rape he told us about in Lincoln County?"

Gabby felt her pulse quicken. "Of course."

"Well, as you suggested, the sheriff over there got Klinger's DNA from the cops down in Nebraska. And guess what?"

"It's a match."

"You got it."

"YES!" she blurted, sticking her folded fist into the air, drawing startled looks from Jesse and Jennie across the way.

"Hey, calm down," he said. "But you should be proud. You have their thanks."

"Tell me about it. The rape."

"Pretty much like the one in Nebraska. High school girl on the way home from a game. Small town of Hayburn. Assaulted and left lying in the street. She survived, but had no clue about her attacker. There's now a warrant out for Klinger, but no one knows where the hell he is."

"Can you do me a big favor?"

"I'll try."

"Hold off on your story, if you can. Until I get a chance to do my own."

"That's not a problem. We don't publish for another three days. But I can't guarantee someone else down here won't do it."

"I'll have to take my chances. But another thing. Would you get me everything you can about the rape?"

"Sure. I know the sheriff in Lincoln County, too. I'll get you the details as quick as I can."

"Thanks." Then. "Have I ever told you that you remind me of my father? Who was also a newspaper guy?"

"No."

"Well, you do. And that's a big compliment."

She glanced at her watch and hurriedly placed a call to Barclay. "I thought you were on vacation," he said.

"I am, but I have some news," repeating what she had just learned. "That means we can do the Klinger story, and do it before somebody else down there does it."

"What'd you mean?"

"I'd like to do a piece for the ten o'clock show, if you could save me some space."

"How much space?"

"Two minutes, maybe a little more. I'll need to use some of the footage from the funeral and the farm...so you should alert Zach, if he's around."

"I don't know, Gabby, it's almost two o'clock now and where the hell are you?"

"I'm at The Haven with Jesse and Jennie, but I can be back at the station in a half hour or so. There should be time to put the piece together by ten."

A moment passed. Then another. She could sense his doubt in the silence.

Finally, "We'll give it a try. But remember, I'll need to see the piece before it goes on the air."

"I understand."

She tucked the phone in her pocket and walked back to Jesse and Jennie. "Something important has come up and I need to get back to the station. So what do you two plan to do?"

"We're going to talk to Mrs. O'Connell," Jesse said, standing up. "Tell her what we've told you. And I'll tell her where I'm staying in case the child protection people schedule a visit. And in case I don't get to see them, I'll be working on the affidavit you asked me to write, telling them about my own bullying by our dad."

"That's great," she said. "And where are you staying?"

"At the Hilton, across from your station."

"All right. I'll give you a call in the morning and see where things stand." And to Jennie, she said, "Stay strong, young lady. I'll be back as soon as I can. Meantime, be patient. Be good. And enjoy this time with your brother."

When she walked into the newsroom, she could feel the urgency in the air. Barclay had alerted the ten o'clock producer and the rest of the nighttime staff of what could be coming. She found Zach in one of the editing rooms, rolling through the funeral video, searching for any shots that included the image of Arnold Klinger. "Are you sure you're up to this?" he said as she looked over his shoulder. "I hope so," she replied. "I'm going to give it my best shot."

She slipped off her coat and settled in at her desk, flipping on her computer to find an email from Howard Hooper with the criminal complaint on the rape from Lincoln County. She quickly scanned it and found a few more details than she already knew, including the fact that the rape had occurred in early September, about a month before Klinger's attempted rape of Hannah. And, not surprisingly, that he was now the subject of a widespread search.

She made a copy of the complaint and sat back, trying to get her thoughts together. Where to begin? How to tell this story as compactly and as understandably as possible? As she mulled this over, Barclay came across the newsroom. "Need some help?" he asked.

"Not yet. Just trying to figure things out. Getting started is always the hard part."

"Well, I'll be here," he said. "Right up until ten o'clock. So if you need me, or anything, just give me a shout."

As he was about leave, Harry Wilson, the assignment editor, walked over. "Don't want to bother you, Gabby, know you're in a crunch, but I thought you should know that you've gotten a couple of strange calls."

Barclay stopped in his tracks. "What kind of calls?"

"Male. No name. Asked for her, then hung up without another word. Three calls, all this morning before Gabby got in."

"Did you get a number?" she asked.

"Yeah. After the second call. Tried it several times since but got no answer."

"Shit," Barclay muttered. "What's *that* about? Probably just one of your fans."

She wasn't so sure.

"I'll get you the number," Wilson said as he walked away.

The rest of the afternoon and the early evening were a blur, the hours passing by quickly as she crouched over her computer, mostly unaware of what was happening around her. As if she was in her own little space capsule, floating, emerging only to make trips to the bathroom and to accept cups of coffee and cans of Diet Coke from Zach—who also brought her a video shot-list of scenes from the funeral. Her back and shoulders ached and her fingers felt numb from the writing and rewriting.

Get it right, she kept telling herself. Get it right.

As it approached six o'clock, Barclay stopped by. "You almost finished?" he asked. "You've got to give Zach time to put the piece together."

"I know. I'm almost there."

"Anything for me to see?"

She looked at her watch. "Twenty minutes, max."

She knew she had precious little video to work with. Most of the report would have her live on the news set, telling the story she had so yearned to tell. Time to see justice for Hannah, she told herself. Time to tell the truth. Finally.

True to her word, within twenty minutes she brought the finished copy to Barclay, waiting as he read it. "So?" she said.

"I think it's great. I'll make a couple of quick suggestions and get it back to you and to Zach. Meantime, why don't you head over to The Local and get something to eat. I don't want you fainting on the set when ten o'clock rolls around."

"All right, but instead of that, can I run home to eat? I need a fresh change of clothes, too. Feels like I've been in these for days."

"That's fine. Just don't get lost on your way back or we'll have to find something else to fill your couple minutes of the newscast. Or go to black."

When she arrived at the apartment and put the key in the lock, the door opened slightly. No more than an inch. Surprised, she quickly stepped back and glanced down the hallway. She saw or heard no one. Just the muted sounds of a guitar from the apartment next door.

Her mind quickly raced back to the morning. *Think!* Of course, the phone call from Jesse, the rush to meet him at the station, her thoughts jumbled at the time. But could she have forgotten to lock the door? Maybe, but not likely. She never had before.

Now, cautiously, she used a toe to push the door fully open, ready to flee or scream if she saw or heard anything. But there were no sounds, no movement. Even the poodle, which normally would be jumping at her feet, lay quietly on the sofa, staring at her. Was that fear in his eyes?

"Hey, buddy," she whispered. "What's up? What's going on? Come over here."

But he lay unmoving. Only when she crept closer and knelt next to him did she see the swelling and a trace of blood next to his right eye. She gently put her fingers beneath his jaw and raised his head. "My, God, what happened to you?" His answer: a slight whimper as he tried to lick her fingers.

Shaken, and fearful of venturing farther into the apartment, she picked up the dog and held him to her chest as she reached for her phone and punched in the apartment manager's office. It was answered immediately. "This is Gabby Gooding in apartment 206. I need someone up her now! I think the apartment's been broken into."

He was there in less than two minutes. A man she knew only as Vince, young, probably in his early twenties, with close-cropped hair and muscles to spare. He carried a golf club in one hand, like a weapon. "Best I could come up with," he said with an apologetic smile.

"I don't think you'll need it," she replied. "But thanks for the quick response." While they had met only once or twice before, he knew who she and Zach were and where they worked.

As she gently put the poodle back on the sofa, she quickly told him what she had found. "Have you looked farther?" he asked. "Have you called 911?"

"No, neither. And no 911 'til we see if anything's missing. Just walk with me."

They quietly moved through the apartment, feeling a little foolish as they checked behind furniture and carefully opened closet doors. But as they paused outside the office, there on the floor, next to the desk, lay a broken picture frame, upside down, pieces of glass scattered around it. Without a word, Gabby moved to it and carefully turned it over. Torn to shreds were the fragments of what had been an 8X10 copy of a selfie she had taken of herself and Zach the night he'd proposed to her.

"Damn," she whispered, gathering up the pieces, avoiding the shards of glass.

Vince stood back. "Are you okay?"

"I guess. It was a picture of my fiancé and me."

"Are you kidding? That's pretty strange, huh? An old, jealous boyfriend, maybe?"

Without replying, she put the remnants of the photo on the desk, knowing it was no old boyfriend. And already suspecting who it was.

They continued their tour, seeing nothing more until they stopped outside the bedroom door. Inside, one of the dresser drawers had been thrown onto the bed and its contents spread across the floor.

Her underwear.

Panties, bras, slips and nighties. Scattered about, but some bunched in a ball, as if they'd been held and maybe fondled.

She moved inside and began to gather the pieces up.

"This is really weird," she heard from Vince behind her. "I gotta call the cops."

"No, not yet," she said. "Give me a minute to think."

"I have no choice," he replied. "This is breaking and entering. We've got rules."

"Then you're going to have to be here to meet them. I've got to get back to the station, like now. I'm going on the air at ten and I have to show up."

After a moment, he said, "I'll call my boss. Maybe we don't have report it since it looks like nothing was taken. The cops have enough on their hands without dealing with some creepy pervert."

"That would be great…"

"Also, I'm off duty in a half hour…but if you'd like me to babysit your apartment and your dog until you get back later tonight, I'd be happy to do it."

"We'd pay you…"

"No need for that. Least I can do."

"If you're sure."

She hit the speed dial on her phone and Zach answered immediately. She quickly reported what had happened. *Are you kidding me?* he blurted. *"Are you okay? Is the dog okay?"*

156

"Calm down," she said. "We're both okay. But he must have kicked Barclay or something," explaining his bruise and cut. "We'll get him to the vet tomorrow."

"Not tomorrow. Tonight," he said. "I've finished editing your ten o'clock piece. It will be waiting for you when you get back here. I'll head home now and try to find an emergency vet."

"Fine. Vince from the office downstairs says he'll be here waiting and the two of you can figure out what to do next."

"This is incredible," Zach replied. "Was it Klinger?"

"That's my guess," she said. "But there's no proof."

"I'll kill the bastard!"

"Better hurry. Before he kills *me* with his lust and love."

"Oh, yeah? Just watch that twisted love turn to twisted hate once he sees what you're reporting tonight."

She could feel a shiver pass through her body.

TWENTY-TWO

. . .

At ten minutes to ten Gabby climbed onto her chair on the news set, to the right of the two seats soon to be occupied by the show's coanchors, Andrea Neusem and Scott Gilgrist. The studio was cool, lighted by big fluorescent lights and all but deserted— except for a floor director who would be giving the camera cues and who already had given Gabby the earpiece she wore.

Off to one side, in the weather center, one of the station's meteorologists was preparing that night's weather graphics. Unseen in the control room, the director/technical director had run through the intricacies of the pending newscast with an automated system that would code and control virtually everything: the graphics, the TelePrompTer, and the three robotic studio cameras. All to prevent possible human error, and also, in the case of the cameras, to cut costs. Before her time, Gabby knew the cameras were operated by humans, and she still found it strange and a little spooky to see the big unmanned cameras moving and turning, dancelike, across the studio floor.

The drive from the apartment to the station had been nightmarish. Blinding headlights piercing her eyes and the darkened streets, snow pellets pounding the windshield. Driving as if by remote control, gripped with the fear of what she had left behind and the fear of what lay ahead. Could she really go on the air after this?

There was no choice.

By the time she'd arrived at the station, Zach already had left and Barclay had met her at the newsroom door, offering both comfort and confidence. "Everything is ready for you," he'd said. "Everyone knows what you've gone through and stand ready to help in any way. You'll be fine, trust me."

Trust myself, she'd thought.

"And you should know," Barclay had added, "I had to tell Ryan, our esteemed general manager, that we were going with the story. I had promised him that."

"And?" she'd replied.

"He's nervous, afraid of offending his buddy on the governor's commission, but he made no effort to try and kill it. I'll give him that."

She had spent the past twenty minutes in the Green Room, in front of the mirror, touching up her makeup, fussing with her hair and clothes, and then, once again, reviewing the script in her hand. As she'd left for the studio, she ran into the newscast director, who would be in the control room, calling the shots. "You'll be great, Gabby," he said. "You're a pro. You've done it dozens of times."

Yeah, she thought, but not often at the top of the newscast— leading the show with a story that had been promoted all afternoon as an exclusive new development in the Hannah Hendricks murder.

At seven minutes to ten, Andrea and Scott arrived in the studio, greeted her and took their places, adjusting their chairs and plugging in their ear pieces. *They're the pros*, Gabby thought. Andrea was lithe and statuesque, although that was hard to tell as she sat behind the anchor desk, and brunette, unusual for a woman in television, where blond was the hair color of choice. While she certainly was attractive, Gabby thought of her features as more wholesome than beautiful, her skin fresh, absent the overdone makeup often seen on the television screen. Scott, Gabby had to admit, was downright gorgeous. In his late-thirties, he could have walked out of any catalog or movie set but, in fact, had been on the street covering the news in one city or another for the past fifteen years. While she didn't know either of them well, she had learned to respect their on-air ease and the reporting she had seen them do. And unlike other anchors in the market, they tried to keep the inane chatter to a minimum and concentrate on the news.

Barclay would have had it no other way.

After the control room did a quick microphone and TelePrompTer check, the studio lights came up and the wait began. "You okay?" Andrea asked. "We heard what you've just gone through. Scary stuff."

"I'm fine, thanks," Gabby replied. "I just hope this goes well."

Despite the tension that had gripped her earlier, while writing the piece, and later, while living through the turmoil at the apartment, she now felt a strange calm. She was pleased with the script and excited by the chance to tell the story. Before she'd walked to the set, she had called both Rosemary Klinger and Howard Hooper to tell them the story was about to go on the air. Mrs. Klinger, it turned out, was by then aware of the new rape charges against her husband and said she and her sons were now trying to cope with that news. Gabby promised to call again as soon as she could.

At thirty seconds before ten, the floor director shouted "Stand by! Comin' at yah." Then, at precisely ten o'clock, the Channel Seven News open rolled by and the studio scene opened up to a two-shot of the anchors with the photo of Hannah Hendricks over their shoulders, between them.

SCOTT: *"Good evening everyone. There are new developments tonight in the brutal murder of Hannah Hendricks, the eighteen-year-old whose body was found in a Minneapolis parking lot ten days ago.*

ANDREA: *Before her murder, she had been wanted in Lyon County for the October fifteenth stabbing of her stepdad, Arnold Klinger, on a night while the rest of the family was away. She fled to Minneapolis where weeks later—before law enforcement could find her—she was killed.*

THREE SHOT, INCLUDING GABBY: *Here with the background and the new developments that could shed light on what happened to Hannah Hendricks is reporter Gabby Gooding, who has been following this fascinating case from the beginning.*

GABBY, LIVE ON CAMERA: *Hannah came from the small western Minnesota town of Delroy, where on that October night she stabbed her stepfather and fled to Minneapolis before she could be arrested. There seemed to be no doubt that she had committed the crime, but no official motive for the stabbing was ever revealed, or known, and Hannah went to her grave a few days ago suspected of trying to kill her stepfather for no known reason.*

VIDEO OF FARM: *The stabbing happened at this isolated, rural farmhouse where Hannah lived with her mother, Rosemary Klinger, two younger brothers and her stepfather. According to local law enforcement, the stepfather, Klinger, said he was stabbed after a heated argument with Hannah over a boyfriend...late that night.*

GABBY LIVE: *However, after fleeing to Minneapolis, Hannah befriended a young runaway from northern Minnesota, to whom she told a quite different story: that the stabbing happened as her stepfather tried to rape her. That she kept a knife under her pillow because she was so afraid of him. But who in her hometown would believe her? There was no proof. And because she had made the decision to flee...she was not there to defend herself or to report the assault to authorities. At the time, while we were not free to report on the allegations made by Hannah to the young runaway, we decided to investigate further.*

VIDEO OF FUNERAL: *Before Hannah's funeral, as stepfather Klinger sat with the rest of the mourning family, our investigation moved forward and revealed that several years before he married Hannah's mother, Klinger had been convicted and imprisoned for raping and almost killing a seventeen-year-old girl in Nebraska. Hannah's mother would later tell us that she knew nothing of his past record at the time of their marriage or after. Nor did local law enforcement in Lyon County, where the stabbing happened.*

GABBY LIVE, with pic of Hannah over her shoulder: *But it did raise a crucial question: did Klinger's past rape conviction give credence to Hannah's claim that she stabbed him only as he tried to rape her? Of course it did, but again, there was no proof. And we may never know for sure…because Hannah was murdered in Minneapolis before she could tell her story to anyone besides the young runaway. Who told us.*

Now, however, we can report, exclusively, that Arnold Klinger is being sought for the rape of yet another young woman, this one in neighboring Lincoln County, in the town of Hayburn, less than a month before Hannah Hendricks claimed that he had attempted to rape her. A warrant has been issued for his arrest and at last word he is on the loose and the subject of intensive search. He is said to be driving a 2014 Ford F-150 pickup, license number 348-WFT. If you see him, please call 911 or the Lyon County sheriff, whose number you see on the bottom of the screen.

GABBY LIVE, close-up on camera: *Now, finally, if I may be allowed a personal word. This investigation began because of Channel Seven's interest in the plight of homeless children in our cities…where several hundred are on the streets or in the shelters every night. Often ignored, often exploited. It was because of one of the homeless youth we met that we were able to learn the apparent truth about Hannah Hendricks and to now report it, in the hope that the truth will live on in the little town of Delroy and beyond. But in the meantime, Hannah's murder in Minneapolis remains unsolved…and we will continue to follow that investigation, as well.*

THREE SHOT, SCOTT: *A couple of quick questions, Gabby, if I may. What is the current status of the murder investigation?*

GABBY: *To my knowledge, there have been no breakthroughs. No suspects. But I do know that several Minneapolis Homicide detectives are working on the case as we speak. So hopefully something will break soon.*

SCOTT: *And what about the young runaway whom you met and who gave you that information about Hannah? What has happened to her?*

GABBY: *She is safely in a shelter here in the metro area and will soon be talking to child protection people from her home county up north. She's a wonderful young woman and I continue to be in contact with her and helping her in any way I can.*

ANDREA: *Thank you so much, Gabby. We know you'll continue to keep on top of this story.*

As the three-shot became a two-shot and the anchors moved on to the next story, Gabby heard the director in her earpiece, "Good job, Gabby. But hang tight until we go to the commercial break in about four minutes. Okay?"

She gave a quick nod and settled back in her chair with a quick glance out into the semi-darkness of the studio—seeing Barclay standing behind the big cameras, giving her a thumbs-up.

By the time the first commercial popped up, the four minutes had seemed like a half hour. But before she could step off the set, Andrea rose up out of her anchor chair and leaned across the desk. "Excellent job, Gabby. I just hope they get this guy...or both guys, I guess. The killer *and* the rapist."

"So do I," Gabby replied. "The sooner the better."

Then, as she walked across the studio to join Barclay, she paused to check her phone—finding three texts, from Howard Hooper, Rosemary Klinger and Sara Chan, all congratulating her on her story. Then a fourth showed up, from Julie O'Connell, "Wadena County child protection here at ten tomorrow morning. Can u and Jesse be here?" Gabby quickly thumbed in a reply, "We'll try."

When she reached Barclay, the commercial break was over and the floor director was giving them a finger-to-the-lips signal. So she had to be satisfied with a firm handshake from Barclay, who then, in her ear, whispered, "Just got a text from Ryan. The jerk thought you did a good job." Despite herself, she couldn't help but let out a quick but audible giggle, drawing a sharp glance from the floor director.

As they walked out of the studio and into the newsroom, Gabby hurriedly placed a call to Jesse Nystrom at his hotel, repeating the text message from Julie O'Connell. "Is it okay if I pick you up a little after nine in the morning?" she asked.

"Sure," he replied. "Should I bring anything?"

"Only those affidavits, if you've finished with them."

"Gotcha."

"One more thing," she said, as an afterthought. "Did you bring your Army uniform with you?"

"It's in my suitcase."

"Wear it, please," she said. "That might help."

Later, as she was packing up her things, both the ten o'clock producer and the show's director stopped by to add their thanks for her quick and hard work. "I can just see everybody else in town scrambling to catch up on the story," the producer, Sam Allard, said. "And I hope we can stay ahead of the game."

"I'll give it my best," she replied.

A few minutes later, as she walked out of the station, she again ran into Barclay, this time at the back door, bundled up in a heavy overcoat, thick gloves, earmuffs, and a wool scarf wrapped around his nose and mouth. "Is that you?" Gabby said, leaning in close, with a smile, "Sure you'll be warm enough?"

"Don't be wise," he said. "I gotta' walk eight blocks home while you're riding in your toasty warm car."

"Do you want a lift?"

"No thanks. My wife thinks I need the exercise. But you'll notice she's not out here freezin' *her* ass."

Gabby laughed as they started to walk away.

"Wait a sec," he called out. "In the middle of everything, I forgot to tell you that Wilson checked on those phone calls you were getting this morning. He tried calling the number several times during the day, but never got a response. And whoever it was never called back after those first few calls."

"Probably some crank," she said, more confidently than she suddenly felt, especially in light of the apartment break-in. She didn't get those types of hang-up calls often, but when she did, they gave her pause. It was only a few months before when she'd received similar calls from the old boyfriend who had followed her from

California, eventually dying in his foiled-attempt to abduct her.

"You okay?" Barclay asked, studying her.

"Sure," she said, shaking off the memory. "I'm fine. I need to get home to Zach."

"Can I have one of our security people drive you there?"

"No, no. Just walk me to my car. It's right over there."

By the time she got to the apartment, it was after eleven. She found the door unlocked, the lights on, and Zach and the poodle sound asleep on the sofa, the dog snuggling against Zach's chest. She quietly closed the door, slipped off her coat and knelt next to them, gently touching Zach's knee.

"Hey, guys, it's me. Time to wake up and go to bed."

The dog's eyes opened first, then closed again as Zach stirred and stifled a yawn. "Well, hi there," he said, groggily, taking her hand from his knee and kissing the back of it. "Welcome home. I saw your piece. You did great."

"Thanks, but forget about that. Is everything okay here?"

"The pup's going to be all right. The vet says the bump on his head and the cut around his eye will both heal with time, but it may take a bit longer for him to get over the shock of the attack. He keeps looking at me with those sad, sort-of-fearful eyes."

"Poor thing," Gabby said, stroking his soft fur. "Don't worry. We'll spoil the hell out of you."

Zach got up and stretched, then bent to pick up an empty wine glass from the floor next to the sofa. "Vince from downstairs stayed here while I was at the vet. Says they'll put in a new lock on the door tomorrow, which he claims will be pick-proof."

"Yeah, right," Gabby replied, rolling her eyes.

"I took all of the undies you threw in the washer and put 'em in the dryer. They should be dry by now."

"I'm not sure I'll ever wear them again. Even after the washing. The thought of his hands on them makes me want to vomit."

He took her hand and walked her into the kitchen, pouring

each of them a small glass of red wine. "We need to talk about this," he said.

"Tonight?" she asked plaintively, sipping the wine. "I'm beat. You must be, too."

"That's true," he said, pulling out a chair for each of them. "But it's best while things are still fresh in our heads."

She let out a sigh. "Go ahead."

"If it was Klinger…and who else could it be…then it's an all-new ballgame, to use an old cliché. He's got some kind weird attraction to you, which could make him more dangerous and more unpredictable than even your old boyfriend."

"But what can we do?" she asked. "We have to live our lives. We have to do our jobs. We can't go into hiding. We can't go to and from the station in an armored car."

"Maybe we'll have to do some of those things," he said. "At least until Klinger's behind bars."

"And when will that be? And what about Jennie? What about Hannah? We can't leave Jennie in the lurch and forget about Hannah's murder. Especially after what I've just reported about Klinger."

"I know, but…"

"We've got to get to bed, Zach. My eyes won't stay open and this wine isn't helping. I have to pick up Jesse in the morning and try to deal with Jennie's situation. We both need some sleep. Please."

"Okay, but this discussion isn't over. Promise me."

She held up her right hand. "I promise. Now go undress me."

He perked up. "I thought you wanted to sleep."

"First things, first," she said, with a coy smile. "I'm not *that* tired."

TWENTY-THREE

• • •

In the morning, when Gabby pulled up in front of the Hilton, she found Jesse already outside, all six-plus-feet of him, standing almost at attention in his Army service or dress uniform—his Sergeant stripes on the sleeves and gold braids running down the sides of his slacks. On his chest, a couple of rows of colored ribbons. On his head, a black beret. A topcoat was draped over one arm.

The sight of him didn't quite take her breath away, but close. And this time, she felt like it should be her giving him the salute.

After a quick beep of the horn he spotted her and hurried over as she leaned across to open the door. "Good morning," he said, as he slipped onto the passenger seat. "Thanks for picking me up."

"Not a problem," she replied. "And I have to tell you, you look dashing."

"Thanks. I wasn't sure I'd need the uniform, but I'm glad I brought it along."

She slipped the car into gear and eased onto the street. Traffic was light as they moved out of downtown and toward the suburb of Brooklyn Park. "So, tell me, how do you like the Army?"

"It's okay. I've made a lot of friends and have grown up a lot in the last few years. It can get a little scary at times on some of our missions, but you soon learn to keep your head down and watch where you're walking. And hope for the best, I guess."

"I can't imagine what it's like."

"It's probably best you not know."

"You plan to make the Army a career?"

"Not really. I'm pretty good at technical stuff, so maybe I can make a living in the software or computer business. I've been taking online classes to try and get prepared. And I have a few months to decide."

Neither spoke for a few moments as she navigated the downtown streets. Finally, he said, "Do you know what's going to happen when we get there?"

"I have no idea," she replied. "This is all new to me, too."

"I finished the affidavit you asked me to do."

"Terrific. Could you read it to me while we're driving?"

He reached into his breast pocket and pulled out a sheet of paper. "I should have told you that while I'm okay at technical stuff, I'm not very good at writing. Almost flunked English in high school."

"That's no problem. Go ahead."

He held the paper up and read. *My name is Jesse Oliver Nystrom. I am the son of Curtis and Marion Nystrom and the older brother of Jennifer, Jennie, Nystrom. I currently am serving in the U.S. Army, stationed at Fort Hood, Texas, and have returned to Minnesota to support my sister in what she says our father has done to her and why she has had to run away. I left my home more than three years ago and joined the Army because of my father's continued physical abuse of me, including punching and kicking me, twisting my arms behind my back until I thought they would break, and, if you can believe this, once putting my fingers on the top of the hot stove burner because he thought I had smoked weed.*

He stopped there and turned. "You should know my chaplain friend helped me write this. He wanted to make it as good as I could and still be me."

"You're doing fine," she said. "Keep going."

He refocused on the paper.

And these things did not happen just once, but often. Especially when he'd been drinking and lost control of himself. And while I did not personally see him physically abuse Jennie, I did witness him attacking her verbally and insulting and threatening her on numerous occasions. When she was only eleven or twelve years old. I also saw him attack my mother several times when she tried to stop his abuse of me and Jennie. Including breaking her arm once. I know I should have spoken out before this, and I take full responsibility for not doing so, but I cannot believe that anyone who is responsible for a child's safety and welfare would consider returning Jennie to my parents' home. Based on my own experiences, I am not exaggerating when I say Jennie could very well end up dead at my father's hands. I am willing to testify personally to all of this, if asked.

Gabby looked across at him. "Those are powerful words, Jesse."

"They're all true," he replied. "You can't know what it's like, living in that house."

"You're right, I can't. But Jennie does. And between the two of you, maybe you can convince the child protection person that she can't go back there, not the way it is."

"Maybe so, but I bet my dad's already filled their ears with a bunch of bullshit. Probably claims Jennie is just a spoiled, troubled kid that he can't control. Hangs out with the wrong kids. Lies and manipulates people. He can be a pretty convincing, Gabby. I've seen it often."

"And I can believe it," she replied.

Now, as they pulled into The Haven parking lot, she was surprised to spot Sarah Chan, in plain clothes, standing by her unmarked squad car. Gabby parked next to her. "Didn't know you were going to be here."

"Julie asked me to come. Thought it might help to have somebody from law enforcement here. To report on how Jennie has helped in the Hannah investigation."

"Perfect."

Then, as Jesse unfolded himself and stepped out of the car to stretch, Gabby could hear a quick catch of breath and a low whistle leave Sarah's lips. She laughed, "Easy, girl, easy," she whispered.

And as he walked around the car, and before she could introduce them, Sarah stuck her hand out. "You must be Jesse. I'm Sergeant Sarah Chan, with the Minneapolis Police Department. I've been working with Gabby and Jennie."

He returned the handshake with an approving once-over. "I know. Jennie told me about you, that you're a friend and not like a lot of cops she's heard about. That's quite a compliment."

"Thanks, I guess."

Before they went further, Gabby said, "I should tell both of you about what happened last night," describing the apartment break-in and the clues left behind.

"Your underwear?" Sarah said.

"Yeah. You believe that? It had to be Klinger."

Jesse stood back, looking puzzled.

"It's a long story and we'll tell you about it when we have a chance," Gabby said. "But it has nothing to do with Jennie or why we're here."

As they walked toward the front entrance, she noticed a car on the other side of the lot with a Wadena County logo on the driver-side door. "They've already arrived," she said, pointing it out. "I thought we were early."

Sarah said, "They may have to do some paperwork with Julie before they can actually see Jennie. We'll soon know."

Mrs. Hansen, the stern-looking receptionist they had met once before was on duty again, but this time she was expecting them and buzzed them in, politely leading them across the lobby to their chairs. "Mrs. O'Connell will be with you as soon as she can," she said. "She's in a meeting at the moment."

"That's fine," Gabby replied. "Thank you."

They were left with nothing to do but look at one another and wonder what would come next. Finally, to Sarah, Jesse said, "I suppose they've already talked to my parents and gotten their side of the story."

"I'm sure they have," she replied. "It's been, what? Six or seven days since I brought Jennie here...since the county people were notified...so I suspect there have been several conversations, some of them stormy, I would guess. Knowing what we've heard about your father and his anger issues."

Jesse put his head in his hands then looked up at both of them. "All *we* can do is to tell the truth, if we get the chance."

Another twenty minutes passed. Gabby spent most of her time on her cell, scanning the web news sites while Sarah and Jesse chatted quietly, trading information about one another. Gabby would hear only snippets of their conversation, but sensed they were getting along quite well. Which made her smile.

She knew little about Sarah's personal life, but did know she was not married and had never mentioned any kind of serious relationship. But something seemed to be happening now.

After another fifteen minutes, the door from the offices opened and Julie O'Connell walked out in the company of a short, stout, matronly woman wearing a white fuzzy sweater over what Gabby could only describe as a house dress, the kind she remembered her grandmother would wear. Hanging loosely, comfortably on her body.

While she had a serious, all-business look about her as she and Julie approached, Gabby was surprised by the soft, gentle voice that greeted them. "I'm Eleanor Gladstone," she said. "From Wadena County, here, as you know, to see and speak to Jennie and, of course, to any of you who would like to speak to me."

With that, they all introduced themselves.

"Perhaps we should sit for a moment," she said. "Before I see Jennie. And to give me time to tell you where we are in the process."

"That would be great," Gabby said as they pulled their chairs into a small circle.

"As Julie may have told you, I would have been here sooner were we not so busy with other cases in our small county. Like many child protection agencies, we are overburdened and short-staffed and do our best to keep up." She paused, surveying the circle of faces.

"So here is the plan for today. I will spend some private time with Jennie, seeking as much information from her as possible. And then, as time allows, I'll speak to each of you for whatever insights you can provide. I would hope to complete all of this by mid-afternoon, to give me time for the long drive home."

Gabby leaned forward. "Will you take Jennie with you?"

"Not today. I'll need to report to my supervisor to decide what the next step will be. Julie has assured me that Jennie is welcome to stay here until a decision is made."

It was Jesse's turn. "Have you spoken to my parents? To my father?"

"Yes," she replied, with what Gabby thought was a small passing scowl, "several times. He is quite outspoken and eager to see Jennie returned home. But I can say no more about those conversations at this time."

"I've written an affidavit," he said, pulling out the paper. "I want you to have it whether we have time to speak or not."

"Good," she said, "I'll make it part of the record."

As they watched Julie lead her away, Sarah asked, "So what did you think?"

Jesse didn't hesitate. "I think she looks like somebody Jennie may trust. Like our Grandma Harriet, on my mother's side, who died several years ago and who Jennie loved. I think this lady will remind Jennie of her."

"She struck me the same way," Gabby said. "And my guess is, my hope is, that she'll try to comfort as well as question Jennie."

Before she could say more, her cell, tucked away in her bag, sounded. And once in her hand, she saw the now-familiar number of Howard Hooper, catching her again at The Haven.

"Hey, Howard. How goes it?"

"Fine, Gabby, thanks, but I have a little news for you."

She got up and walked away, just as Jesse handed Sarah a copy of his affidavit.

"So tell me," she said.

"You remember our county commissioner friend, Lester Updahl?"

"Of course. The guy who told Rosemary Klinger about Klinger's past."

"And the guy," Howard added, "who Klinger apparently thinks may have spread the word to others down here."

"And?"

"He has a farm outside of Travis…and very early this morning, while it was still dark, his barn caught on fire and burned to the ground, killing two of his prized sows."

She caught her breath. "No kidding," she whispered. "Was it arson?"

"I don't know. I'm not sure anybody does. Updahl wasn't home at the time. He and his wife were in the Cities visiting one of their kids. A neighbor spotted the flames and got there in time to save three horses before the barn collapsed, but he couldn't save the pigs."

"Did he spot anyone?"

"Not that I know of."

"Where did you learn about this?"

"Your friend the sheriff, Duane Henderson, called me just a few minutes ago and gave me what little information I have. One of my reporters is on his way there now."

"So what does Henderson think?"

"Nothing more for the record, but he did tell me something else, which is also why I'm calling."

"What else?" Gabby asked.

"He told me what you already know, that Klinger left a note to his wife before he fled. But he also told me what you don't know… that the note blamed two people for his problems. And I quote: 'Scumbag Updahl. Bitch reporter.' Want to guess who he's talking about?"

She sucked in her breath. Which left her speechless for a moment.

Hooper: "Are you there?"

"Yes, I'm here." Her voice wobbly. "Feeling a little shell-shocked, actually. I knew he'd left a note, but I've never seen it. Or knew what it said."

"Now you know. It could be a coincidence, but if this fire *is* a case of arson, and if it turns out that Klinger set it, Henderson wanted you to know what the note said. And the possible implications."

It was all making sense: the strange hang-up calls at the station and, of course, the invasion of the apartment.

"Thank you, so much, Howard. Thank the sheriff and please let me know what your reporter or the sheriff's people may discover about the fire. You should also know this—because it may be connected. Our apartment was broken into yesterday, which looks like the work of Klinger," explaining what they had found.

"Hey, I'm sorry. Are you okay?"

"I'm fine, but who knows? If it *was* him, he may have driven down to Updahl's farm to set the fire after leaving our apartment. Considering what he said in the note about the two of us, it seems possible."

"I agree," he said. "I'll pass that word on and keep in close touch."

"Thanks."

"One more thing, if I may." In a halting voice. "I Googled your father's name and learned about his work and reputation at the *Oregonian*. He was quite a guy and quite a journalist, and I'm proud that I remind you of him."

Before she could respond, the line went dead.

As she tried to absorb what she'd been told, Sarah walked over and sat next to her. "What's happening? You look a little distressed."

She shared what Hooper had reported.

"That's downright scary," Sarah said. "If this dude is out raping young girls and setting barns on fire...and fondling your underwear...and is that pissed off at you...or that bewitched by you...or both...I'd start to pack a piece."

174

Gabby couldn't help but laugh. "Oh, good. Should I wear the holster inside or outside my coat?"

"It's no joke, Gabby. I'm a cop. I see bad things happen to good people. And you should be the last person to flip off a possible threat after what you went through with that old boyfriend of yours, who—think about it—may not have been that different than Klinger. A psycho who thinks he's been dealt a bad hand, and that you're the dealer."

"You don't waste words, do you?" Gabby said.

"I also know that in your case, your particular psycho was brought down by a retired cop who *did* have a gun."

"Don't think I haven't thought about all of that. How could I not? It wasn't that long ago and it's never far out of my mind. But I'm not going to live in constant fear. I didn't then and I won't now."

"Being vigilant doesn't mean living in fear," Sarah said. "Watching your back, or having someone watch your back is not cowardly, it's smart. And from what you've just told me, it may be past the time to be smart. And alert."

TWENTY-FOUR

. . .

A full hour passed before Eleanor and Julie emerged through the door leading to Jennie's room, chatting softly, their expressions revealing little. Gabby flipped off her phone and stood with the others, waiting. "Please sit," Eleanor said as she and Julie each grabbed a chair, forming the same small circle.

Gabby sat, but then leaned in. Impatiently. "Tell us. How did it go?"

If Eleanor was surprised by the abrupt question, she didn't show it. She simply smiled and settled back in her chair. "I can only tell you that the interview went well. Jennie was very composed, considering her age and the situation she finds herself in. She answered all of my questions more calmly than I would have expected, and described in some detail what she claims has been happening at her home. That's about all I am free to say."

"That's good to hear," Gabby said, "but the crucial question is: did you believe her? Did you believe what she's told all of us and what she must have told you about her father and his abuse?"

"You know I can't answer that. I recorded our interview and it will go into the record...as will the interviews with her parents and all of you. Along with Jesse's affidavit. It will not be up to me, alone, to decide what is true and what is not. And what should happen with Jennie. I can only gather the best information on which to base those decisions."

Sarah looked at Julie. "You were there the whole time?"

"Yes, but I said nothing. I just chose to listen."

"But do you agree with what Eleanor has just told us?"

"About Jennie's demeanor, yes. There were no outbursts, no temper tantrums. I was quite proud of her for that."

Gabby stood up and faced Eleanor. "You know that she'll run again if she's sent back to that house…to that man."

As she was about to answer, Jesse, who was facing the front door, jumped to his feet, his face a sudden twisted mixture of surprise, anger, fear…and what? Hatred?

Then, from across the lobby, a booming voice, so loud, so penetrating that it seemed to reverberate off all the walls and ceiling, surrounding them, closing in on them from every direction. *"Where is she? What have you done with my girl?"*

Gabby later tried to decide how long it took for those still seated in the circle to realize what was happening. Five or six seconds, at most. In those vital seconds, total confusion. But then they all scrambled and stood staring across the lobby, seeing what Jesse already had seen: a big man, six-foot-four, at least, broadshouldered, big-bellied, spread-eagled like a gunslinger standing at the barroom door in the Old West. And, like the Old West, a holstered pistol clung to his belt.

Curtis Nystrom, Jennie's and Jesse's father had arrived.

Mrs. Hansen, at the reception desk, shrieked and slowly sank behind the desk. And from Sarah, who was now reaching for her own service pistol, a shouted, "Get down, get down. Now!" Gabby, Eleanor and Julie fell to their knees behind their chairs. But Jesse stayed upright, defiantly. Then he began to move forward, one purposeful step after the other, his head up, shoulders back.

"Jesse, get back!" Sarah shouted.

To no avail. He kept moving. When he was within about five feet of his father, the man smiled and said, "Well, lookie here. What'-d'-ya know? The soldier boy is back in town. All dressed up in his fancy uniform. Here to protect his little sister, right? Give it

177

up, Jesse boy. Little sister's coming home with daddy. Like now, as soon as I find her. These social worker jerks have had her too long. I'm done talkin'."

Jesse stood, unmoving, smelling the man's beery breath even from that distance. "'Fraid not, dad. She's staying here. Away from your bullying hands. And if I have my way, you may never see her again. You're not going to keep doing to her what you did to me. Those days are over."

"Up yours, son. I'm her father. I have rights."

By now, Sarah had moved up behind Jesse, her Glock held loosely by her side. "I take it you have a permit to carry that pistol, Mr. Nystrom?"

"Damn right," he said. "And who are you?"

She held out her badge. "I'm a police officer and I'm ordering you to unbuckle your holster and drop it to the floor. You must not have seen the sign on the door—that no weapons are allowed in here."

After a moment's hesitation, he did as he was told. "If you're a cop," he said with a sneer, "go find my little girl and bring her out here."

It was only then, looking over Sarah's shoulder, that he noticed Eleanor Gladstone. His ruddy face paled and he stepped back. "Eleanor! I didn't know you'd be here."

She marched up to him, stopping within inches of his face. "How did you find this place, Mr. Nystrom?" she demanded.

He stepped back. "None of your goddamned business," he sputtered. "I have my ways. And I'm here to get my daughter."

"I'm afraid that's not possible," she replied, staying in his face. "And you're not helping yourself by being here, barging in like this. Your daughter is here in protective care until a decision is made in her case. You've been told that more than once."

"And I'm tired of waiting. I wanna see her. Talk some sense into her." With that, he started to push past her, only to be met chest-to-chest by Sarah. "Mr. Nystrom, this is not my jurisdiction, but if you don't walk out that door immediately I will alert the Brooklyn Park police and have you arrested on a variety of charges, including breaking-and-entering and carrying a weapon into a prohibited space. Do you get that?"

For a moment, she thought he might spit in her face. But, then, with a "Screw you," he turned away and stooped to pick up his pistol.

"Hold on," Sarah said. "I'll hand you the weapon once you're outside that door."

"Pussy cops," he muttered as she picked up the gun and followed him to the door.

Once he was outside and walking to his car, Mrs. Hansen was back on her feet behind her desk. "I don't know how he got in," she exclaimed. "That door is always locked. I must have forgotten. I'm so sorry."

"And I have to apologize as well," Eleanor said. "I have no idea how he found us. I know none of our staff would have told him."

Julie stepped forward. "Forget that, but thank God Sergeant Chan was here. What would we have done without her? And what do we do if he comes back?"

"Make sure the door stays locked," Sarah said, "but I'll also give the Brooklyn Park PD a call to see if they'll keep an eye on the place."

"Thank you," Julie replied.

Eleanor took a deep breath. "Now that the excitement is over, can we get back to business? I need to record each of your interviews and be on my way."

As they turned to their chairs, they were startled to find young Jennie standing outside the door leading to her room. Erect, back against the door, noiselessly sobbing.

Julie was the first to react, and rushed over to her. "Jennie! My, God, how long have you been standing there? You're supposed to be in class!"

What did she see? Everything?

She took her in her arms. "Hey, calm down, okay? He's gone. We're here. Everything's going to be all right."

Jennie clung to her, the sobs slowly subsiding. Then she pulled away. "Why does he have to be such a shit? Why can't he be nice, like other dads? My friends' dads?"

As she struggled for an answer, and with a pleading glance at Eleanor, Julie finally said, "We don't know that, Jennie. Maybe he needs some help. Maybe Eleanor and others can find him some help."

At this point, Jesse walked up and took one of Jennie's hands. "C'mon, kiddo, let's let Julie wash those tears away and get you back to your class. And after that, we'll have more time to talk."

With a quick look back at the others, she gave a shy wave with one hand and clutched her brother's hand with the other, as he led her back through the door.

For the next two hours, Gabby, Sarah, and Jesse, one by one, told Eleanor of their experiences with Jennie. For Gabby, from the first moment she appeared at the television station through the search for Hannah, and—then—the devastating news of Hannah's murder. She admitted Jennie never did reveal many details of her father's abuse, except that it was pervasive and that her mother would not, or could not, do much to intervene.

"And I have to tell you that I never once doubted the essential truth of what she told me. She may have fudged here and there, but it was clear to me that she is an abused child."

Sarah picked up the story from the time Gabby first brought Jennie to her attention to her role in getting the girl safely to The Haven. "She's also been very helpful to our homicide detectives who are trying to solve Hannah's murder," she said. "In fact, the lead detective is still hoping Jennie can listen to the voices of their suspects, one of whom may have made that threatening call to her. That could happen any day now."

Jesse, for his part, basically elaborated on what he had written in his affidavit. "From what we just saw, you can understand the anger, the outrage he's capable of. And try to put yourself in my place, or Jennie's, home alone with him, surrounded by four walls where no one can hear or see the kind of abuse he can dish out, especially when he's had too much to drink or a bad day at the shop."

Eleanor recorded each of their interviews, interjecting questions of each before finally putting the recorder back in her briefcase. "I think that's all I need," she said. "I'll take all of this back to my boss and we'll see what happens next. I deeply appreciate your time and candor, and I'm very pleased to see that Jennie has such wonderful friends and such a safe place to be."

As she stood up to leave, Gabby asked, "When will we hear something?"

"Impossible to predict. It's a complicated case with no easy answers, I'm afraid."

"There is *one* easy answer," Jesse said. "She can't go back to him, not the way he is. She will only run again and once again be lost in that world of homeless kids. You can't let that happen. Please."

"We will do our very best," she replied.

As she walked away, Gabby caught up with her and pulled her aside. "Tell me, Eleanor, please, off the record, how does a guy like that have the kind of power and prestige I'm told he has in that county of yours?"

"I really can't discuss that," she said, turning away.

"Please!" Gabby said. "I have to understand."

Eleanor stopped. "Then you have to understand rural Minnesota. People live apart and are very protective of their privacy. Especially in small towns like Elsa. Your business is nobody else's business. As Jesse said, your home is your castle. Your walls are your moat. What happens inside those walls, that moat, is like, sacred.

"I will not speak directly about Mr. Nystrom, but it is entirely possible for a man to be highly-respected and liked in a small community, or in the county, by those who have never seen or ventured behind those walls. Whose personal privacy has been protected, by whatever means. Fear, threats, lies..."

"Still," Gabby protested.

"I'm sorry. I can say no more."

And with that...she was gone.

TWENTY-FIVE

...

When Gabby returned to the newsroom, she found Andy the intern at her desk, his facial bruises still showing but fading. The hair on the shaved the side of his head was returning, but his lips were still puffy and the skin around his eyes still dark. "Hey, big guy," she said, with a grin, "I thought I told you to stay away."

He got up and gave her a quick hug. "I'm bored and I missed you, okay?"

She settled into her chair. "Sorry I didn't get back to the hospital. I've been on the run ever since. But I hope you got the flowers from all of us."

"Yes, thanks. My mom took them home."

"So how are you?"

"On the mend, but as you can see, my good looks have not yet returned."

She smiled. "And how are the ribs?"

"Still sore as hell, but I'll survive. And ready to go back to work."

"What about school?"

"I'm getting caught up. And the profs have given me a lot of support."

"Great. And as you can guess, a lot has happened since I last saw you."

"I know some of it. I saw your report on the news. About Klinger and the fact that he's on the fly. But tell me more."

As best and as rapidly as she could, she reported on everything from Jennie's current situation… to Rosemary Klinger's visit …to the apartment invasion and then on to the latest from Lyon County on the farm fire.

"Wow," he said. "And they think Klinger may have set the fire?"

"I'm not sure. I haven't had the chance to call back. Or to tell Barclay or Zach about it. There's been no time. And I'm still officially on vacation."

"So what can I do to make myself helpful?"

She took a moment to think. "When you have time, sit down with the video from all of those interviews you've done and try to make some sense out of them. Edit them, bleep out all of the profanity, and make them flow for the eventual homeless youth piece I hope to do. At least get a start on it."

"I'll do that, but you should know I'm not done doing interviews. I've got a law school buddy who's as big as the guy who beat on me. And who's willing to serve as a kind of bodyguard when I'm out on the street."

"No kidding?"

"For real. He's got a kid brother who ran away a while back and got into some scrapes on the street. So he's interested in working with me."

"But you do understand that you're on your own."

"I understand."

"So beat it and get to work. I've gotta go find Barclay."

She found him standing at the assignment desk, chatting amicably with Harry Wilson. "Hey," he said when he turned to find her waiting. "Seems like you're here more on vacation than you are when you're working."

"Very funny," she replied. Then, "We need to talk."

He turned serious. "Why does that not surprise me? Your desk or my office?"

"Your office, please."

"Lemme grab a cup of coffee and I'll meet you there. Want one?"

"No, thanks."

She was sitting at his desk when he returned, coffee in hand. As he sat, he said, "You're looking even more serious than usual. So what's up?"

"You're not going to be happy," she replied.

"Why does *that* not surprise me?"

"It's going to sound like déjà vu all over again," she said, quickly repeating the phone call she'd received from Howard Hooper on the farm fire and the implied threat to her in Klinger's note to his wife. "He apparently referred to 'a bitch reporter,' which the sheriff thinks could be me. That he thinks I was the one who exposed him."

"Well," Barclay said, "it does sound familiar, like another guy who wants a piece of you."

"It's possible, I guess. Especially when you put it together with those strange calls and the thing at the apartment. I'm sorry to lay all of this on you, and it may be nothing, but I wanted you to be aware of it."

"Does Zach know about this?"

"No. He's on assignment and I just got back from Jennie's shelter. That's where I got the call from Hooper."

"And the sheriff thinks Klinger could be responsible for the Updahl farm fire?"

"That's the suspicion, but no proof, as far as I know. But it does seem like a strange coincidence, considering everything."

"Klinger's still on the loose?"

"Yes, I guess so."

He settled back in his chair. "It appears your little Jennie is not the only one who needs protection. Unfortunately, J.J.'s not available."

He was talking about John Jacobs, a retired St. Paul cop who became Gabby's bodyguard while she was being stalked by the old boyfriend…the man who fired the fatal shot that ended her ordeal. Although justified in what he had done, J.J. never did recover from the trauma and had since moved to Florida.

"I don't need a bodyguard," she said. "I'll stick close to Zach and watch my back."

He was clearly not convinced, but could think of no immediate alternative. Finally, "I'll grab a still-frame shot of Klinger off your video and give it to our security people at the doors. But promise me you'll never be alone. If you're not with Zach, you'll be in some public space, with people around you."

"Deal," she replied.

There could be no more public space than the crowded skyways linking the downtown office towers and apartment buildings. So she felt comfortable as she wound her way across town, by skyway and street, to City Hall, dodging in and out of the human traffic for a hastily arranged meeting with Homicide Detective John Archer. He had sounded harried and surprised by her phone call, but reluctantly agreed to give her twenty minutes, no more.

As it turned out, he kept her waiting for about forty-five minutes, which gave her time to flip through a couple of magazines and check her phone before he finally opened his office door and ushered her in. "Sorry for the wait," he said, "but I tried to warn you that things are kind of busy around here."

"No problem," she replied as she took a seat across from him. "I just appreciate any time you can give me."

"So what's up?" he said.

"A couple of things, but first can you tell me where you're at with the Hannah Hendricks investigation?"

"Off the record, more or less at a dead end," he admitted. "As Sergeant Chan has probably told you, we've interviewed several people, a few of them as a result of our talk with your young friend, Jennie. But we still have no results on possible DNA from the murder scene, and no other real leads at the moment."

"And you've heard about the attack on our intern, who was beaten up apparently for asking questions about the murder."

"Yes, I've read the report."

"Of the suspects you've interviewed..."

"Not suspects. Persons of interest."

"Okay, do any of them match the description of our intern's attacker?"

He considered the question. "I would say two or three would come close."

She shifted in her chair. "I'm no detective and don't pretend to be, but something occurred to me the other night after I did a report on the search for Arnold Klinger."

"I happened to see the report," he said. "You did a nice job."

"Thanks. And this may be off the wall, but what occurred to me is this: maybe her killer wasn't some pimp or random guy she met on the street, but," she paused, "someone who was determined to keep her quiet about her alleged rape?"

He smiled, clearly amused. "Are you talking about Klinger? I told you before, we checked him out. He's clean."

"I know, and I'm not talking about him actually. Even before you eliminated him, I never believed he could have done it. I haven't checked, but I'd be surprised if he's ever been in the Cities or away from the farm for any length of time. Certainly not long enough to find Hannah and kill her. Or to even know where to look."

Archer leaned across the desk, cupping his chin in his hands. "So, detective, if not Klinger, who would our mystery killer be?"

His benevolent skepticism was not lost on her. "Maybe a friend of Klinger's, or an acquaintance of some kind. Someone who lives here and could be capable of a murder like this."

"Like? You say Klinger's a farmer who never gets to the Cities."

"Like someone he may have met in prison years ago. You knew that he spent three years in the Nebraska State Penitentiary, didn't you? For rape?"

"Yeah, I remember. That was part of your TV report," he replied.

"Well, it may be worth your time to see if any of your persons of interest has spent time in there with him. Someone he's kept in touch with over all these years, someone who is now living here, in the Cities. Who may fit the description of our intern's attacker or whose voice might match the one Jennie heard on her phone. Someone who might be willing to kill to repay a long-ago debt to Klinger...or for money."

She started to get up. "I know it's a long shot and that you're probably regretting the short time you've given me, but I wanted to get it off my chest."

"Sit down, please," he said, his amused expression changing to one of respect. "You may not be a detective, but you've just shown me you have the instincts of one. Your hunch could be off the wall, but it's certainly worth checking out. And I will, as soon as I have the chance. I only wish that I or one of my detectives had thought of it first."

She got up and shook his hand. "One other thing," she said. "I have a personal interest in this. The sheriff in Lyon County thinks there's a good chance Klinger has a personal grudge against me for the reporting I've done...that he thinks I might have helped expose him...and, that he may want a chance to get even. So the sooner you can get to the bottom of all this, the better I'll feel."

On her way back to the station she decided to forego the skyways and brave the fresh but chilly November air and swirling snowflakes, ignoring Barclay's orders to stay in crowded spaces. Not to worry, she told herself. No one knows where I am or where I've been, and the sidewalks are virtually deserted. Still, she kept a watchful eye.

As she made her way up the Nicollet Mall, she suddenly realized she'd had nothing to eat since a quick breakfast hours before. So she stopped at the Starbucks, shed her coat and cap and ordered her cappuccino and a blueberry muffin. But before she could take a bite or a sip, her phone sounded. Sarah Chan.

"Hey, Sarah."

"Hey, yourself. Where are you?"

"At Starbucks, why?"

"I just got a call from Archer. He said you paid him a visit."

"Man, that was fast."

"He told me about your theory…that it sounded plausible."

"Good. I hoped I wasn't wasting his time."

"After you left, he arranged a visit with Jennie in the morning, to have her listen to the audio of the guys they've interviewed. He'd like to have you there."

She took a sip of the cappuccino, thinking ahead. "Sure, I guess so."

"He thinks you'd help put Jennie at ease. He'd like me there, too."

"Fine."

"I'll pick you up, like at eight, okay?"

"Great."

"One more thing," Sarah said. "Jesse and I are having dinner tonight…at the Hilton…and wondered if you and Zach would like to join us?"

It took Gabby only a moment. "Gosh, thanks but no thanks. I haven't seen Zach in ages and we have a lot to catch up on. Besides, I think it might be nice for the two of you to have some more time together. Like alone."

She laughed. "Okay, match-maker, match-maker. I'll see you in the morning."

TWENTY-SIX

. . .

Zach came through the door with no more than a brush of a kiss for her. "Anything you'd like to tell me?" he said, slipping off his coat and gloves, but leaving intact the irritation in his voice.

"Well," she replied innocently, "there's a pepperoni pizza ready to go in the oven and a glass of wine waiting for you on the kitchen table."

"That's it?" Ignoring the poodle trying to climb up his legs.

She picked up the dog and held him close. "Oh, no, lots more. But I thought we could talk over that glass of wine."

"I hope so," pushing past her. "Because I've just spent a half hour talking to our boss, who told me some scary things. Things I should have heard from you, not him."

"Hey, hold on," following him. "You've been gone all day and I've been running all over town. I'm not trying to keep any secrets... so let's shed the attitude, okay?"

"You could've called..."

"These aren't the kind of things you talk about on the phone. Besides, you were working and I was not about to get in your way."

They picked up their wine and returned to the living room sofa, one on each end, keeping their distance. "So what did Barclay tell you?"

"That Klinger not only left a note calling you 'a bitch reporter,' but may have set a goddamned barn on fire and is still on the loose. Who knows where, planning to do what? All of that on top of his wandering around in here like he owned the place, cuddling your panties." He took a sip of his wine. "I gotta tell you, Gabby, living with you can be like living in a war zone."

She burst out laughing, spraying him with a sprinkle of red wine. "God, give me a break!"

"Oh, yeah? How many months ago, now? Six? Since your old boyfriend…"

Her laughter suddenly turned to anger. "C'mon, that's history! Done and gone."

"Not that far gone."

She settled back and settled down. "Okay," she admitted with a sigh. "You're right. I do seem to be a magnet for trouble."

"And I always end up in the middle of it," he replied with some pique.

She leaned over and poked a finger in his chest. "Listen up. You don't have to be. You're the one who proposed to me, not the other way around. I can be out of your life tomorrow." Then, with a pause and a grin, "Of course, I get to take Barclay with me."

That broke the tension. "Fat chance. Do I get my ring back?"

"No way. It goes with me and Barclay. For the next guy who comes along."

He picked up the poodle and moved next to her. "Okay, smartass, so until then, what else do you have to tell me?"

She told him what had happened that morning with Jennie's dad.

"See what I mean! There you are, in trouble again. Facing a guy with a gun, for God's sake."

"It's not my fault," she shot back. "I just happened to be there. Luckily with a cop who also had a gun."

With a shake of his head, "You ought to write a memoir, 'The Life and Adventures of an Intrepid Reporter.' Except that it's going to sound like fiction."

She got up and took his empty glass. "I'll get each of us another one and put the pizza in the oven while you wash up. Because I've got more to tell you."

"I can hardly wait."

As they finished the last piece of pizza, she told him about her visit with Detective Archer and her theory of Hannah's murder.

He listened carefully but clearly was doubtful. "That seems like a stretch to me, Gabby, but who knows? Klinger seems capable of almost anything."

"I know it's a stretch and I admitted as much to Archer, but he seems to think it's worth checking out. Maybe he was just being nice, but it didn't strike me that way. And he did make the quick call to Sarah."

"How did you come up with this idea?"

"Hard to explain, but the more I thought about it, it didn't seem that implausible. There's apparently no other ready explanation for her death that the cops can figure out, and no obvious suspects. Of course, it could be just a random killing or done by one of the bad dudes that Jennie said they'd run into."

"If I were a betting man, I'd bet on that."

"I know, but one thing does seem clear. Whoever killed Hannah stayed around long enough to phone Jennie and to beat the hell out of Andy. So he could still be here."

"Or long gone. Those things happened days ago."

"True."

"And how did this killer find Hannah? To know where to look?"

She shrugged. "Got me, but she was pretty well known on the street."

He learned back. "So what's next for our intrepid reporter?"

"Archer's going to ask Jennie to listen to those persons of interest recordings in the morning and wants me and Sarah to be there, to help keep her calm. That's where I'll be, safe and sound with a couple of cops by my side. So you can relax."

"Oh, yeah? I've decided I can never relax, living with you."

Archer was already at The Haven, in the lobby talking to Julie O'Connell, by the time she and Sarah arrived. "Glad you could make it," he said as he stood to greet them. "Mrs. O'Connell said Jennie is waiting for us and knows why we're here."

"How is she doing?" Gabby asked Julie.

"About the same. She's made a few new friends, but still sticks pretty much to herself. Despite our efforts to draw her out. I think it'll just take more time, until all of this is finally decided."

"Her brother plans to visit this afternoon," Sarah said, "so that should help."

"Good," Julie said.

"What have you heard from Wadena County?" Gabby asked.

"Nothing. And I've made no effort to contact them. They've got some difficult decisions to make and it will take time."

With an impatient nod toward the lobby door, Archer said, "Can we see her now? I don't have a ton of time."

"Of course," Julie replied, leading the way.

They found Jennie sitting on the edge of her bed, wearing a baggy but clean sweatshirt and a too-long pair of jeans Gabby had left for her. There was a slight smile as Sarah and Gabby came across the room to give her a quick hug, then backed away to make room for Archer, who pulled up a chair next to her. "It's nice to see you again, Jennie. I can't tell you how much we appreciate your help as we try to find out what happened to Hannah."

She swiped away a single tear on her cheek. "Why is it taking so long?" she whispered.

"These things do," he replied, "but we're doing our best."

He removed a digital recorder from his briefcase and put it on a table next to them. "I'm going to play the voices of several men we have questioned about Hannah's murder. We asked each of them to repeat some of the words you told us you remembered from that phone call at the library. Remember?"

"Yes," she said.

He went on. "Since they'll all be saying the same words, they may sound much alike, but their voices will be different and we hope that you might recognize a voice that sounds like the man you heard on the phone. And I'm going to give you a pencil and a sheet of paper with the numbers one through five on it. You should put a check by the number of one or more that bring back that memory. Can you do that?"

"I'll try."

"This is Number One," he said, touching a button on the recorder. *"Forget her. Stop hunting for her. Don't screw with me. For your sake. You've got a life…so give it up."*

Gabby leaned in and listened carefully, watching for Jennie's reaction. The voice sounded normal, neither high-pitched nor low, with no particular accent that she could discern. Jennie made no mark on the paper.

"Here's Number Two."

This one was more nasal than the first, as though he was fighting a cold. But, again, it was not the low, gruff voice that Jennie had described to Gabby weeks before. She also knew that any one of these guys could and probably would try to change his voice for the recording, but probably not this much, she thought. And, again, Jennie made no check mark.

It was the fourth voice that brought Jennie straight up, with a quick of pivot of her head, her eyes suddenly wide open, her hand to her mouth. "That could be him, I think," she burst out. "Play it again, please."

He reset the recorder. This voice was lower than the others, the words spoken with what—had you seen him—could be pictured as a sneer.

"What makes you think so?" Archer asked.

She didn't hesitate. "The way he said, 'Don't screw with me.' I can't explain it, but that's exactly the way it sounded to me. The way he said screw, like he was standing right next to me, saying it in my ear."

"Okay, good," he said, "so now let's play number five…"

"So who is he?" she blurted. "The one I just heard?"

"I can't tell you that, Jennie. Not until we know more. I'm sorry."

The fifth voice was similar to the first and drew no reaction.

Archer put the recorder away, stood, and shook her small hand. "Thank you, again, Jennie. You've been a great help. And I can only wish the best for you."

"Will you find him? The man with the voice?"

"We'll certainly try. But don't get your hopes up too high, please. He may sound like the man on the phone, but he may not be the man who hurt Hannah. It's my job to find out for sure. And Gabby and Sergeant Chan will keep you informed."

Leaving Julie with Jennie, Gabby and Sarah escorted Archer through the lobby to the front door. As they walked, Gabby asked, "So now can you tell us any more about the mystery voice?"

"Strictly between us, the guy's name is Julius Winthrop. A gang banger with a record like a foot-long hot dog: burglary, car theft, domestic abuse. You know the song-and-dance. Not somebody you'd want for your next-door neighbor."

"No murders or attempted murders?"

"Not that we know about. But we've got a lot of unsolved murders."

"Did he happen to be wearing cowboy boots?"

"I have no idea. Why do you ask *that*?"

"Because I remember that our intern said the guy who attacked him was wearing boots that looked like cowboy boots. It should have been in your report."

"I'll have to check, but I don't remember reading that."

She went on. "Does he have any known connection to Klinger?"

"If you're talking about your Nebraska state penitentiary connection, it's too soon to tell. We've talked to the people down there, but remember Klinger did his time some ten years ago, so it's like trying to find a bad needle in the prison haystack. Digging through their old records, looking for names of guys he may have had a relationship with, like former cellmates of whatever. It's a thankless task and they're not exactly eager to help."

"Then what are you going to do?"

"I may have to send one of my guys down there to go through the records ourselves. But I'll have to get the okay from somebody higher up than me on the police food chain."

"Well, good luck," she said.

He opened the door and looked back. "Thanks, but I think it'll take more than luck. Like more time and a little more manpower."

As they watched him drive away, Sarah asked, "What are you up to now?"

"I wish I knew," Gabby replied, looking off into space. "I'm still officially on vacation, I guess, but I'm not sure what my next step should be. It doesn't look like there's much more we can do for Jennie at the moment, and not much more to do on the investigation itself. Everything is kind of at a standstill, so maybe I should just go back to work...and wait to see what happens."

"And keep watching your back," Sarah said. "Don't forget that."

"Don't worry. Barclay and Zach won't let me."

"And I'll be there if you need me. Day or night."

TWENTY-SEVEN

...

It was on her third day back at work that Gabby got a call from Julie O'Connell, reporting that Wadena County Child Protection had—as a result of its investigation—demanded that Jennie's father take a series of anger management classes and counseling as a condition of Jennie's return to the family home. And, that he had profanely refused the demand, calling it "pure bullshit."

"What does that mean?" Gabby asked.

"It's unclear," Julie replied. "Our friend, Eleanor, says he's threatened to sue the county to get Jennie back...so the case could end up in court."

"Jesus," Gabby said. "And he's a big man in that county, with lots of friends, including some judges, I would guess."

"That would be my guess, too."

"She'll never stay," Gabby said, "unless they put her in chains. And what's more, how would any foster family dare to keep her with her father around? We've seen what he can do."

"I know."

"You've got to do something, Julie. Talk to your attorneys or whatever. We can't let her go back there."

"Gabby, with all due respect, I can't make this my battle. We don't have the money and we've got a bunch of other kids here who need our attention. I feel deeply for Jennie, but there are limits to what I can do."

"Does Jesse know about this?"

"Not yet. I just got off the phone with Eleanor."

"He'll go nuts."

Gabby had seen Jennie's brother virtually every day, at lunch or breakfast or at dinner with Zach and Sarah. And she knew his emergency leave from the Army was about to end.

Frustrated, she finally said, "I hope you'll keep in touch."

"I will," Julie replied, "and I'm sorry I can't do more."

Gabby put the phone down and stared at the newly-falling snow outside her window, obscuring the view and reflecting the gloominess that seemed to be overtaking her. For three days, Barclay had largely confined her to the newsroom, working with producers and writing the routine stories of the day. She had been allowed to cover two nearby news conferences, but only in the company of Zach or one of the other photographers and an extra security guard the station had hired. She increasingly felt like a prisoner housed in a newsroom isolation cell.

And Barclay had gone one step further, suggesting or ordering that she and Zach take different routes to and from home and, again, to stick to public places or around other people, even when they walked their dog.

The extra precautions and her continuing presence in the newsroom had not gone unnoticed. A few people had asked about it, or expressed their sympathy and support, but most—by and large—had left her alone.

Now, sitting there, she finally decided she had had enough and headed across the newsroom to Barclay's office. She found him nose-deep in a stack of spread sheets, which she guessed must be budget bullshit. She rapped on the door and said, "George, I can see you're busy, but we need to talk."

He looked up, irritably, but then smiled. "No problem. I need a break, anyway. C'mon in."

As she took a chair across from him, she noticed for the first time that he seemed to have lost weight and what little remained of his summer tan, giving his face a tired, pallid look. Running a newsroom in these increasingly tight, competitive times was clearly having an impact. Not only did he have to worry about the competition from the other television stations and newspapers, but from all the digital sources of news and entertainment, some of them real, some fake, but all of them taking a piece of the audience and the advertising dollars that once largely belonged to local stations like Channel Seven.

And she knew she was only adding to the pressures he must be feeling.

Breathing deeply, she said, "I know you've got a lot on your plate and I don't want to add even more, but you've gotta set me free, George. I'm going crazy sitting over there, doing almost nothing, like a freaking prisoner. I know you're trying to protect me, but it can't go on like this. And it's not just me. Zach is getting twitchy, too, always looking over our shoulders. And it's having an impact on…you know…our relationship."

He listened intently but betrayed nothing. Finally, he said, "This Klinger guy is still on the loose, isn't he?"

"Yes. I would have heard if he wasn't."

"And that means you could still be in danger, right?"

"I suppose so, but nothing has happened in days. No more threats, no more strange phone calls. Nothing suspicious, as far as I can tell."

"But there's still the chance he has some buddy up here, right? The one who attacked our intern? The one who may actually have killed Hannah?"

"That's also true. But this uncertainty could go on for weeks. Keeping me cooped up in here like some…"

He gazed across at her. "So what do you want me to do?"

"Loosen my leash a little. I'll keep taking the precautions you suggest, but let me get out and about, doing whatever you want me to do, but also giving me the freedom to pursue some other stuff."

"Like what?"

"A couple of things. I'd like to hook up with a reporter down in Nebraska to help check out those prison records, if the cops don't do it. Maybe even go down there myself, on my own dime. And, also, to see if there's a story in what Jennie is facing up in Wadena County. The whole dilemma child protection people face in trying to keep an abused child out of the reach of an abusive parent. I know there are a lot of others like her and it could make for a larger story."

He leaned back, clearly torn. "You've got to give me time to think, Gabby. If something were to happen to you, you know where the blame and guilt will fall. Right on top of this slowly-balding head. You have to keep yourself safe, for your sake and mine. And then there's this," he added, pointing to the spread sheets, "our beloved GM is on my ass to keep expenses down or cut them. That means we have to cover the news with the reporters we have, or maybe even fewer."

"I understand. I'll do everything you ask. But let freedom ring. Please."

"We'll see. But for now, hang around the newsroom for the rest of the day and give the producers a hand. And give me that time to think."

Later, as she and Zach drove home, she got a call from Howard Hooper. "I just got off the phone with Sheriff Henderson and he says they've confirmed the fire at the Updahl farm was arson. It took a few days, but they finally found traces of gas or some other accelerant in the rubble."

"That's no great surprise, I guess," she said.

"No, not really. But, so far, they can't tie the arson directly to Klinger."

"Anything new with him?"

"As a matter of fact, there is. The sheriff said they found his truck in a used car lot in Rochester. He apparently left it there and stole another pickup, a black F-150 with a new set of plates. So that complicates the search for him."

"Damn."

"One other thing. I don't know if you've talked with Mrs. Klinger recently…"

"No, I've been meaning to call her."

"She's decided to sell the farm and move in with her sister in Marshall temporarily. Apparently her boys are having a tough time at school, getting flack from other kids. You know, 'like father like sons'. That kind of thing. So she's found a friend who's tutoring them at home until she can make the move."

"It never ends, does it?"

"I'm afraid not. It's really sad."

"I'll call her when I get the chance."

"I think she'd appreciate that."

One of the most troublesome and irritating aspects of their stay-safe regimen was finding a secure spot to walk the dog. They could no longer simply step out the front door of the apartment building, but now had to put him in the car and take him to a different local park or dog park where there were other people around.

Morning and night.

On this evening, as they walked around Lake Harriet, Gabby got a call from her mother in Portland. They hadn't spoken in days, and Gabby apologized. "I'm sorry, Mom. It's been really busy. Long days. Lots of stuff going on."

"Like what stuff?" she asked. "Are you okay?"

"I'm fine. I've just spent a lot of time on that complicated story I told you about earlier. The homeless story and the murder of that young woman."

"Did they find who killed her?"

"Not yet."

"And what about the stepfather, the rapist?"

"He's still on the loose."

"And how about that young girl you've been helping? Jennie. Is that her name?"

"Yes. Jennie. She's still in a shelter, waiting to see what will happen to her."

"I've been worried about you. Your sisters have, too. Are you getting your rest? And how is Zach?"

Gabby gave Zach a beseeching look. "Yes, I'm getting my rest and Zach is fine. He's right beside me, actually, walking Barclay."

"Please say hi for me," she said, again leaving unasked any question about marriage plans.

After another few minutes of conversation, Gabby was able to ring off, with a promise to keep in closer touch.

"No questions about a wedding ?" Zach asked.

"No, thankfully. But I know she's wondering."

"So am I," he replied.

"As they pulled out of the parking lot, with the dog spread out in the back seat, neither of them took notice in the approaching darkness of a black F-150 pickup sitting idling across the lot.

TWENTY-EIGHT

...

Ｔhe next morning, after checking in with Wilson at the assignment desk, Gabby settled in at her desk, clicked on Google and punched in the number of the *Lincoln Journal Star* in Nebraska.

Transferred to the city desk, she identified herself and asked if she could speak to one of their reporters who covered the crime beat. "And what is this about?" the woman at the desk asked.

"It's about a story I'm working on up here in Minnesota," Gabby replied, "that might have ties to Nebraska."

"And you're with a television station?"

"That's right. Channel Seven in the Twin Cities."

There was a pause and she could hear the newsroom hubbub in the background. Finally, the woman said, "I'll try to connect you with Paul Cornell. But I'm not sure he's in yet."

Gabby waited for a minute or so before she heard, "This is Paul. How can I help you?"

She reintroduced herself and got straight to the point. "I don't want to take a lot of your time, but as I told the woman at the desk, I thought you might be interested in a story I'm working on."

"Really? You're a long way away. Tell me more."

"I'll be brief and then you can tell me if you have the time to hear more."

"Sounds good."

She went on to describe Hannah's murder and the fact that—earlier—she may have been raped by her stepfather, who happened to be a convicted rapist from the little town of Hershall, Nebraska ten years before.

"That was well before my time at the paper," he said, "but I do remember the case. It was pretty brutal. But what that does that have to do with *your* story?"

"Maybe nothing. But so far there are no obvious suspects or motives in the girl's murder and the stepfather, a guy named Arnold Klinger, has an alibi and could not have committed it himself. You know, to protect him from her rape accusations."

"I'm listening."

"As I thought about it, it occurred to me that if he didn't do it, and if he really did want to get rid of her, he might have enlisted the help of someone else. Like one of his old buddies…like someone he might have served time with in your penitentiary. Like a cellmate, maybe."

"Wow. Forgive me, but that does seem like a reach to me. A long reach."

"I know I'm reaching. But the cops up here haven't rejected the idea and may even send someone down to check it out."

"And you'd like to beat them to it."

"If true, it would be great story. For me. And maybe for you. Think about it. An old Nebraska rapist now in Minnesota, who may have recruited a killer that he met while serving time behind your bars."

"Where is this Klinger guy now?"

"On the run. From another rape in Minnesota. Which they connected him to through DNA from the Nebraska rape."

"Jeez."

She waited.

"What would you want from me?" he finally asked.

"If you or someone else at the paper has contacts at the penitentiary, and have the time, I'd like to get the names of anyone they might remember as being close to Klinger. You know, like a cellmate. I know it's been ten years and I know a lot of guys have come and gone through those prison gates, but Klinger may be remembered because of the publicity his rape case got."

"And then?"

"Then we'd try to tie those names to any of the persons of interest the cops here have in the girl's murder. Especially a guy named Julius Winthrop."

She could almost hear his mind churning in the silence that followed.

"You still there?" she asked.

"Sorry. I'll have to talk to my boss. They run a pretty tight ship down here. Like all newspapers, I guess."

"I understand. But if you do get the approval, let me know and I'll send you everything we have on the case. But in any event, I appreciate your time."

"That's no problem, but could you do me a favor in return? Between us, if you hear of any openings at the *StarTrib* or the *Pioneer Press,* let me know. Nebraska is not the garden spot of the world."

"Will do," she promised.

Across the newsroom, Jeff Parkett, the assistant news director, stepped into Barclay's office and leaned against the door. "So what's going on with our friend, Gabby?"

"What do you mean?"

"I mean, does she still work for us? Or is she on vacation again?"

Barclay could only smile. "You never give up, do you?"

Parkett would be the first to admit that he'd never been one of Gabby's fans, not from her first day of work. Not since talking to a couple of his friends at the San Jose station from which she had come, hearing numerous stories of her aggressive, in-your-face, go-it-alone personality that had left her with respect but not many friends.

And to see some of those same traits emerge here.

Neither her success in the Ponzi expose' nor her reporting on the Klinger story and Hannah's murder had changed his mind. She might be a good reporter, he admitted, but she was a prima donna who was hired because of her friendship with Sam Ryan's daughter. And who'd been given far too much freedom by Barclay to do as she pleased. It had been a point of contention between them from the day she stepped through the door.

"So what's your problem now?" Barclay asked.

Parkett glanced across the newsroom. "Can't you see? She just sits there on the phone while the rest of us are scrambling to cover the day's news."

"Has she refused to do anything you've asked?"

"No," he said, "but she doesn't volunteer any ideas, either. We're out there beating the streets, getting enough stories to fill six or seven newscasts a day. And she just sits there, or is out running around who knows where. It hasn't gone unnoticed by the rest of the staff, George."

"Really? And are they aware of what she's dealing with? What I'm dealing with? The possible threats against her? That I've asked her to stay close?"

"Some of them are, I guess. Word gets around. But it's been what? Damn near a week and people have started to wonder what's going on."

Barclay leaned across the desk, face flushed, rare anger in his voice. "Then you better tell `em. That's your job. I know we have to cover the news. I know we're stretched thin. But we're also here to *break* news. Which is what this station is all about, what Gabby is all about.

"So it's about time you flush this attitude of yours," he growled. "She's a hell of a reporter, maybe one of the best who's ever sat in this newsroom. On the phone or otherwise. Working on what could be a hell of a story. *So get over it.* And don't let the door hit you on the ass on your way out."

Gabby, of course, was not privy to that conversation, but she *was* aware of Parkett's feelings about her. They had been evident, if unspoken, from the beginning. Not that he was downright unfriendly, but he was more aloof and indifferent than she would have expected as a newly arrived employee. She knew he'd spoken to some of her former colleagues in San Jose, at least a couple of them not her greatest fans. And that he suspected it was her connection to Sam Ryan that had brought her here. He rarely spoke more than necessary words to her, and was seldom among those to congratulate her for an outstanding effort or story.

She had tried to close the gap between them, but finally gave up, deciding—perhaps self-indulgently—that it was another case of a male not enamored of an aggressive female. So she more often worked around him than with him. She never ignored his orders, but never went out of her way to accommodate him. Instead, she tried to deal directly with Barclay as often as possible, which she suspected also pissed Parkett off.

In the end, she no longer cared. He could do his job. She could do hers. And they could work together when absolutely necessary.

Parkett had no more than left Barclay's office, with a hardened stare at her across the newsroom, than she was back on the phone, this time answering a call from Detective Archer. "Glad I caught you," he said. "And to thank you."

"For what?"

"For that heads-up about a pair of cowboy boots. Remember?"

"Sure. The guy who kicked our intern was wearing a pair."

"Guess what? That intrigued us. So we brought our friend Julius Winthrop, he of the mystery voice, back into the shop for some follow-up questioning..."

"And, lo and behold," Gabby said, "he was wearing cowboy boots."

"You got it. A little worn but with nice pointy toes."

"I shouldn't laugh," she said, laughing, "but don't tell me he came in on a horse."

"No," with a chuckle, "he was on foot."

"Did you hold him?"

"For wearing cowboy boots? No, but he did suddenly become more of a suspect than a person of interest."

"And where is he now?"

"Back on the street, but with a warning from us, you know, in cop-speak, not to leave town."

Doubtfully, "I'm sure he'll honor that request."

"We didn't have much choice. But we did take a discreet picture of his boots and would like your intern to take a look at the photo."

"I'm sure he would. Just email or text me the picture."

"Good."

"One more thing," she said, telling him of her call to the Lincoln, Nebraska newspaper reporter. "Maybe I shouldn't have, but I didn't know if you'd be sending any of your guys down there, and I wanted to test my unlikely theory."

"That's fine with me. I still don't have the funds to send any-one, anyway. So let me know what you hear, if anything, about that and also the cowboy boots."

"Will do."

A few minutes later, she forwarded the photo of the cowboy boots on to Andy, with a brief explanatory note. Almost immediately, she got his reply: "I don't know, they sure look like the ones, but, hell, it was all too quick, like a blur. I certainly could never swear to it in court. Sorry."

TWENTY-NINE

...

Later, Gabby could not remember much in the moments before it happened. The car radio was on, with local news, she did remember that, and the snow was coming at them horizontally, plastering the windshield, challenging the wipers. Zach was mumbling under his breath, about the weather, she guessed now, but her mind then was elsewhere. She couldn't remember where.

The impact was so sudden, so jarring, with such force that her head flew to the side—as if it had left her neck, her body, momentarily erasing any thoughts, any memories. She heard her own scream, a screech really, piercing, mixed with the explosive grinding of metal and the shattering of glass.

And Zach's "What the..." before he was swallowed up by his air bag, both of them surrounded, engulfed by the smoky powder from the bag.

The car was flung to the side as though slung from a giant slingshot, careening to the right, then back, then back again, sliding on the slick pavement as if on skis, not tires. And, finally, fishtailing into a snow-covered car parked along the street. Another impact, this one less severe, still lifting her, but held secure by her seat belt.

Suddenly, it was over. The only sounds now—the grinding of more crumbling metal and falling pieces of shattered glass.

Dazed, filled with fear and a stabbing pain in her shoulder, choking on the powder, Gabby tried to regain her senses, looking quickly over at Zach, whose head still lay on the steering wheel's deflated bag. She struggled to unsnap her seat belt and to reach across to him, her voice shrill, as though it belonged to someone else. "Zach, Jesus, Zach! Are you okay? Talk to me, Zach!"

No response. His eyes were closed, an almost serene look on his face. But, as she leaned closer, she could hear his labored breathing. Thank God, she thought. She touched his face, wiped away the traces of powder and splinters of glass that clung to his cheek, seeing a small trail of blood leaking from his nose.

Only then did she hear a shout from outside of the broken passenger-side window. A woman, scarf tight around her head, nose bright red from the cold, "Are you all right? I've called 911. Help should be on the way."

"Thank you, thank you," she responded, reaching for the door, but finding it wedged against the car on the curb. "My friend is hurt. He needs an ambulance."

"I can see. It shouldn't take long. Are *you* okay?"

She stretched her legs and ran her hands over her mid-section, finding her ribs intact, but grimacing at the sharp pain in her right shoulder. "I think so, yes." Then, "Please tell me, what happened?"

The woman shook her head, eyes wide, as she stared over the caved-in hood of their car. "A big black pickup with big bumper guards with two guys in it ran the red light and hit you in the middle of the intersection. T-boned you. It was a horrible sound, almost like a bomb exploding. It was terrible."

Gabby looked around but saw no sign of a black pickup. "Where is it?"

"It backed up and took off down that way," pointing to her left. "But I got the license number."

She knew immediately. Klinger had finally found them.

By then, more people had gathered around the wreckage. And she could hear a siren drawing closer. A big Black man in a Vikings stocking cap fought to get the passenger door open far enough for her to squeeze out. But it was not enough. She was tempted to crawl over the seat and escape through one of the back doors, but the headrest was in the way and she wasn't sure she had the strength, or if the injured shoulder, would allow her to get over it. And she didn't want to leave Zach.

"Hang tight," the Black man yelled. "Here are the cops."

The squad car, lights flashing, slid to a stop just in front of them. Another, a moment later, came from the rear. And then one of the officers, a woman, was at Zach's fractured window, looking across at her. "Are you okay, Miss?"

"I think so," she said, trying to focus on her, "but my friend isn't. He needs help."

"The ambulance and paramedics are a few minutes away. They'll take care of him. And you. Try to stay calm. Don't want you going into shock."

As it turned out, the first fire truck arrived minutes before the ambulance. Two firemen were at Zach's door, using some kind of steel bar to pry it open. Another fireman was at *her* door, working with the Black passerby to force it open.

Zach's eyes remained closed, but his breathing seemed easier. She felt for his pulse, which, despite the chaos of the moment, seemed regular. And the blood flow from his nose appeared to have stopped. She leaned close to his ear, "Zach, Zach, it's me. Help is here. Please, hang in there!"

Try as she might, she could never remember the next several minutes with clarity. Perhaps it was the early signs of shock or simply the confusion that surrounded her, but suddenly both her door and Zach's were open. The ambulance was there. One paramedic briefly checked her over, gently touching the injured shoulder, making her look into his eyes and speak to him. "Sit tight," he said. "Stay calm. I'll be back after I help with your friend."

One minute passed, maybe two, maybe more, and she was on the sidewalk, ignoring the orders to stay put, finding herself in the grasp of the woman with the red nose. "Take it easy, honey," the woman said, holding her tight. "Everything will be okay."

She tried to hold herself steady, to keep her balance, but her legs wobbled. She was able to stay upright only because the woman refused to let her fall. She tried to focus, to ignore the pain in her shoulder, to see through the whipping snow and the confusing movement of the first responders who milled around the wreckage. "Please let me go," she said frantically to the woman. "I have to check on my friend!"

"Not a good idea," the woman said, refusing to release her. "Trust me. You'll only be in the way. Let them do their job."

By now, Gabby could see that Zach had been lifted out of the car and lay stretched out on a flat board, covered by a blanket of some sort, and then being lifted onto a gurney. Pushed slowly toward a waiting ambulance. She searched for some sign of movement but saw none. "They're taking him away! I need to go with him!"

As she struggled to free herself, the woman officer who had first spoken to her was now by her side, blocking her way. "I'm afraid not. Another ambulance will be here shortly to take you to the hospital. But first, if you're up to it, I need a little information. Is that okay?"

"Will I see him there?"

"I'm sure you will, after they check both of you out. But first give me your name and the name of your friend."

"He's my fiancé, Zachary Anthony. And I'm Gabriel Gooding. We both work for Channel Seven News. He's a photographer and I'm a reporter. It's Zach's car and all of the information about it should be in the glove compartment. And here's my ID," pulling out her driver's license. "We both live at this address."

The cop was taking notes. "Did you see what happened?"

"No. There was just the crash. But this lady said it was a black pickup with big bumpers that ran a red light and hit us. You'll have to talk to her."

"We have. And others who saw it. We're looking for that pickup now. Anything else you can tell me?"

"Yes. I think I know who the driver may have been. A man who has been stalking me. A man police all over the state are looking for. His name is Arnold Klinger. You can check it out. It's a long story, but now I need to get to the hospital to see Zach and to make an important phone call."

"Okay," the officer said. "Someone else from the traffic division will talk to you there, but I'll get this information out now. I'm glad we've got the license plate."

As she waited, but before she brought her phone out of her purse, she picked out two business cards and a pen from her purse and gave them to the woman who held her and the Black man who had tried to pry the door open, both still standing by her. "I can't thank you enough," she said, her voice shaking, "and I hope you'll write your names and phone numbers on these cards so I can get back to you later with a proper thank you."

"No need for that," the man said, handing back the card. "I'm just glad we happened to be here."

"Me, too," the woman added. "I just hope your fiancé is okay. And besides," with a smile, "I've never met a real TV person before."

"Especially one who can barely stand up," Gabby replied, grinning. "Just know that I won't forget your kindness."

Barclay picked up on the first ring.

"George, this is Gabby."

"Hey, Gabs, what's up?"

"I've only got a minute. We've been in a horrible accident."

"What?"

"Zach's on the way to the hospital. He's hurt bad, I think."

"Damn! What happened? Where are you?"

"Somewhere on Hennepin Avenue. A black pickup, Klinger's, I think, crashed into us and took off. The car is crushed and Zach was unconscious when they took him away. They're going to take me in a minute or so."

"My, God. How are *you?*"

"Okay, I think. Except for a bad shoulder."

"I *knew* something like this was going to happen," he said, angrily. "I just *knew* it."

"We did take a different route, but he must have followed us from the station, got ahead of us somehow and then plowed into us. The cops have his license number and are hunting for him now."

"All right," he said. "I'll leave now and meet you at the hospital. Stay calm, okay?"

"I'm doing my best. And praying for Zach."

As she was rolled from the ambulance in a wheelchair, she found the emergency room at the Hennepin County Medical Center surprisingly calm and quiet for such a wintry, slippery day. Barclay was already there, walking beside her as she was wheeled toward an examining room. "How is Zach?" she asked. "Do you know?"

"No, nothing. No one will tell me anything. I've been on the phone trying to pull some strings, but, so far, no luck. I'll keep trying."

"We have to call his parents up in Duluth," she said.

"I know, but let's wait until we know more. It may not be as bad as you think."

At that point, he was left behind as she was pushed through a door and into the interior of the emergency complex.

Two hours later, she came out the same door, walking now, her right arm in a loose sling. Barclay got up to meet her. "What did they say?"

She sat down in a chair next to his. "They examined me from head to toe and did a bunch of x-rays, but the only really bad thing they found was this," lifting the sling, "a badly bruised shoulder. Not even a break. But it still hurts like hell, and I probably won't be doing much typing for a few days."

"Glad it's not worse," he said. "And forget about the typing. You're off-duty until I tell you otherwise."

"And what about Zach?" she asked.

"Good news there, too. At least better than we might have thought. I finally talked to one of the mucky-mucks here, a Doctor Ben Harrison, a guy I've known for years and who I've done a few favors for. He hasn't seen Zach himself, but did talk with those who have. He's conscious and out of the emergency room.

"Thank, God," she whispered.

"No apparent long-lasting brain damage, but he does show all the signs of a fairly serious concussion, plus a broken left wrist and lots of facial and abdominal bruising. The air bag may have saved his life, but it didn't prevent some of those other injuries. But he's going to survive, which is the crucial thing, of course."

"Can we see him?"

"Not for a while. Probably not today. They have to do more workups and monitor the concussion effects."

"He probably doesn't remember anything about the accident," she said.

"That'd be my guess, too."

"Do you want me to call his folks, or you?"

"Should be you," he said. "You're his fiancée and know them. I don't."

She looked away. "I hate to, but I'll call them from home." Then, "Will someone tell us when we can see him?"

"My buddy, the doctor, says he'll let me know. And, by the way, I called your friend, Sergeant Chan, and the Homicide guy, Archer, to tell them what happened. They'll be giving you a call."

"Thanks."

As she got up, she said, "You know, a couple of days ago Zach said living with me was like living in a war zone. I laughed then, but he was right. And now he's paying the price once again."

THIRTY

. . .

By the time Barclay had dropped her off at the apartment, and after her call to Zach's parents in Duluth and to her own mother in Portland, it was now the middle of the evening—and Gabby felt as low as she had in many weeks. Low and alone in an empty apartment with the scents and shadows of Zach in every corner. Touching her, whispering to her. The world she had known only hours before had collapsed around her like the crushed car, leaving only the poodle, now sitting in her lap, to provide any trace of comfort.

Zach's parents, Joseph and Judith Anthony, had accepted the news of the accident with predictable alarm, but were relieved to know his injuries were not life-threatening. Gabby assured them she would let them know when a hospital visit or phone calls would be possible, and of any further changes in his condition.

She did not tell them, *could not tell them*, that the crash was deliberate, and that she was largely responsible. They would learn all of that soon enough. And when they did, they would almost certainly wonder why she had avoided telling them now? Not the best way, she thought, to endear herself to her future in-laws. If, after this, they were ever to be.

Gabby's mother took the news more calmly than she would have expected—once she knew her injuries were relatively minor. But Zach was a different story. "My, God, how bad is it?"

"We're not sure, Mom. But he's going to live and that's all that counts. I'll let you know more when we know more."

Before making the calls to Duluth and Portland, she had ignored three messages waiting on her phone: one from Sarah, another from Detective Archer, and the third from Paul Cornell, the Nebraska reporter. She decided the last two could wait until the next day and that Sarah could wait until she had taken the dog for a short walk, and until she had taken a warm shower.

But, it turned out, the walk and the shower would have to wait. Sarah was on the phone. "Are you okay?" she asked. "I talked to your boss and he told me what happened. That's terrible."

"I'll be fine, but Zach isn't. He's in the hospital."

"I know. I checked."

"You must also know it was Klinger and some other guy in the pickup."

"That's one of the reasons I called. To tell you the cops out in Shakopee found it abandoned in a Walmart parking lot."

"But no sign of them?"

"No. They're checking any reports of stolen vehicles in the area, and doing the forensics on the truck. We still don't know who the second guy is."

"Will this never end?" Gabby asked, plaintively.

"Everybody's doing their best, Gabby. Trust me on that."

"I know."

"One other piece of news. Brace yourself."

"What now?"

"Julie O'Connell called. A deputy sheriff from Wadena County showed up at The Haven this morning with a court order requiring that Jennie be surrendered to his custody."

Gabby sank to her knees. "That can't be! Is she gone?"

"Yes."

"Back to her family?"

"No. That's the only good news. She's going to a foster family in the county."

"But within reach of her father?"

"I can't tell you that."

Tears filled her eyes. "Does her brother know?"

"Yes. We've stayed in touch. He's going to try and get another leave."

"She'll run again. I know she will. Back to nowhere. Just like Hannah."

"Are you okay?" Sarah said. "You sound like you're crying."

"It's not been my best day."

"Want me to come over and have a drink? I can do that."

"No, I have to walk the dog and get myself cleaned up and into bed. But thanks for the offer."

"I'll talk to you in the morning. Try to buck up."

After her shower, she stayed up long enough to watch the late news, which—about four minutes in—carried the following story, voiced by anchor Andrea Neusem.

We're sorry to report tonight that two of our Channel Seven News colleagues were injured in a hit-and-run accident on Hennepin Avenue in south Minneapolis today. Reporter Gabby Gooding and photographer Zach Anthony were in a car that was rammed by a pickup truck that police say ran a red light and then raced away. The driver has yet to be found, but we understand tonight that the truck was discovered abandoned in Shakopee. Gooding was treated and released at the Hennepin County Medical Center, but Anthony remains in the hospital with serious, but non-life-threatening injuries. We wish them both well and a speedy recovery.

Then it was off to bed, but if she'd expected to get a restful night's sleep after the tumultuous day, she would be sadly disappointed. The minutes, then the hours, dragged by with agonizing slowness in the darkened bedroom. Her shoulder ached and the images and sounds of the crash would not leave her. Virtually every minute of the ordeal played over and over in her mind—from the moment of impact to the sight of Zach being lifted into the ambulance. She painfully tossed and turned and was up twice for a glass of warm milk and a Tylenol PM. To little avail. She wasn't sure when sleep finally came, but the last numbers she remembered seeing on the bedside clock were 3:12.

Four hours later it was the phone, not her alarm that brought her out of a short, but blessedly deep sleep.

"Barclay here, how are you doing?" came the voice.

"Barely awake," she replied, still groggy.

"Well, listen up. I talked to my doctor friend and he says Zach should be able to take phone calls and maybe see some visitors about noon or a little after. He'll be getting more tests before then."

"That's great. Thanks."

"He's been told we're thinking about him and will be there to see him as soon as it's allowed. And I've ordered some flowers to be sent over."

"He'd probably prefer a beer."

She could hear his chuckle. "I get that."

As she hoisted herself out of bed, phone in hand, she made her way to the kitchen. "I appreciate the call and your help, George."

"No problem. Did you talk to his parents?"

"Yes. Last night," she said, repeating the essence of the conversation. "But they don't know the crash was probably deliberate. I couldn't bring myself to tell them that on the phone. Better in person, I decided."

"I understand. I'll try to be there with you."

"Thanks."

"So, how are you doing?"

"Feeling guilty," she replied. "And about as low as you can get."

"Then get over it. This is not your fault. We're dealing with a psycho here. You were just doing your job."

"You've told me that before."

"I know, and I mean it."

"But I can just hear the buzz in the newsroom. Gabby's curse strikes again."

"Stop that. Everyone is worried about both of you and realize it's not your fault."

"Does that include my friend, Mr. Parkett?"

"Forget about him. He's not your problem. Relax, and I'll see you at the hospital."

Once she'd dressed and taken the dog for his walk, she returned the two calls from the night before. Detective Archer was not in, but Paul Cornell of the *Lincoln Journal Star* was. "Hey, Paul, I'm sorry I didn't get back to you sooner, but we've had some issues up here that have kept me tied up."

"I understand. But I wanted you to know that I, or we, may have struck gold."

Her mind raced. "How's that?"

"The one name you gave me. Julius Winthrop. Turns out he *was* one of a few guys who shared a cell with your man, Arnold Klinger, during his three-year stay at our friendly state penitentiary."

"Yes!" she blurted.

"My source at the prison tells me they were together for about a year, and apparently were the best of buddies. In fact, Klinger was something like Winthrop's bodyguard, watching his back."

"That's great, but how does your source know all of this? It's been years since Klinger was there."

"Strange thing. Small world. Whatever. My source happens to have relatives in a town not that far from Hershall, where Klinger raped the girl. So he kept a close eye on Klinger while he served his time. He remembers him well."

"Terrific. The cops up here will be delighted with this piece of news and will want to get on top of it themselves. Does your source have a name?"

"Your cops can contact me and I'll put them in touch. By the way, Klinger briefly had two other cellmates while he was there. I'll email their names and some details after I get off the phone."

"You've been a great help, and if it turns out Winthrop is our man, you'll have yourself a nice little story. Two Nebraska ex-cons involved in a Minneapolis murder."

"Thanks. I'll look forward to it…and, remember, you promised me any leads to job possibilities up there."

"I'm still working on that," she lied, "so why don't you send me a clip file of some of your stories and I'll try to pass it on to folks at the newspapers up here."

"It'll be in the mail tomorrow."

As soon as she clicked off, she placed another call to Detective Archer. This time he answered on the first ring with a gruff "Archer."

"Hey, Detective, this is Gabby Gooding."

"Hey, yourself. Did you get my message?"

"Yes. I tried to get you a few minutes ago."

"I was sorry to hear about the accident. Are you doing okay?"

"Yes, but it was no accident."

"I know. We're still looking for the guys."

"That's not why I called. I have some good news."

"'Really? Tell me."

She shared with him what she'd just been told by Paul Cornell. "Winthrop could be your man."

"No shit! That's great work, Gabby. But there's one problem."

"What?"

"I'm going to have to tell my boss that you've done what we should have done. He'll be pissed."

She laughed. "I'd like to be a fly on the wall for that."

"May be funny to you, but not to me."

"My reporter friend, Paul, will tell you his source when you give him a call. I'll give you his number and the names of the other two cellmates as soon as I get them."

"Good. I just wish we'd known all this when we had Winthrop sitting here in his cowboy boots. Now, if he was the one with Klinger in the pickup, we may have a tough time finding him again."

"Two things, Detective. First, if and when you do get them, the whole story is *my* story first, right? Like exclusive. No newspapers, no other TV."

"I understand."

"Second, I'll feel better if you find the two of them before they try killing me again. I don't have nine lives."

THIRTY-ONE

• • •

S he arrived at the medical center well before noon, but it took her another half hour to navigate the medical maze of buildings and skyways to a small fourth floor waiting room—where she found Barclay on the phone and Andy the intern thumbing through the latest issue of *Minnesota Monthly*. Once he spotted her, he got up and gave her a hug, avoiding her arm in the sling. "I'm so sorry," he said. "I didn't know anything until I saw the news last night. I feel so badly for both of you."

She smiled and wiggled free of his hug. "Thanks. I would have called you, but I just haven't had the chance."

"I understand. I should be the last thing on your mind."

"Have you heard anything about seeing Zach?"

"I don't know. Mr. Barclay's been on the phone since I got here."

There were only a few other people in the waiting area and no sign of any hospital personnel, aside from a woman at the reception desk. Gabby was tempted to go talk to her, but assumed Barclay was on top of things. Glancing at him, she saw he was still holding the phone with one hand and pointing with the other to one of the lobby television monitors—where the Channel Seven noon news had just begun. Gabby and Andy moved closer and heard the opening story from anchor Tony LaForge.

We have learned that Minneapolis police now believe the hit-and-run driver who plowed his pickup into a car carrying two Channel Seven employees yesterday may have been Arnold Klinger, the fugitive from western Minnesota who is wanted for sexual assault in Lincoln County. The pickup truck, which was found abandoned in Shakopee, is believed to be one stolen by Klinger in Rochester a week or more ago. But there has been no sign of Klinger or the unknown male who was in the pickup with him. Also, we've been told unofficially by law enforcement in Lyon County, where Klinger lived before his flight, that he was angered by some of the reporting on his case done by Channel Seven's Gabby Gooding, and that she may have been a target of the hit-and-run. Gabby was injured but not hospitalized in the crash. However, her companion, photographer Zach Anthony, was seriously hurt and is now at the Hennepin County Medical Center.

As she turned from the monitor, Barclay was standing next to them. "Wow," she said, "that was kind of risky, wasn't it? A little speculative, I'd say."

"What's he going to do, sue us? It's all true."

"Yeah, but… "

"No buts. Forget it."

As they waited, she told him about the call from Paul Cornell and her subsequent call to Detective Archer. "It looks like this Winthrop guy could be the second man in the pickup and—who knows?—maybe the guy who actually killed Hannah."

Barclay looked at her with admiring eyes. "So your idea of searching the prison records paid off. That's more nice work, Gabby, you should be proud."

Ten more minutes passed before the receptionist walked over. "Mr. Barclay?"

"That's me."

"Doctor Harrison called and said it will be okay for you and your guests to see Mr. Anthony now. He's in Room 206. The elevator is just down that hall."

223

"Thanks so much."

Andy held back. "You go ahead. I'll try to see him later, but give him my best."

"If you're still here," Gabby said. "I'd like to sit down and talk. We've got some catching up to do."

"I'll be here."

They approached Room 206 tentatively, tapped softly on the closed door, then slowly pushed it open, to find Zach upright in bed, greeting them with a lopsided grin. "About time you got here!"

Gabby couldn't help herself, exploding with a laugh. "Oh, my God, he's alive!" Then she rushed to him, ready to throw her free arm around him, but stopped short.

Afraid.

The cast on his broken left wrist was in a sort-of sling and a large bandage covered the left side of his face, hiding his eye. A dark bruise colored his forehead and his lips were puffy.

"Do I dare kiss you?" she said.

"Probably not on the lips, but if you can find an open space, I'd love it."

She leaned over with a lingering kiss on the un-bandaged side of his face, and then defied him by softly touching his swollen lips with hers. "Did that hurt?"

"Terribly, but you can do it again."

She grinned. "Just wait `til you get home. You'll get more kisses than you can count."

"And? That's all?"

"When you're able."

"Careful, we're in mixed company."

Barclay still stood by the door watching, saying nothing. But the grin would not leave his face. Finally, he moved across the room and took Zach's hand with the unbroken wrist. "I bring greetings from the newsroom. Everybody's thinking about you and worrying about you."

"Thanks, but tell them I'll be fine and back there once they let me out of here. Maybe I can do some one-handed editing."

"Let's not even think about that."

"You know," Zach said, "I still don't know what the hell happened. With this concussion thing, they won't let me read, watch television, or do anything that strains my eyes and brain. And no visitors until now. I don't remember anything. It's like I just returned from outer space."

Then I'll fill you in," Gabby said as she recalled details of the accident and the aftermath. "I was so afraid. You were unconscious and bleeding, trapped in the car. I didn't know if you were going to make it or not."

"And you're okay?"

"This sore shoulder, that's all. I was on the right side of the car."

"And they think it was Klinger?"

"Yes. And, sadly, you know it was me, not you, he was after. Yet look who's in the hospital."

Barclay then reported what had happened since the abandoned pickup was found, and on the search for Klinger and the second man, possibly Klinger's former cellmate in Nebraska. "They're on the run and there's a several-state search for them as we speak."

"What about my car?" Zach asked.

"Totaled. The HR people at the station are in contact with your insurance company and are taking care of everything. You're going to end up with a new set of wheels."

"Has anyone talked to my folks?"

"I have," Gabby said. "Last night. I told them you or I would get back to them as soon as we knew more."

"Good. I'll call them after your leave."

"I also called my mom. She sends her best wishes."

"I appreciate that. And how's my dog?"

"You mean *our* dog. Well, he's missing you, but maybe not that much. He loves your side of the bed."

"I should have known. You spoil the shit out of him. Just wash the sheets before I get home, okay?"

"Deal."

At that moment, a nurse was at the door. "Sorry," she said, "but I think he's had enough attention for awhile. And his lunch is on the way."

"No problem," Barclay said. "I was just leaving. I'll talk to you later, Gabby, and I'll try to stop by tonight, Zach."

"Don't worry about me, boss. You've got a newsroom to run, and I'm told I'm not going anywhere for now."

He paused at the door. "One more thing, Gabby. Unlikely as it may be, these dudes may try again. Stay away from the station for a while and stay as close as you can to that lady cop friend of yours. And watch your back, every minute."

Gabby lingered by the bed for a few minutes more, leaning over to whisper, "I'm so sorry, Zach. Seeing you lying here tears my heart out. It's my fault and I'm not sure I can ever forgive myself."

He touched her face with his good hand. "Bullshit," he said with a smile that was also a grimace. "You had no way of knowing what this crazy idiot was going to do. And, think about it. It could have been worse. He could have used an AR-15, not a pickup. And you gotta believe they'll get him sooner than later and it'll all be over."

"I wish," she said, softly stroking his cheek and then fluffing his pillow.

He tried to raise himself up. "Now get out of here. Go walk *our* dog. And get some rest yourself. You were in that car, too."

"I'll be back tonight. And, oh, yeah, have I told you lately that I love you?"

"You don't have to tell me. I know."

True to his word, Andy was still in the waiting room, and glanced up from his phone as Gabby approached and sat next to him. "How's he doing?"

"He looks worse than you did when we saw you here," she said, "but better than I thought he'd be," describing how they'd found him. "I think he's going to be here until they decide how serious the concussion is."

Confusion was written across his face. "I just don't get it. Why does this lunatic Klinger hate you so much?"

She paused for a moment. "Trust me, that's all I've been thinking about," but then repeated her theory. "I think it may have started when he saw me talking to his wife after the funeral. I've never asked her, but I think she must have told him what I told her…about Jennie and Hannah's friendship in the Cities. And then he saw some of my reporting and maybe correctly figured it was me who learned about his Nebraska rape conviction and alerted the sheriff. That's all my speculation, of course, but it's clear he somehow sees me as the source of his troubles and wants to make me pay."

"I'm certainly no shrink," Andy said, "but there has to be something of a love-hate thing going on here. Like you say, he may hate you for exposing him, but loves or admires you in a way for the attention you give him on television." He looked away for a moment. "Remember the times he's tried to call you? And he must have been watching and following you often enough to know where you and Zach live and where you'd be when he plowed into you yesterday. It's like a nightmare that never ends."

"And probably won't until they finally get him," she replied. "But enough of that. What have you been up to?"

"Back at school, but also back on the street when I have the time, doing more interviews with homeless kids. Never without my law school buddy, the bodyguard. We've probably talked to at least a dozen or more kids since I've seen you. Gotten to know a few of them pretty well, including a couple who have let us follow them around, see some of their haunts and meet some of their friends. I think we've started to earn their trust. They don't seem to see us trying to exploit them, but, instead, honestly trying to tell their stories."

"Jeez, Andy, that's great, but…"

"It's all for you, you know. For the series you said you hope to

227

do. We're just collecting the interviews. You're going to have to put it all together and make sense of it. But a couple of my profs are also interested in the project, especially in how law enforcement and the courts treat these kids. They've given us some breaks in terms of our class schedules, but it still may take me another semester to finish."

"I don't know what to say."

"Don't say anything. You've got enough on your mind. Just stay safe and help Zach get well. When you want to see the video of the interviews, just let me know."

This time it was she who gave the hug.

THIRTY-TWO

• • •

O nce out of the hospital parking ramp and on her way home, her cell sounded and she pulled over. It was Julie O'Connell from The Haven.

"I'm so sorry," she said, "about what happened. I would have called sooner, but I just learned about it on the news. Are you okay? Is Zach?"

"I'm doing all right and I just left Zach at the hospital. He's doing better, but he's going to be there a while."

"Please give him my best when you see him next."

"Thanks. I will."

"But that's not the only reason I called. I hate to tell you this, but I have more bad news."

"About Jennie?"

"Yes.'

"I know. Sarah told me that she'd been taken back to Wadena County..." Gabby began.

"That's only the beginning," Julie said, "and not the latest. Eleanor Gladstone just called, and said Jennie's on the run again."

"What? So soon?"

"Yes. Last night. After her foster family was asleep. She slipped out of the house and took off. The family didn't know she was missing until this morning. And alerted Eleanor. But that's not all. Jennie took one of the family's cell phones and some cash. So now the sheriff is involved."

"It never ends."

"They think an older kid, a friend from the high school, may have been waiting and took her to who knows where. They're questioning him now."

Gabby leaned back, trying to compose herself. "Do they know why she ran? Was there a problem with the foster family?"

"No, they don't think so. But apparently they've spotted her dad driving by the farm several times, and once as she was getting off the school bus, defying orders to keep his distance. Spooking Jennie."

"Gets worse and worse. What can we do?"

"Probably nothing. But Eleanor wanted you to know in case Jennie makes it to the Cities and tries to contact you."

"And then what?"

"Contact me, I guess," Julie said. "We can't let her wander the streets again. Not if we can help it."

"I'll also alert Sarah. In case she does make it down here. And she can also let Jennie's brother know."

Returning home, Gabby retrieved two messages and a text she had ignored until then. The first message was from Rosemary Klinger, Hannah's mom, expressing regret at what had happened to her and Zach.

"I can't tell you how sorry I am and how ashamed I am that my husband did this to you. Something must have happened to his mind. Despite what he did to those girls and tried to do to Hannah, I can't imagine the man I knew and once thought I loved would do something like *this* to you," she said, sorrow evident in her tone. "But perhaps I never knew him at all. I've filed for divorce, the farm is up for sale, and my boys and I are living with my sister in Marshall. Please call me when you have a chance and tell me how you and Jennie are doing."

Gabby thought about calling her back then, but decided to wait until she knew more about Jennie. The lady didn't need something else to worry about.

The text was from Sarah, saying simply: "Got time for a drink? Bet you need one. I know I do. I'll pick you up."

She shot a text back. "Six o'clock. Before I go back to the hospital. Thanks."

The second message was from Detective Archer. "I wanted you to know we're still looking for Klinger and his friend. There's an all-points out for them and I'll let you know when we know something. And I haven't forgotten that we owe you a story."

She put the phone down and picked up Barclay, looking into his tiny eyes, seeing what she was convinced was deep sadness. "I know," she whispered. "I miss him, too. But he'll be back. Be patient, little guy."

A low whimper was his response.

As she faced the rest of the afternoon with nothing urgent to do, she decided to take on the household chores that had been left undone for days. She was about to begin with a load of wash when her phone sounded again.

Zach.

"Hey, you," she said. "I thought you'd be resting...or hustling the nurses."

He laughed. "I'm not much up to hustling right now."

"So what are you up to?"

"I want to get married..."

"What?"

"On Christmas Eve. Outside, in the snow. Then take a sleigh ride and make love under the blankets."

She doubled over, holding her stomach, the giggles escaping like bubbles. "Are you crazy?" she finally managed. "People don't get married in the snow!"

"This is Minnesota. And why not? Your wedding dress could be fake fur."

She couldn't control herself. "What kind of pills are they giving you over there? Are you hallucinating?"

"No, I'm quite serious. Maybe not about the snow, I admit. But about the wedding, yes. We've waited too long, Gabs. Lying here, knowing what almost happened, made me realize time's too precious. Life's too short."

For a moment, she felt woozy, as though she'd stumbled and hit her head. It was all too sudden, too unexpected. She had never been caught more off-guard. Finally, "Can we talk about this? Like when I get there tonight?"

"Sure, but we've talked about it before. So unless you have second thoughts, I want to stop talking and start doing. Making plans, setting a date, telling your Mom and your sisters, my folks, our friends. You have one ring on your finger and I'd like to put another one there, like soon."

"Okay," she said. "But please give me a chance to catch my breath. Everything's happened too fast and this kind of takes the cake."

"Are you having second thoughts?"

"Of course not," she assured him. "But, forgive me, almost seeing us get killed by some maniac took my mind off marriage momentarily."

She could picture his lopsided grin. "Okay. I'll see you tonight."

From the day Zach had proposed and she had accepted, she'd never doubted that they would end up married. But she had never felt the urgency that Zach was now feeling. They'd only been engaged for a few months and much of that time had been consumed by their jobs and the past threats from her California stalker, leaving little time for them to actually come to know one another in ways a longer, less-stressed relationship would have brought. And, truthfully, she had always dreamed of a big, traditional wedding, perhaps in a location where friends and family from Oregon, California and now Minnesota could gather and celebrate. And she wasn't sure Minneapolis was that place.

But could or should she share those thoughts with Zach now? As he lay in a hospital bed, impatient to move on with life as he had envisioned it before the crash? No, she decided, now was not the time. Play it cool. Don't dismiss his ideas, but don't embrace them, either. Let him fully recover. Let the current drama, the current threats play out, and hope they could agree on a time and place to recite those vows.

Sarah and Gabby were each nursing glasses of red wine as they sat at The Cellar bar, just down the block from the hospital, each picking at a plate of happy hour hors d'oeuvres. Between bites, Sarah reported on a long telephone conversation with Jennie's brother at his Army base in Texas. "He's very upset, as you'd guess, but like all of us, doesn't know quite what to do. He's thought about trying to get another leave, but figures it would be a waste of time until we know where Jennie is."

"I agree," Gabby replied. "There's not much any of us can do until we hear from her…or about her."

"For what it's worth, I've already circulated a picture of her to all of the precincts with a personal plea to watch out for her. And to grab her if they see her."

"And I called Andy," Gabby said, "to also be on the lookout if he goes back on the street for more interviews."

"Maybe she'll call."

"Maybe. But I'm not counting on it."

"Have you thought about going up to Wadena County yourself?" Sarah asked. "You know, as part of the homeless kids story?"

"Yes, but they probably wouldn't talk to me about Jennie's case or those of any other kids under eighteen. As you well know, juveniles are pretty much off-limits to the media. So I'm not sure what I could get out of it."

"I understand that, but you could put a little pressure on them, knowing you've got a personal interest in how they've been dealing with Jennie and her dad."

233

"They already know I've got a personal interest, but it may be academic, anyway. I don't think Barclay would let me go."

They sat quietly for a few minutes as the crowd noise picked up around them. Finally, Gabby said, "Anything else you'd like to tell me about your chat with Jesse?"

Sarah smiled. "Well, he did ask me if I'd come down for a long weekend in Texas."

"And?"

"I told him I'd think about it. Maybe when I get a break."

"He seems like a sweet guy, Sarah, and obviously a little smitten by you."

"You think?"

"Yeah. I'd go for it."

As they got up to leave and push their way toward the door, Sarah asked, "Tell me, what are you doing to protect yourself?"

"Being watchful, I guess. I try never to be alone on the street, walking the dog or whatever. I take Uber or Lyft whenever I can. There's only so much I can do."

"Well, keep doing it," she replied.

When she walked into his room, Zach was in a chair next to the bed, wearing a broad smile, humming "Here comes the bride, here comes the bride..."

"You goofus," she said, smiling, as she walked over to him and planted a wet kiss on his forehead. "You're obviously feeling better."

"A lot better," he replied, pulling her halfway onto his lap. "They say I might get out of here tomorrow after a couple more tests. It won't be soon enough."

The large bandage that had covered half of his face was now off, and she cupped his head in her hands, studying the bruises on his forehead and his black eye below it. She grinned. "I don't know. I'm not sure I want to marry somebody who looks like you."

"I'm afraid you're stuck with me, but I'll be good as new before you know it."

She pulled herself off his lap and brought a chair over next to his.

"My folks stopped by after you'd left," he said. "They're sorry they missed you, but had to drive back to Duluth before we get more snow tonight."

"Sorry I wasn't here, but did you tell them the bad guys were after me, not you?"

"Of course not. We're a team, remember?"

"Did you tell them about your wedding ideas?"

"Sure. They think a winter wedding would be great, but they think Christmas Eve is a bad idea. People want to be with their families, not at some wedding. So I think we should aim for New Year's Eve. Bring in the New Year with a splash."

"Or with a blizzard."

He laughed. "Seriously. What do you think?"

"I think I'd better talk to Mom and my sisters. And they're going to want to talk to my aunts and uncles and cousins. This wouldn't be an easy thing for them."

"Then let's make it a small wedding. Just the immediate families and a few close friends. We can hold a celebration in Oregon next summer for your other relatives."

"Let me think about it and call my Mom. But don't send out the invitations yet."

"If you insist."

She went on to tell him about Jennie's disappearance. "I don't know what to do but wait," she said.

"I bet you won't have to wait long. She'll be on the phone to you or at our door within a day or two. Where else is she going to go?"

"That's what I'm worried about. She's not even sixteen yet. Who knows where her mind is? She could do anything or go anywhere."

After another half hour of conversation, and as his eyelids began to droop, she got up. "If they let you go tomorrow, I'll be here to pick you up and get you home. But after that, after we get you settled, I'm going back to work. Despite Barclay's orders. I'm a reporter, not a nurse, and you'll do just fine home alone, recovering."

"No problem. I've got a ton of books to read and *our* dog to keep me company. I'll be just fine."

THIRTY-THREE

· · ·

Zach was right.

The call came shortly after one in the morning, as she once again slept fitfully, her mind a jumble, rushing from what to do about a wedding to more vivid flashbacks of the crushing crash. Of Zach's face buried in the air bag. As she tried to shake off the tangled thoughts, she reached for the phone on the bedside table and saw an unfamiliar number, but then, as she put the phone to her ear, heard an all-too-familiar voice.

"Gabby?"

"*Jennie?*" She pushed herself upright. "Where *are* you? Are you okay?"

"I'm okay. Tired, but okay."

"Thank, God. But where are you?"

"You won't tell?"

"I can't promise that. I just want to know you're safe. And to help you."

"I'm in Fargo… "

"*Fargo?*"

"A friend got me part way here, and I hitched a ride the rest of the way. I'm squatting with a couple of friends I met on the street."

"What kind of friends?"

"They're okay, Gabby. They got me some food and clothes at one of the drop-in centers. Watching out for me."

By now, Gabby was out of bed and in the kitchen, fully awake. "Jennie, I don't know what to say. You shouldn't have run again. You're in even more trouble now, and I don't know what I can do to help."

"I couldn't stay, Gabby. My dad kept coming around, watching for me. Yelled at me when I got off the school bus. He was supposed to stay away. I didn't know what he might do next. So I took off. And I didn't know who else to call."

"You have to give me a minute to think, Jennie. Just hold on."

She put the phone down and opened the refrigerator to grab a glass of juice, trying to fight off not only the fatigue of sleeplessness, but an overwhelming sense of helplessness. Finally, she was back on the phone. "I'm glad you called and I'm glad you're safe, but you can't stay there. You're too young and something bad could happen to you. Like Hannah… "

"I can take care of myself!" she blurted.

"You keep saying that, and maybe you can for the moment. But not forever. And I need some time to figure out how to help you. Promise me you'll take care of yourself until I do. Don't do anything foolish. Stay away from bad people. You have your whole life to live, Jennie."

"I know. I will." There were tears in her voice.

"Can I call you at this number?" Gabby asked.

"Yes, but the phone's not mine, you know."

"I know. Stay safe until you hear from me."

After several days free of snow and freezing cold, the weather had again turned wicked by the time Gabby pulled up in front of the hospital. She found Zach waiting just inside the doors, in a wheelchair with an attendant by his side. She got out and quickly opened the passenger door as he was wheeled through the snow and slid into the car, profusely thanking the retreating, shivering attendant as he did.

Once inside and before buckling up, he leaned across to give

Gabby a kiss. "Free, free at last," he said. "And turn up the heat!"

"It's as high as it can go," she laughed. "And, remember, this is *your* Minnesota!"

"You gotta love it, right?"

"It's seventy-two and sunny in San Jose. I checked."

"Sissyville."

As she pulled away from the curb, straining to see through the wind-whipped snow, she managed a quick glance at him. Except for the remaining traces of the facial bruising and black eye, he looked fairly normal. "What did the doctors say?"

"Nothing more than I told you on the phone. Get plenty of rest and let my body heal. Don't strain my eyes and watch out for the headaches. The normal post-concussion stuff. They want me back in a few days to change the cast on the wrist and do some more tests. But everything seems to be A-Okay. How about you?"

"Aside from being awake most of the night again, I'm fine," she replied, and then recounted the early-morning phone call from Jennie.

"She's in Fargo?"

"Yes. And I don't know what to do. I was hoping you'd have some ideas."

He could only provide a look of frustration. "I'm sorry. This is so out of the blue."

"I know. That's what kept me up the rest of the night. I haven't talked to anybody else and I can't call the people in Wadena County without revealing where Jennie is. But they also have the right to know she's safe, at least for the moment. I'm stuck."

"You think Barclay or Sarah or Julie at The Haven would have some ideas?"

"Doubtful. But I'll try after I get you home and settled. I'd planned to go into work anyway...so maybe I can get Barclay and Sarah together."

Barclay the poodle was waiting impatiently as they opened the apartment door, his tiny tail waving frantically, jumping at Zach's legs as they stepped inside. "Hey, buddy, hold on," he laughed as he picked him up and held his wiggling body to his chest, ignoring the sloppy licks on his neck. "Yes, your daddy's home. And, yes, I'm going to save you from this wicked lady."

He continued to hold the dog as he walked through the living room and into the kitchen, smelling the succulent aroma of the freshly-baked cinnamon rolls Gabby had prepared during her sleep-less early morning hours. "God, it's great to be home," he said, finally putting the poodle down and giving Gabby a hug. "Feels like I've been gone for weeks, not days."

"I do know the feeling," she replied, still vividly recalling her own days in a San Jose hospital almost a year before—after being battered by the boyfriend who later followed her to Minnesota. "It's great to have you home. And, believe it or not, I'm as excited as that dog. I just don't have a tail to wag."

"Oh, yeah?" he laughed. "I think you've got a nice tail."

As they walked through the rest of the apartment, she said, "Everything's been washed. Your clothes. Your bedding. With that broken wrist and all your aches and pains, you may want to sleep in the other bed for a while."

"Are you kidding?" he said. "No way. In fact, I'm ready to jump in right now. How about it?"

"Down boy. Patience. I've got to get to work. Call me if you need anything."

"I will, but have you talked to your mom about…well, you know?"

"Not yet. But tonight, if I can."

Gabby wasn't quite sure what to expect when she walked into the newsroom. It was her first day back since the crash, and in that time she'd received only a few calls, texts and emails from coworkers. Which didn't come as a complete surprise, knowing full well she was not the most popular figure in the place.

But now, as she stepped through the doors, she immediately drew a crowd, surrounded by everyone in sight, all of them offering handshakes or quick hugs. With words of concern for her and, of course, for Zach—with questions about how each of them was doing.

Even her nemesis, Jeff Parkett, welcomed her back, though with noticeably less enthusiasm than the others.

The reception was a bit overwhelming, but she graciously and patiently tried to answer all of the questions thrown at her, reporting that she had just taken Zach home and that both of them were doing great—considering what could have been. "I just want to get back to work," she told them.

Barclay finally interrupted the reception and led her back to his office. "I thought I told you to stay away for a while," he said.

"I know, but here I am."

"How's Zach?"

"Home and more frisky than he should be."

He laughed.

"But I need your advice."

"Shoot."

She quickly reported on Jennie's late night call and the dilemma she faced.

He didn't hesitate. "You've got to call Wadena County or go find her yourself and bring her to them. Or alert the child protection people in Fargo. She's a kid, for God's sake. You can't keep her whereabouts a secret..."

"I know, but... "

"No buts. What if something really bad happens to her up there? And you're the only one who knows who she is and where she is? You want to carry that kind of guilt?"

As she was about to respond, her cell phone sounded. A quick glance. Detective Archer. "I should take his," she said. Then, "Hey, Detective."

"Hey, Gabby. Remember my promise to give you that exclusive story?"

"Of course I remember."

"Well, I'm about ready to make good on that promise. But it will have to remain between you and me."

"I understand. But what's the story?"

"In the next hour or so, we hope to arrest Julius Winthrop for the murder of Hannah Hendricks."

"What?"

Barclay gave her a quizzical look.

"I'll tell you more when I see you, but I suggest you get yourself a photographer and meet me outside City Hall as quick as you can. Call me when you get here."

"I'll be there. And thanks!"

"No thanks needed. If it weren't for you, this might not be happening. At least not this soon."

She turned to Barclay, disbelief written on her face. "I need a photographer quick, George. Maybe more than one."

"What's going on?"

She repeated what Archer had told her.

"Holy shit!" He was out of his chair and rushing across the newsroom to the assignment desk, with Gabby trailing behind.

The assignment editor, Harry Wilson, looked up with surprise as Barclay approached. Rarely did anyone see him walk fast, let alone run. "Who's the closest photog?" he demanded, breathing hard.

"Les Leonard," Wilson said. "Ten minutes out."

"Is he all geared up?"

"Should be, sure."

"Then have him meet Gabby at the front door, stat!"

Wilson got on the phone and passed on the instructions to the photographer. Then, to Barclay, "Can you tell me what the hell's happening?"

He leaned across the desk and, in almost a whisper, told him of Archer's call. "I don't want anybody else, except Parkett, knowing. I don't want to risk a leak. Got it?"

"Got it. Wow!"

Barclay then turned to Gabby. "I want you to stay in constant touch. Call me as soon as you know what's going down and where. I'll have some other people standing by to assist, if needed."

"That's fine," she replied. "But don't let them get in the way and screw things up. Or my pretty ass will be in the wringer."

THIRTY-FOUR

...

L eonard had the station's cruiser parked in front of the station by the time Gabby got out the door and into the front seat. "Hey, Gabby, welcome back."

"Thanks, Les. Good to be back."

She had worked with Leonard several times in the past on routine assignments, but did not know him well. In his early thirties with a stern, no-nonsense look about him, he had the reputation as a hard worker and a consistent if not brilliant photographer. She knew Zach respected and liked him, largely because he rarely failed to produce useable if not always great video.

He put the car in gear. "So how's Zach?"

"Good, considering what he went through. I brought him home from the hospital this morning."

"I hope you'll give him my best."

"He'll appreciate that."

Then, with a glance over his shoulder, "You should probably tell me where we're going."

"To City Hall. We're supposed to meet a detective there. Fellow named Archer."

He pulled out into the street. "And then?"

She told him what she knew, little as it was. "He's going to tell us more, but as far as I know we're going to be alone on this story... so it could be a big deal."

"Jeez, I guess. How'd we luck out on that?"

"Long story short, I helped them find a connection between this Julius guy and Hannah's stepdad, going back to their days in a Nebraska prison. Archer says he owes me a favor for that. And this is it, I guess."

As they pulled in next to City Hall, behind a string of squad cars, Gabby phoned Archer. "We're here," she said, "on the Third Avenue side."

"I'll be right down."

Three minutes later he was in the car and was introduced to Leonard. "I'd rather not be seen with you guys," he said, "so why don't we circle the block a few times."

Gabby said, "So tell me. What's going down?"

"We got word from one of our snitches that Winthrop is back in town, hunkered down in an apartment in the Seward neighborhood. We set up surveillance and sure enough, we've seen him come and go several times, usually with a woman we're told is his longtime honey. Unless he skipped out during the night, he should be there now. And as far as we know, he thinks he's home free."

"But you said you're going to charge him with Hannah's murder. How's that possible?"

"Ahh, yes. Since we've talked, we finally got a report back from forensics. Believe it or not, the DNA on a paper cup left under the back seat of the SUV where Hannah's body was found had gone unmatched with anyone until we got a sample of Winthrop's DNA from your prison friends in Nebraska. Bingo. Proves he was in the murder car. We know that."

"And that's enough to charge him?"

"The county attorney says yes."

By now, they'd been around the block twice. "So what's the plan?" she asked. "And how do we fit in?"

"There's only a few of us in the department who know you're going to be involved. It has to stay that way or we're going to get crap from every other reporter in town. Since we can't have this news car anywhere in the vicinity of the bust, we're going to put you in the back seat of an unmarked squad car, driven by a sergeant who knows the score. Hopefully, he'll get you close enough to get some video, but far enough away to keep you safe if things go wrong."

She looked at Leonard. "Are you okay with this?"

"Of course. I'll just need a lane to shoot and hopefully be close enough to keep the shot steady."

Archer checked his watch. "We plan to make our move in exactly an hour. At twelve-forty-five. We have cars in the area now and are continuing our surveillance from an apartment across the street. We hope it will go down quietly, but we're prepared if things get out of hand."

"And then?"

"Then, when you see him being led out of the building in cuffs, you can hustle over to get him on the perp walk. We'll take it slow to give you time. It would be best if none of the other officers there see you get out of the squad. You'll just suddenly appear…and then you can find your own way back to the station."

"What about Klinger?" she asked. "Any sign of him?"

"No. He's still in the wind. The two of them must have split after abandoning the pickup in Shakopee."

She still couldn't quite believe this was happening. "And if this does work out, how are you going to explain that we were the only ones here?"

Archer simply shrugged. "That there must have been a leak in the department and that we're launching an internal investigation." He smiled. "That's our story and we're going to stick to it."

"And you could end up in deep…"

"Not to worry. I've got thirty-two years on the job. And the chief has my back."

"If you're sure," she said as they returned to City Hall. "What's next?"

"Park somewhere around here. My sergeant will spot your car and make the pickup. His name's Jim Andrews. Nice guy. Good cop."

As he started to get out, she said, "I appreciate this. You know that."

"As I told you before, no thanks are needed. I just hope it all works out."

As Les tried to find a parking spot, Gabby had a moment to consider the implications of what was about to happen. From her days in journalism school through her years in the news business, she had been taught never to get too cozy with the cops you cover. To avoid potential conflicts of interest. Yet here she was, about to jump into a squad car driven by a cop, and taken to a crime scene about to unfold. A crime scene she apparently would have all to her journalistic self. And all because of her friendship with Archer the cop. Oh, well, she thought, guiltily savoring the idea of the exclusive, it's too late to worry about it now.

Fifteen minutes later, they heard a quick tap of a horn as an older Mazda CX-5 with darkened windows pulled up behind their parked cruiser. They scrambled out and quickly climbed into the back seat, Les with camera and backpack in hand. The sergeant, in full uniform, turned in the seat with a "Welcome aboard. I'm Jim Andrews. You got everything you need?"

"I think so, thanks," she said. "I'm Gabby Gooding and this is Les Leonard. Thanks for doing this."

He grinned. "Just following orders, but I hear you helped us nail this guy…so I'm pleased to be of service."

He pulled away and headed south.

After that first glance, she could only see the back of his head and upper body, but his shoulders were broad, his neck thick and his hair graying. Kind of how you'd picture a big, strong cop. "So where are we going?" she asked, leaning across the seat.

"To around 27th and Oak in the Seward neighborhood. There are several apartment buildings in the area and our suspect is in one of them. At least we hope he's still there. One of our guys is supposed to have saved a parking spot for us about a half-block away—with a clear view of the building."

"Then what?"

"At twelve-forty-five, if all goes as planned, four marked squads will pull up in front of the building. Four officers, fully armored–up, will enter and move to the apartment on the third floor, hoping to take our friend by surprise. Four more officers will remain outside, front and back, in case he's somewhere else in the building and tries to make a break. Others will be standing by in the neighborhood."

"That's pretty impressive," she said. "Like you're expecting trouble."

"Better safe than sorry, as they say. But this isn't some drug bust. A murder suspect gets special treatment. And from what we know, this guy could be a tough takedown."

"Why don't I hear any radio traffic? I thought there'd be some chatter."

"We're on a separate frequency," he replied. "And radio silence for now. Just in case he's got a receiver and happens to be scanning the channels. You never know."

It took about fifteen minutes to get to Seward, one of the older neighborhoods of Minneapolis, and an area that Gabby could not remember being in before. New snow had begun to fall, whipped around by a strong north wind. She glanced at her watch. With about twenty minutes to go, they pulled into an empty space along Oak. Andrews pointed to an older, red brick building on the opposite side of the street that looked to be about five stories high.

"There she be," he said, checking his own watch.

"Do you know which apartment it is?"

"Third floor, second window in, facing us. Looks like the shades are down."

Les rolled down the back window and, while staying low, tried to adjust his position to get the clearest possible view, keeping his camera at his side. "This should work," he said, "but I can't keep the camera totally out of sight."

"I understand," Andrews said, "but just wait until the last possible minute."

Those minutes ticked by. Les fiddled with his gear. Gabby stayed silent. At precisely twelve-forty-five, the car's police radio awoke. "All cars move in. Stay alert."

Les raised his camera to the window as four marked squad cars, two from each direction, came to a stop in front of the building, blocking the street. Two officers from each car scrambled out, four raced to the front door, two toward the rear, and two remained in front—just as Andrews had promised.

Gabby turned to Les, silently mouthing, "You getting this?"

She got a quick nod.

The four cops in the front pushed open the door, which apparently had been left ajar by some pre-arrangement. Two carried assault rifles, the other two handguns.

They disappeared inside.

Andrews had a small pair of binoculars trained on the third floor apartment window. But he saw no movement. The shade remained down.

Two minutes passed. Then three. There were no sounds they could hear. No shots, no shouts.

Then.

A muffled blast. The shaded-window shattered. A woman's screams. Angry shouts, indistinct at this distance.

Gabby leaned over, her voice barely a whisper. "What's happening?"

Andrews already had the car door open. "Stun grenade. Stay here and stay down until I see what's up."

Les had not moved, the camera still trained on the building. She fought the urge to leap out of the car, but held back, straining to see over his shoulder. Then, suddenly, the front door of the building swung open and people started to stream out, two men, then a woman carrying a toddler, another man helping an older woman with a cane. Then more. The cops outside intercepted them and directed them down the street and into another apartment building, out of danger and out of the weather.

Les pushed the back door open, camera on his shoulder still rolling. "Screw-it," he said. "I'm heading down there."

She hastily followed, pulling her jacket around her body and her hood over her head, fighting the wind, trying to keep up. Two of the cops in front saw them coming, clearly surprised to see the camera on Les's shoulder. They held up their hands, bringing them to a halt about a hundred feet from the building. "Where the hell did you come from?" one of them shouted. "Stay back."

Gabby pulled a five-by-seven PRESS card from her jacket pocket and held it up. "Channel Seven News," she yelled.

One of the cops moved toward them, anger on his face and in his voice. "I don't care where you're from. Are you crazy? This is a crime scene. Get the hell away!"

But Les kept on shooting.

Hearing the commotion, Sergeant Andrews, who was by now at the front door, turned and started back, shouting at the uniforms. "It's okay, it's okay. They've got a right to be here. Keep your cool."

Despite his efforts to calm things, she could see he was also pissed that they had ignored his orders to stay in the car. But before he could say anything, the front door was pushed open and two officers emerged with a woman between them. A minute later, two more officers came out with a handcuffed Julius Winthrop in tow.

"Okay," Andrews said, "they've got him. Follow me. I'll clear the way."

The woman, who was not in cuffs, was led toward one of the squads. Her head was covered by a scarf and her upper body wrapped in a black parka. She kept her head tucked into her chest, hiding her face from view and from the wind, shuffling in what—from a distance—looked like bedroom slippers.

Les moved quickly ahead of Gabby, following Andrews.

The officers holding Winthrop had stopped at the bottom of the steps, pausing, as promised, for a minute or so before following the woman toward another squad car. Unlike the woman, Winthrop held his head high, defiantly looking around him and then, squarely into the lens of Les's approaching camera. He wore an old, oversized Army fatigue jacket and a pair of baggy jeans tucked into, yes, a pair of cowboy boots. And when he spotted Gabby he stopped short, with first a look of surprise and then, a twisted grin, shouting, "You'll get yours, bitch!"

Gabby stood back, smiled, and discreetly put her middle finger in the air.

Once he was safely tucked into the back seat of the squad car, Les finally took the camera off his shoulder. "Jesus," he said, "that was one hell of a scene."

"You got it all?" Gabby said.

"Should have. I'll check it now."

As she waited, she took out her cell and hit Barclay's number. He was clearly waiting. "It's all over," she told him. "Les is checking the video as we speak."

"And?"

"Not quite sure what happened, but I think they used a stun grenade to get at him. Blew out an upstairs window. The cops evacuated the building. But Winthrop and a woman who was with him are in custody, and I hope to get an interview."

"And we're all alone?"

"Far as I can see, yes."

"That's great. I'll send a cruiser to pick you up."

"Don't bother. We'll Uber back after we try to get that interview. And after I do a couple of promos. It'll be quicker that way."

"I'll have things ready here. Good work, both of you."

As she put the phone away, she spotted Detective Archer standing with a group of uniforms by the unmarked Mazda they had arrived in. There was a frown on his face as she and Les approached, and before she could say anything, he barked, feigning genuine anger, "I want the name of your boss. You had no business being here, and I want to know how the hell you learned about this?"

"My boss's name is Barclay, George Barclay, and we have our sources."

As he glanced at those around him, scowling, he said, "Well, you could've screwed the whole thing up, you know that? And got hurt, too. I'll get to the bottom of this, trust me."

"Good luck with that," Gabby said, "but in the meantime, can we talk to you about what happened here?"

"You gotta be kidding."

"Look, Detective, be reasonable. Our sources tell us this suspect has something to do with the murder of Hannah Hendricks. The public deserves to know if that's true. You don't want us to broadcast misinformation, do you? We have the video and now we need the facts. They'll all come out anyway, so why don't you give us a break?"

"I don't know," he replied with the quickest wink in history. "I guess you've got a point. But I can't tell you much."

"I understand, and I appreciate that. Why don't you stand over here, in front of the building, with the squad cars in the background, while Les gets the camera set."

With an exasperated sigh, he said, "All right, but make it short. I've gotta get back downtown."

THIRTY-FIVE

. . .

For the second time in just more than a week, Gabby found herself at the anchor desk, slumped in her chair, physically exhausted and emotionally spent, waiting as the countdown continued for the opening of the five o'clock news.

In the hours since Winthrop's arrest, she had braved the wind and the snow to record two off-the-cuff promos from the scene that would run during the afternoon and evening, promising exclusive coverage. And after a hurried phone call to check on Zach, it was a rush back to the station, an hour in the editing booth with Les viewing all of the video he had captured, and agreeing on a shot-by-shot sequence for her story.

Then to the computer for an hour of writing, working to keep her words to a minimum and letting the natural sound video of the chaotic capture carry the story. In this case, she knew the pictures were worth more than a thousand of her words. Never far away were Barclay and the five o'clock producer, encouraging her and relaying information from another reporter, who was at City Hall for Winthrop's booking. Waiting to know if he'd been officially charged, so they could be free to use his name.

By four o'clock, he was. Second degree murder. Being held without bail for now.

"Ten seconds to air…nine….eight…" came the call from the floor director. Gabby straightened up and perked up as the news open rolled and anchors Andrea and Scott appeared on the screen.

SCOTT: *Good afternoon everyone. We have breaking news to bring you at this hour…the arrest and charging of a suspect in the weeks-old murder of Hannah Hendricks, the young rural Minnesota woman who was found bludgeoned to death in a Minneapolis parking lot.*

ANDREA: *The dramatic arrest came early this afternoon in the Seward neighborhood of Minneapolis…and Channel Seven reporter Gabby Gooding and photographer Les Leonard were there to witness it all, and to bring you an exclusive report. Gabby?*

GABBY (with picture of Winthrop behind her): *The name of the suspect is Julius Winthrop, thirty-three-years old, who was living on the twenty-seven-hundred block of Oak Avenue and has been a person of interest in Hannah's murder for some time. Our sources tell us his arrest finally came after a trace of his DNA was found in the stolen car where Hannah's body was discovered.*

VIDEO OF THE SCENE: *The arrest came shortly after twelve-forty-five this afternoon as several squad cars closed in on the apartment building where Winthrop was known to be staying. Heavily armed officers in body armor rushed into the building while others covered the front and the back.* (NAT SOUND UP FOR FIFTEEN SECONDS). *Several minutes passed before a blast was heard from a third floor apartment, blowing out a window and triggering shouts and screams from inside.* (NAT SOUND UP). *Within minutes, confused and frightened residents began to run out of the building, met by waiting officers who escorted them to safety down the street* (MORE NAT SOUND OF FLIGHT).

SHOT OF GABBY AND ARCHER: *Homicide detective John Archer oversaw the operation.* GABBY TO ARCHER: *So what happened up there…in the apartment?* ARCHER: *I don't know all the details, but the suspect refused to comply with our orders to open the door and come out. So they forced the door open and used a stun grenade to neutralize the suspect and to protect themselves. He surrendered moments later. Neither he nor the woman who was with him…or any of the officers…were injured. We'll know more when we can view the officers' body camera video.* GABBY: *So what about the woman?* ARCHER: *I have no information on her.* GABBY: *Can you confirm that Winthrop is a suspect in the Hannah Hendricks murder?* ARCHER: *Yes, I can confirm that.* GABBY: *Do you believe he acted alone?* ARCHER (with a sly smile): *I can't comment on that.*

VIDEO OF THE SCENE: *The woman who was taken into custody with Winthrop has not been identified, and as far we know, has not been charged. And her relationship with Winthrop is also not known at this time. Minutes after she was escorted out, Winthrop himself was brought out of the building in handcuffs, pausing long enough to mouth an expletive at our camera…and moments later…at this reporter.* (NAT SOUND OF WINTHROP WALKING TO SQUAD CAR). *We can confirm that Winthrop once was a cellmate of Howard Klinger in the Nebraska state penitentiary. Klinger, as you may remember, was the stepfather of Hannah Hendricks, and who allegedly had attempted to rape her before she wounded him and fled to Minneapolis weeks before her murder.*

GABBY LIVE: *Klinger spent time in the Nebraska penitentiary for the rape of a young woman more than ten years ago and is now accused of assaulting another young woman in Minnesota's Lincoln County. He is still at large and the object of a widespread search.*

THREE SHOT LIVE, SCOTT: *That's a remarkable story, Gabby. Congrats to you and Les for the exclusive. I know our viewers and others* (with a small smile) *must be wondering how you happened to be there when all of this was going down?*

GABBY: *I'm afraid I can't reveal that, Scott. But I will say some of the police were not exactly happy to see us there.*

ANDREA: *So what happens next?*

GABBY: *That will be up to the county attorney, I guess. We're told he may hold a news conference tomorrow. So we should know more then.*

SCOTT: *And we'll be there covering it, I'm sure. Thanks so much, Gabby.*

Barclay waited in the wings as she left the set during the first commercial break. Jeff Parkett was there, too. Both sporting broad smiles. "Nice job, Gabs," Barclay said. "You make me proud to be in this business."

"I agree," Parkett said. "And I'm sorry I haven't said it before, Gabby, but you're a terrific reporter. Which doesn't mean you're not a pain in the ass for someone like me, trying to keep a daily newsroom going. But you do make us a better place, for sure."

She smiled, surprised at the compliment. "Can you put that in writing?"

"Not likely. You know me. I'll deny I ever said it."

"You must be bushed," Barclay said, "but I'd like you to stay for the six o'clock show. I've taken the liberty of rewriting a somewhat shorter version of the story that you can voice on set. Then we'll do an anchor-read for ten o'clock. Is that okay?"

"Sure. Just give me a minute to catch my breath."

"Of course. Get a pop and relax for awhile. Then I'll show you my revised script."

"First I've got a couple of calls to make. To Zach, to see how he's doing. To my reporter friend down in Nebraska, to let him know he's got a story. And, finally, to my friend, Howard, in Lyon County. In case he didn't see the news. He'll want to know they've got a suspect in Hannah's murder."

"That's fine, but get some rest too."

Two hours later, when she opened the door to the apartment, she stood stock still, mouth agape. Zach was on the couch, the poodle in his lap, a glass of wine in his hand and—huddled in a corner of the couch—*Jennie.* Momentarily lost for words, Gabby could only stare, not quite believing what she saw.

"Hi, honey," Zach said with a smile, clearly enjoying her shock, "welcome home. And say hello to our visitor."

She shrugged off her coat and left it in a heap at her feet. Still befuddled, she slowly walked across the room and knelt before the two of them, grabbing one of Jennie's hands. "My, God, Jennie…"

The girl managed a shy grin. "Hi, Gabby. I'm sorry…"

"Don't be sorry. I'm just glad to know you're safe. But how did you get here?"

Zach answered for her. "She hitched a ride with some guy she met in Fargo, a nice guy, she says, who sort of adopted her on the street and kept her safe. She says he reminded her of me."

"And I told him about you two," Jennie said, "that you were my friends and had been helping me. He agreed to bring me here. I didn't know what else to do or where else to go."

Gabby lifted herself from her knees as Zach got up, making room on the couch. "I'll get you a glass of wine," he said. "You've had a hell of a day and I want to hear more. It was quite a scoop and I wish I could have been there."

"Les did a great job, both the shooting and editing."

"Good. I'll send him a text."

As he walked to the kitchen, Gabby turned to Jennie. "Can you stand up and let me get a good look at you?"

She hadn't changed much. A little lighter, maybe, and what? Somehow more mature, more grown-up than she'd been just a couple of weeks before. Living on the streets *had* left its mark. Her smile seemed more forced, her features more hardened. No longer with the look of a sweet, innocent young girl. And how sad was that? Always on the run, missing those wonderful teenage years surrounded by giggling girlfriends, raucous sleepovers, wooing or rebuffing boys overflowing with hormones, and cheering at Friday night football. All of those things and more that had been part of Gabby's own growing-up years in Oregon, all of them a part of her adult DNA. Memories of the kind that Jennie was now missing and might never recover.

"Where did you stay? How did you… "

"In and out of shelters. In a couple of empty houses. Squatting with friends I made on the street. Never stayed long anywhere. You know, to keep from getting caught and sent back. Spent the money I stole and finally sold the phone. I had to eat."

"Wow," Gabby marveled. "You're one tough kid."

That drew a small smile.

Gabby got up. "Wait here. Give Barclay a little loving while I talk with Zach."

He was still in the kitchen, holding her wine, cocking his head, shrugging his shoulders. "So what do we do now?"

She took a sip of the wine. "I have no idea. Keep her here for the night…and then, I don't know. Try to persuade her to let us take her back to Eleanor in Wadena, I guess. Maybe she'll be okay with that if we're with her, to make sure the folks up there know we've got her back. That a Twin Cities television station is interested in her case and will be there to see that she's treated right."

"So we've become full-time social workers?"

Frowning, she said, "You have a better idea?"

"No," he admitted. "Unless we take her back to The Haven and let Julie O'Connell deal with her."

"Julie's already said she doesn't have the time or resources to take Jennie on."

As she glanced into the living room, she saw Jennie was now lying to one side of the couch, eyes closed, clutching the poodle like a furry rag doll. Fast asleep.

She put her wine down and took his from his hand, then put her arms around him and looked into his eyes, kissing his cheeks, then his lips. Lingering, touching his tongue with hers. Feeling his warmth as she moved her hips against his. "Enough about her," she whispered. "What about you? Are you better?"

"Much better, thank you, oh, yes," he breathed, moving his hand to gently touch her breast, his caress causing her breath to quicken. But only for a moment. Then, stepping back, "Whoa, big guy. Hold on. Not on the kitchen table. Once she's in bed and asleep, I promise you."

"It's been way too long," he said, pulling back. "I've missed you."

"And I've missed you. But, remember, you've been on injured reserve for a while."

"And you've been out chasing murder suspects. Maybe we should both get normal jobs."

258

She laughed. "What fun would that be?"

Watching Jennie sleep on, they took their wine to the small office area off the living room. "I saw your five o'clock piece," Zach said, "but Jennie arrived before the six...so I missed that one. You've had a big day."

"And I feel it in every bone in my body."

"Did you get anything to eat?"

"Yes. George ordered in some food for all of us. I hadn't eaten anything since breakfast."

"You must feel pretty good about it all."

"I do, but the whole thing was kind of surreal. Like being on a Hollywood set and watching a bad movie unfold. Everything seemed so choreographed. I kept waiting for someone to shout 'Cut, that's a wrap.'"

"Funny."

"But the best thing is that Parkett actually congratulated me and apologized in his own way. I never thought I'd see that."

"That should make life a little more pleasant for you."

"I hope so." She paused. "But what about you? Have you talked to the doctors?"

"I did, actually. They're going to give me a soft cast tomorrow, and since the headaches have stopped, they say I should be able to go back to work."

"Like when?"

"Like in a couple of days. After one more checkup."

"That could give us time to drive up to Wadena County."

"You're really serious about that?"

"If Jennie will agree, yes. I don't know what else to do, except to turn her over to local child protection or let her go back on the streets. And we can't do that."

"You should talk to Sarah and to Eleanor up in Wadena..."

"I will. Tomorrow. After the county attorney's news conference in the morning."

Once Jennie had awakened and eaten something, they were back in the living room, Jennie again with the dog clutched in her arms. Gabby leaned close. "We have to talk, Jennie, about what will happen next. You may still be a teenager, but you'll have to listen to us like an adult. Is that okay? Do you understand?"

Tears formed in her eyes. "I understand. You want me to go back."

"That's true. We don't think you…or we…have any choice. You can't go on living on the streets, here or in Fargo or anywhere else. It's too dangerous and you're missing out on too much. Christmas is not that far off. You have to get back to school, to your Mom and to your friends, to the kind of life you deserve to live. If you don't, you could end up like Hannah, or alone and sick in some alley or as somebody's sex slave, turning tricks to stay alive."

She stuck out her jaw. "How often have I told you? I can take care of myself."

"Then why are you here?" Gabby challenged her. " Why come back to us?"

She had no answer, and simply looked away.

Zach took one of her hands in his. "We're not asking you to go back alone. We want to take you back, to make sure you're protected and treated right. And that means keeping your dad away until he changes, or until you're old enough to live on your own."

She pulled her hand away, defiance in her voice. "And how can you do that?"

"Because we're from a television station," Gabby said. "Because we will make sure Eleanor and her people know that we'll follow your case closely, that we're prepared to go public if you're abused in any way, by your father or by their system."

Zach gave her a look, aware she was promising far more than they could probably ever deliver. But he said nothing.

"What if I say no?"

"Then we will have done all we can for you. I'll call Sergeant Chan right now and have her come pick you up. Get you to child protection. You have to understand that Zach and I are taking a big risk keeping you here. We could go to jail ourselves. And we can't afford that. And you wouldn't want that."

She clearly was torn and started to get up, the tears falling freely now.

"You should think about it," Gabby said. "Sleep on it. But if you walk out that door, please don't consider coming back. You'll be on your own. And think about the life you have left to live. Please don't throw it away."

"When would we go?" she asked.

"Probably the day after tomorrow. I have to cover a news conference in the morning, and then I'll call Eleanor to tell her we'll be bringing you to her."

"Okay," she said, picking up the poodle. "Can Barclay and I go to bed now?"

"For sure. But first, let's get you a shower, change the bed, and find some fresh jammies for you."

As they themselves prepared for bed, Gabby did what she had promised Zach: to call her mother in Portland. "Hey, Mom. Hope I didn't get you from anything."

"No, no, I just finished cleaning up the dinner dishes."

"I won't keep you long," Gabby said, "but we have some important news."

"Really? What's that?"

She glanced at Zach and swallowed hard. "We're getting married, like maybe soon..."

"Yes!" Almost a shriek. Then, after a moment, "You're not... "

Gabby laughed. "No, Mom, I'm not. We just decided we've waited long enough. Especially after the close call with the car crash. It's time. Life is too unpredictable."

"That's wonderful. I can't tell you how pleased I am...and how pleased your sisters will be. When are you thinking...?"

"That's still a question. But maybe as early as New Year's Eve, or Valentine's Day at the latest."

"But…"

"I know it's a surprise and short notice, but we're thinking of a simple, small wedding here in Minnesota with just our families and some of our friends. Then, next summer, a reception in Oregon for the rest of the family and our friends back there."

"Gosh, Gabby, I don't know," disappointment in her voice. "This isn't what I was hoping for, I guess. I need to talk to your sisters and the rest of our family."

"Do that and get back to me when you can. Nothing is for certain. We're still really busy, but we wanted you to know what we're thinking."

"I appreciate that." Then. "And how is Zach?"

"Sitting next to me, smiling. And recovering. I think he'll be fine."

"Good. Tell him hi."

The conversation went on for several more minutes before Gabby finally ended it with the need to get some sleep. "Let's keep in touch," she said.

With the phone aside, she leaned over to give Zach a kiss on the cheek.

"Thank you," he said simply. "Now can we go make love?"

"I thought you'd never ask."

THIRTY-SIX

• • •

By the time Gabby and Les Leonard got to the atrium of the towering Hennepin County Government Center the next morning, they found every other TV station already there, setting up their cameras and putting their microphones on the pedestal where the county attorney would soon hold forth. "Wow," she whispered to Les, "this is quite a crowd."

"What did you expect?" he said, unloading his gear. "After our story."

Despite her efforts to stay in the background, she couldn't help but notice some curious, not entirely friendly stares, coming her way. Finally, a reporter from Channel Ten, Sean Holister, whom she knew only slightly, wandered over. "Hey, Gabby, remember me? Sean… "

"Sure, Sean. Nice to see you. How goes it?"

He gave her a quirky smile. "I'd be better if I hadn't gotten ten lashes and a kick in the ass from my news director yesterday. That was quite a beat you got."

"Thanks. Got lucky, I guess."

His smile turned one shade short of sour. Smarmy. "Rumor has it that you've got an inside track in the cop shop. Gorgeous lady like you. You know, a little quid pro quo, as the lawyers like to say."

Recoiling, stunned by what she'd just heard, she leaned into him, her face flushed with anger, the words flowing before she had a chance to control them. "I don't know what you're trying to say, Sean, but if it's what I think it is, fuck off. And if you get one inch closer to me, you'll get my knee in your balls."

Clearly shocked, he backed away, unconsciously letting one hand fall to his crotch. "Hey, hey, no offense intended. I was making a joke... "

"Bullshit. It was no joke. Stay away from me and stick those rumors up your ass. And tell your friends I get my stories the hard way. By working at it. You ought to try it."

With that, she turned and walked away, taking a seat in the back of the crowd, struggling to quiet her nerves and ease her anger as she stared up into the heights of the atrium. Nice going, she told herself. That little scene will spread like a five-alarm fire. And, Barclay, she was sure, would be among the first to hear about it. Parkett, too. She'd be the talk of the local news world by noon.

Let 'em talk, she thought. She'd seen and heard enough of that kind of sexist crap for years now, from her days as a teenager through her years in the news business, perhaps less now than before and seldom as blatant as this encounter. But, still, there wasn't a woman she knew who hadn't been verbally or sexually assaulted or harassed at some time in their lives. And she was sick of it.

As she waited for the county attorney to show, she called Eleanor in Wadena County. "Eleanor, this is Gabby Gooding in Minneapolis."

"Hey, Gabby."

"I just have a minute, but I wanted you to know that Jennie is with us again."

"What?"

"She showed up at our door last night. She'd been squatting in Fargo and bummed a ride to the Cities."

"She's at your apartment?"

"For the moment, yes, but unless she runs again, we plan to bring her to you tomorrow."

"Is she okay?"

"As okay as a fifteen-year-old runaway can be, I guess. She's not been abused as far as we can tell, and seems ready to return."

"I can send someone down for her," Eleanor said.

"No, please don't do that. She'll run again. The only reason she's agreed to go back is because we're bringing her."

"And why is that?"

"Because we've told her I'll be watching out for her, as a reporter as well as a friend. As you know, I'm hoping to do a series on homeless kids and she could be the star of the show. How she and others like her are treated and protected in counties like yours."

"You think we've mistreated her?"

"Not you personally, of course, but I know the county hasn't been able to keep her father away from her, and that's why she ran again."

"She's a difficult child, Gabby... "

"You're right. A child. Who's gone from living with an abusive father, to living on the streets, to seeing her friend dead. I'm not defending everything she's done, but she deserves a chance to be a normal kid. Who shouldn't have to live in fear of her father."

At that moment, she saw a group of people cross the atrium, led by a tall, thin, snappily-dressed man she recognized as the Hennepin County Attorney, Marshall Mantis.

"I've gotta go, Eleanor. I hope to see you tomorrow. I'll call to set up a time."

"Wait... "

"Sorry, I can't. I'm at a news conference that's about to begin."

Mantis was accompanied by a woman Gabby had seen at the parking lot murder scene, whom she had then thought might be from the county attorney's office. Behind her was a man she didn't recognize, likely a Mantis aide. And trailing the group, Detective John Archer.

In her relatively brief time at the station, Gabby had never met Mantis or knew that much about him. But in her Google Search, she'd discovered that he was fifty-two years old, a native Minnesotan, a graduate of the University Law School who had clerked for a federal judge and worked for the state attorney general before winning election to his present post. Word in the newsroom was that as affable as he might appear in public, he had a hard edge that made him both tough to work for and tough to face if you happen to cross a legal line.

He stepped to the podium, adjusted his blue-and-red tie, brushed back his graying hair, and scanned the crowd of reporters and onlookers. "Thank you all for coming," he began, "on such relatively short notice. I wanted to meet with you as soon as possible, but I'm afraid that also means we will have to be brief—since this investigation is ongoing and there are still many unanswered questions."

He turned to the woman who stood behind him. "When I'm done, Margaret Jacobsen, who will personally prosecute this case, will pass out a news release detailing the facts as we now know them. But let me first say that we are grateful to Detective John Archer, who is here, and to the Minneapolis Police Department for making this arrest and resolving some of the mystery surrounding the brutal murder of Hannah Hendricks, a young woman whose promising life was cut short in a most vicious way. Her family and friends deserve resolution and justice in this case and we hope to provide it."

He went on to identify Winthrop as the suspect. "He has a lengthy criminal history, which is detailed in the news release, but until now, has no known crimes of violence in Minnesota. He was charged late yesterday with second- degree murder and is being held without bail until his first court appearance, now scheduled for tomorrow morning. At present, we plan to ask a grand jury to consider possible first-degree murder charges against him. I should add that the woman who was taken into custody with Winthrop has been released without charges for now."

Before he could go on, a woman three seats to Gabby's left raised her hand.

"Yes?" Mantis said.

"Marjorie Nester from the *Star Tribune*. Can you confirm a media report that Winthrop spent time years ago in the Nebraska state prison with Hannah Hendricks' stepfather, and that it was that information that led to Winthrop's arrest?"

"I'll let Detective Archer respond to that."

Archer came to the podium with a quick glance at Gabby. "That report is correct. The Nebraska prison officials provided us with a sample of Winthrop's DNA, which we were able to match with evidence found near Hannah's body."

"And how did you discover the link between the two in Nebraska?"

"Through our investigative process. That's all I can say."

Nester persisted. "Does that mean the stepfather, Arnold Klinger, might also be involved in her murder?"

He paused and glanced at the county attorney. "We have no direct evidence of that, but as you know, Klinger is wanted for the sexual assault of a young woman in Lincoln County, and is the subject of an intensive search. Based on what we now know, we certainly would consider him a person of interest, and would like to question him once he has been apprehended."

Before he could step away, Sean Holister got up abruptly. "Detective, a number of us wonder why it was that only one media outlet, Channel Seven, happened to be at the scene of Winthrop's dramatic arrest yesterday? And whether you're playing favorites these days?"

Gabby stared straight ahead, ignoring the heads turned in her direction.

Archer's face reddened slightly. "Funny you should ask. We wondered the same thing, and I've ordered an internal investigation to get to the bottom of it. And, no, we don't play favorites." Then, with a laugh, "We hate all of you media types just the same."

Once the news conference was over, as Gabby helped Les pack up his equipment, she was approached by Marjorie Nester, the *Strib* reporter, who took her aside. "I overheard part of your encounter with that Channel Ten guy and wanted to laugh out loud. On behalf of all of us women, I want you to know how proud I was of you." Then, with a grin, "And while I'm not sure I approve of your language, you certainly put that prick in his place."

Gabby couldn't help but smile. "Thank you, I think. My mother would have been aghast, but I was taught all of those words from my dad, God rest his soul."

"Well," Marjorie went on, "Trust me, it will be the talk of our newsroom and probably every other newsroom in town. You'll be the gal gunslinger from out West who takes no prisoners."

"That's what I'm afraid of."

"Don't be. And when you get a chance, give me a call. I'd like to buy you a drink."

"Thanks. I'd like that." Then, "Oh, one more thing."

"Sure."

"Can you give me the name of the person at the *Strib* who takes reporter applications?"

She smiled. "Are you interested?"

Gabby returned the smile. "Not me. There's a reporter in Lincoln, Nebraska who gave me a hand in the Winthrop story. Paul Cornell, by name, who'd love to work up here. I promised I'd give him a name and a good word."

Nester said, "You or he should talk to Hank Abbot in personnel. He'd be a good place to start, but as you know, things are tight and we don't have a lot of turnover."

"I understand. But I told him I'd try." She then took a moment to tap Abbot's name into her phone.

As she expected, or feared, in the twenty minutes it took to get back to the station, the word had spread like it had wings. Barclay was standing by the assignment desk as she sheepishly approached, he sporting a grin as wide as the newsroom. "Is it true?" he asked. "Did you really say you'd 'knee him in the balls'?"

"I'd rather not talk about it," she replied as she headed for her desk.

He followed her, clearly enjoying the moment. "C,mon, 'fess up. 'That he could stick the rumors up his ass'?"

She threw her coat on her chair and faced him, finding it hard not to smile herself. "I'm not proud of it, but I don't regret it. It pissed me off that he thought I was screwing some cop to get my story. I'll apologize to the newsroom, if you'd like, for any embarrassment it's caused, but I sure as heck won't apologize to the Sean guy."

"Apologize to *us*? Hell, no. I just wish I had it on video."

"Funny, except I've made another enemy. And I have enough of those already."

"Don't worry about it. I know the guy. He's a harmless blowhard."

As he turned to leave, she said, "The news conference didn't produce much new and I'll do whatever you want for each of the newscasts. But I'd like to take tomorrow off, if I could. Maybe the next day, too."

He looked puzzled. "Really? Why's that?"

"I haven't had the chance to tell you, but Jennie showed up at our door again late yesterday. And we've persuaded her to let us take her back to Wadena and get her off the streets. But she won't go unless we go with her, and I've promised the people in the county that we'll do it tomorrow."

"Okay, I guess. We'll have to find somebody else to cover Winthrop's court appearance."

"I know. And I'm sorry. But I don't have much choice."

As she sat at her computer writing her report for the noon news, her phone buzzed. "Gabby, this is Marshall Mantis."

She took a breath. "Yes, sir. Hello."

"I had hoped to speak to you after the news conference, but I got sidetracked. And by the time I looked around, you were gone."

"I'm sorry," she said. "We had to get back to the station."

"My problem, not yours. I just wanted you to know that I'm aware of the part you played in the Winthrop investigation. And I wish I could have publicly thanked you for that, but I know it's a sensitive subject right now."

"I guess so."

"But I did want to personally thank you on behalf of my office and the people of Hennepin County."

She didn't know what to say.

"So," he continued, "if you need a favor from me at some point, just let me know. We *do* occasionally play favorites."

"I appreciate that," she said, finally finding the words. "And I'll keep it in mind."

"Good."

With that he was gone.

THIRTY-SEVEN

. . .

The trip to the city of Wadena, the county seat of Wadena County, took the better part of four hours, with Jennie bundled up in the back seat, saying little, apparently content to stare out the window at the snow-covered fields and the towns they passed along Highway 10. In fact, she had said almost nothing since getting up, showering, and dressing in the early morning hours. And neither Gabby nor Zach had pressed her, knowing there was little they could say to cheer her up, or to ease the grave misgivings she must be feeling.

There were no tears, no angry outbursts, and no final pleas to undo what was being done. Her only show of emotion came as she put on her coat and picked up the poodle, holding him close, rubbing his ears, and whispering a soft goodbye.

Looking at Gabby, "Who's going to take care of Barclay while we're gone?"

"Our neighbor. Mrs. Pendelton," Gabby said.

"Will I ever see him again?"

"Yes. I'll make sure you do. He'll miss you, too. With all of your cuddles."

Before they left, Gabby asked for the name of the foster family Jennie had briefly stayed with before she fled to Fargo. "Why do you want to know that?" she'd asked, an edge to her voice.

"Because I'd like to call them to see if we might stop by before we get to Wadena itself. Just to talk to them and to thank them for letting you stay with them."

Jennie scoffed. "You gotta be kidding. I screwed them over, stole their money and phone. They must hate me."

"Don't be so sure. I know they called the sheriff and reported the theft, but they must also know, or suspect, why you ran when you did. That your dad was hanging around and that you were very scared."

"I don't know if I can face them now."

"C'mon. It'll give you a chance to apologize for running off."

Reluctantly, "Their name is Jamieson. Corinne and Gerald. They have two boys, Jamie and Roger. They have a farm a few miles outside of Elsa. On County Road D.

"I'll try to call them as we get closer. But, first, tell me about them and how you got along?"

"They're okay, I guess. Mr. Jamieson is a nice, friendly man, but I didn't see that much of him. He was always doing something on the farm. Chores and stuff. They don't have any hired help. Just the two boys and they're not old enough to do much. And Mrs. Jamieson, well, she's nice too, I guess. She never was mean to me or anything like that. But she's a very strict lady. To her boys. And to me. Doesn't smile much, kinda like my Mom. And I don't think they have much money. I heard them talking a few times about how hard times were, with the bad weather and prices and all."

"That's too bad."

"Which makes my robbing them even worse. Like I said, I'm sure they hate me."

"Hate is too strong a word, Jennie. Disappointed may be closer."

The long trip was eased by the fact that the highway was four lanes for all but the last few miles into Wadena itself. And largely snow-free. They passed larger cities like St. Cloud and Long Prairie, smaller towns like Motley and Verndale, and by tiny towns like Aldrich, population, 48. At times, they were accompanied to one

272

side by never-ending BNSF freight trains, many of the railroad cars decorated with elaborate and artsy graffiti that seemed to capture Jennie's attention. Even made her giggle.

After two hours, Gabby pulled out a copy she'd made of the Wikipedia report on Wadena County, the first time she'd taken the time to learn about their destination. Small, with a population of fewer than fourteen thousand, but beautiful, with low rolling hills, woods, lakes and trails, bordered by the Crow Wing River. A favorite tourist destination. The city of Wadena was once a trading post in the late 1800s and was named for Chief Wadena, an Ojibwe Indian chief in those same years.

She also learned the county had been hit by an EF4 tornado years before, the 170 mile-an-hour winds damaging or destroying dozens of homes and demolishing the high school in the city of Wadena.

In another half hour, as they passed a signpost indicating they were now entering the county, Jennie spoke up from the backseat. "County Road D is about five miles ahead. You should take a left and go about another mile. The farm is on the left. You'll see the big silo."

"Thanks," Gabby said. "Can you give me their phone number?"

"I guess so," she said, reciting the number, "but I wish we wouldn't be doing this."

The phone was answered by a woman. "Mrs. Jamieson?"

"Yes. Who's this?"

"My name is Gabby Gooding. I'm a reporter from Channel Seven in the Cities."

"Really?" Curiosity, maybe disbelief, in her voice.

"Yes, really."

"I've seen you on TV. And Eleanor Gladstone has told us about you and Jennie."

"That's why I'm calling. I know this might come as a surprise, but we're a few miles from your home and wonder if we might stop and speak to you?"

There was a long pause. "About Jennie?"

"Yes. In fact, I have her with me."

An even longer pause. "I thought she was long gone."

"She was, but she came back to us the night before last. We're taking her back to Eleanor and the child protection people in Wadena, but I'd hoped to see you, or you and your husband, first."

"You must know she's not welcome here. She stole from us before she ran away... "

"I know. And I'd like to repay you, if I could, and if you'd let us stop by."

"I'll have to talk to my husband," she said, hesitantly. "He's in the barn working."

"Please do. And if you choose not to see us, simply wave us away."

The farm was easy to spot. A two-story white-framed house, the tall, red-brick silo and a large pole barn at the other end of the long driveway, with an older John Deere tractor parked next to it. The red lettering on the black mailbox said simply, "Jamieson."

Zach paused before turning in. "You sure this is a good idea?"

"No," she said. "But I don't see how it can hurt."

As they approached the house, a couple emerged from the back door and stood waiting on the porch. The man, big and burly, was clad in bib overalls and a heavy Carhartt jacket; the woman, short and slight compared to her husband, was wearing a heavy knit sweater and slacks, her arms clutching her chest against the cold.

Gabby said, "I think you should stay in the car, Jennie, until we have a chance to speak to them. We'll let the motor run to keep you warm. Is that okay?"

"I guess so. Will you be long?"

"I don't think so, but we'll come get you if it looks like it might be a while."

With that, they headed for the house, treading carefully on the snow-slicked sidewalk. The man stepped off the porch and held out his hand. "Hello, there. I'm Gerald Jamieson, but most people call me Jerry." Then, leading them to the porch, "And this is Corinne." With a smile, "And most people call her Corinne."

Gabby returned the grin. "And I'm Gabriel Gooding, but most call me Gabby. And this is Zachary Anthony, but we call him Zach."

"C'mon in and get out of this cold," he said. Then, looking back, "Isn't Jennie coming in?"

"We thought we should talk first," Zach said.

Confirming what Jennie had said, Jerry's apparent warm welcome was in contrast to Mrs. Jamieson—who stood unsmiling, stoic, as she turned to lead them into the house and into the kitchen—a large, warm, open area bordered on one side by a row of white cabinets, and on the other by the string of appliances, including a large gas stove, the kind Gabby imagined you'd see in a farmhouse like this. In the middle, a large oak table with four chairs. And on one of the counters, a framed eight-by-ten color photo of the couple and their two boys, one of whom looked about ten, the other a bit younger.

"Take off your coats and grab a chair," Jerry said. "The coffee's brewing."

Slipping off her coat, Gabby said, "Thanks so much for seeing us on such short notice. We won't keep you long."

Corrine spoke for the first time. "I don't mean to be impolite, but I still don't understand why you're here."

"We're here," Gabby said, "because we care deeply about Jennie and her future. As I'm sure Eleanor has told you, Jennie went through a great deal before coming to you. From the first time she ran away from home weeks ago and came to us for help in finding her friend, Hannah."

"The girl who was murdered, right?" Jerry said.

"Yes. Jennie had spent days on the streets looking for her, braving the cold and all of the dangers a girl like her can face, alone, in a city like Minneapolis. She was crushed by the news of Hannah's death, to an extent I'm not sure any of us will ever truly understand."

"She never did talk much to us about it," Corrine said, "even though we asked. In fact, she never really talked about much of anything in the short time she was here. Kept to herself mostly, with her books from school and the library. Sometimes playing video games with our boys."

"Did she tell you about the encounter with her father at the shelter? When he barged in and threatened all of us?"

"No," Jerry said. "But Eleanor did."

"And Jennie saw it all," Gabby said. "So you can you understand how afraid she must be of him."

"He's a mean bastard, that's for sure," Jerry said. "Damn near everybody in the county knows about his temper."

"But he *is* her father," Corinne said. "And that must count for something."

At that, Zach spoke up. "So why did you agree to take her in? If you knew about him and his tough reputation?"

Corinne said, "I guess because once Eleanor told us Jennie's story, we felt sorry for her and thought she might be a good companion for our boys. I've always wanted a daughter, but it's too late for that now."

"And, frankly," Jerry broke in, "we can use the help the county was going to give us. It's been a tough year for farmers like us. We're barely making it."

"Did she tell you she saw her dad hanging around? Driving by, watching for her?" Gabby asked.

"Yes," Corinne replied. "After the last time, she came to us in tears, said her dad had seen her get off the school bus and tried to talk to her, yelled at her. So I immediately called Eleanor. She said she'd be out the next day to talk to Jennie, but Jennie took off that night with one of our phones and about a hundred-and-fifty dollars of our savings."

"I'll repay you for what she took," Gabby said, with a quick glance at Zach, "but I first have an important question. If Eleanor and child protection would agree, and if Jennie would agree, would you be willing to take her back?"

Both were clearly startled by the question and remained silent for a moment. "Gosh, I don't know," Jerry finally said, staring across the table at his wife, who was shaking her head, whispering, "No, no." "She's not the easiest girl to deal with," he went on, "and after what she did…the trouble she caused…I just don't know…"

"But you *do* know what she's been through," Gabby argued. "She deserves every chance she can get to lead a more normal life. With a family like yours. I know she's sorry for what she did, and while there's no guarantee she won't cause more trouble, you have the opportunity to make a lasting difference in a child's life. Think about it. What if one of your boys a few years from now was in a similar place? Wouldn't you want a family like yours to step in and help save him?"

Corinne continued to shake her head.

"And if you don't take her back," Zach said, "who knows what kind of family she might end up with? We know you must be a decent, loving family or Jennie wouldn't have been placed with you. There's no guarantee she'll find another family like yours."

"I hear what you're saying," Jerry replied, "and I appreciate your nice words, but there's that other factor. Her dad. What if he comes around here again, this time with a gun, like he did at that shelter? Threatening us and our boys?"

"I have no answer for that," Gabby admitted, "but we do plan to speak to the sheriff when we're in Wadena."

Zach checked his watch. "And we have to get going. But, first, could we bring Jennie in to say hello and to apologize for what she did? I know she'd like to do that."

"Sure," Jerry said. "I'd like to see her again, but you should understand we have not agreed to anything."

"We understand," Gabby replied.

When Zach walked through the door with Jennie, she hesitated, looked around and then drew into herself. Shoulders scrunched, eyes to the floor, leaning into Zach for support.

It was clear she would like to be anywhere but here. But here she was.

Surprisingly, Jerry crossed the kitchen and took one of her hands in his. "Hey, Jennie, nice to see you again. We've missed you."

She looked up at him, then around him to see Corinne still standing by the table, stern, sober. Gabby stood off to one side, watching and waiting to see what Jennie might do and say.

Finally, in a quivering voice, she said, "I'm so sorry. That I stole from you and ran off. I'll give you your money back, I promise, as soon as I can get a job."

"Not to worry," he said. "Not now. We're just happy that you're back and safe."

She freed her hand and stepped around him, facing Corinne. "Let me finish, please. I know how angry you must have been. And maybe you still are. You were nice enough to take me in and make me part of your family. And then I ran off." She paused, wiping at her eyes. "I was stupid and selfish, and I hope you can forgive me some day. But thanks to Gabby and Zach, I am done running. I know now that I can't run away. That I could end up like my friend, Hannah."

"We're sorry, too," Jerry said. "That we didn't do more to keep your dad away. To truly realize how terribly afraid you are of him."

Corinne finally stepped forward. "It's brave of you to come and apologize, Jennie, although I'm guessing it took some persuasion by your friends here. And I want to believe what you say, that you've stopped running. But, as my dad used to say, the proof will be in the pudding. You hurt us by what you did, and we can only hope that it's a lesson learned."

At that point, Zach got up and reached for his coat. "Time to go, I think. We've got a lot to do yet today."

"You guys go ahead," Gabby said, reaching for her purse. "I'll be out in a minute."

As Jennie reached the door, she turned and said, "Thank you again and please say hi to Jamie and Roger for me."

"We surely will," Jerry said, "and you take care of yourself, young lady. Okay? We'll be thinking of you."

THIRTY-EIGHT

• • •

B ack on the highway, they had gone no more than a couple of miles before a sign announced Elsa was coming up on the left. They crossed over and went another mile before a new sign welcomed them to the town itself, speed limit 30 mph, population 1676.

As Zach slowed, Jennie leaned forward and said, "Please don't stop. Please."

"We won't," Gabby replied. "But will you show us where you lived?"

"It's down the next street, next to the water tower. But please keep going."

The town's homes were spread out on both sides of the street, most of them one-story and compact, none of them looking new. A Mobil gas station was on one end of the street, next to a small convenience store, and farther on were a series of small shops, a grocery store, a café, a bar and an American Legion post. At the far end stood the one-story brick school and football field, its bleachers blanketed by snow. A line of yellow school busses stood by, ready to carry the students home.

Driving through, it reminded Gabby of Travis, where Hannah's funeral was held.

"Have you always lived here?" she asked.

279

"Yes. My mom was born here and we live in the same house as her folks did."

"What about your dad? You told us he runs a machine shop…"

"It's down the next street, on the right. He fixes farm machinery, cars, all kinds of things. He worked for my grandpa until he died, then took over the shop."

"And he's the mayor?"

"Yeah," she said, with bitterness in her voice. "A big man in a small town."

As they passed the last business on the outskirts of town, a small farm implement dealer, Gabby's ringtone sounded. Sarah Chan.

"Hey, Sarah."

"Where are you?"

"On the way to Wadena with Jennie. What's up?"

"Two things. Sheriff Henderson called. Said he tried to get you, but your phone must have been off."

"It was," she said. "While we visited Jennie's foster family."

"Well, get this. Our friend, Arnold Klinger, confronted his wife this morning after she'd dropped her boys off at school in Marshall…"

"What?"

"He followed her and forced her into his truck. Demanded money, his share, he said, of their bank account. Said he was broke and needed to get out of the country. Threatened to take one of the boys if she didn't come through."

"I don't believe this."

"She somehow got out of the truck, I don't know how, and called 911. He's still on the loose and she and the boys are under police protection. I thought you'd want to know."

"Of course. Thanks. He's a maniac."

"And increasingly desperate, it seems."

"I'll call Barclay right away, in case he doesn't know about it."

"I doubt that he does. Henderson said it happened less than an hour ago."

"He'll get somebody on it."

"One other thing," Sarah said. "Jesse will soon be heading your way."

"Up here? To Wadena?"

"Yup. He called this morning. He was able to get another leave after hearing of Jennie's latest flight to Fargo. Says he's going to settle things with his dad, one way or another."

Gabby turned away, holding the phone close, hoping Jennie would not hear. "Jeez. Did you try to talk him out of it?"

"Of course, but he's determined."

"Did you tell him Jennie's with us, on our way to Wadena?"

"I told him you were going, but I didn't know you'd already left."

"Do you know when he's arriving?"

"Not really. He said he'd call me from the airport."

Gabby took a moment to think. "Let me know when you know. I'll alert Eleanor when we see her. This could get ugly."

"I know. I'll try to calm him down when I see him."

With ten miles to go to Wadena, and another half hour before their scheduled meeting with Eleanor, Gabby briefed Zach and made her call to Barclay—relating what Sarah had just told her. "The cops in Marshall should have the details. I wish I was there to make the call, but I'm still on the road with Jennie."

"No problem," he said, "I've got a couple of guys sitting on their ass. I'll put one of them on it. And good luck with Jennie."

"Thanks. I should be back sometime tomorrow."

"I hope so."

Zach looked across at her. "So what else did Sarah say?"

With a glance back at Jennie, she replied, "I'll tell you later."

The courthouse in Wadena was an attractive, modern, low-slung white building with tall windows facing Jefferson Street, the city's main street. Zach managed to find a parking space a half-block away—with still a few minutes to spare before their meeting with Eleanor.

Gabby turned in her seat. "Are you ready, Jennie?"

Her face was pressed against the window.

"Jennie?"

She turned back, eyes brimming with tears. "What will they do with me? Where will they put me?"

"I don't know where, but I do know they'll keep you safe. And that's the most important thing right now."

"Will I see my mom?"

"I'm sure you will, but I can't say when. We'll find out more when we see Eleanor."

Gabby took a quick glance at Zach, hoping he wouldn't notice the welling of her own eyes. Everything, she thought sadly, had come full circle, from her first sight of a half-frozen Jennie hunkered down in the station lobby to this, the frightened teenager, still a child in many ways, fighting her tears and fears in the back seat of their car. Now, as then, facing the unknown.

"C'mon, Jennie. Show us your courage. Eleanor will be waiting."

And she was. Standing erect and alone in the lobby, wearing a different version of the "grandma" dress she'd worn when they'd first met her at The Haven. But the stern, no nonsense expression she had worn then had now become a soft, warm, welcoming smile.

Jennie held back as Gabby and Zach moved ahead to meet her. "Hey, Gabby, hey, Zach," she said as she grasped each of their hands, "welcome to Wadena." Then, looking beyond them, "And who's that lovely young lady you have with you?"

Gabby glanced over her shoulder, showing a small smile. "I think you've met her. And I think she may have something to say to you. Right, Jennie?"

She stood motionless, eyes on her toes.

"C'mon, child," Eleanor said, brushing past Gabby and Zach to approach Jennie, bending to look into her eyes. "You have something to say to me?"

Jennie looked up and straightened up, her expression a mixture of anguish and defiance. "I'm sorry. I'm sorry I ran. I'm sorry I stole. I'm sorry I disappointed you. I'm sorry to the whole world. Is that good enough? That's all I've said today. And is it okay if I tell you I'm damned sick of saying I'm sorry?"

Eleanor grinned. "Well, I wish you would have used other words, but I do understand what you're saying. And I think the only other person you'll need to say you're sorry to is your mom."

"Is she here, my mom?"

"Not yet, but she will be. Be patient. We've got some talking to do first."

She took Jennie by the hand and headed down the hall, stopping to tell Gabby and Zach they could come along for a time.

"Are you sure?" Gabby said.

"Just follow me. I want you to meet someone, and also give you a piece of news."

They trailed her to a small conference room with two windows that looked out onto the street and, in the center, an oblong steel table surrounded by five chairs, one of them occupied by a tall, younger man in a uniform almost identical to the one worn by Sheriff Henderson in Lyon County. He rose as they walked in and waited for Eleanor's introduction.

"This is Deputy Irving Stanland," she said, "who's assigned to the Sheriff's Juvenile Division and works with us in Child Protection." He stepped up to shake hands as she quickly introduced Gabby and Zach.

"Eleanor has told me a lot about you two," he said. "How you've tried to watch over and protect Jennie..."

Who still stood by the door, fear on her face.

"...that you've been with her almost every step of the way, getting her off the streets and into a shelter. That it was you who finally persuaded her to come back here." Then he walked over to Jennie and knelt down. "I'm glad you're back, Jennie. We're going to take care of you, keep you safe, so you'll never have to run again. Ever."

"Thank you," she whispered, and then, looking over his shoulder at Eleanor, again asked, "When can I see my mom?"

"Soon," she said, "but let's all sit down for few minutes first."

As each took a chair, Eleanor said, "In just the time it took you to drive from the Jamieson's farm here, we've received a call from Jerry Jamieson. After you'd left, he and Corinne talked and—first of all—agreed to drop those theft charges against you, Jennie, and secondly, that if you're willing, they're willing to have you come back and live with them again. As your foster family. Would you like that?"

Her face broke into a grin, the first one any of them had seen. "Yes!" she said. "I would like that." But then the grin evaporated. "Can they keep my dad away?"

The deputy leaned in. "They can't but we can, Jennie. I promise you. I'll explain later, but you'll have a special phone that will connect you to us if you ever see your dad nearby. At the Jamiesons, at school, or wherever. You'll have it until Eleanor is sure your family situation is safe. Do you understand that?"

"I think so."

Gabby turned to him. "That's good to hear, deputy, because that's part of the reason we came, not just to bring Jennie back, but to be assured she'll be safe. And it's not just us, personally, who have a stake in this, but our television viewers as well."

"I understand," he said.

She looked into his eyes. "I hope so…because Jennie has come to be a symbol to us of the hundreds of kids just like her, from abusive homes who are caught up in a system that often seems more interested in getting the child back to the family than ending the abuse."

Eleanor started to object, but Gabby waived her off. "I'm not talking specifically about you, Eleanor, or Wadena County. I think you know we have great respect for you, but I also know not enough was done to keep her father at bay. And we know—we've seen—the kind of man he can be."

The deputy's warmth turned frosty. "Are you threatening us in some way? Using the power of your television station?"

Aware she was on dangerous journalistic footing, she went on. "Not threatening, deputy. I'm simply telling you that we hope to make our audience aware and care about what becomes of Jennie and others like her."

Eleanor broke in. "You've made your point, Gabby. We'll do everything in our power to keep Jennie safe and healthy, not because of you or your station's interest in her, but because it's our job. You don't know, because I haven't had the chance to tell you, that we've obtained a court order prohibiting Jennie's dad from being anywhere near her until the family issues are resolved."

"That's great news," Gabby said.

Eleanor went on, "I do hope you'll do your series on homeless youth, and I do hope it will make the public even more aware of the challenges we and others like us face in dealing with situations like Jennie's. It ain't easy."

"Even in a small county like ours," the deputy continued, "we have dozens of kids who go missing in any given year. Some are runaways from bad home situations, like Jennie; some are taken as the result of parental custody fights; some get kicked out of their homes because they're gay or transsexual and flee to the Cities or wherever. Others disappear for no apparent reason at all. And I can tell you, as Eleanor will, we simply don't have the resources to try to find them all."

Before he could go on, there was a light knock on the door and a woman poked her head in. "Mrs. Nystrom is here, Eleanor. I put her in your office, if that's okay?"

"Of course, Jan. Thanks." Then, turning to Jennie, "Ready to see your mom?"

A big smile popped up on her face. "For sure!" Then, looking across the table. "Is it all right if she meets Gabby and Zach?"

"If she'd like to, yes. But I want the two of you to spend some time together first."

As they got up to leave, Deputy Stanland did as well, but Gabby put her hand out. "Can you please wait to go until Eleanor gets back? We have something to report that you'll both want to hear."

He glanced at this watch. "Fine, but I don't have a lot of time."

Eleanor was back within five minutes, stopping just inside the door, not bothering to wipe away a tear. Her words weren't needed to describe the emotional reunion of mother and daughter she had just witnessed. She slid into a chair, took a deep breath and said, "Jennie's mother would like to meet you two, but I'd give her some time now to be alone with Jennie."

"Of course," Gabby said. "But are *you* okay?"

"I'll be fine, but it's a day like this that makes me think of retiring. To know that the two of them in that room will likely not see one another again for days, maybe longer. That their splintered family may never be made whole again. I see it too often and it makes me want to weep." Then she straightened up. "But enough of that. I'm sorry. What is it that you have to tell us?"

"This won't make your day any better," Gabby said, "but we've learned that Jennie's brother, Jesse, may soon be on his way here. Angry and determined, we're told, to confront his dad…to have it out with him."

The deputy leaned in. "Why?"

"Because he learned that Jennie had run away again…after the dad tried to accost her at the school bus. Jesse stood up to him once, at the shelter, and apparently is set on doing it again."

"We can't let that happen," Eleanor said. "One of them could get hurt or worse."

"I understand…"

"Can you stop him? Talk to him?" she pressed, leaning in.

Gabby looked at Zach. "We can try, but we don't know where he is now."

Stanland stood up. "Please try and please let one of us know. If we know when he's coming, we'll try to intercept him, or at least put someone in Elsa to keep them apart. Everybody in the county knows

Nystrom is never without a pistol at his side. It's the last thing this family needs."

"We'll do our best," Gabby said, but knew her words had a hollow ring to them.

THIRTY-NINE

...

She and Zach had no idea of what to expect when Eleanor led them down the hall to meet Jennie's mom. They only had Jennie's brief description of a loving mother but—also—of a dour, sad, often angry woman who lived with an abusive husband. To their surprise, what they found as the door opened was a tall, lean, attractive woman with light brown hair and dark eyes that seemed to find their way across the room. She held Jennie closely, displaying a shy smile that didn't seem to come easily.

Eleanor stood aside and said, "Marion, I'd like you to meet Gabby Gooding and Zach Anthony. As you know, they've been important people in Jennie's life...and I know she wanted you to meet them."

First Zach, then Gabby stepped up to shake her hand. "You have a wonderful daughter, Mrs. Nystrom," Gabby said, "and it's been a pleasure for us to get to know her and to be able to help her when she needed it."

The shy smile took on more life. "She's told me all about you... and what you've done for her. And about your poodle..."

"Barclay," Jennie offered. "A teacup poodle, Mom. You'd love him."

"I'm sure I would," she laughed. "And maybe we can get one someday."

Gabby looked at Eleanor. "May we sit for a minute or two?"

"Sure, if Marion has the time. I have to tend to some other business and will be back in, say, a half hour. Is that okay?"

They all nodded.

"What happens to me?" Jennie asked.

"You'll be at the same shelter as before," Eleanor said. "Until we can make sure things will work out with the Jamiesons. And after that, we hope, you can get back home. But when that will be," with a glance at Marion, "none of us knows yet."

Once she left, there were a few awkward seconds of silence. Then Marion said, "Jennie thinks that you paid the Jamiesons for the money and phone she took. Is that right? I'd like to pay you back."

"Please don't worry about it," Gabby said. "We can settle up later. What we'd like to know, if you're willing to tell us, is how you're doing in all of this? How you're coping?"

She leaned back and turned toward the window, considering her response. "Coping is probably the right word," she finally said, turning back. "It's pretty lonely, pretty scary, if you want to know the truth. Missing Jennie, never knowing for sure where she is or how she is. Whether she'll ever be back with me for good."

She turned and stroked Jennie's cheek. "I miss her friends, her school, of being part of her life, of watching her grow. It's only been weeks that she's been away, on the run, but I can see the changes in her. And it makes me sad."

Jennie took her hand and squeezed it.

"We feel sorry for both of you," Zach said, "and can only hope things work out. But may I ask another question? Which you should feel free to ignore."

"About my husband?"

"Yes."

"If you're asking if he's changed, the answer is no. He's still as stubborn and as angry as ever about Jennie, as much as I and others have tried to reason with him. He feels he's being unfairly deprived of his daughter, and that everybody, including me, is against him. He says the way he and Jennie get along, the way he treats her, is nobody else's business. Certainly not the county's."

A soft sigh escaped Jennie's lips as she went on. "And I suppose your next question will be: why do I stay with him?"

Gabby started to protest. "You don't need to… "

"It's okay. Jennie and I have talked about this often. The simple answer is that I don't have anywhere else to go. I have no job, no real skills. I've simply been a mom. Divorce is probably out of the question. He would try to leave me with nothing. So I simply sit at home, watching the hours pass, waiting for night to come."

"You must have friends to go to," Zach said.

"I did have. And still have a few. But most of them know of our situation, the problems with Jennie, and they simply choose to stay away. Knowing my husband and his temper, they're afraid to pick sides."

She paused again. "Jesse does call as often as he can, but if my husband happens to pick up the phone, he hangs up and tries again later. Stationed in Texas and sometimes serving overseas, he's in no position to offer much comfort or support…and I understand that."

Zach gave Gabby a quick glance, but she shook her head. She didn't want to mention the possibility of Jesse heading this way. Not now. Not until they knew more. Then she asked, "Is there anything more we can do to help?"

"Not really," she said. "I just don't know what will happen to our family. My husband and I seldom speak…and when we do, it's often in anger. So I simply try to survive, if that's the word, until this nightmare finally ends. If it ever does. Meantime, I want to spend as much time with Jennie as I can."

Gabby and Zach got up. "Then we'll leave the two of you alone," Gabby said, "but know that we'll be thinking of you and keeping track of what happens to Jennie. Please take care of yourselves. And, Jennie, remember what you promised: that your running days are over. Right?"

She nodded and got up to give each of them a hug. "Thank you," she whispered. "You're my best friends, you know."

"We know," Zach said. "Please take care."

Back in the lobby, Gabby put in a call to Sarah. "Glad I caught you. What have you heard from Jesse?"

"He arrives at the airport at a little after seven tonight. I'm going to pick him up."

Gabby put the phone on speaker. "You can't let him come up here, Sarah! We had to tell Eleanor and a sheriff's deputy what he's planning. They're going to try to stop him."

"I'll do what I can. But it won't be easy. Like I said before, he's intent. Hellbent. He's going to stay with me tonight and plans to drive to Elsa in the morning."

Gabby sucked in her breath, releasing it in a rush. "Somebody could get hurt or killed, Sarah. His dad is armed and angry and the sheriff's people could be there waiting. Who knows what might happen in that situation?"

"I understand, but I can't arrest him or tackle and hold him down. What do you suggest?"

Gabby looked pleadingly at Zach, who shrugged his shoulders. Finally, she said, "Look. We'll be seeing Eleanor again soon, and maybe she can arrange a private meeting with Jesse, Jennie and their mom. To defuse this thing before it turns really ugly. To convince Jesse that Jennie's going to be safe. Protected this time. That confronting his dad will only make a bad situation even worse."

"I'll do my best," Sarah said. "Cross your fingers."

As she put the phone down, Zach said, "You know, this is out of the blue, but I've been doing more thinking. At what point are you, or we, crossing some kind of ethical line here? Are we pursuing your homeless kids story or are we becoming more advocates than journalists? Like threatening to use the station's power to protect Jennie and others like her? I don't know, Gabby, the more I think about it, the more uncomfortable I get. Supposedly, we're getting paid to pursue the story, but I haven't shot a stitch of video and you haven't done a single interview."

She was clearly taken aback and gave him a sharp look. "I hear what you're saying, but Jennie and others like her *are* the story. We may never be able to tell it through her eyes…since she's so young… but knowing what she's gone through and is still facing will help us tell the larger story. At least I hope so. Besides, what would you have us do now? Pack up and leave like good journalists? Or stay and try to prevent a shootout at the OK Corral?"

"Now you're being silly and insulting," he replied, with some heat. "I think it's a legitimate question. Right now, I feel more like Jennie's guardian than a news photographer. And as admirable as that might be, I'm not sure it's right."

Before she could respond, her phone sounded. Barclay.

"Hey, George."

"Hey, yourself. Just wanted you to know that your lunatic friend Klinger is still on the loose. I've got Max Jordan and Les Leonard heading down to Marshall to interview the cops and whoever else will talk to them. Mrs. Klinger is unavailable, of course, but apparently is doing okay. She and her boys are in a safe house, under guard."

"Good."

"Max is filing a report for the five o'clock show, but you may miss it if you're on your way back."

She took a breath. "I don't think we're coming back tonight, George," she said with hesitation, explaining what had happened and why she thought they had to stay.

There was a pregnant pause. "Shit, Gabby. Sorry to hear that. I thought you and Zach might be able to replace Max and Les in Marshall. I want to keep somebody down there until they catch this looney tunes. And it really is *your* story."

"I know and I'm sorry. But I don't think we have much choice."

"I guess. If you say so."

"What's happening with Julius Winthrop?" she asked.

"He's still behind bars on a million-dollar bond. They're apparently going to ask a grand jury for a first-degree murder indictment. We'll have to see."

At that moment, Eleanor walked into the lobby and moved in their direction.

"George, I've got to go. I'll talk to you later today, if that's all right?"

"I'll be here." Not bothering to disguise his disappointment or irritation.

Zach gave her a long look. "He's pissed, isn't he?"

She met his gaze. "Sounds like it. Can't blame him, I guess."

"I guess not. He's the one paying us."

Eleanor was talking before she reached them. "So you're still here?"

They got up. "Yes," Gabby said. "We have more information on Jesse."

"Please sit," she said, taking a seat across from them. "So what is it?"

"He's still coming," Zach said, "in the morning. Heading directly for Elsa."

"And you can't stop him?"

"Sarah has tried on the phone, but she won't actually see him until tonight," Gabby said. "But we've thought of a way you might be able to help."

"How's that?"

Zach said, "Let us try to convince him to meet with you, the deputy, Jennie and their mom. To assure him that everything possible is being done to protect Jennie. That there's no need to confront his dad."

"And if he refuses?" Eleanor said.

"Then we all head for cover," Gabby replied.

"So you're staying the night?"

Gabby looked over at Zach. "I suppose so. Until we hear from you and Sarah."

"There's a Country Inn down the street. It's as good as any place in town."

"That's where we'll be," Gabby replied. Then, as they got up, she reached into her briefcase and pulled out a DVD and gave it to Eleanor. "This is a copy of my story on Hannah's funeral. I promised Jennie I'd show it to her at some point, but I've never had the chance. If and when you feel she's ready, please let her see it. I know it would be mean a lot to her."

"Thanks," she said. "I'll try to decide when the time is right."

FORTY

. . .

By the time they got to the hotel and checked in, it was almost five o'clock. And as they threw their bags on the bed, Gabby suddenly remembered. "Quick," she said, "Max is supposed to be doing a Klinger piece from Marshall."

After a short search, Zach found the TV remote, and within a couple of minutes the opening of the five o'clock news rolled across the screen, revealing a two-shot of anchors Andrea Neusem and Scott Gilgrist.

SCOTT: *Good afternoon everyone. We have some breaking news at this hour.*

ANDREA: *According to law enforcement, Arnold Klinger, the man wanted for the rape of a western Minnesota girl and as a person of interest in the murder of his stepdaughter, Hannah Hendricks, attempted to abduct his estranged wife in Marshall, Minnesota, earlier today.*

SCOTT: *Reporter Max Jordan and photographer Les Leonard are in Marshall with the latest.*

MAX: *Scott, Mrs. Klinger had just dropped her two children off at this school in Marshall, and was getting back into her car when police say she suddenly was confronted by her estranged husband and forced—at knifepoint—into his pickup truck, which had pulled up behind her car.*

At that point there were video scenes of the Klinger family farm outside of Delroy, taken before Hannah's funeral.

Mrs. Klinger had moved to Marshall to live with relatives after putting the family farm up for sale outside of Delroy, where her husband allegedly had attempted to rape his stepdaughter, Hannah, who was later murdered in Minneapolis. He is also accused of another rape in an adjoining county and has been on the loose ever since.

It has not been revealed exactly how, but Mrs. Klinger was able to escape from the pickup and run into the school, calling 911 as she ran. By the time police arrived minutes later, Klinger had fled...and at this hour is still missing, despite a widespread manhunt. Leading the investigation is Marshall Police Chief Stephen Rider.

MAX: *Chief, tell us the latest on the search for Klinger.* CHIEF: *Despite our efforts on the ground and in the air, he remains at large. He knows this part of the state very well, and may be difficult to find.* MAX: *How did Mrs. Klinger manage to escape?* CHIEF: *It's still unclear, since we've been unable to question her closely. She's still quite shaken. But I believe she was able to knock the knife from his hand with her purse and exit the vehicle. He chose not to chase her.* MAX: *Is it true that he was demanding money?* CHIEF: *That's what we understand, but the investigation is ongoing at this time.*

Rolling video now appeared of downtown Marshall and activity on the streets.

MAX: *As you might expect, word of this encounter spread quickly on the streets of Marshall. Mrs. Klinger's two sons were immediately taken out of school and they and their mother are under guard at an undisclosed location.*

Arnold Klinger may now be the most-wanted fugitive in the state, and law enforcement is warning that he is armed and dangerous and should not be approached. Anyone having information about his whereabouts should call 911. We will continue to bring you updates as the search continues. This is Max Conrad with photographer Les Leonard for Channel Seven News in Marshall, Minnesota.

Zach lowered the TV volume and turned to Gabby. "What do you think?"

"Not much more than we already knew," she said. "But they

didn't have much time to do more. It's a long drive from the Cities."

"I assume they'll stay overnight in case the cops figure out where Klinger is."

"Don't count on finding him. He's like a ghost. He's probably already dumped his pickup and is off and away in somebody else's car or truck. He could be in Nebraska by now."

"I don't know, Gabs. I think if he'd wanted to leave the state, he would have done it by now. I'm no psychologist, but I'm betting he's almost waiting for a final showdown of some kind. A dramatic surrender or shoot-out or whatever."

"If you're right, I'd certainly like to be there when it happens. Whatever it is."

"But we're up here, aren't we?"

"Don't push it, please. I'm feeling enough guilt already."

"Then let's forget all of that and go get something to eat. I'm starving."

"No argument there," she replied.

An hour later, with two beers and a burger under their belts, they sat in the small lobby of the hotel waiting for phone calls, for whatever might happen next. Having been up since daybreak, they were both exhausted. Gabby's head rested on Zach's shoulder, her eyes closed, aware she was moments from sleep.

That's when her ringtone sounded. Like someone jabbed her in the ribs. She checked the phone, hoping for Sarah. But it was Eleanor, who quickly asked, "So what have you heard?"

"Nothing, so far," Gabby replied, stifling a yawn. "He must have landed by now, but we're still waiting on a call from Sarah."

"Okay." Weariness in her voice. "Jennie's mom has agreed to come in tomorrow to meet with Jesse, if he shows up. But she sounded frightened on the phone. Her husband apparently suspects something is up."

"That's not a surprise, I guess."

"Deputy Stanland is taking no chances. He plans to have

another deputy in Elsa, once we know Jesse is on his way."

"I hope that won't be necessary."

"So do I. For the sake of everyone. Please call me when you know more."

Another hour passed. They'd moved from the lobby back to their room, and were now sprawled on the bed. Zach was sound asleep when the call finally came from Sarah. Gabby wasted no words. "Talk to me."

"Jesse is with me, and we're heading to my place for the night. Then it's on to Elsa first thing in the morning, he says."

"He can't!" Gabby snapped. "We've got another plan."

"What?"

She told Sarah of the proposed meeting. "It may be our only chance to prevent a really bad scene."

"You're preaching to the choir," Sarah said. "You'd better talk to the altar boy."

Gabby hoisted herself up and sat on the edge of the bed as Jesse came on the phone. "Hey, Gabby. How are things back home? Touchy, I hear."

"It's no time to be cute, Jesse. We're not here for the fun of it. We should be doing our jobs. We're here because we care about Jennie and to help keep you alive and out of jail."

Before he could respond, Zach rose up and took the phone from Gabby. "Jesse, this is Zach. Listen up. You know what your father is capable of…what he did at the shelter. And that was in neutral territory. Think about it! If you try to face him in his own backyard, there'll be hell to pay. Don't let that happen. That's the last thing Jennie or your mom need. There has to be another way and we think there is."

"Yeah, well… "

"Jennie has promised she won't run again. Her foster family is willing to take her back. There's a court order keeping your dad away from her, and the deputy we spoke to has promised to keep an even closer eye on her."

"I've heard promises before…"

Zach put the phone on speaker as Jesse went on.

"…but the next thing I hear, she's run off to Fargo because our father put the fear of God into her. This has to stop, and I'm not sure more words, more promises, will do it. He needs to know somebody is going to stand up to him."

"Do you really think he's going to be impressed by your bravado?" Zach demanded. "Gimme a break. He'll laugh at you now just like he did at the shelter. And what are you going to do when he puts his gun in your face? He's an angry man and I don't think anybody really knows what he's capable of."

"He's a bully, but he's also a coward," Jesse said. "I don't think he's ever fought anybody his own size. He carries the gun as a sign of strength, but it's really a sign of weakness."

"That's what you *think*, but you don't *know*," Gabby said. "And what if the worst happens? If one or both of you gets hurt or killed? Or thrown in jail? Think about your mom, think about Jennie."

There was silence on the line. Until Sarah came back on. "I think Jesse's done talking for now. We'll call you in the morning as we're leaving."

"I'm telling you again," Gabby said, "you can't let him stop in Elsa, Sarah. They'll be waiting for him unless you promise to bypass the town and meet us here in Wadena. We'll be at the courthouse waiting, and by then we should know more about a meeting."

"I hear you, and I'll do my best."

"Are you carrying your weapon?" Zach asked.

"Of course. I always do."

"Do me a favor. Put it in the glove compartment and lock it, okay?"

The phone went dead before they could hear a response.

FORTY-ONE

• • •

They got Sarah's call as they were eating breakfast at a place called Billie's, about two blocks from the hotel. Gabby put aside her scrambled eggs and bacon and picked up the phone. "Hey, we've been waiting."

"We're on the road, heading out of town."

Gabby put the phone on speaker. "And?"

"Jesse has agreed to bypass Elsa and meet you in Wadena."

"That's *great*," Gabby said with a sigh of relief. "But how did you persuade him?"

There was an audible chuckle on the other end and a whispered conversation. "I'll let him tell you."

Jesse came on the line. "Want to know the truth, do you? Well, she told me flat out that she'd never consider a lasting relationship with a vengeful man. And if I insist on confronting my father, it would be an act of vengeance, not courage." A long pause. "And since I *do* hope we can have a lasting relationship, I want to do everything possible to avoid the confrontation."

"Congratulations," Zach said, "first, for agreeing on a possible peaceful solution to this mess, and, second, for recognizing a golden opportunity with a terrific woman." Laughing, he added, "who happens to have a badge and a weapon."

"Enough of that," Gabby said, breaking in. "Here's the deal. We talked to Eleanor last night and the meeting is set for one this

300

afternoon at the courthouse. Your mom will be there, but not Jennie. You can see her later at the shelter, Jesse."

"Good."

"And since you've promised not to stop at Elsa, we'll also see if Deputy Stanland can be at the meeting. But one caveat. It's possible your dad may know something is going on. If that's true, and if he shows up, we'll let the sheriff's people deal with it."

"That makes sense," he said. "But don't underestimate him. He may not be smart, but he can be clever."

After the call, Zach and Gabby lingered over breakfast, downing more coffee than they probably should, and then, with a few hours to spare and nowhere in particular to be, they started to wander the streets of downtown Wadena, taking in the sights on Jefferson Street and beyond. There was the old Cozy theater, the Boondocks Café, the Glamor Full Service Salon, among others. And a couple of blocks off Jefferson, a cluster of three churches, including St. Ann's Catholic, with its soaring and beautiful steeple. As they drew near, they heard the muted sounds of an organ playing "It Came Upon a Midnight Clear," a sudden reminder of what they had almost forgotten: Christmas was not far off.

And in the distance, looming above the town was the huge water tower with **Wadena** emblazoned on its rounded sides.

The walk was made more pleasant because an overnight December thaw, not unheard of in Minnesota, had left temperatures in the fifties and the streets and sidewalks largely bare. Not exactly the tropics but warm enough for only light jackets.

Twice, as they walked, Gabby called Barclay to check on the situation in Marshall and was told nothing had changed...that Klinger was still among the missing. With the second call, the irritation in his voice was hard to miss. "So what's happening up there?"

She briefly described the situation. "We hope this can end peacefully, but we'll know more by early afternoon."

"I hope so," he said, "because I may still need you two to

replace Max and Les in Marshall. I'd even pay for a charter to come and get you, if I had to."

She was puzzled. "A charter? Really?"

"I told you before. This is *your* story. If they ever find Klinger, I'd like you and Zach to see it happen. You deserve that. There would be no manhunt if you—we—had not exposed him in the first place. I like tidy endings. Besides, Max and Les are now on their second day there and are itchy to get home."

"I hear you," she said. "I'll call when we know how all of this is going to end."

"I'll have the plane standing by."

She put the phone back in her jacket and told Zach what had been said.

"That's Barclay," he replied. "He may have his faults, but lack of loyalty is not one of them. And he's right. It is your story, *our* story, and we should be there to see it end."

"But it may not end," she argued. "They may never find him. Or if they do, he could be dead."

"Then, hopefully, we'll be there to report it."

Later, as they approached the courthouse, they saw no sign of Sarah and Jesse. But they did see a sheriff's car parked in front of the sheriff's office, which was next to the courthouse itself. And across the street, a black-and-white patrol car belonging to the Wadena Police Department. On seeing them, Deputy Stanland got out of his car and gave them a quick tip of his hat. "Nice to see you again," he said.

"And the same to you," Gabby replied as she glanced at the Wadena squad car. "You have reinforcements?"

"I hope he won't be needed," he said, "but seeing that we're on city property, I thought the local cops should know what's happening."

"What *is* happening?" Zach asked. "We haven't talked to Eleanor since this morning."

"The meeting is still on, as far as I know, but Mrs. Nystrom has not shown up yet, and that's causing a little concern."

"Has anyone tried to call her?" Gabby asked.

"There's been no answer, the last I heard."

"That *is* strange. Do you have one of your people in Elsa?"

"Yes, but he hasn't tried to contact her. He's simply standing by in case Jesse decides to violate his promise to you."

"I'm sure he won't," Zach said. "We talked to them a half hour ago and they were just passing by Elsa."

No sooner were his words spoken than they saw Sarah's green Jeep turn the corner and pull in behind the sheriff's cruiser. Gabby and Zach walked over as Sarah and Jesse got out, and introduced them to Deputy Stanland. "Happy to see you," he said, as he shook each of their hands. "I'm glad you kept your word."

No sooner were *those* words spoken, and before Sarah or Jesse could reply, than a voice broke over the sheriff's shoulder radio. "Irv, we may have a problem."

"What?"

"Mrs. Nystrom just left their house, but she's in a pickup with her husband, and a couple of his buddies are following them. And he gave me the middle-fingered salute as he passed by. Do you want me to stop 'em?"

"No, too risky. Keep on their tail, but let 'em come. We've got more people here."

"*I knew it!*" Jesse shouted. "He's got my mom as a damned hostage."

"Settle down," Stanland said. "We'll handle things. You should get inside the building." Then he spoke into his mike. "Base, we may need another car down here."

Hearing that, Zach, without a word, rushed down the street to retrieve his camera gear. And Gabby was on the phone to Eleanor inside the courthouse, explaining the situation. "My God," Eleanor said. "I knew something was wrong when I spoke to her. I could hear it in her voice. You should get inside now."

"I don't think that's going to happen, Eleanor. Not now. And I hope Stanland doesn't try to force us inside. We could all end up in jail."

Jesse and Sarah still stood defiantly on the curb, face-to-face with the deputy, who said, "Jesse, I don't really know you, but I do know you're an Army guy who's used to taking orders. And I'm ordering you and the others to go inside the courthouse. Now."

"I'm afraid not, Deputy. I did my part, kept by word, and I'm not ready to back off. Not again. He needs to know I'm here. And not afraid."

"You're going to make me arrest you?"

"Go ahead, but like you say, I'm an Army guy who knows how to take care of himself."

Before Stanland could say or do anything more, his radio squawked again. "They're into town, heading your way."

"Copy that," he replied.

At that same moment, two more sheriff's cars and another Wadena squad car pulled up on both sides of the street, the officers starting to gather around Stanland for instructions. But before they could take their positions, Nystrom's pickup and his buddies' car turned the corner and headed toward them. The trailing sheriff's car was immediately behind them, its lights now flashing.

At that sign of trouble, and as all of the officers took cover behind their cars, weapons drawn, Gabby and Zach, his camera rolling, scurried back toward the doors of the courthouse—where Eleanor and others were standing on the steps just inside the doors, staring out at them.

Jesse and Sarah remained in place, ignoring shouts to move back.

As the pickup and car came to a stop, Nystrom's two friends, apparently surprised by the armed reception, tried to do a quick turnaround, but were blocked by the trailing sheriff's cruiser. They clambered out of the car, arms raised. "This is a mistake!" one of them shouted. "We're just here as Curt's friends. We don't want no trouble."

"Drop to your knees," the deputy behind them ordered. "And stay that way."

They quickly did as they were told.

Both were in their late forties or early fifties, Gabby guessed from a distance. Both, like Nystrom, were big and well-built, wearing heavy jackets and stocking caps. From what she could see, neither was armed.

Nystrom had pulled his pickup next to Stanland's cruiser and rolled his window down. The deputy, still crouched behind the car, slowly raised himself up, his Sig Sauer pistol in his right hand.

"Hey, Irv," Nystrom said with a sly grin. "What's all the fuss? Looks like you've got a freakin' army here. Even got that brave little soldier-boy son of mine with you."

Stanland called back, "Are you armed, Curt? Show me your hands."

"What the hell?" Nystrom said as he slowly put his hands on top of the steering wheel. "Yeah, I got a gun, but you know I've got a permit to carry."

"Two things, Curt. And don't screw with me. Drop your holster and gun out the window, and then let your wife out of the truck and have her walk toward me."

"'Fraid not, Irv. Not going to happen. Not until I see my girl Jennie walk out of the courthouse doors and get in the truck. I've had enough of this bureaucratic bullshit. Screw the county. I want my family back together and nobody's going to stop me this time. Right, Marion?"

She was huddled next to him, barely visible, her face buried in her coat.

Stanland started to walk around the cruiser, his pistol by his side, finger on the trigger-guard. "You damn well know there's a court order keeping you away from your daughter..."

Before he could finish, Jesse suddenly forged ahead, roughly pushed past the deputy, and covered the next ten feet like a sprinter—all before either Stanland or Nystrom could react. He reached through the pickup window and put both hands around his dad's neck, lifted him out of his seat, and tried to pull him through the window.

Retribution. At long last.

Nystrom's strangled shout, more of a gargled scream, could be heard even inside the courthouse doors. His face reddened, his eyes bulged. Spittle was on his lips.

Holding on, Jesse yelled, "Get out of the car, Mom, now! Hurry."

She looked up, scared, befuddled. Finally, crying out, "Jesse, please, let him go!"

"No, not 'til you're out! Come on, quick!"

Suddenly, Stanland and the Wadena cop were at Jesse's back, struggling to free his grasp. "Give it up, Jesse," Stanland shouted. "This ain't helping. We've got him!"

But he held on until he saw his mother slide out of the passenger door. Then he let go and watched with a small smile as his father fell back in the seat, gasping for air. Stanland pushed Jesse aside, opened the door, and retrieved the pistol cradled in Nystrom's lap. The Wadena cop had Jesse in a bear hug as his mother ran for the courthouse, met by Eleanor, who had come out to lead her inside.

As Stanland tried to pull Nystrom out of the truck cab, he'd regained enough of his breath to shout, "He tried to kill me! Didn't you see? My own son, for Christ's sake."

"Calm down," Stanland said, "We'll take care of Jesse, but right now, I want you out of the truck."

In fact, the Wadena officer had just freed Jesse and pushed him aside, ordering him, "Hands behind your back. You're under arrest for assault."

Until then, Sarah had stayed back, unwilling to show her own badge, but did shout, from a distance, "You gotta be kidding. He was just trying to get his mother out of the truck."

As the officer slipped handcuffs on Jesse, he turned at her words. "And who the hell are you?" he barked.

"His friend," she said as she moved ahead, finally showing her badge. "But also a Minneapolis cop. And," glancing back, "I'm sure another friend has this whole thing on video."

"That's fine," he said, "but I saw what I saw. He had him in a choke hold, and in my book, I don't know about yours, that's an assault. He's going to jail and somebody else can decide what to do with him."

He then took Jesse by the arm and led him across the street to his squad car.

Nystrom continued to cling to the steering wheel, refusing to get out. "Listen to me, Curt," Stanland snapped, "don't make this situation even worse. You're under arrest for violating a court order, for the attempted abduction of your wife, and for making terroristic threats. Want me to add resisting arrest?"

"What about my buddies back there?" Nystrom asked, looking over his shoulder.

Stanland glanced back. "They'll be free to go once you're out of the truck."

"This is all crap, you know. Do you have kids, Irv? Would you like to see them kidnapped by the goddamned government? Shit, no! You'd be sitting here just like me."

"Nobody has accused *me* of abusing *my* kids, Curt, so quit the squawking and get the hell out of the truck before I fill your face with pepper spray."

Nystrom finally released his grip on the steering wheel and slid out of the truck. "I should have known. You're just like all of the rest of these freakin' do-gooders."

FORTY-TWO

. . .

O f the group standing inside and outside the courthouse, only Zach had moved more than a couple of feet during the angry standoff. He'd advanced cautiously toward the street, stopping about a dozen feet from the pickup as Nystrom got out and was handcuffed by the deputy.

Predictably, Zach and his camera did not go unnoticed.

"You're that prick from Channel Seven, aren't you?" Nystrom shouted. "Jennie's friend, right? Well, you know what you can do with that camera. And if I see my face on your shitty television station, I'll sue you 'til you bleed blood, not cash. Hear that?"

Zach kept shooting, knowing the chance of the video ever making the air was doubtful at best. But you never knew.

As Nystrom was led to the sheriff's office, Sarah walked across the street to the Wadena squad car, still parked with Jesse sitting calmly in the back seat, his window open a crack. "We'll bail you out as soon as we can," she told him. "But it could take a while, maybe overnight."

"Don't sweat it, Sarah. I'll be fine. I just hope they don't put me in the same cell with my dad. I might kill him this time."

"No more jokes, Jesse," she warned. "This is serious business."

"I know that. But it had to happen, and my mom's okay. That's what's important."

Gabby was inside the courthouse, standing in a small crowd that had gathered to watch the drama unfold outside. Off to one corner of the lobby, Eleanor sat with a sobbing Marion Nystrom, arm around her, handkerchief in her hand. Gabby wandered over and knelt next to them. "Is there anything I can do?" she asked.

Marion reached out and took her hand. "What can anyone do?" she asked plaintively, freeing her hand to brush away a tear. "My husband's in jail. My son's in jail. My daughter's in a shelter…"

"Easy, Marion, easy," Eleanor said. "We'll figure things out. We will not abandon you. We will not abandon Jennie."

The sobbing suddenly stopped. She froze, as though struck by a bolt of internal lightning. She turned and stared into space, her face a study in—what? Resolve? Anger? Then she erupted. "I don't want to see him again!" she blurted. "I want a divorce, Eleanor. I will not live my life like this. No more. I have no idea what I will do, but I will not share a house or a bed or a life with him again." Her expression hardened. "I have some money put away, not much, but some, and my family's house is still in my name. Perhaps you or Jesse can help me, but I will not go back to that house if he is there."

"Relax, Marion, please," Eleanor said, an arm around her shoulders. "First things, first. I want you to spend some time with Jennie at her shelter. Then, if Curt is still in jail, as I suspect he will be, and if you are as determined as you say you are, I'll ask one of the deputies to take you home to collect some of your clothes and other things you'll need while you're away."

"Away?"

"Yes. If you're willing, and if they have an opening, I'd like you to go to the Heyword Women's Shelter, on the south side of town, until all of this is resolved, in the courts or wherever. You'll be safe there and they'll provide some volunteer legal help, if you still think you need it. And, who knows? Maybe Jennie could be there with you for a time. Would you like that?"

"Of course. It would be wonderful, but I'm not sure I can pay…"

"Not to worry. It's a non-profit and you'll need to pay only what you can."

Marion turned to Gabby. "I think it's a great idea," Gabby said, "until things settle down. And I wouldn't worry too much about the money now. If you do decide on a divorce, you could end up getting some alimony. And child support for Jennie."

Eleanor got up. "Let's get you to the shelter to see Jennie, and then I'll see if I can make this all work out."

As they prepared to leave, Gabby said, "Marion, we may not see you again for a while. We have to get back to the Cities to do our jobs, but you know we'll be keeping tabs on you and Jennie and hoping for the very best."

Marion stepped up to give her a hug. "I'll never forget what you've done for us. For Jennie. Never."

Zach waited across the lobby, camera by his side, watching but not wanting to intervene in the scene across the way. But even at that distance, while he could not hear the words, he could see and feel the emotion.

"Wow," he said when Gabby finally joined him, "is she going to be all right?"

"I hope so," she said, revealing what had just transpired.

"A divorce? Nystrom will go crazy," he said. "Once he gets out of jail."

"That may not be for a while. Not with the charges he may face. And who knows? Maybe the prospect of losing both a wife *and* a daughter will make him finally realize he's fighting a losing battle."

He shook his head. "I hope you're right, but my guess is that he'll never accept that reality. Guys like him never do. He's going to end up in even deeper shit...and we can only hope mom and daughter survive."

"What *I'm* hoping," she said, "is that Jesse can somehow come to their rescue. Eventually take them under his wings. He told me once that he might leave the Army when his time is up and get into the technology business. Maybe in six months, I think."

"That could be the answer," he agreed.

Minutes after speaking of him, Gabby got a call from Sarah. "Jesse's due in court in about an hour. At which point they may officially charge him and hopefully set a bail amount."

"Charge him with what?" she asked.

"A misdemeanor of some kind, I hope. Disorderly conduct or something else short of assault. Deputy Stanland gave me the name of a lawyer, and I hope to be in contact with him shortly."

"What about your job, Sarah?"

"No sweat. I've got days-off coming and I've checked in with the precinct."

"Here's what's happening at this end," Gabby said, repeating the essence of what Eleanor and Marion had decided to do. "Once Jesse is out of jail, you should contact Eleanor right away. She'll give you the latest information."

"What about you?"

"We'll be gone in a few minutes. I have to check with Barclay to see what he wants us to do."

"Well, good luck. And thanks for everything. "

"The same to you. Keep in touch."

Barclay got to her before she could get to him.

"Hey, George, I was just about… "

"Are you done up there?"

She couldn't remember hearing that kind of urgency in his voice before and quickly switched on the speaker. "Yes. As I was about to say… "

"Do you know where the Wadena airport is?"

"No, but… it shouldn't be hard to find."

"It's just outside of town, I'm told. Follow Highway 29 to County Road 77."

"Okay."

"Get there as quick as you can. We've got a Cessna charter in the air that should be landing within the half hour, I would guess."

"George," she pleaded. "Slow down. Please. What's going on?"

"Sorry. I've been trying to get you, but your phone's been off. Zach's, too."

"I know. It's a long story... "

"I don't have time for a long story. We need to get you two to Travis as quick as we can."

"Travis?"

"Yeah, Travis. Klinger is holed up there, at Lester Updahl's farm."

"Where the barn burned down... "

"Right. He's holding Updahl and his wife hostage. He's barricaded the doors and claims he'll torch the place, just like the barn, with them inside, unless..."

She already knew what was coming. "Unless *what*?"

"Unless you're there. In person. On the phone with him. FaceTiming. Letting him tell his story, with the promise to broadcast it."

"We can't make that promise," she argued. "You know that. And what story? And why *me*?"

"Your friend, Sheriff Henderson, says what we already know, that the dude is fixated on you. Won't talk to anyone else."

"This is ridiculous, George. I'm a reporter, not a hostage negotiator. What am I supposed to do? Stand in the open and talk to a maniac barricaded inside a farmhouse? A guy who's already tried to kill us once!"

"I understand," he said. "And I sure as hell won't force you into it. But trust me, you won't be standing out in the open. Henderson says you'll be totally protected. And, Gabby, it'd be a hell of a story. *Your* story."

She looked at Zach, who provided only an unhelpful shrug.

"Does Henderson really believe that he'll set fire to the place?"

"He doesn't know what to believe. Nobody does. But he sure as hell doesn't want to take the chance, not with the Updahls inside."

There was a long pause on her end of the line.

"Are you there?" he asked.

"Yes, I'm here." She turned to Zach again. "Please. What do you think? Speak."

"It's your call, but I think you'll kick yourself if we don't go."

With a deep sigh, she was back on the phone. "You win. Who do we look for at the airport?"

"A blue-and-white Cessna 182 Skylane. Jimmy Nelson's the pilot. The airport is fenced in with a security gate. The code to get in is 5544. Jimmy will be looking for you near the office. And a deputy will be waiting at the Travis airport to pick you up."

She put the phone down. "This is crazy," she said to Zach. "Like some Grade-B flick. I've only seen the guy once in my life, at Hannah's funeral. For what? A half hour? Most of it at a distance. And he's fixated on me? Give me a break."

"C'mon," Zack said, "we've talked about this before. You may have seen him only once, but he's probably seen *you* every time you've been on the television screen, talking about *him*. Wow, he thinks, this gorgeous babe is talking about *me*." Zách went on, "I can just picture him—sitting in some sleazy motel room, fantasizing. Thinking about your panties." He paused for a moment, sickened by the image. "And remember what Andy the intern once suggested…that this could be some kind of love-hate thing. That he hates that you've exposed him, but is nonetheless smitten by you."

"Yeah, right."

He smiled. "Hell, I was smitten by you the first time I saw you. And it didn't take *me* five minutes."

"C'mon, I'm serious."

"You said it yourself. He's a maniac. A crazy man who goes around raping young women. Women who, like you, he was probably also fixated on. And don't forget your old boyfriend. Talk about crazy. He was so fixated on you it got him killed."

"And almost you."

After a moment, Zach said, "What I'm curious about is the

313

story he wants to tell. And be broadcast. What the hell could that be? A confession? An apology?"

"I guess we'll see," she said. "If listening to him can help save his hostages…"

"Amen to that."

The Cessna was easy to spot near the small airport office. And Jimmy Nelson, the pilot, was standing next to it, puffing on a cigarette. Zach had flown with him before, but this was a first time for Gabby. He had to be well over six feet tall, probably in his early thirties, slender, with a bushy mustache and eyebrows that looked like a couple of unshorn hedges. He dropped his cigarette and stamped on it before he walked over to greet them. "Hey, Zach. It's been a while." Then, "And this must be Gabby. I've heard about you and seen you on the air, but haven't had the pleasure."

She returned his smile and handshake. "Nice to meet you, Jimmy," she said with a glance at the plane, "Does this thing fly?"

He laughed. "Like a charm. You a little nervous?"

"I had a couple of scary moments when I worked in California. So I'm not a big fan of light planes."

"Well, relax. This baby has a lot of miles under her wings and never a close call."

"Good."

"Besides, we don't have that far to go. It's only about a hundred-and-fifty miles to Travis…so we should be there in about an hour or so, once we're underway."

He held the small door open as first Gabby, then Zach, climbed aboard and settled into two of the plane's four seats, buckling up and putting on their headsets. Minutes later, the engine caught and they were rolling down the runway.

Next stop: The unknown.

FORTY-THREE

. . .

They'd been in the air for for less than an hour, at some four-thousand feet, moving over snow-covered fields, scattered farms and small towns before Jimmy spoke to them over the intercom. "Hope you're doing okay back there. We're about fifteen minutes from touchdown and will be passing within sight of the Updahl farm a couple of minutes before that. You'll know it when you see all of the squad cars and fire trucks and other vehicles surrounding it. It'll be on the left side of the aircraft."

Gabby had a chart in her lap, with a line she'd drawn between Wadena and Travis, a line which had brought them over towns like Parkers Prairie, Glenwood, Benson and others that would suddenly appear through the openings in the clouds.

"Barclay said the pool helicopter is going to be over the farm, getting some aerial shots," she said. "Do you know if it's there yet?"

"Don't think so," he replied. "If it was, I think I would have heard on the Unicom frequency. There's no airport tower in Travis so we and the other traffic in the area are pretty much on our own, flying VFR,—visual flight rules. So I'll have to keep an eye out."

"I hope so," she said, not hiding a nervous laugh.

Zach took her hand in his. "Try to relax," he said. "This is the easy part."

Easy for him, she thought, because she had never told him that once—on a flight between San Jose and San Francisco—their charter plane, not unlike this one, had lost power at about three-thousand feet. It was only through the superb skill of their pilot, who somehow managed to get the engine restarted and land safely at a small town airport of the kind she could picture in Travis. It was an experience she would never forget and continued to give her tremors in a plane like this.

She kept her eyes on the ground, relieved the weather had remained calm with no new snow flurries or strong winter winds. Which made for a smooth flight and, she hoped, a smooth landing.

The minutes and miles passed quickly. The sound of the engine was mesmerizing. Her eyelids begin to droop until...

"Stand by," Jimmy said. "The farm will be coming up in about thirty seconds, on your left."

She quickly came awake. She was on the left side of the plane so she moved over and back so Zach could share the window.

They were lower now, at about a thousand feet above the ground, and the first thing they saw—besides the ring of emergency vehicles—was the burned-out shell of the barn where Updahl's prized sows had been destroyed. By Arnold Klinger. The farmhouse looked larger and more elaborate than the Jamieson's home they had visited the day before. There were three other out-buildings, two silos, and a fenced-in area where three horses stood in the snow. A prosperous farm, by all appearances.

Now under siege.

Once it was safe, with no other planes in sight, the Cessna turned ninety degrees for its final approach to the single runway. Gabby tightened her seatbelt and stared out the front windshield, seeing at the end of the runway three small hangars to the right and what appeared to be an office on the left, a windsock hanging limply from its roof.

The runway had been cleared of snow and the touchdown was smooth, the plane stopping and turning about a hundred feet from the office. Jimmy shut down the engine and turned in his seat. "That wasn't bad, was it?"

"It was great," she replied, unbuckling her belt. "Nice and smooth. Thanks so much."

"When all of this is over," he said, "I'll be here waiting to take one or both of you back to Wadena to pick up your car."

"That may be someone else," she said. "My guess is that both of us are going to be pretty busy for a while. The car may have to wait."

At that, the door to the office opened and a sheriff's deputy emerged, walking over as they stepped out of the plane. He held out his hand. "I'm Adrian Comstock," he said. "Welcome to Travis. I wish it could be under other circumstances."

"So do I," Gabby said before she introduced herself and Zach. "Believe me."

"Sheriff Henderson sends his greetings and his appreciation for your willingness to help out. It's a tough situation, as you know."

"So I've heard. I'm just not sure I can help."

A state patrol helicopter and several other planes were parked near the hangars, but there was no way to tell if they belonged to other media. And there was no sign of the pooled helicopter.

Zach said, "I'll need a couple of minutes to get our bags and my camera gear out of the plane." But as he turned around, Jimmy already had them on a small cart heading for the squad car.

The deputy checked his watch. "We should be on our way. The Updahl farm is about fifteen minutes away and sunset is coming in just a couple of hours. We hope we can resolve all of this before dark."

Henderson had set up a small command post in a tent behind one of the fire trucks that formed a partial circle around the farmhouse. A sheriff's or highway patrol car was parked on each side of the house, the officers standing or crouched behind the cars, helmets on their heads, vests on their chests, weapons in their hands.

Waiting.

As was Henderson when Gabby and Zach arrived. "Thanks so much for doing this," he said, reaching out to her as she walked up. For a moment, she thought he might give her a hug. Stepping back, she wasn't quite sure what to say. "I don't know, Sheriff, this is all so strange. I'm pleased you think I can help, but if it doesn't work, I don't want to carry the blame."

He scoffed. "Trust me. If it doesn't work, there's only one person to blame. And that's Arnold Klinger."

"Tell me the latest," she said.

"Nothing has changed, as far as we know. We haven't spoken to him for," glancing at his watch, "forty-eight minutes. That's when we told him you were on your way and willing to speak to him. We've tried to contact him since, but he won't answer."

"And what about the Updahls?"

"We think they're still okay. At least we have no reason to believe otherwise. There've been no sounds from the house, no signs of smoke or fire. He *is* armed. We know that. He showed us his pistol on one of our early FaceTime conversations."

As she and Henderson talked, Zach, with camera in hand, spotted Max Conrad and Les Leonard standing behind another fire truck with a few other reporters and photographers, all confined to a roped-in space. He walked over and was met by Conrad's greeting, "What do you know? The heroes have arrived."

Zach smiled, "Barclay decided to send the A-Team, so here we are. You can head home now."

"Fat chance," Leonard said. "And you can put that camera down. We've shot everything there is to shoot."

"Yeah, but is any of it in focus?" Zack shot back. "Barclay wanted to make sure, so he sent us."

"Right," Leonard replied, grinning.

Among others standing there were photographers and reporters from Mankato, Marshall and Austin, a few of whom Zach had met at Hannah's funeral just a few weeks before and a few miles away. So far, there were no other Twin Cities media he could see. But he knew that wouldn't last. The question was: would they get there in time?

Also there, standing a few feet away, was Howard Hooper, Gabby's friend and newspaper editor. After greeting Zach, he asked, "Do we have this right? That Gabby's supposed to talk Klinger out of the house?"

"That's the hope, I guess," Zach said. "But it's fair to say she's not exactly eager to play the role. She's as mystified as all of us are."

"All Henderson will tell us," Conrad said, "is that Klinger wants to tell Gabby some kind of story…and that she has to promise to broadcast it."

"That's really all I know," he replied, looking over his shoulder. "She may be learning more as we speak."

"They're keeping us here, like cold horses in a corral," Leonard complained. "Promising to free us when the time comes."

"Neigh, neigh, is all I've got say," Zach laughed.

Gabby couldn't take her eyes off the farmhouse. Not that she could see much. Curtains or drapes covered all of the windows, hiding any signs of movement within. Only one door was visible, toward the back of the house, opening to a deck that extended for about ten feet to either side.

She turned back to Henderson. "So tell me again. Why do you think the Updahls are still alive?"

"We don't know for sure. But they were two hours ago. Klinger turned the camera on them to prove it."

"So tell me, what *is* the plan?"

"We've linked into the farm's power supply to heat our little tent, and have set up a system that will connect you by FaceTime to Klinger, while at the same time recording the conversation for both legal, evidentiary, reasons, and also to provide the media with everything that was said. We're trying to be as transparent as possible."

"I mean, what do you expect me to say? To do? This is like asking me to fly to the moon with no training. And I'm scared to death that I'll screw it up and cost an old couple their lives."

Henderson took her by the shoulders and looked directly into her eyes. You *will not* cost them their lives. You may *save* their lives. Do you understand?"

"I can only hope," she said nervously.

"From what Klinger has told us, he wants you, and only you, to hear what he has to say…and to promise to broadcast it. And if you do, he will free the Updahls. We don't know what he wants to say. You will have to play along. We hope you can get assurances, if not proof, that the couple *is* still alive before you let him tell his story, but that may not be possible. You are a smart woman. You have to trust yourself, as we trust you, to do everything within your power to make this a happy ending. That the couple is freed and Klinger is captured without the loss of life."

At that moment, filled with doubt and fear, Gabby remembered what she had told Jennie outside the Wadena courthouse:

Show your courage.

FORTY-FOUR

...

As Henderson and his deputies made final arrangements for the virtual encounter, Gabby took the time to head over to the media corral to meet Max, Leonard and the others, giving a warm hug to Hooper, who responded with, "Chin up, Gabby, you'll do fine. Your dad's watching, I know."

"I'll give it my best," she replied. "But it's come a long way, hasn't it? From the first time we talked on the phone? Remember? About Hannah?"

"I won't forget it," he said. "And you're right. Who could have imagined it would come to this?"

Zach said, "While you talked to Henderson, one of his deputies told us two pool photographers would be allowed to shoot your actual conversation with Klinger. I'm one of them and Tad from Mankato will be the other. Les will be making the video dubs for everybody once this is over."

"Sounds good," she replied.

"And I just got a call from Barclay. Our live truck is about a half hour away, and the pool chopper is just minutes away. It will stay clear until all of this is done, then make some video sweeps for all of us. And the Minneapolis Air Traffic Control Center in Farmington has ordered other aircraft to stay away until they give the word."

Which meant, she thought, that their Twin Cities competitors might not make it.

Too bad, too sad.

Henderson was suddenly at her shoulder. "We're set, Gabby, if you are?"

"As I'll ever be," she replied, following him back to the command tent.

Ten minutes later, she was seated at a small, makeshift desk in the tent, facing a large-screen computer. Adrian Comstock, the deputy who had met them at the airport, and who was serving as the department's hostage negotiator, sat to her left. "If things go as we hope," he told her, "you will simply talk to Klinger on the screen in a very normal way. But don't be a patsy. Be tough, if you have to be. He will be speaking on a cell phone, so the audio may not be perfect. But in our earlier conversations with him, it was adequate. Understand?"

"Yup."

He straightened up and looked around. "Is everyone set?"

Zach and his camera were directly behind Gabby, shooting over her shoulder at the computer screen. Tad, the other photographer, was off to one side and to her front, where he could record her voice and expressions.

Both nodded. As did Henderson, standing next to Zach.

The deputy punched in a FaceTime number, and all listened as the rings sounded. Finally, after the third, the face of Arnold Klinger filled the screen.

"Mr. Klinger, this is Deputy Sheriff Adrian Comstock. As we promised, I have Gabriel Gooding with me, ready to speak to you and broadcast what you have to say in return for the safe release of Mr. and Mrs. Updahl. And for your peaceful surrender to the officers who now surround the house. Is that understood and clear?"

"I guess so, yeah. That's the deal," Klinger replied.

Gabby stared at the screen, witnessing an entirely different man than she had seen at the funeral. True, that sighting had been brief and before his weeks on the run, but the tanned, healthy, haughty image of that time had dissolved into a gaunt, long-haired, unshaved shadow, with blood-red eyes and teeth that may never have seen a brush.

He could have been looking up at her from a shallow grave.

But then he spoke. "Hello, Gabby, it's nice to…"

"Hold on!" she snapped. "I won't talk to you or hear your story until you show me that Mr. and Mrs. Updahl are safe. Turn your camera to them and ask them to wave. Do that now!"

"Okay, okay," he said, "take it easy, okay? But they can't wave. They're tied up."

"Then have them say something," she demanded.

The cell phone turned to reveal the couple, bound in two chairs, their faces portraits in fear.

"Say something," Klinger told them. "She wants to know you're still alive."

"Please help us," Updahl pleaded. "My wife is having trouble breathing."

"We hope you'll be free soon," Gabby said. "Stay calm, please. And brave."

The camera swung back. "Satisfied?" he said, his haggard face again looking back at her.

"Not until they're standing beside me," she replied. "And I mean *standing*."

"They will be, if you live up to your part of the bargain."

"I will."

"Okay. I'm trusting you."

"So tell me," she said. "It's getting dark and colder out here."

He looked away, then back. "I am not proud of the way I have lived my life," he began. "I have done some bad things. Assaulting those girls, living a life that is a lie. I don't deny that, and I will die knowing I have lived in sin. I have prayed about it and hope that I will be forgiven."

Gabby listened intently. Skeptically. To her, it sounded like a written script.

"But this is what I want to tell you, to tell the world. And, most of all, to tell my wife and my two boys. I *did not* intend for Hannah to die. Never. Ever. It broke my heart, if you will believe that. I loved her in my own way, in my heart, despite the horrible thing I tried to do to her.

"I admit I told Julius to put a scare into her, but *never* to hurt her. I don't know how or why he or others did what they did. He would never tell me. And he will have to live with that as I will have to live and die with what he did. With what I did."

As he finished, tears began to trail down from those bloodshot eyes. He looked away, staring into what? A past he could never relive? Acts he could never take back? Or a life ruined by lust and a moral compass that had given him no direction?

Gabby waited and watched. "Are you done? Have you said what you wanted to say?"

He wiped the tears away with a swipe of his dirty sleeve. "Yeah, I'm done."

She then repeated what the deputy had told her to say, "Untie the Updahls and lead them to the side door. Let them out and watch them walk to safety. When they are safely behind the fire truck, throw out your gun and walk out with your hands raised. Do you understand?"

"I guess."

"No guesses. We've done our part. Now do yours."

The screen went dark. Deputy Comstock leaned over. "Nice job, Gabby. Perfect."

"We'll see," she replied.

Five minutes passed. Perhaps the longest five minutes in her life. The curtains and drapes remained closed. No movement. No sound.

"He's going to screw us over," she whispered, more to herself than the deputy.

But he'd heard. "Patience," was his whispered reply.

At five minutes and forty-seconds by her watch, the side door to the deck opened. A patch of gray hair appeared. Then the full head and shoulders of Lester Updahl, looking confused, as though he saw what lay before him for the first time. He had a cane in his right hand while he held out his left to a woman who clutched a woolen shawl around her neck with her other hand—Margaret Updahl.

Gabby had seen neither of them before, but instantly felt a kinship. They became, in that moment of first sight, her grandparents back in Oregon.

They gingerly made their way down the steps, Lester leading, making sure his wife did not stumble and fall. The distance between the house and the fire truck was only a matter of fifty feet or so, but the ground was pitted and still snow-covered and potentially treacherous. One of the deputies started to walk out to help, but was called back by Henderson. "Let 'em come. We don't want to do anything to spook Klinger."

Despite stumbling twice, they made it safely—embraced immediately by a man Gabby would later learn was their son, who had just arrived from the Cities. Blankets were wrapped around their shoulders as they were slowly led to an ambulance which had been summoned from Marshall.

Now, all eyes were refocused on the farm house, waiting for Klinger to emerge, to finally end the pursuit that had frustrated and exhausted law enforcement across the state. The man who had made Gabby's and Zach's lives a nightmare.

The minutes passed. Darkness closing in. No one spoke. No sound was heard.

Then.

A single gunshot. It rang out from inside the house, splitting the air, shattering the stillness.

The shocked, stunned silence was broken only by the frightened cries of a single crow fleeing from the rooftop.

Climbing, disappearing, in the cold, winter sky.

EPILOGUE

...

Two days later, the remains of Arnold Klinger were transported to his hometown of Hershall, Nebraska, accompanied by his wife, Rosemary, but without his two stepsons, who remained with an aunt in Marshall. He was laid to rest in St. Mary's Cemetery, next to his parents. Only Rosemary and a local priest were at the graveside for the reading of the last rites and a closing prayer. Not a single tear was shed.

Julius Winthrop remained in the Hennepin County jail, charged with second-degree murder, held on a million-dollar bond, awaiting a first-degree murder indictment. His court-appointed attorney would later demand a change of venue for his trial—based on the reporting of Gabby and others from the Updahl farm, which he called "sensational." He also demanded that Klinger's broadcast implication of Winthrop in Hannah's murder be thrown out as "hearsay," uttered by a deranged man now dead.

Ten days after the standoff, Gabby and Zach were in Portland for Christmas with her mother and sisters—to discuss plans for a June wedding in Portland, with a small reception to follow in Minnesota after their honeymoon. Gabby's two sisters and Sarah Chan would be the bridesmaids, and Jesse Nystrom and two of Zach's boyhood friends from Duluth the groomsmen. George Barclay had agreed to walk Gabby down the aisle in lieu of her late father, and her editor friend, Howard Hooper, so much like her dad, would serve as ring bearer. Jennie Nystrom would be the flower girl.

Before Christmas, Marion Nystrom officially filed for divorce. And shortly after Christmas, she left the women's shelter in Wadena and moved to Minneapolis, where Sarah had found both an apartment and a job for her as a caretaker in the complex where they both now lived. Three months later, Jesse Nystrom would be honorably discharged from the Army, and would return to Minnesota to help out his mother and Jennie, who was back living with the Jamiesons for the balance of her school year.

Her father served six days in jail after the Wadena encounter, was put on probation for six months and required to surrender his permit to carry a firearm. He was allowed to see Jennie once every two weeks in a neutral location, but only with supervision. He contested the divorce and the sale of the family home, and went to live with one of the friends who had followed him into Wadena on that fateful day.

Paul Cornell, the Nebraska reporter, applied for jobs at both Twin Cities newspapers and is still waiting to hear from them.

After their return from Portland in early January, Gabby and Zach were given permission to devote full time to her planned series on homeless kids, or youths, as the professionals refer to them. By then, Andy and his law school friend had collected dozens of additional on-the-street interviews, which Gabby spent the bulk of her time reviewing and editing. She also spent more hours interviewing experts in the child protection field, people like Eleanor, and with the law enforcement officials, and with still others working for non-profits, whose lives were devoted to finding and helping the scores of kids who populated the urban streets and shelters on any given night.

Finally, by early April, the series was ready….and on a Sunday night, after the first commercial break, Gabby again sat alongside anchors Andrea and Scott, her first time on the set since she had flown back from Travis to report on the standoff at the Updahl farm.

SCOTT: *Tonight, we begin a four-night special series on the plight of homeless kids in the Twin Cities, scores of them, many as young as twelve or thirteen, often without food, without shelter, without homes. Without love.*

ANDREA: *Reporter Gabby Gooding, photographer Zach Anthony and interns Andy Simmons and Jack Gordon have spent weeks on the streets of the Twin Cities, talking to the homeless youth, seeing where they live and how they survive. And to all of the people who are trying to help those kids, to give them a chance at life.*

THREE SHOT; SCOTT, ANDREA AND GABBY.

ANDREA: *Here with that first report is Gabby Gooding....*

GABBY, ALONE ON CAMERA (with a deep breath): *"It all began with a girl named Jennie...."*

ACKNOWLEDGEMENTS

As always, I am indebted to a number of family, friends and former colleagues who have supported and encouraged me as this story unfolded over many months. Chief among them is my wife Carol, whose love and patience never ebbed. And to those who provided crucial criticism and suggestions, including our son Greg; grandsons Nate, Tony, Zach, and Sam Louwagie; their aunt and my friend, Pam Louwagie; fellow-author Bob Junghans; Maui friend Sharon Nesbit; the late Fred Webber; Brian Bellmont; Judge Herbert Lefler; and my editor, Sherri Hildebrandt. Add to them my long-time friends and former television colleagues David Nimmer, Nancy Mate, Don Shelby, Carol Johnson, Don and Petie Kladstrup, Gary Gilson, Jerry Bowen, and Tom and Cheryl Zigler. And, finally, to those in the homeless community, who assisted in my research for the book: Dr. Heather Huseby of YouthLink, Katherine Meerse and staff of Avenues for Youth, Carolyn Marinan and her colleagues at Hennepin County, and Stacy Sweeny, formerly of the YMCA Youth and Family Services.

About the Author

Ron Handberg has spent his entire career in broadcast journalism, beginning as a writer/reporter at WCCO Radio in Minneapolis all the way to News Director and, finally, as VP/General Manager of the television station. Over those years, the station's news department became one of the most honored in the country, winning numerous national and international awards for its reporting and documentary productions and earning Ron a place in the Minnesota Museum of Broadcasting Hall of Fame. This is his seventh novel.